BORN IN SALT

T. C. Weber

To contact the author, visit https://www.tcweber.com/

Born in Salt / Weber, T. C.
Freedom Thorn Press, 2021.
ISBN 978-1-7369017-1-7

FIC040000: FICTION / Alternative History
FIC055000: FICTION / Dystopian

Cover design by Robert E. Smith

Acknowledgments

Thanks to Eric Bakutis, Wayne Martin, Eric Guy, Warren Schmidt, Julie Miller, Renni Browne, Shannon Roberts, and Jane Knuth for reading drafts and providing feedback, and the critique groups at the Baltimore Science Fiction Society (www.bsfs.org) and the Annapolis Fiction and Poetry Writers, as well as others who read portions of the manuscript.

Broke the deep slumber in my brain a crash
Of heavy thunder, that I shook myself,
As one by main force roused...
For certain on the brink
I found me of the lamentable vale,
The dread abyss, that joins a thunderous sound
Of plaints innumerable. Dark and deep,
And thick with clouds overspread, mine eye in vain
Explored its bottom, nor could aught discern.

- Dante Alighieri, *Inferno*

Chapter Zero

Sgt. Jacob Adamson stared out one of the bulletproof side windows of the ATH-3C 'Retribution' airborne assault helicopter as it flew over green hills and fields. The other 'copters in their formation—more 'Retributions' and an escort of gunships—were close enough that Jake could see other faces staring back. Beyond rose the lush forested peaks of the Escambray range, some areas scarred raw from past battles. They flew below mountain height, to make it more likely they'd catch the enemy by surprise, but high enough to make the 'copters less vulnerable to ground fire.

As usually happened en route to landing zones, images of Rachel's beautiful face and trim body drove everything else from focus and gave him a raging hard-on. "I love you," her ruby lips intoned between orgasms their last night together, right before Jake got shipped out to Cuba. As he boarded the bus from New Bethany to Scott Air Force Base in nearby Shiloh, her last words were "Come back in one piece," a psalm that still echoed in his mind.

Jake was due for leave soon. He couldn't wait to hold his fiancée again, kiss her warm lips and perfumed neck, and most of all, drive between those smooth white thighs. *Two weeks of non-stop sex with the hottest dish in New Bethany!* He had to see family, too. *Go hunting and fishing with my brother, watch his band play, say hi to Sarah and the rest.*

Strapped in next to Jake in the cramped cargo section, PFC Seth Bowen, a fellow survivor of the Hill 249 disaster, shouted over the noisy rotor blades, "Anything interesting out there?"

"More of the same," Jake yelled back.

"What do you think?" Bowen asked.

"It's mop-up. We'll be fine." It was Jake's job to ensure this, that all his men went home alive.

Ben was right, I shouldn't have re-enlisted. The Army had given Jake a sizable bonus, though, which his family needed to pay off the bank. And now that he was serving overseas, he'd be eligible for VFW membership, practically the only way someone from a poor farm family could secure the connections needed to get ahead in the world. Like to run for county council like Rachel had suggested, and stand up to goons like Sheriff Johnson.

Alpha Company's helicopters cut over the mountain spine and headed south. The knuckleheads in headquarters had decided one company was enough for the mission. Their destination, the village of San Isidore. According to Captain Tannin, the battalion's military intelligence liaison, it was an insurgency stronghold, and the home town of one of the rebel commanders.

The village came into sight—a few dozen red-tiled roofs atop white houses, nested among fruit and palm trees, with a Catholic chapel and a school in the center.

A squadron of Viper ground support jets zoomed in low at an angle. The deep thuds of explosions carried over the whine of the copter rotors and rattled Jake's bones. Giant fireballs blossomed upward from the village, angry fists of orange and black thrusting into the sky.

Did they have to use such heavy ordnance? Jake turned from the window and made hand signals to his quad, to get ready to deploy.

The 'copters dropped into bean fields about a mile from the village, forming a double semicircle. The rear door swung down. Jake waved his arm toward it and led his ten men out the back of the helicopter. As soon as all boots hit the ground, it took off again.

Every building and tree in the village belched flames and smoke. Even a mile away, Jake felt rippling heat, smelled burning gasoline, and heard faint screams.

Just beyond Jake's hearing range, Captain Tannin, a narrow-faced man who never smiled, and the German S.S. adviser, Hauptsturmführer Krüger, peered through binoculars and conferred with the company commander.

The radio operator relayed orders and the platoon commanders gave the order to march. "No one gets past us," Lt. Wheeler, the new commander of 3rd Platoon, told Jake and the other two squad sergeants.

Jake took point for his squad—he was the most seasoned, as well as the best shot. He moved carefully, scanning ahead for partisans and searching for mines. No gunfire came their way. There didn't seem to be any resistance at all. The company's gunships circled the burning village, laying down machine gun fire.

A horse galloped across the bean fields toward Jake, fire trailing from its back and tail, eyes wide with terror, froth spitting from its mouth. *Poor creature.* He braced his rifle, aimed at its head, and pulled the trigger. The horse dropped and burned in place, smelling like gasoline-soaked barbecue.

The flames had died down by the time the infantry reached the outskirts of the village, or what was left of it. Jake spotted no signs of life, not even birds or insects.

Accompanied by Captain Tannin and the Hauptsturmführer, Lt. Wheeler called his sergeants over. "We're on head staking duty."

What? "Excuse me, sir," Jake asked the lieutenant, "did you say head staking?"

"Orders. Cut off every head you find and place it on a stake outside the village. Divvy up your men accordingly."

The Hauptsturmführer spoke in barely accented English, more to the officers than the sergeants. "The key to pacifying resistance is the precise yet overwhelming application of fear. When the natives see what we've done here, they'll think twice before supporting the rebellion. It has worked well elsewhere."

"Sir," Jake said, "may I speak frankly?"

The lieutenant frowned. "Go ahead."

"That's fucking barbaric, sir." *We're Americans, not Nazis, even if Germany is our ally and controls a third of the world.*

The lieutenant's eyes widened, then narrowed. "Just do as you're told. I'm not in the habit of repeating orders."

Inside the village, the houses and other buildings had all collapsed into piles of blackened bricks and wood, some of it still smoking. The trees were charred fingers stabbing at the sky. Burnt corpses lay amid the bricks. They smelled like the horse, only a thousand times worse, people who just an hour earlier, might have been smiling or laughing or expressing love or perhaps arguing about pointless things that didn't matter anymore. There wasn't much in the way of weapons, only a few old carbines and shotguns.

The bodies were thickest inside the collapsed church—stiff blackened limbs, frozen screams and scorched bones. *Maybe they heard we were coming, and went inside to pray.* Most of the corpses were small. Children. Jake's squad picked through the church, not speaking.

Jake unsheathed his combat knife and knelt by the blackened eyeless corpse of a child, blade trembling. He couldn't tell if it was a boy or a girl.

I'm not going to do this. Or anything like this, ever again. My squad's not going to do this either. Jake lowered the knife and scanned the burnt church. "If you're watching me from above, Mom, please forgive me."

He gagged, stumbled to his feet, then threw up his breakfast on the remains of the altar.

Chapter One

"Benjamin," our slick-haired preacher said into the pulpit microphone, "you have some words to share?" He stepped aside, offering up his post.

I couldn't tear my eyes from the casket in front, draped with an American flag and surrounded by flickering candles and white lilies. The Army had sealed it, saying the remains hadn't been recovered right away and weren't suitable for viewing. Only a hint of disinfectant, a faint chlorine smell beneath the flower scent, gave away the presence of a body inside.

My brother's body.

Jake's face, blue-eyed and strong-jawed like a Hollywood cowboy, smiled from a framed photo displayed to the right of the casket, *1962-1983* beneath his name, then the national motto, 'Love of God, Love of Country, Love of Duty.' My eyes lingered on that smile, which was more of a smirk, like Jake had been thinking, "the world isn't so hard if you play the game right."

"Benjamin?"

I stood up from the pew, welcomed by a few coughs and lots of sniffles. Jake had been the family's Big Hope and we'd never imagined him to get snuffed out like this. Sitting next to me in the front, Pop, who had refused to cry at Ma's funeral, shuddered and choked.

My stomach tightened. What was the point of this church stuff? It didn't help when Ma died and it didn't help when poor Abby died either. Jake deserved better than a catalog funeral.

I patted Pop on the shoulder and edged past him. My feet dragged me across the red carpet, past my brother's casket, and up the steps to the pulpit.

Preacher Bill glared at me and tapped his index fingers together. Did he have better things to do? Or was he bent out of shape 'cause I hadn't set foot in his church for so long? As if his smarmy Bible waving should make me appreciate my lot in life.

I hesitated at the microphone. A cough escaped me and echoed off the pale blue walls.

I'd held my share of audiences, but never this large, and never by myself, without even a guitar for help. Every pew was filled: easily a couple hundred people, all clothed in dark suits or dresses. Everyone in New Bethany knew my brother, or had at least seen him play football. In the entrance hall earlier they'd said one after another that Jake's death was a damn shame, though most added that dying for one's country was the greatest of honors.

Behind me, the preacher sighed.

Better get this over with. I unfolded my two-page speech, written in barely legible cursive and full of corrections. My eyes drifted to Rachel, Jake's fiancée, sitting in the front row across the aisle from Pop and Grandpa. Her face, normally so flawless and assured, was wracked in agony, tears smearing her makeup.

I laid the speech over the open Bible on the lectern and started to read. "Jacob Adamson was a rare figure. He was smart, handsome, and popular. He had a beautiful fiancée, land to till, and probably a career in politics down the line. It is a terrible tragedy that his life was cut short ..."

An image flashed in my mind: the whole family, Ma and Abby too, gathered around the Christmas tree Pop said he'd planted the year Jake was born. I was six and my wool pajamas itched. But I was happy. We all were. Jake tore the paper off a model tank with moving treads, a present from Grandpa.

Tears blurred my vision. He's never, ever coming back.

In the back pew, close to the door, a solitary dark face urged me forward. Sarah. They'd let her in or she snuck in. She mouthed something, probably akin to 'the stage is yours.'

I gave up on the speech and stuffed it in my pocket. "You all knew Jake. He was the guy I wish I was. I won't lie and say he was perfect, but he was a lot closer than most people."

A lot closer than me.

"He shouldn't be lying in a coffin at twenty-one," I said. "He should be sitting on a porch well into next century, grandkids and great-grandkids gathered 'round, telling his life story and farting dust."

No one laughed. Jake would have.

"Pop taught me how to fish and trap and shoot a gun and lots of other things." I cast a glance at Pop but he was too lost to notice. "But Jake was the one I did most of that with. We were a team, me, Jake, and Sarah, all the way up to high school. Jake was the leader of course since he was oldest. But he never bullied me and even stuck up for me. Can't ask for more from a big brother."

In the back, Sarah wiped her nose. Up front, Rachel sobbed.

My knees grew weak but I locked them rather than lean against the podium. "I'm supposed to quote Scripture and say how this is all part of God's plan." I stared at the Bible in front of me, open to 1 Corinthians 15. *Where, O death, is your victory? Where, O death, is your sting?*

My shoulders tensed. We'd been robbed. Again. And the preacher and government thought it was glorious.

"Death is victorious." I gripped the mike and words spilled out. "Death always wins, and misery, and pain. That's the world we're stuck in."

The whole room seemed to hiss inward. Even Sarah and Rachel stared at me with open mouths. I eyed the cross on the wall behind the podium and nearly gave it the finger.

I couldn't stop my tongue, though. "If there's a God, he's a sadistic son of a bitch."

Pop's face reddened and I stomped back down the pulpit steps. With all the scowls directed my way, I almost kept going. Out the door, out to freedom, where I could take off this damn noose they called a tie, run to one of my ponds, and take my peace in single combat with whatever largemouth bass I hadn't bested yet.

Wouldn't be right to abandon my brother, though. I took my seat, Pop's eyes still glued on me.

Preacher Bill examined the ceiling, as if gathering strength, then shook his head and trudged to the microphone. "The Lord is my shepherd; I shall not want …"

People were still staring at me. I slunk against the back of the pew.

"…Yea, though I walk through the valley of the shadow of death, I will fear no evil."

My rod and my gun, they comfort me.

* * *

Most people had avoided me at the burial at New Bethany Baptist Cemetery, and now avoided me at the reception. Preacher Bill had offered to pray for my soul but I told him to pray for his own damn soul. His entourage of Praise the Lord housewives kept peering at me like I was a three-legged dog.

I wasn't up to talking anyway. I could still hear the shots fired by the honor guard at the grave site, each one piercing my heart like I was a mourning dove in season.

I kept by the front window of our crowded living room. Grandpa and the other seniors sat on the tattered sofa or quilt-draped stuffed armchairs. The younger guests stood in trios or quartets, talking quietly without smiles. Throughout the room, embedded in baskets of goldenrod and blue monkshood, fragrant sprigs of rosemary hid the mold and mildew that had flourished inside the walls since Ma's passing.

Pop, standing with hunched shoulders, got most of the attention. He'd stopped crying and started drinking.

"Picked up this bourbon on the drive through Kentucky," one of his old Army buddies told him. "Supposed to be one of the best." He poured a golden liquid into two aluminum mugs decorated by war eagles. The man, who had a flesh-colored patch over his left eye, thrust his mug toward the portraits of Presidents Lindbergh and Clark on the fireplace mantel, then turned to Pop. "Strength and honor."

Pop tapped mugs with him, but didn't return the toast. He took a swig, exhaled, and said, "People die in war ... but Jake, he was special. No one with more potential on God's whole earth. We thought for sure he'd come back without a scratch, and a fuller man. Like us when we came back from Haiti—stronger, more appreciative."

He gulped down more bourbon. "Shoulda been someone else who stepped on that mine."

Pop had been drinking the day we got the news. We'd delivered twelve thousand bushels of corn kernels to the Midland Grain Corporation, but they'd only paid half what we'd hoped, well below the break-even point. Two Army officers in dress uniforms, one of them a gray-haired chaplain, knocked on our door. The old chaplain sat us down in the living room and told us Jake had died instantly. Pop had kicked over the coffee table and swung the hat rack around and the officers had called in reinforcements from the car out front.

A hand touched my shoulder. It was the Army grief counselor, a young guy with glasses and lieutenant bars. I couldn't remember his name.

"How are you holding up?" he asked.

I shrugged off his hand. "Fine." I was only nineteen but I was a veteran at grief and didn't need his help.

When Sarah stepped in from our screened-in front porch, I lightened a little. She wore her winter dress, which was long and dark blue, not happy and flowery like her summer dress. A matching felt hat hid her short kinky hair. Her wide cheeks drooped and her molasses eyes were puffy from crying.

I waved her over. Her parents and two older brothers followed her into the room. And behind them, a tall man dressed in a charcoal suit with a white fedora. His skin was deep black, darker than Sarah's. His name eluded me but he looked familiar.

Sarah threw fierce arms around me. "I'm so sorry, Ben."

She almost never called me Ben. Usually it was Deerslayer, which Jake had come up with. I almost never got skunked, and even if I went for a head shot, I never missed.

"Thanks," I managed.

Sarah smelled her normal earthy self, no perfume. She squeezed my shoulder. "Why didn't you read your speech? It was good."

"Didn't feel right, just leave it at that."

"Yes but... You know you shouldn't go cursing God, especially in a church."

She meant well so I didn't get mad. "Maybe God shouldn't keep cursing me and mine and all the other folk who don't deserve it."

Sarah stepped back as her parents and brothers offered condolences. "The rest of the family, they're all sorry too," her mother said.

Then the tall man with the white fedora clasped my hand. "I'm Paul. Do you remember me?"

He wore gleaming white shoes to match the hat. City slicker all the way.

"Cousin from the Turners," Sarah said.

Now I remembered. Must have been ten years ago I last saw him, maybe more. I was a kid then, Ma and Abby still alive.

"Paul's been living in Chicago," Sarah said. "Just moved back and got a job tending bar at the Deer Head."

That was the only saloon in the county, part owned by Sheriff Johnson. I wasn't twenty-one yet and had never been inside.

She winked. "He knows every cocktail invented. They couldn't resist."

Paul nodded. "Being a war vet helped too. Though things being as they are, I wouldn't expect to make management."

Sarah's mother interrupted. "You come by the farm any time, Ben, and I'll cook you a nice meal and we can all sit down together. Any time you want."

Food wasn't what I needed. I stepped forward and twined my fingers with Sarah's. "Come get 'faced with me. We got all manner of homebrew and shine in the kitchen. Got food from two dozen families too if you're hungry."

She smiled. "Blaze the way, Deerslayer."

Her smile tore away some of the heaviness crushing my ribs. Then Pop tramped over and stuck his aftershave-drenched face in mine.

"What's all these... people... doin' in my house?"

My skin flushed with embarrassment. "Sarah's come with her family to pay respects."

Grandpa frowned, and my aunts and uncles did too. Dumb ass racists, the whole family, even though we lived in the Land of Lincoln.

"What's the big windblow," I said. "We're all equally poor." And our families had lived near each other for generations. Sarah was practically my sister.

8

"We'll be on our way," Sarah's pop told me. "Ain't a time for confrontation."

"No, stay," I said.

Sarah squeezed my hand. "I'll stay."

Pop glanced at our clasped hands and grimaced. He knew we weren't a couple, but might be afraid things would head that direction. We'd thought about it, naturally, but sex would have felt weird, like incest. And what if I broke her heart? Or she broke mine? It would be too much to bear.

"Go on and drink with your old buddies," I told Pop. "Let me drink with mine."

"These are your buddies?" He exhaled bourbon fumes. "That's the best you can do?"

Sarah gritted her teeth and let go of my hand. "What did you say?" She'd never been one to take shit.

My toes clenched, then my fists, but sadness and fatigue won out. "Truce, Pop. Sarah was Jake's friend too. He'd want her to stay."

Pop's face sagged and he took a swig from his eagle mug. He threw up a hand. "Have it your way."

Grandpa waved him over and he retreated.

Sarah's folk hugged me one by one and said goodbye.

"I'll wait outside for you," Paul told Sarah.

"Wait on the porch," she said. "I'll bring you a drink."

As Paul left, Rachel approached. I hadn't spoken to her at the funeral, not knowing what to say. Her shoulder-length raven hair was still tangled from the wind at the cemetery. Her face was slack, emerald eyes blank like a doll's. "*Why*, Ben?" Water oozed into her eyes and started to drip.

My body tensed as the horror returned. Jake was gone. Forever. Poor Rachel. Even though they were an odd match in a lot of ways, she'd been Jake's steady since tenth grade and had a whole life planned with him.

I wrapped my arms around her, breathing in her rose-scented hair. "You know I'm here for you." I wondered if I would still be her confidant, or if she'd leave my life too.

"I'm real sorry about Jake," Sarah told her.

Rachel turned her head. "Thank you." Her watery eyes returned to me. "I have to find out what happened. You have to help me."

"He stepped on a mine," I said. "What else is there to know?"

She wriggled out of my embrace. The grief counselor studied us, but I shook my head and he stayed put.

"That's all they'll tell me, he was killed in action." Her lips quivered as she grasped my left arm. "Nothing about what he was doing. Whether someone could've stopped it."

His death could have been prevented if he'd quit the Army after the mandatory two years instead of signing up for more like a dumb ass. If I had a girl like Rachel, no way would I spend one minute apart from her.

"Jake's last letter," she continued in a shaky voice, "had more redactions than usual, and then I didn't get anything at all." Her pink-nailed fingers remained wrapped over my forearm.

"Well," I said, "the Army chaplain told me they try to keep spies from seeing anything sensitive in the mail." The pictures Jake had mailed after he first arrived at his post depicted a tropical paradise: green mountains, blue seas, and endless fields of tall sugarcane. He and his squad buddies smiled like they were having a good time.

"Why Cuba?" she asked. "What's the point of that?"

"You might as well ask why a tornado comes down and smashes up one side of a street but not the other."

Her eyes widened and she let go of my arm. "I thought you were on my side."

Should have said something comforting. This was why I'd never had a girlfriend more than a couple of weeks. Never said the right thing. That and being skinny and not having a nickel to my name.

Still by my side, Sarah came to my rescue. "You ain't the only one who lost someone, you know." She put a hand on my arm. "Let's get those drinks."

Rachel's face fell. "Are you leaving?" She bit her lip, one of her worry gestures.

"I'm getting a drink," I said. "Want one?"

Rachel hesitated, then sniffled. "You're more like your father than you think."

My toes clenched again and I walked off, leading Sarah into the adjacent kitchen.

The heavy wooden table in the middle was covered with food, mostly casseroles. We'd hauled a second table up from the basement and piled booze on top. Folk congregated around the tables, heaping food onto plates and pouring homebrew or moonshine into glasses, teacups, and mugs.

"We should start slow," Sarah said.

"Yeah." After my outburst at the church, I was in enough trouble without passing out in the living room or throwing up on Preacher Bill's wingtips.

I opened the old refrigerator and pulled out three bottles of factory-brewed Budweiser. Better than the local homebrew and a treat since it cost money.

I led Sarah through the living room again. Rachel was talking to my crazy Aunt Sybil, who was wearing a wide-brimmed hat sprouting a circle of egret feathers. She was Pop's oldest sister but she almost never visited.

"I have a book you should read," my aunt told Rachel as we passed. "It really explained things for me."

We continued onto the covered porch, which ran along the front of the house and down one side. The screen was supposed to keep out bugs but it had too many holes. Paul was sitting in a weather-beaten rocking chair, the only one that still had both armrests.

Sarah opened one of the beers and handed it to him.

"St. Louis's finest," he said, and took a swig.

Sarah and I sat on the swing. The chains creaked but they wouldn't break. We dove into our beers without talking.

The porch faced east so we couldn't see the setting sun. But the sky had darkened and the trees around the house cast long shadows onto the patchy yard and the two dozen cars and trucks parked there. Beyond, our hard-packed dirt driveway ran a hundred yards through fields of corn stubble to the county road.

"You got a nice house, Ben," Paul said, leaning slightly forward in the chair, feet planted to keep it from rocking.

"Everything needs fixing," I said. "But it's been in the family a hundred years. My great-grandpa put the porch on. It's home."

Each ancestor and offshoot had a picture on one of the walls, ghosts watching the generations pass. I half expected their sepia eyes to weep blood.

"No matter now," I continued. "Bank's threatening foreclosure, they wanna take the whole farm."

Paul shook his head. "That ain't right, to take a man's home away."

Sarah nodded.

My teeth gritted. "Banks, government, they see us as hogs for the slaughter." I finished my beer.

Sarah finished her bottle too. "Want me to get more?"

"I'm ready for something stronger."

"I thought we were gonna pace."

"You call downing a beer in two gulps pacing?"

She frowned. "Wasn't two gulps."

Paul fixed eyes on me. "You've got Lindbergh and Clark over the fireplace."

"Not my say." Pop and Grandpa worshiped President Lindbergh, National Leader for four decades until cancer took him. They even worshiped his cleft-chinned, slogan-spouting replacement, Andrew Clark.

"And if it was your say?" Paul asked.

I couldn't help but feel bitter. "Why pay tribute to men who let the banks and grain buyers grind us down? And send people off to die when they're needed here?"

I didn't mention that Pop and Grandpa loved Clark's 'master race' speeches. No matter how bad our lives got, they relished that there were whole races of people beneath them.

Paul scooted the rocking chair close and spoke quietly. "There's more of us than them. We could stand up and say no."

Was he serious? "That what they do in Chicago?"

"Sometimes."

"And I bet they get their heads kicked in."

His eyes narrowed. "Nothing worthwhile's easy."

"Nothing's easy, period," Sarah added.

The door opened behind us and Pop stomped out. He stabbed a finger at me. "Get back in here, boy. We got guests."

That was true. Today was for Jake, not me. I slid out of the swing, rocking Sarah in the process. "I got circulating to do," I told her and Paul. "Why don't you come inside?"

Paul shook his head. "I don't need to stir trouble with your kin. We'll pick this up later."

While Pop stood with crossed arms, Sarah stood and hugged me. "See you tomorrow?"

I whispered in her ear. "I'll stash enough shine to last a while."

Paul tipped his fedora at me and led Sarah down the porch steps. They followed their shadows toward the road.

Chapter Two

The pond had no official name. It was an unlabeled blue teardrop on the county map. But just the place to shake off a three-day drinking spree, especially on a warm cloudless day. And I was tired of re-reading Jake's letters.

We called it Lake Livingstone after the farm it was on. It wasn't actual lake size, but was still over five acres, and full of fish since the owners kept it stocked and ran off anyone not in the co-op. Pop hadn't paid maintenance dues for years, but the Livingstone Boys cut me slack as long as I brought my band over to the barn twice a year.

I pulled my bait cage out of the water, hauling it by the string staked to shore. Water streamed out the bottom grate and two dozen shiners I'd netted from the shallow end wriggled and flopped around inside, silvery scales flashing in the sun. I unhooked the top of the cage and snatched one out, then eased the cage back in the water.

I stuck the hook through the shiner's lips and cast it out beyond the weed line, right where the bottom dropped off. This time of year, the bass were active and hungry, so I expected to catch my limit. I let the shiner swim down a bit, then started walking it along the bank, not letting it get in the weeds.

Somewhere behind me, my hound Bandit barked. I turned and spotted Sarah hiking down the dirt track toward the pond, wearing jeans, a checkered flannel, and a wide straw hat; rod, net, and tackle box in her hands. Her cousin Paul walked by her side. He had denims and boots on, but still wore that white fedora.

I waved. Normally I liked to fish alone, but I made an exception for Sarah. She took it as seriously as I did, and even though poorer than me, she'd saved for a near-pro rod and reel. Fishing gear was one thing you couldn't skimp on. And with proper care, it would last forever.

Bandit wagged his tail and escorted Sarah over, though he eyed Paul with suspicion.

"Paul wanted to come talk to you," Sarah said. "Hope you don't mind."

Paul's hands were empty. "You could have helped Sarah carry something," I said.

He turned away and asked her, "Can I take your box or something?"

She ignored him and pointed at the string leading out to the submerged bait cage. "You got shiners to spare?" she asked me.

"Help yourself."

"Thanks, Deerslayer. I'll net the next batch." She set her net and tackle box on the grass and adjusted her split shots, the two tiny lead weights that held the line underwater.

Paul stepped close. "Sarah told me a lot about you."

I glared at her. "Yeah, she does have a mouth."

Sarah looked up and gave me the finger.

"She only had good things to say," Paul said. "Like how you write honest songs. Honest songs in a dishonest world."

I reeled in my bait. "I just write about life, nothing fancy." I swung the shiner inches from Sarah's face.

"Pond's that way." She pointed.

I chuckled inside and told Paul, "Sarah's the star in our band. She plays a mean fiddle."

"Yeah, she's got talent. She says you're the front though."

I walked along the bank a dozen yards or so, searching for the perfect spot.

Paul followed me. "You're tight, the two of you."

I cast the shiner out again. You couldn't keep fish out of water long or they'd die. "What do you mean by that?"

"Just saying."

I cast him a glance. "Well, we ain't grinding love muffins if that's what you're getting at. Not that it's any of your business."

He held up a hand. "You're right, it isn't."

"Ain't a lot of suitable men around here." It was illegal for blacks and whites to marry, or even have sex, and our county was ninety percent white.

I reeled the bait back in. Its tail was still flopping. I walked a little further and cast it just past the drop off.

"You guys got fishing licenses?" Paul asked.

I laughed. "Government wants a license for everything. Hunt, fish, farm, even to play music." The shiner swam toward the weeds for cover. I led it a few feet to a bare spot where it couldn't hide. "We played a dance hall and cops shut us down 'cause we weren't properly authorized. They took me in for making a fuss about it."

"Yeah, it's like that everywhere. What about your songs? Any trouble with the censor board?"

"Haven't pitched anything to the record company or the Radio Bureau. We ain't at that level and I'm getting drafted by next May anyway." The service board had given me a deferral since I had a brother serving and was needed on the farm, but I still had to go in by twenty.

I turned to Paul. When would he get to the point? What did he want?

"I heard about your punishment for helping the colored school," he said. "They had the worst of everything when I went there."

My shoulders tensed. I'd liberated surplus band equipment from a storage closet in high school, and donated it to the three-room New Bethany Colored School, where Sarah went. It was the perfect heist, but a so-called friend turned me in. The principal had expelled me from school and the police had whipped me in front of half the town.

"I admire that," Paul said. "You're a good man."

"Thanks." I winced a little inside. I'd burgled the band equipment more for the thrill than anything else. Every prank I pulled in school, like dumping salt in the teachers' coffee or switching snooties' padlocks, had to be topped by the next.

"Sarah said you're a natural at opening locks."

"Practice, like anything." Sports had been my brother's thing. Cracking locks was one of mine, learning a secret skill that none of the jocks knew.

I returned my attention to the pond. No bites yet, but from vibrations in the monofilament line, the bait was still alive. I moved farther down.

"So how'd you end up in Chicago?" I asked over my shoulder.

"I joined the Army the day I turned eighteen. A black man can't get a decent education or job in this country, but he's welcome to die for it. Army pays better than anything 'round here, and if you volunteer you get a bonus and more say about your service branch."

"Jake should have joined the Navy," I said. "Been years since they've been in a fight." And even then, nothing like the Pacific War in the Forties.

"You worried about going to battle?" Paul asked.

"What do you think?" Jake was a crack shot and handy in the woods like me, and a lot stronger and faster, but none of that kept him alive.

"I saw plenty of action," Paul said behind me, "the type that changes a man. But when I got out, I learned what suckers we all were. And that things can be different."

Still no bites. I reeled in the bait and cast it out again. "What do you mean?"

"Let me ask this," he said. "You said the bank's taking the family farm?"

I met his eyes. "Not yet, but it doesn't look good. We're more in debt each year, can't pay off the loans, and have to take out more to pay the interest on the first ones, plus cover our costs. Now they're sending letters with deadlines we can't meet."

He nodded. "You're not alone. And like I said the other day, there's more of us than them. We could stand up and say we've had enough."

I couldn't help but survey for eavesdroppers. Talk like that, even joking, could land you ten years in a work camp.

No one visible besides me, Paul, and Sarah. "We sold our corn right before we got the news about Jake," I said, feeling bitter. "We had a decent yield, but couldn't get a good enough price to pay what we owe."

"That's all by design. I bet you the bank will get a better price once they take your land and put tenants on. Who do you think controls the markets? A handful of families own nearly everything. They won't be happy 'till they own what's left and people like you and yours are nothing more than sharecroppers with barely enough to survive."

"I'll never do that, no way. And Pop will never give up his land, no matter what the bank says."

"Good for him. If there'd been more resistance in the Thirties, if people had marched on Washington to throw down the coup, we wouldn't be living like serfs today."

"Why would they have?" I asked. "Grandpa told me no one knew about the change till afterward. And Lindbergh brought jobs, hospitals, roads, schools... He ended the Depression and kept us out of the war in Europe. He was a national hero before; all that made him a superhero."

Paul's nose wrinkled. "Daily doses of radio propaganda from his enablers like Father Coughlin. It sure wasn't a positive change for unions and Jews and the other scapegoats. And while Lindbergh and his cronies were distracting people with the left hand, they were picking their pockets with the right, dismantling democracy and rewriting the Constitution. All at the bidding of the bankers and industrialists who financed the coup."

"I'm not saying I agree with Grandpa and Pop, I'm just saying what most people think."

"Until they realize how they're being screwed, and that they can say no, you can't take my land. No, you can't tell me what to say. No, you can't keep me poor and dance on my back."

"Ain't gonna be any rise up." I recited the official mantra. "'Love of God, Love of Country, Love of Duty.' Most folk either believe it or pretend to."

He half smiled. "You don't, obviously."

His expression irked me. "And what'll happen if anyone sticks their neck out? Look what happened in Poland last year. Big movement to throw out the Germans, and they ended up a testing ground for the latest plague weapon. And those dockworkers in L.A. two years ago, striking for higher wages? The National Guard went in and shot anyone who didn't surrender. The survivors got ten years in the coal mines."

He raised an eyebrow. "How'd you know all that?"

Rachel. She knew all kinds of things. "My point is, nothing ever gets better."

"That's what they want you to think. From hope follows success."

The line tugged beneath my index finger and the rod tip bent down.

"Woo doggy!" I snapped the rod up, setting the hook, then started reeling in. The tip jerked up and down. Not a monster but no doubt a keeper.

"Fetch the net, would you?" I told Paul. I'd left it over by the bait cage along with everything else.

The fish broke the water, just the dark green back visible. Bass, maybe two pounds. Not waiting for the net, I kept reeling, then lifted the fish out of the water and onto the bank. It flopped around in the grass, probably wondering what the hell was going on.

"Two pounder," I yelled over to Sarah, who was working the bank in the opposite direction.

She gave me the thumbs up. Paul brought the net.

"A little late now." I took the bass off the hook and carried it over to where I'd left my tackle box.

"There's an organization," Paul said behind me.

"What?" I pulled my hand scale out of the tackle box and held up the bass with it. The needle swung to two and a quarter pounds.

"People are preparing for revolution," he continued. "The fiftieth anniversary of the coup is coming up, and there will be a fire like this country's never seen. The regime's already hobbled by corruption and bureaucracy. It just needs finishing off."

He looked serious. Which made him dangerous.

"You can be a part of it," he continued. "You've got skills and motivation, you can help set things right."

"Set off bombs and kill people?" I scanned the surroundings again. "You can't bring that here."

He frowned and shook his head. "If you're talking about Kansas City, that was a government frame-up—"

I cut off his spiel. "Look, you wanna fish, you can split with Sarah. I had enough jawing for today."

I had enough burdens to carry without some Chicago zealot adding more.

Chapter Three

A week passed. I set leg traps in the woods for foxes and other furbearers, and waited for deer season. I practiced songs with Sarah and the rest of our band. Grandpa directed the soybean planting, saying Pop should have held off selling the corn till prices went up. We used the Army's death gratuity to cover our losses and pay down the bank loan. We were still way behind.

My Aunt Eunice, youngest of Pop's three sisters, moved in to help out. She brought her husband Floyd along, who was unemployed, often drunk by noon, and all around useless. According to Aunt Eunice, he didn't even have sperm for children.

I hadn't seen Rachel since the funeral, and she hadn't been taking phone calls. After Sarah left the reception, Rachel and I had sat together, apologized for cranky words, and cried on each other's shoulder.

I finally went to check up on her. It was after ten, so she'd be at the family bookstore on Main Street.

We had two trucks on the farm, both long past retirement age. I took the smaller one, a dented white pickup covered with fiberglass patches. I followed the county road into town, two miles past fields of harvest debris, sprawling brown beneath leaden skies. The entrance to New Bethany was marked by a billboard of Lindbergh holding hands with two children, 'PRESIDENT LINDBERGH SHOWS THE WAY' inscribed above.

I turned right onto Main Street, the twelve-block strip of downtown commerce. It was lined with black-painted aluminum lampposts, erected after the coup but before the Pacific War's metal rationing. Each lamppost held an acrylic-encased black and white photograph of a New Bethany war hero, with 'Love of God, Love of Country, Love of Duty' inscribed beneath. As soon as it could be arranged, a letter from the mayor's office informed my family, Jake's picture would end up on a lamppost somewhere in town and there would be an official ceremony.

I parked in front of Inside Stories. Like other stores in the oldest section, it was brick, flat-topped, and snug against its neighbors.

The bookstore never had many customers. With television, you didn't have to imagine the setting and action, it was all laid out for your eyes. And school was so damn monotonous, studying the same writings by Lindbergh,

Pelley, and Hitler over and over, that most people I knew avoided books after graduation.

Rachel was New Bethany's number one exception. I spotted her through the plate glass window, sitting behind the counter and reading a hardback. A couple of elderly women, one trailed by Rachel's mustached father, browsed the cramped aisles.

When I entered and set off the jingly bell, Rachel met my eyes. Violins played some classical dirge over the speakers.

"Hi Rachel."

"Hi." She sounded tired. She looked eye-catching as ever, wearing a sky-blue dress that hugged her curves, but her face and shoulders sagged. She slipped an Inside Stories bookmark between the open pages and shut the cover. *Three Soldiers* by John Dos Passos.

"How've you been?" I asked. "I called your house, but your mom said you didn't want to be disturbed."

"I did call back, but your father said you were out fishing." Her lips came close to forming a smile. "I'm glad you came over. I've been thinking about you. If not for you, Jake and I might never have lasted so long."

"I just told him he'd be a fool to give up the best catch in southern Illinois. And he was smart enough to realize it."

Her smile deepened, then disappeared. She called her dad over. "Can I take a break?"

"Sure." He stepped toward me and offered his hand. "Hi, Benjamin. Sorry again for your loss."

That phrase again. I wanted to move on, but every mention ripped open my guts. Mr. Tolson had been at the funeral service and reception, and he'd said "sorry for your loss" then, too.

I shook his hand, though. "Ain't fair. Jake had a great life ahead."

Rachel pulled me away and led me to the stairwell, then up the wooden stairs. She smelled like wildflowers.

We passed the open second floor doorway to textbooks and stationery. On the third floor, the stairs ended at a door marked 'Employees only.'

Rachel opened the door and we entered a dusty chaos of sagging bookcases, boxes, and piled books. Cast-iron pipes ran below the raw lumber ceiling, from which protruded a legion of overshot nail points.

She closed the door and stared in my eyes. "Jake's been talking to me."

"What?"

"Almost every night since the funeral. When I'm asleep, when there's no distractions."

"So you've been dreaming—"

She gripped my arm. "No, not just dreams. Messages! I don't remember dreams so vividly. And sometimes I see him in the mirror behind me. He died wrong and he's too upset to rest in peace."

Of course he died wrong. He got his legs and nuts blown off. But I wasn't going to say that. "You said you see him in the mirror?"

She loosened her grip. "Sometimes, yes. He doesn't say anything then, he just appears behind me in his uniform. He can only talk to me when I'm asleep."

"What does he say?"

Instead of replying, she led me to a small table piled with books and sat in a wooden chair. I took the one next to her.

"Have you heard of *yuan gui*?" she said.

I had no idea where she was headed, so I said, "Go on."

"It's Chinese for 'ghosts with grievances.'" She opened a thick leather-bound book titled *The Way of Ghosts*.

"Where'd you get that?" I asked.

"Your Aunt Sybil loaned it to me."

"She's crazy, you know."

Rachel's eyes narrowed.

Said the wrong thing again. "I didn't mean... You know she was committed, right?"

"For what?"

"You know what happened with my grandma?" Before I was born, she walked into our woodlot in the middle of winter with only her nightie on, lay down, and froze to death.

Rachel nodded.

"After she died, Aunt Sybil had this breakdown. She told us her mother had sent instructions from beyond, that the End Times had already come but most people had chosen to follow Satan's minions and been left behind, along with their progeny. She claimed there were monsters everywhere, spreading evil, and the only chance at salvation was to beg God's forgiveness and depart this world for the next. Grandpa was afraid she'd kill herself too, and had her committed."

And after the electroshock, my other aunts claimed, she was never the same.

Rachel stared at me. "Jake never mentioned that."

Couldn't blame him. "She doesn't live around here, she lives with my Aunt Joanna's family. The reception was her first time at our house since, uh, since Ma's funeral I guess." I started feeling sick, the way I always did when I thought about Ma.

"Did she say where she got the book?" I asked then. I'd never seen it. Had it triggered my aunt's ghost stories? Was it doing the same to Rachel?

Rachel turned the pages carefully, like it was a museum piece. "She said a friend gave it to her when she was a girl. It's on the ban list. Anti-Christian."

She stopped at a page titled *YUĀN GUǏ* in curlicued letters, with Chinese characters below. "*Yuan gui* have been recorded back thousands of years in China," she said. "They're the spirits of persons who died wrongful deaths and can't move on to the afterlife. They often contact a living person, someone they know, and ask for their help. Once their grievances have been redressed, when justice is done, they can rest in peace."

"Jake wasn't Chinese."

She sighed. "The point is, the Chinese have been studying ghosts for thousands of years. There's a lot more wisdom in their teachings than there is in, say, the *New Bethany Bugle*."

Not a high bar to jump. "Okay," I said, "so what's Jake telling you?"

"He needs help to move on. He wants his death to mean something." Her lips trembled. "He told me he doesn't want what happened to him to happen to anyone else."

Was craziness contagious? Or transmitted by books? Would I catch it too? "So what are we supposed to do?"

She dabbed her eyes with a flowery handkerchief. "I had a long talk with Paul last week."

He sure got around. "Oh?"

"He said he hasn't given up on you."

"It's crazy," I said, "someone from New Bethany thinking they could overthrow the government."

Rachel shook her head, swishing fine black hair against her neck. "Paul said the government may seem invulnerable, but they're weak from complacency and corruption, and most people are so bad off these days, they'd jump at a chance for change."

I wasn't sure about that. Pop and Grandpa would gladly take a bullet for President Clark.

She continued, "Paul agreed with me that Jake shouldn't have died the way he did. He said whether it's Jake talking or my subconscious, he'd want an end to the war in Cuba, and all wars of occupation and colonialism."

"He ought to watch where he says things like that." Informers were everywhere.

"The store is safe," Rachel said, "especially up here."

"Maybe you should run for Congress or something," I suggested. Jake had talked about a career in politics after he got out of the Army. Rachel was smart and beautiful, and maybe she'd change things for the better.

"Don't be stupid."

The room pulsed and constricted. "Just 'cause you went to college and I got kicked out of high school..."

She flinched.

I tried to control my anger. "School was a waste anyway. I don't need anyone telling me what to think."

Morality, Hard Work, Respect. Crib to casket subservience, and if you were born with an adventurous streak, regimens of punishment and shaming.

"I'm sorry, I didn't mean to say that." She reached out and held my hand, her skin warm and soft. "I've always thought highly of you. You're right, you think for yourself, which is sadly rare in New Bethany. And you're clever, all the pranks you pulled in school."

"A lot of good that did me." Ruined me for life.

I rubbed Rachel's hand and fell into her deep green eyes. I wished for the millionth time she was my age instead of two years older, which wasn't a big deal now, but had been a huge matter in high school.

Rachel blushed and broke eye contact.

My fingers froze. She was Jake's fiancée. What the hell was wrong with me?

"Anyway," she said, "what I should have said was, I'm too young to run for Congress, and don't have the connections."

Of course. "Maybe down the road?"

"That's flattering, but I'm not social the way Jake—um, was. He was a football hero for God's sake. I was kind of a nobody before we started dating."

"I doubt that."

"It's true. I wasn't in any clubs except the mandatory ones like Young Homemakers. Boys would ask me out or act stupid around me because I'm pretty. But Jake was the only one who liked me for more than that."

"There's a lot more to you than being pretty or being Jake's girl. You see more than most people and don't just repeat dumb slogans."

Rachel bit her lip. "You've managed to completely derail me. We were talking about how to help Jake move on to the afterlife, how to address his grievances."

My heart clenched. Thoughts scattered like dead leaves in a gust.

"Paul told me," she continued, "Jake died to keep Cuba under the control of the sugar plantation owners."

Paul again. "How would he know? He wasn't there."

"Cuba's one of the world's top sugar producers. According to Paul, the industry's run by U.S. corporations. But they only pay the workers two dollars a day, which no one can live on. There was a strike, it was put down by force, and it turned into a rebellion."

Rachel pulled her hand away. She strode toward the far wall, turned down one of the aisles, and knelt behind the bookcases, disappearing from sight. She returned clutching a thick book, with *A History and Primer of Yarn-Knitting Techniques* printed on the dust cover.

She got up for that?

Rachel's eyes crinkled like she was amused. "It's not about knitting," she said, opening the book. The first page read *The Roots of Injustice,* by Dr. Solomon Biafra. "Paul gave me this. It's consistent with some of the other shadow lit I've seen over the years, but a lot more incisive."

I waited for a connection to Jake.

She studied me, maybe sensing I wasn't along for the ride yet. "Do you remember that memoir I showed you, the one by the *New York Times* journalist?"

"Yeah." Jake had only shown passing interest in the half dozen banned books Rachel had gotten hold of, but I'd thought it was fun, uncovering lies we'd been taught.

She flipped through *The Roots of Injustice.* "Biafra confirms the journalist's descriptions of the coup, that a clique of rich bankers and industrialists admired Mussolini and Hitler, and were so scared of Roosevelt and the labor unions, they put an army of veterans together. They took over Washington and forced Roosevelt to resign. All to protect their fortunes and bring back the gold standard."

I didn't know what the gold standard was, but didn't want to look stupid by asking.

"There's more, though," she said. "Biafra claims Garner was assassinated."

John Garner had been Roosevelt's conservative VP. He'd declared a state of emergency and brought in Lindbergh as the new vice. A week later he died in a plane crash.

"What's his proof?"

She fumbled through the text. "Biafra doesn't lay out proof per se, just says it was too convenient for coincidence..."

Her forest green eyes fixed on the pages as words rolled past her red lips and perfect teeth. She was too angelic for this world. I lost the string of her words, something about Roosevelt's ties to the Soviet Union, which they said in school was one of the reasons he had to be replaced.

Rachel stared in my eyes. "Are you listening to me?"

My cheeks turned warm. "Sorry. I'm tired, that's all."

Her eyes dropped. "Me too. I can't sleep after Jake talks to me."

That.

"I was saying," she said, "what they teach about stopping a communist takeover was all made up. Roosevelt established diplomatic ties with the Soviet Union, but all the 'Support Comrade Roosevelt' brochures were fakes, and the newspaper and radio accusations just propaganda. He wasn't transforming America into a socialist dictatorship, he was trying to pull us out of depression."

"My Grandpa was around back then; he says that's what Lindbergh did—put people to work, fed the hungry, built apartments for the homeless."

She let out a huff. "Now that's a socialist dictatorship, because they also shut down opposition papers and arrested anyone who spoke out."

"Where'd Paul get this book?" I asked. "I thought we were capitalist." Everyone was supposed to work together, teachers told us, but capitalism rewarded the best ideas and best people. Crap, of course—connections were the actual key to success.

"We're both," she said. "Once Huey Long was assassinated and the Depression ended, Ford, the du Ponts, and the rest of the business clique wrote a new constitution. Protections for property but not for people."

I'd never seen the original constitution. Our schoolbooks claimed it was outdated and needed modernizing. But they didn't let us see for ourselves. "So how does this help anything?"

Rachel closed *The Roots of Injustice.* "This is how we start, to help Jake rest. Knowing the facts and telling other people. The past created the present. Biafra describes how the government uses the military to enforce the exploitation of foreign workers and the theft of their natural resources. Only a handful of people benefit."

"Just like New Bethany." First Consolidated Bank used the Sheriff's Office and Pinkertons to evict debtors and shut down any grumbling about unfair corn prices.

She nodded.

"So, did Paul ask you to join some organization?" I hoped she'd had the sense to say no.

"Yeah, but I don't know, I mean, he didn't even say what they do."

I slid my chair close. "Forget that guy. We'll get through this, you and me."

She finally smiled and guitars pounded major triads in my head. It would be a while before Rachel was ready to move on, but when she was…

Would that be betraying Jake? Or would he be fine with it?

For now—and Jake would agree with this—I'd make sure she didn't do anything to get herself jailed.

Chapter Four

Someone's in my room.

I sit up in my narrow iron-frame bed, hurl the quilt aside. The guns are all downstairs in the mud room. Stupid of me. I try to stand but can't leave the bed, like I'm sitting in a grave.

My brother Jake sits on the wicker chair by the window, wearing his Army uniform, the formal one with the peaked cap, black tie, and olive drab jacket with corporal stripes. I can only see his face in the moonlight. The rest lies in shadow.

I try to say something, tell Jake he's dead and buried, but nothing comes out.

"Look after Pop," he says in a raspy voice. "And Rachel. They need you."

My eyes adjust to the dark. Ragged stumps protrude from his pelvis instead of legs.

My heart pounds, throat screams, but nothing comes out.

"Go away," I manage. I can't tear my eyes away from the stumps.

"Help," he says. The room darkens. Obscures his mangled body. Only his face remains.

What kind of an asshole rejects their only brother? My brother who died for his country, while I sit around home doing nothing? "I'm sorry, I didn't mean it."

"Help." My brother's dead face fades into blackness.

I sat up in bed and threw the musty blanket aside. The sheets were damp with cold sweat. Just a dream. But it felt real, and I could still see Jake's face. Maybe Rachel was right.

I threw on jeans and crept downstairs, bypassing the creaky boards. I hurried to the heavy black telephone box on the kitchen wall, lifted the handset off the hook, and dialed Rachel's house. I hung up after the first number. The wall clock hands were still short of four a.m. Better to tell her in person anyway.

I glanced at the open mud room doorway, drawn toward the protective shotgun standing in the rack with the rifles.

Don't be stupid. I turned and trudged back upstairs.

I never did get back to sleep.

* * *

Once the sun rose, I made myself presentable and drove to Rachel's house on Chestnut Street, a block west of their store. Thick gray fog cloaked the world. Even with the headlights on, I couldn't see more than twenty feet or so, and hoped no one else was on the road.

The Tolson house wasn't any bigger than my house, but made mine look ramshackle. It had freshly applied creme-colored paint and windows so clean, you could hardly see the glass. I climbed the concrete steps to the front porch and rang the doorbell.

Mrs. Tolson opened the door with a glittering smile. "Benjamin. What brings you here?"

"Uh, is Rachel here?"

"It's only seven o'clock. The store doesn't open until ten, so she's still asleep."

Of course. I was too tired for this.

"Come on in. I'm getting the other kids ready for school. You drink coffee?"

"When we got it. Usually with chicory." I had never actually been inside Rachel's house and it was like entering foreign territory. Everything was warm and plush and spotless and smelled like fresh lemons.

"We've got regular coffee, Colombian. I'll pour you a cup."

Mr. Tolson was sitting at the dining room table with coffee and a copy of the *Chicago Tribune*. The top headline read, 'New Victories in Cuba and The Philippines.' We'd been fighting in the Philippines as long as anyone could remember, decades after kicking the Japanese out. The other headlines read 'Jap Atrocities in India' and 'Canadian Jews Behind Detroit Unrest.'

I smelled oatmeal cooking in the adjacent kitchen. Rachel's two sisters, Serena and Samantha, fraternal twins in high school, and her long-haired middle-school brother, Jimmy, darted around the house in their blue and white uniforms. They cast suspicious looks at me.

I didn't belong here. "I should leave."

"Nonsense," Mrs. Tolson said. She waved a hand toward the table and I sat. She placed a flower-painted cup of strong-smelling coffee in front of me. "Sugar and cream?"

"Just milk, thanks."

As she poured milk in, Mr. Tolson put down his paper. "Hello again, Benjamin."

"Hi, Mr. Tolson. I just had something I wanted to talk to Rachel about."

He stood. "I'll go get her, then."

"No, that's okay. I can wait."

He headed up the stairs anyway. The sisters, who had Rachel's perfect cheeks and nose, plopped down at the table and picked at their oatmeal.

Their brother Jimmy joined them and stared at me. "What are you doing here at breakfast?"

Serena and Samantha eyed me and smirked.

"Just some news for Rachel." I turned my attention to the coffee, which was hot but not scalding, and surprisingly mellow-tasting.

"What's it like living on a farm?"

Mrs. Tolson wagged a finger. "Hush, Jimmy. Don't be rude."

Didn't seem like a rude question. "You have this house and the book store," I said. "We've got 216 acres of land, been in the family five generations. Most of it's rotated between corn and soybeans, with wheat or rye in the winter, but we also have twenty acres of woods and our own creek and pond. Pond's too small for good-sized fish but Jake and me had plans to dig a bigger one."

Everyone was watching me. "Are you still gonna do that?" Jimmy asked.

"At some point." Assuming I wasn't killed overseas. "It falls on me to take care of the place once Pop gets too old."

Mr. Tolson stomped back down the stairs. "She'll be down in a minute."

"No hurry."

"Apparently there is, otherwise you wouldn't be here this early." He drained his coffee. "How are things with you at the farm?"

"Doing okay." I didn't want to talk about my freaky dream—or whatever it was—or the farm's money troubles.

"Ever thought about returning to school, getting a degree?"

"They won't let me back. Besides, I have to help at the farm." And school was a waste, not a thought he'd appreciate.

Mr. Tolson frowned. "Rachel started community college late thanks to your brother. And now, who knows when she'll be ready for a degree program. The University of Illinois accepted her application, but she's in no condition to study now."

"Her fiancé was killed less than a month ago." I decided to change the subject before I got mad. "Deer season's starting soon. I know where to find them and never miss. I could bring you some steaks."

He smiled. "That's awfully nice of you, Ben."

Rachel padded down the stairs, wrapped in a thick white bathrobe. She'd brushed her long hair, but hadn't put on makeup. She was even prettier without it, more relatable.

She approached without smiling. "What is it?"

Her father's stare transfixed me as I rose. "I should have come later."

"Well, you're here now," she said.

"Best we talk alone."

Mr. Tolson held up a hand. "Say what you have to say."

I met Rachel's green eyes. "Just wanted to say I had the same dream." This would ramp up the squirm factor, so I pushed in my chair. "We can talk later."

"You came here about a dream?" Mr. Tolson asked.

Rachel deflated inside her bathrobe. "We can talk now," she told me.

"Shouldn't you put some clothes on first?" her father said.

Rachel rolled her eyes. "Why don't you wait for me in the library, Ben?"

I started to ask what library, but she motioned for me to follow her. She opened a door, flipped a light switch, and led me down creaky steps into a finished basement.

We entered a spacious room ringed by floor-to-ceiling bookshelves. The shelves were packed, thousands of books, a chaos of color that wrapped the room like a quilt. Rachel steered me by the arm to a circular table with a bright ceiling lamp above, and sat me in one of the four padded chairs. "Wait here and my family won't interrogate you. I'll be back soon."

"You have your own library?"

She grinned. "We're booksellers, you know." Her eyes swept the crowded shelves. "Truth comes from reflection, and books accumulate our reflections. They're how humanity grows."

"Humanity just grows in numbers. Nothing ever gets better."

Her smile faded. "If you don't control it, of course life can be hard. But that's why we have minds. Direct your thoughts toward an outcome and you can shape it." She turned and hurried back up the stairs.

I got up and browsed the book titles. Most I hadn't heard of, and half weren't even in English. *Kritik der reinen Vernunft. Logische Untersuchungen. Sein und Zeit.* I'd taken two years of German like everyone else, but I was never much good at it.

I didn't see anything by Solomon Biafra. Or the obligatory Charles Lindbergh for that matter. Nor *Mein Kampf*, which was so boring and pointless that I'd taken an 'F' in European Studies rather than finish it. I'd received an 'F' in American History that semester too, having decided from talks with Rachel that it was mostly lies. The Spirit Administrator punished me, making me lead the singing of 'Onward, Victory' during morning assembly the rest of the year, arm raised to the flag in salute. And if I hadn't received 'A''s in Machine Shop, Military Drill, and Music, they would have held me back a grade, an unbearable humiliation.

I pulled down a random Zane Grey novel, sat back down, and started thumbing through it.

A sharp clip-crop of iron-shod hoofs deadened and died away...

"I should have figured you were a Western fan," Rachel said behind me.

I was well into the book. I turned. She'd exchanged the bathrobe for a short-sleeved, pastel-striped dress.

I closed the book and stood. "Just killing time."

"Everyone's gone now," she said. "Except Mom."

"Your sisters are a lot younger than you." I'd never met them.

Rachel glanced toward the stairs. "I was an accident. My sisters were planned, after my parents settled and saved money. Brother, another accident."

I didn't have any siblings now. My little sister Abby, gone close to ten years now, was born with a broken heart. At least that's what the coroner said, she had a hole in her heart that no one knew about. She got tired easily but her phys-ed coach pushed her like everyone else and she collapsed. A tragedy but no one's fault, the school said. She's in God's hands now, Preacher Bill said. America is better off without inferior specimens, the Eugenics Department would say.

Rachel was rocking on her feet. "So what did Jake say?"

I described the vision. "He said to look after you and Pop. He kept saying, 'Help,' though I wasn't sure if that meant him or you or both."

I hoped it was just a dream and I wasn't going crazy like my Aunt Sybil. No way could I deal with electroshock.

Rachel hugged me, then started to cry. Soon she made bawling and gasping noises, and tears dribbled down her cheeks.

Poor girl. I held her and stroked her hair. I hoped her mother couldn't hear the crying, but maybe everyone was used to it by now. "It was like you said. It was a dream but it felt real afterward."

"Jake needs us," she managed. "We have to help him."

"We should talk to his Army buddies. Maybe they can help."

She pulled away, wiped her eyes with her wrist, and sniffled. "How?"

"To find out more, like how he died, so we have a better idea what he might want."

"I told you, he wants to end the colonial wars."

"That's what Paul told you. Jake was quite a patriot."

"He was more open than your father." Her shoulders tensed. "I didn't mean—"

I waved off her apology. "Pop's brainwashed."

"How do we contact his fellow soldiers?" she asked. "They're all in Cuba."

"Who knows, maybe they'll send me there when I'm drafted."

Jake had been lucky to spend his first two years stateside. America had over six million people in uniform, and half of them were overseas managing an empire that sprawled the globe and occasionally butted heads with the Japanese, Soviets, or ungrateful equatorials. At least we hadn't traded nukes with anyone yet.

Rachel turned paler than usual and gripped my arm. "You have to avoid that. Jake doesn't want you to die the way he did."

"I doubt I'll have a say." I dropped the unpleasant topic. "We can write Jake's Army buddies. Or call, that would be quicker. I have postcards and letters at home, they have some of the names."

"I'll get mine." Rachel hurried upstairs, leaving me to the silent warehouse of Tolson wisdom.

She returned before I had time to get bored. She laid a gilded box on the center of the wooden table top, sat in one of the chairs, and opened it. "All his letters and postcards since the day he started basic training."

I took the chair next to her. "He sure was full of hellfire when the drill sergeants got through with him. Better dead than Red, mercy's for the weak, that sort of shit."

The letters were neatly organized in the box, as if filed up for inspection.

Rachel flipped through them. "He was back to normal in a few days. His first leave, after boot camp, was the closest we'd ever been." She smiled. "Stupid rocky times forgotten."

Her smile disappeared. "Last I saw him was the week before he shipped out to Cuba."

Six months ago. That was the last anyone in New Bethany saw my brother.

"I asked if he was scared about being sent to a combat zone," she said. "He said no, but they fly back caskets almost every day." Tears beaded in the corners of her eyes. "I miss him so much."

I scanned the library for a handkerchief but she pulled one out of her purse.

"He shouldn't have signed up again." I'd told Jake that from the beginning, and now the thought wouldn't leave my mind.

Rachel dabbed her wet eyes. "He said he had to, and I should be proud he was fighting for our country."

Jake had sent his signing bonus home to pay off the bank, but Pop bought a new tractor instead. I'd told him to take it back, but Pop never was one for listening. Had to show up the neighbors, especially Sarah's family.

Rachel slipped the handkerchief back in her purse and opened one of the letters. She placed it on the table between us so we could both read. Jake's handwriting was better than mine, although not as neat as Rachel's.

Dear Rachel,

Saw my first combat. It was a piece of cake, nobody hurt on our side. We took out a bunch of rebels, though. They're cowards and dress like civilians instead of soldiers, but shoot at you anyway. You have to be careful and get them before they get you.

I enclosed some photos of me on the base and in a helicopter. Those things can carry a whole squad and all their gear, have enough armor to resist ▉▉▉▉▉▉▉▉▉ *▉▉▉▉▉▉ and fly over* ▉▉▉ *knots. I look at your picture all the time. I wish you were smiling more in it, but a half smile is better than no smile. You look pretty sexy actually.*

Can't believe I'm here a whole year. I get a two week leave, but no word on the date yet. At least they cover transport home, all the way to my house. I can't wait to be in your arms again.

I decided no way am I doing another two years. I've got big plans for the farm and like we talked about, thought I'd run for county council. I'll be VFW eligible and they have a lot of pull.

Have to go. More later!

Love,
Jake

"Did you get a letter about a mission he said he couldn't get out of his head?" I asked. "Mine was half censored."

She searched the box. "Yeah. Mine had a lot of redactions too, and I've wondered why." She pulled out an envelope. "Here it is."

She unfolded the letter on the table: three sheets of cursive front and back.

Dear Rachel,

Ever had something happen that you might never get out of your head? My mom's death was like that. Today's mission was too.

An image flashed in my mind, me and Jake finding Ma lying on the hen house floor, eyes shut, cheeks clammy white, flower-print work dress crimson between her legs. The chickens wouldn't stop pacing and clucking. We lifted our mom off the blood-soaked straw and red glop slid out of the skirt, then a cord with a tiny pink baby attached, lifeless little arms, legs, and face. Sepsis took Ma not long after.

We got intel the rebels were planning to hit a sugar mill in Santa Rosa Valley, one of the main production centers. They're just hurting their countrymen if you ask me, but they're too yellow to attack our bases.

"Why attack a sugar mill?" I asked.

Rachel looked up. "To pressure the companies into a settlement, I presume." She returned to the letter, and I did too.

They flew the whole battalion into the valley. The helicopters flew in V-formations, like geese, and I was thinking if the rebels had anti-aircraft weapons, how easy it is to pick off geese in formation once they're in range.

No one fired at us, and the copters dropped us in a cleared field. Raining as usual, though not more than a drizzle. The gunnery and squad sergeants gathered the platoon together. Sgt. Armstead yelled at us, 'Quit standing around and get your shit together,' that sort of thing. Lt. Higgins, our platoon commander, a young guy fresh out of the academy, stared at his map, probably having no clue what to do next. Capt. Tannin, the battalion's military intelligence liaison, grabbed the map out of his hand and called all the sergeants over.

The way it works is the officers tell the sergeants what to do and they tell the sloggers—the rest of us—what to do. Sgt. Armstead pointed at this big aluminum-sided factory the rebels were supposed to hit. The sarge said we'd do a perimeter sweep and interrogate the locals to see what they knew. Other units would sweep the hills.

We followed a cart path into the sugarcane, which was thick and ten feet high. They put me on point as usual since I've been hunting my whole life. Some of the others took flanking tracks so we wouldn't get ambushed.

About a mile past the landing field, we saw a bunch of mulattoes—men, women, and children—hacking sugarcane with machetes and piling them into ox-drawn carts. I hoped we'd get perimeter duty, but no, the gunnery waved us in.

Capt. Tannin shouted at the workers in Spanish, which I'm still trying to learn. The sergeants shouted too. We pointed our guns in case they tried something. The workers dropped their machetes and shuffled toward us with hateful eyes. I counted twelve men, seven women, and ten boys ranging from children to teens. The children were skinny and barefoot.

The oldest man spat in our direction.

The women and children started screaming

"What do you think the censors blacked out?" I asked Rachel as she turned the page.

She shrugged. "Someone must have shot the old man, is my guess."

Not the sort of thing they'd mention on TV.

We led the workers into the middle of the cleared area, which was ankle deep in leaves cut away from the stalks. We made them kneel, hands on head. Capt. Tannin asked them questions in Spanish while I scanned the standing cane along the perimeter.

After a few minutes, the captain pointed at the youngest kid. He couldn't have been more than eight. Two soldiers grabbed him. The other workers yammered in Spanish. This young woman clasped her hands together and shook them like she was pleading.

Sgt. Armstead shot his rifle over their heads and told them to shut up. The captain pointed to the woman with the clasped hands and said "Bring her too."

They took the woman and boy down the cart path from the others. Capt. Tannin questioned them until the woman confessed to something. Sgt. Armstead translated for us: The rebels were there a week ago asking questions and trying to recruit people. They left before the "Yankees"—that's what they call us here—showed up. But they always came back.

The last several paragraphs were blacked out except Jake's signature at the end. "What do you think he said there?"

Rachel gripped the letter and stared at it. "He said something awful happened. Do you think they shot women and children?"

"Jake wouldn't do that," I said. "Although maybe this Captain Tannin did."

Rachel tore a sheet of paper from a notepad on the table. "I'll write down the names on the backs of the photos. Maybe someone will know what's missing from the letters."

Once we finished, we went up to the den, a small room in the back corner of the first floor. It was also full of books, mostly encyclopedia sets, with a polished wood desk and locked file cabinets. A sleek-looking telephone sat on the desk.

Rachel eased into the desk chair and laid her notepad next to the phone. Mrs. Tolson poked her head in. "Aren't you going to the store?"

"Yes, Mother. I just have a call to make."

Rachel had me shut the door. She picked up the phone handset and dialed the operator. "Can you connect me to Camp Santa Clara in Cuba, please?"

"You know someone will listen in," I warned her.

She shrugged. "Yes, I will accept the charges," she told the operator. After a long wait, she introduced herself as Jacob Adamson's fiancée and asked, "Could I please speak with Mark Lowe in the 10th Air Cavalry Division, 103rd Infantry Regiment, 1st Battalion, Company A, 3rd Platoon? I'm not sure what his rank is now."

The first name on the list. A pause, then, "I need to talk to him about my fiancé at his earliest convenience. It's very important." She recited her address and national ID number.

Another pause, then "I'm sorry to hear that." She wrote 'KIA' next to the name. "How about Robert Cole? Same unit."

"I see." She wrote 'UNAVAIL.' next to the name. She kept going through the list, every name that Jake mentioned.

Jaw clenched, she hung up. "They're all either dead or otherwise unavailable."

The door opened. Her mom again. "Rachel, honey, are you done with your call?"

She stayed in her seat. "Yes, Mother."

"Your father needs you at the store. The doctor said working's good for you."

"Okay, mother."

Once I closed the door again, Rachel said, "Some of the men were off-base or reassigned. I'll try to track them down after work."

I nodded, then considered, "I know something that's better for you than working."

She raised an eyebrow. "Oh, do you?"

Sex popped into my mind—not my original intent. From Rachel's expression, she wouldn't appreciate the sentiment.

"Pale Moon Rising," I said. "My band—"

"I know."

"We're playing Friday night at the James barn." We'd planned it before the death notice, but had decided not to cancel. "You should come. It'll be fun."

I'd never seen Rachel at a barn show before. Too Philistine for her, I used to think. But maybe she was just shy, despite her looks.

"Will Paul be there?"

"Probably. He follows Sarah around, and she's in the band. I'm thinking we'll make it a tribute to Jake."

She stood and half-smiled. "Give me directions."

Chapter Five

The James family had one of the biggest barns in the county. That and the fact it had electricity made it popular on the music circuit. It smelled like drying hay, diesel, and mule poop, but once enough people were dancing, all you'd smell was sweat.

They'd cleared the ground floor for the event, and at least fifty people, mostly teenage to thirtyish, gathered inside and shuffled over the straw-covered dirt floor. More would be on the way—hopefully Rachel among them.

The opening band, Glory Stench, had set up on the far end of the barn, backs to the plank wall, hayloft far above, amps snug against the microphone stands. They didn't have a fiddle or bass, just a guitar, a couple of banjos, and a harmonica.

Glory Stench weren't quite in tune, missed a lot of notes, and didn't play entirely in sync, but they had energy—lots of it. A dozen people, mostly couples, danced in front of the band, throwing their partners around and inventing all kinds of new moves.

Wearing denims and her checkered flannel, Sarah strolled up and handed me a mug of beer. There weren't any laws against drinking, just control of selling, so everyone brought their own moonshine or homebrew, or shared with others. "Whatcha think?"

"Breakers are holding." I scanned the crowd again, searching for Rachel.

Most of the crowd were white, but Sarah wasn't the only exception. General rule was, anyone who appreciated bluegrass was welcome, as long as the landowner or one of the bands knew them. Dress was casual townie, the men wearing printed shirts or flannels, leather shoes, and wide-brimmed cowboy or straw hats. Other than Sarah and a couple others, the women wore knee-length skirts or dresses. I guess because it made dancing easier.

I sipped the beer. It tasted like musty grass and wet cardboard.

I must have made a face because Sarah said, "No one around here knows how to brew."

"This is even worse than usual." The skunky aftertaste clung to my tongue like spackling paste.

I smelled cough syrup nearby, someone either too impatient to separate out the codeine, or didn't have a pH meter. Best thing about school, it was widely agreed, was chemistry class.

A handful stumbled around glassy-eyed, probably in the middle of a Smash high. That was the latest craze, but what I'd heard scared me too much to try it. First, it was addictive as hell. Worse, it was the second leading cause of death in Illinois, topped only by suicide.

I abandoned the mug of skank beer. "Let's get some shine. Tastes bad, but you don't have to dwell on it."

Mr. Haskins, an older gentleman who lived on a hundred-acre wood lot, sat in a wicker chair against a support beam and poured clear liquid from a ceramic jug into small plastic cups. It smelled like turpentine. He smiled when we approached, half his teeth missing, and poured a cup for me and Sarah.

"I generally suggest a mandatory donation," he said. "But it's 100% free for performers." He winked.

"Thanks." I inhaled fresh air through my nose, sent a generous sip down my throat, and exhaled. It burned all the way down, then the heat trickled up to my head. No yeasty or metallic aftertaste—Mr. Haskins took pride in his craft.

Paul joined us. He wore his city suit, white fedora, and gleaming white shoes. "Hi."

"You sure stand out," I said.

"Well, next time I'll dress more appropriate."

Sarah elbowed me. "Be nice, he's family."

"How long you in town?" I asked.

"Oh, a while," he said quietly. "I'm staying with my folks. You should come by some time."

"The man can preach," Sarah said. "I'm totally with him."

"You are?" I'd thought Sarah had more sense than that.

"She's not alone," Paul said. "We've all got to work together. And I need to clear up some misconceptions. About Kansas City for starters." His eyes drifted. "Who are the informers here?"

I studied the crowd. "None that I recognize. Darren Walker and Will Coulter and Candy Mallone are banned from the barn circuit—no one will let them on their property. These things are invite-only to keep the rats out. And no recording devices or cameras allowed."

Paul bought a cup of shine from Mr. Haskins, then they got to chatting. Apparently Paul had been a customer as a teenager. Mr. Haskins complained about sheriff's deputies demanding kickbacks and church ladies sticking their snouts where they didn't belong.

He'd always been kind of ornery, having served five years in a labor camp for punching a traveling preacher, then five more for trying to organize a "Throw the Rascals Out" electoral campaign. "Keepin' low to the ground these days," he told Paul.

As if on cue, Glory Stench launched into an illegal union song, "Solidarity Forever." They didn't sing the lyrics so if pressed later, they could say they were playing "The Battle Hymn of the Republic," which the tune was based on.

Paul sang, though. Sarah joined him, her alto voice echoing like the wrath of archangels.

"When the union's inspiration through the workers' blood shall run
There can be no power greater anywhere beneath the sun
Yet what force on earth is weaker than the feeble strength of one
But the union makes us strong..."

Mr. Haskins joined in, then some others, so I added my voice. Why not? Safety in numbers.

Paul's eyes roved from face to face, presumably passing judgment on their sincerity.

"...They have taken untold millions that they never toiled to earn,
But without our brain and muscle, not a single wheel can turn.
We can break their haughty power, gain our freedom when we learn
That the union makes us strong..."

The musicians went into an uptempo jam. Just about everyone picked a dance partner. I wondered where Rachel was.

Sarah grabbed my hand and I led her in a modified two step, left hand in hers, right hand below her shoulder, moving her around the straw floor and whirling her. She grinned the whole time. "You do have your talents," she said.

Interracial dancing was frowned on in town but no one here seemed bothered. That was the nice thing about the barn circuit—people could be themselves.

When the song finished, Alvin James, eldest of the farm's sons, slapped me on the back. "You're up."

"You heard the man," I told Sarah. I corralled the rest of the band: Ash on banjo, Magda on mandolin, and Jesse on standup bass.

Once we were all set and tuned, Jesse, the only band member with a decent-paying day job, switched on his 4-track tape recorder. He recorded all our shows, but we had to edit out anything controversial.

I gazed out at the audience. There were close to a hundred now. Paul leaned against a ladder with crossed arms.

"We're Pale Moon Rising," I said in the mike.

Lots of cheers. Paul clapped but didn't smile.

I took a deep breath. "We buried my brother a couple weeks back. Jake Adamson, most of you knew him or heard about him."

The mood curdled, folks looking down or mumbling condolences.

"So this show's for him. I want everyone to dance and get drunk and have a good time. That's what he'd want."

I caught my bandmates' eyes and strummed the first few chords of "No Geld Sunrise," our usual opener. They joined in, every note in sync. I sang two verses and choruses, then we launched into instrument solos, everyone getting a turn to shine. I recapped the chorus and we ended on a flourish.

The crowd cheered. I got my bandmates' attention and said, "Land."

"This is something new we wrote since our last time here," I said in the mike. I led off in hopeful G major, ascending eighth notes in 4/4, and the others joined in.

"It's a cloudless summer morning
The corn's grown knee high.
I cast for the largemouth
As the sun starts to rise.
The prairie flowers are blooming,
Sweet girls catch my eye,
A life of endless evers
Beneath the blue sky."

Channeling weeks, years of anger, I switched to B major for the chorus.

"Listen Mr. Banker, don't come round here no more.
Listen Mr. Banker, don't come round here no more.
It ain't your land to take,
Give us folk a break,
Listen, don't come round here no more..."

We played all our songs and some covers. We got a grand total of $23.15 in the hat, not an easy sum to split.

Rachel never showed.

As we packed up, Paul strode over and tipped his hat. "Nicely done."

"Thanks."

"You know," he said, "music is the measure of a man's soul."

Not a typical comment. "What are you getting at?"

"Your songs show you care. How angry you are about the injustice in the world."

"They're just songs. I ain't doing anything that'll get me sent to a prison camp."

The James brothers came up and rescued me. They thanked and flattered everyone in the band, then came back to me and slapped me on the back.

"You ought to play full time," Alvin said. "Put out records and get on the radio."

I shrugged. We'd talked about putting a demo tape together, but my heart wasn't in it anymore.

"Trouble is," Paul said, eying the James brothers too, "the government is strict about what airs. Bible thumping and fake news mostly."

Sarah smirked. "And Sousa marches."

John Philip Sousa was the National Composer, even though he was long dead. Pop loved him. I hated him with a passion and had told Sarah one day I'd dig up his bones and nail them to an upside-down cross alongside the highway.

What happened to Rachel? She was normally 110% reliable. "I gotta go," I said.

My bandmates stared at me like I was nuts.

"Party's just gettin' started," Ash said.

"Have to check on Rachel. She said she was coming."

Sarah frowned. "I don't know why you're so surprised. This isn't her scene."

I went outside to my battered truck and hopped in, sliding my guitar case across the bench seat. I glanced back at the barn and spotted Sarah under the floodlights, arms crossed. I waved to let her know everything was cool.

* * *

I pulled the truck up to the Tolson house. None of the inside lights were on. It was close to midnight, though. The family van sat in front, white paint shaded sickly yellow under the streetlights.

Red and blue flashed in the rearview mirror. The hell? Bright floods daylighted the cab interior. I turned the ignition off and waited.

A city cop swaggered up to the driver's window. I recognized him beneath the dark blue uniform. Officer Lance Ferguson, a bully from birth. Like most of the twenty-strong city police, he'd bleached his hair Aryan blond and cropped it close to his skull, then followed with enough weightlifting to bulk his muscles up to freak status.

"Well if it isn't Benjamin Adamson," he said. "We never did get to see you wearing that thief sign."

Not only did they kick me out of school for stealing band equipment, even though it was old surplus, the district attorney's office pressed charges. Being needed on the farm, I avoided work camp, but the judge sentenced me to a public lashing, then made me wear a sign with "THIEF" on it for six months. I took it off as soon as I left his sight and never put it back on.

"I was busy at the farm," I told Bully-Boy Ferguson. "Had no cause to come into town."

"A shame. Maybe we should brand it on your forehead. Once a thief, always a thief. You casing out a place to rob, huh?"

My fists clenched, but striking an officer would get me ten years.

He smirked and thrust out his chest. "Hah, whatcha gonna do? Huh? Maybe you need another lashing. They went light on you."

Rachel, showing why she deserved my worship more than any stymie-eyed Old Man in the Sky, had sold some of her clothes and bribed the whip man to go easy on me. Probably a flutter of those eyelashes was enough.

"I'm not casing anything." I pointed at the Tolson house. "They're family, sort of."

"Hoping to watch one of them girls take their clothes off? Is that what you're up to?"

Ferguson probably peeped all over town. "Of course not," I said. "Can I go now?"

"I can arrest you for loitering, but I'm in a good mood. Twenty-dollar fee for a warning."

The cops were the biggest thieves in town. "I don't have twenty, but you can have what I've got."

I reached into my back pocket. He whipped out his gun, a .38 caliber Smith & Wesson revolver, probably with exploding bullets that would turn my organs to jelly.

"Whoah. Just getting my wallet." I tossed it to him.

He pulled out the cash—four dollars, two quarters, and a dime—my take from the night's show. His nostrils flared like a bull's. "Is that all you've got?"

"Everything I've earned since my brother died." I hoped he wouldn't take the guitar lying next to me.

"Yeah, your brother was the good one." He pocketed my money and threw back the wallet. "Get the hell out of here, you dirt-poor dumb-ass hick. If I see you around again after dark, you're going to jail, no question."

I turned the ignition key and drove home in a rage.

Chapter Six

In a neat hotel room, Rachel unzips her dress, eyes smiling with anticipation. It falls to the floor. A white lacy bra and panties frame a willowy but nicely curved figure and creamy smooth skin. She unhooks the bra, revealing small, upturned breasts, drops it on top of the dress on the floor.

I fumble to catch up, shed my shoes, shirt, pants, and underwear, toss them aside. Rachel slips her panties off. We embrace. Kiss, rub tongues together. Lie on the creaky bed, arms and legs intertwined. I hook fingers between her perfect thighs and she moans.

I am outside myself, outside the pleasure, seeing Rachel on top of me, rocking her pelvis back and forth.

It isn't me. It's Jake. I try to turn away but can't.

Rachel's gone. The hotel room's gone. I'm marching behind Jake, slogging up a steep hill through thick forest. I'm weighed down by something heavy. Not sure what it is. The ground is wet and slippery, the air like steam after a hot shower. Insects buzz and trill from somewhere behind the leaves. They notice that I notice and the noise grows deafening.

Jake's boots and olive drab pants are spattered with mud. He carries an M1969 .30 caliber automatic rifle, muzzle pointed down and to the left. He doesn't acknowledge me. Others are behind me but their faces are blurry.

Our battalion is on a Seek and Obliterate mission. I can't see far. Our squad is alone. I read in a letter that each squad has its own territory to cover. Call in backup if we find anything.

Jake's on point. He's a hunter so he has to go first. I'm a better hunter than Jake. Why aren't I in front?

Birds were singing but now it's quiet. Something's wrong. Ahead, figures move through the undergrowth, dark green phantoms. Jake stops; he sees them too.

Loud crack behind me, some moron stepping on a stick. Muzzles flash lightning and thunder at us. Leaves fly off. Bullets thud into wood and dirt.

I'm going to die. But I can't move. Just stand there, an easy target.

Jake kneels and shoots back with his rifle. I have some kind of weapon on my back but can't reach it.

Explosions on all sides. Hillside shakes. Can't see anything but smoke. Hear trees splintering and crashing to the ground and screams of people in mortal pain. One sounds like mom.

My heart. My heart will stop. I'm going to die! I DON'T WANT TO DIE!

* * *

Thuds. Banging. Knocking against wood.

My door. I'd been dreaming about one of the battles Jake wrote about, the one where most of his squad was killed.

"What?" I shouted.

"Phone call for you." Pop's voice, gruff and loud.

"Who is it?"

"Rachel. Time you were up, anyway."

I threw on jeans and hurried down the stairs to the kitchen. "Hello?"

"Meet me at Jake's grave in an hour." She spoke the words fast.

"What? Why?"

"Just come, okay? It's important." She hung up.

The morning was chilly, although not cold enough for fleece yet. My camo jacket would do. I took the truck to the New Bethany Baptist Cemetery, a savanna of oak trees and mowed turf grass just south of town.

We'd buried Jake with the other Adamsons, next to my ma and sister. Besides the casket, the Army had bought him a rounded marble headstone. It was flanked by little American flags, but someone had taken the flowers away, which would have been unsightly by now.

Rachel stood by the headstone, draped in a black wool coat. Next to her, a man in olive drab Army dress uniform leaned on a polished wood cane. He wore black-framed glasses and looked a year or two older than me. His sleeves had yellow corporal stripes.

He offered a hand as I approached. "Seth Bowen." He had a crisp accent, like a newscaster.

I shook his hand. "Ben Adamson. What brings you here?"

He glanced at Rachel, who looked tired. "Miss Tolson called me. "I served with your brother in Cuba. He was a good man."

My face spasmed, like I'd break into tears.

"I'm so sorry I missed your show, Ben," Rachel said. "Corporal Bowen's bus arrived at five. We got to talking and then I was too upset to go anywhere." Her eyes moistened.

I held her hands in solidarity. They were cold. "Don't worry about it."

"I wanted to come to the funeral," Bowen said. "But I was still in the hospital. Least I could do was see his grave and share what I know."

Rachel stared at the headstone. "The others Jake knew are either still in Cuba or dead. Most of them dead."

"Did you see my brother die?" I asked Bowen.

"No, they transferred him out of the company. Then I took a bullet in the knee and they flew me back to the States. I'm waiting for a metal kneecap, but at least I can walk now, sort of. Then it's back home to Connecticut."

Rachel caught his attention. "Tell Ben what you told me last night. Start with the boy."

"You sure?"

"Jake's brother needs to know everything, same as me."

Corporal Bowen exhaled and settled more of his weight on the cane.

"Jake had already been in Cuba a while when I got there. I was a know-nothing private and Sergeant Armstead, our squad leader at the time, yelled at me a lot. But Jake told me everything I needed to know, like company procedures and how to deal with the heat."

Bowen glanced at the ground, then up at the sky.

"My first field op, they flew our battalion into the Santa Rosa Valley to preempt a rebel attack on one of the sugar mills."

"Jake wrote about that," I said.

"Where do you want me to start, then?"

"The parts that were blacked out," Rachel said.

Bowen flicked dead leaves with his cane. "Captain Tannin interrogated some of the field workers. We made them kneel so they couldn't run off. But one of the boys—maybe ten or eleven—leapt to his feet and bolted for the nearest uncut cane. The captain shouted, 'Don't let him escape—shoot!'

"We looked at Sergeant Armstead. He pointed at Jake, told him to carry out the orders."

"Shoot a ten-year-old kid?" I said. "Who would do that? Why tell Jake to do it?"

"He was the best shot. He lifted his rifle and aimed, but didn't pull the trigger, at least—"

"Of course not," I said, then noticed Rachel's clenched face.

Bowen lowered his voice. "At least at first, I was trying to say. But Captain Tannin said, 'Shoot that runner, Corporal. That's an order.'

"The kid was just a few paces from the cane but Jake hit him with a three round burst and dropped him. Plastic-tipped hollow points, so he died pretty quick."

"I don't believe you," I said, not convincing myself at all.

Bowen stared at me. "I was there. That's what happened."

I turned to Rachel. She wouldn't meet my eyes. A crow called from one of the browning tree tops, *ah ah ah*.

"You're trained to follow orders," Bowen said. "You don't question them. And they told us over and over, if it runs, shoot it."

'It,' not 'him' or 'her.'

"We were going to have kids," Rachel said in a low voice. "I've been thinking about it since yesterday and it still doesn't make sense."

Bowen clasped his hands and looked down. "He wouldn't talk about it afterward. Wouldn't talk about much of anything for days. Then Captain Tannin had a heart to heart with him, told him the kid was probably a spy for the insurgents and he did the right thing."

He opened his hands. "Jake told me he hated dealing with civilians. Hated searching houses, hated watching people intimidated and tortured and executed on the spot."

At least he didn't enjoy it. Didn't turn into a monster. Or did intentions even matter? Wasn't it actions that counted?

"I hated it too," Bowen added.

The crow lurched into the air from its hidden perch and beat its dark wings against the bleak sky, abandoning us.

I had to know more. "There was this battle on a hillside where most of Jake's squad was killed."

"Yeah. It was more a mountain than a hill, at least that's how it seemed to me."

"He hid under a pile of logs," I said, "and wrote that he felt like a coward afterward."

"Corporal Bowen told me last night their own side caused most of the deaths," Rachel said. "That was edited out of the letters."

Bowen nodded. "Me and Jake and Lowe, who was a PFC at the time, were the only ones in the squad not killed or wounded. Mostly from friendly fire. Shouldn't have called artillery in danger range. Then our radio took a piece of shrapnel and we couldn't adjust.

"Jake really hit the rum and marimba—what they call marijuana there—after that. Thought he failed everyone, and like you said, survived by being a coward."

"He didn't do anything wrong," I said. "Did his best, then tried to stay alive. Adamsons aren't cowards."

He nodded again. "He was too hard on himself. Everyone hit the ground when they heard those 155 shells come in. 'Course what we didn't think about was an avalanche of trees coming down on our heads."

"Jake was up for promotion anyway," he continued, "so they fast-tracked it and gave him sergeant stripes and command of the squad. He asked if he could visit home but the company commander told him to wait for his scheduled leave and get the new batch of recruits up to speed."

That was unfair. We never got to see him.

"About the same time," he continued, "our platoon commander, Lieutenant Higgins—young guy, never seemed sure of himself—had this breakdown. Lined us all up and started bawling, saying he was sorry we were all going to die and for no reason. The MP's took him away and we never saw him again." Bowen shifted on his cane again. "Soon after that, Uncle Fritz arrived."

"Who?"

"The Hauptsturmführer. Jake called him Uncle Fritz. Behind his back, of course. Adviser from the German SS sent to work with Captain Tannin, one of hundreds they loaned out. No one knows how to pacify resistance like Nazis, supposedly.

"Our new squad sat in Camp Santa Clara for a while. There were some bombings of bars and whorehouses in nearby towns that killed some of the men. After that, the division commander confined us to base. You've never known boredom till you're stuck on base, huddled in ponchos in rain that never ends."

He paused. "Then it was Jake's turn to crack."

"What?"

"At least that's what the officers claimed. Really, it was one of the only sane moments of my tour."

I met Rachel's eyes. She half smiled and straightened her shoulders. "Tell Ben the whole story."

Bowen focused on the dry grass and fidgeted. "Lieutenant Wheeler, our new platoon commander, told us to prep for battle. Wouldn't say where we were going until right before boarding the 'copters. They gathered the company in one of the ready rooms, wheeled in the bulletin board, and pinned up aerial photos of this village, San Isidore. Small, nothing special.

"Captain Tannin gave the briefing, Uncle Fritz by his side. Told us it was the home town of one of the rebel commanders, and an insurgency stronghold. We were going to make an example. Our orders were to follow an air strike and make sure no one escaped."

"As in kill them?" I asked. "Kill everyone in the town?"

"Just the men. Women and children would be relocated to a work camp. Hostages, I think. But it was a moot point. The Vipers—they're ground support jets—firebombed the shit out of the village, then our gunships finished the job. They killed every last person."

Bowen covered his mouth with the ball of a fist, like he was about to cough. He blinked, then lowered his hand. "Lieutenant Wheeler told the platoon we were on head staking detail. Uncle Fritz's idea."

Head staking?

Bowen pointed a finger at me. "Jake gave him that exact same look, like he'd given an order in Russian. The LT went into specifics, told us to cut off every head we found and stake it outside the village.

"We'd never done anything like that. It was something maybe the Mongols did a thousand years ago, but not the U.S. Army. Jake told him it was barbaric. The LT gave this look like Jake had slapped him across the face. He went into a tirade."

"So he did it?" I asked.

Rachel replied first. "Just let him finish."

Bowen made a fist and gripped it with his other hand. His eyes fixed on the horizon. "Nothing much remained of the village when we got there. The buildings had all collapsed and there were burned bodies everywhere, especially inside the church ruins. None were armed that I saw, and most were women and children.

"Jake took out his knife and knelt by one of the children, or what used to be a child. He muttered something like, 'Forgive me, Mom,' and threw up. Then he turned to us and said, 'Not my squad.' He called the men together and said we were going to bury the dead and the chaplain would give last rites."

A breath escaped me, replaced by pride in my brother.

"Lieutenant Wheeler," Bowen continued, "marched over as soon as we started digging new holes in the village graveyard. He wanted to know what the hell we were doing. Jake told him we were burying the dead.

"Captain Tannin and the Hauptsturmführer came over too. 'In the Wehrmacht,' the Nazi told our officers, 'those who refuse orders are shot immediately.' Captain Tannin nodded like he agreed.

"I remember Jake's response exactly. 'By the rules of war, we never should have bombed this village in the first place. I didn't see a single dead soldier, nor any military hardware.'

"Captain Tannin gave this smirk. 'Rules of war?' he said. 'There's only one rule—Win. This village supported the enemy. Therefore it had to be destroyed.'

"Lieutenant Wheeler—his face was scarlet by this point—chewed out Jake some more and relieved him of command. He called over the platoon sergeant, SFC Parker, and put him in charge of the head removals."

None of this had been in Jake's letters. We didn't get anything after his promotion. "They didn't shoot my brother, did they?" I asked Bowen. "I thought he stepped on a mine."

"No, they just busted him back to corporal and put him on permanent latrine duty. We talked a lot on base, even though they transferred him to a support unit. He was going to speak out when he got back to the States, tell everyone about the atrocities he saw and how un-American the war was."

Bowen spoke to Rachel. "He talked about you a lot. Said you were a freethinker and moral and he didn't want to disappoint you."

He turned to me. "You too. Said you didn't let anyone tell you what to do, especially if they were wrong."

Jake looked up to me? "I need to know how my brother died."

Rachel placed a hand on Jake's tombstone. "That was the first thing I asked him. No one saw it happen."

Bowen's eyes wandered from Rachel to the grave to me. "She's right. All I *heard* was that Captain Tannin asked Jake to deliver a message to a Cuban National Guard unit stationed in Hatillo, a couple of miles away, and he never returned. They found him on the path later—it was a low-visibility shortcut. He'd stepped on a mine."

"What was the message?" I asked.

Bowen blinked. "How the hell should I know? It would have been in a sealed bag."

"Why not radio them?"

He shrugged. "Message bag must have had something, maybe a photo of someone Tannin wanted picked up. He never told us what he was up to, just barked orders now and then."

"So this captain trusted Jake, who'd defied orders, with some secret message and sent him off by himself?" It sounded like a set-up, a way to get him killed.

Rachel pulled her hand from the tombstone and stared at us.

Bowen scratched his head. "Yeah, typically a fire team is the smallest unit. That's three to four men. But this was just an errand in supposedly friendly territory." He gripped the top of his cane and wiggled it in tight circles. "I know what you're thinking. I've thought about it too. But there's no proof. And I've got to head back."

He hobbled toward the Tolsons' car, parked on the footpath beyond. I got back in the truck and followed Rachel to the bus station on Main Street.

Corporal Bowen apologized again for not knowing more about Jake's death. "It wouldn't have been the first time the rebels planted mines outside the base," he said. "I'm sorry Jake didn't make it back."

Chapter Seven

After we left Corporal Bowen, Rachel invited me to the Deer Head to see Paul. It was a low, windowless building just outside town. The parking lot was nearly empty.

"Been here before?" I asked Rachel as we approached the door.

"Jake took me a couple of times. Can't say I care for it."

The bar was dark inside, half the bulbs beneath the dormant ceiling fans burned out. It reeked like geologic layers of spilled beer and cigarette smoke. Ten-plus-pointed deer heads, super-sized bass, and other trophies lined the varnished plywood paneling. A drooping American flag hung on the far wall, flanked by aluminum-framed photos of Presidents Lindbergh and Clark. A grimy jukebox hugged the wall beneath the flag.

The day was still early and the place near empty. A few old drunks hugged the long oak counter along the right side, staring at their drinks or slurring embellished histories at one another. To the left, the wooden booths and tables lay abandoned. Paul was tending bar, as expected. No cops, thankfully.

Paul nodded at us as we entered. Clashing with the rumpled clientele, he wore a uniform of sorts: white shirt with rolled up sleeves, black vest, and a bow tie. No white fedora.

The drunks stared at Rachel, one licking his mustache-canopied lips.

I glared back and clenched my fists, letting them know I was pissed off and ready for a fight. They broke eye contact and I led Rachel to the furthest booth.

"Know them?" she asked when we sat.

"They won't bother us." If they did, they'd be easy to take. What I really wanted to do was tear down those pictures of Lindbergh and Clark, stomp on them and break the glass, then set them on fire.

Paul came to our booth and laid down two tumblers of amber liquid over ice. "On the house." They smelled top shelf, not the paint thinner I was used to.

"Thanks." I needed some liquid medicine and gulped it down. It was cold and subdued, but my face flushed warm all the same.

Rachel sipped hers, trying to hold back a grimace. "Can we talk here?"

Paul sat next to me, across from her. "Sure. Just keep it low."

"Jukebox work?" I asked him.

"Yeah."

I had some gas change in my pocket. "Let me out then."

Paul slid out of the booth and I strode over to the jukebox. I flipped through the record selection. Nothing by black musicians and nothing remotely controversial. I settled on a pair of love ballads recorded last year by Nancy Campbell and a couple of pre-coup classics by Vernon Dalhart, and dropped two quarters in the slot.

The old drunks at the bar counter turned and peered at me as Nancy Campbell's velvet contralto voice drifted from the jukebox speakers and layered sugar over the room's mean dinginess. "Pussy," one of them grumbled.

I sat back down and exchanged solidarity smiles with Rachel. In low tones, she told Paul what we'd learned from Corporal Bowen. I stared at the mounted bucks and fantasized about affording a taxidermist. As Rachel talked about how the Army persecuted my brother for being decent, though, I lost interest in trophies.

"The Nazi said my brother should be shot for disobeying orders," I said, my stomach clenching. "I bet Captain Tannin and his flunkies killed him and reported it as a combat death."

Paul put an arm on my shoulder. "This regime has no sense of morality, despite their claims of being Christian. If they're bringing in SS advisers, things are only getting worse."

"How can I find out what happened?"

He leaned closer. "I served in the Philippines. Mostly Mindanao. Sometimes the military police would take troublemakers into the jungle and arrange an 'accident.' The Army doesn't tolerate dissent. But they also avoid overt executions of soldiers since it would raise too many questions back home. Better to make it seem like they died at enemy hands, a hero for their country."

Rachel finished her drink and made a little choking noise.

"In Mindanao," Paul continued, "they usually deployed a sniper with a Japanese rifle. But sometimes they set up a booby trap, and everyone would say it was just bad luck."

"You seem to know a lot about it," I said.

"My unit set traps for the enemy all the time. Most likely that mine was radio-controlled and someone set it off when your brother walked by."

Rachel stared at him with wet eyes.

From the jukebox, Vernon Dalhart, whose birth name, Marion Try Slaughter, was much cooler, sang long tenor notes about desperate love and prison walls.

We sat a while without speaking. Jake had grievances to redress. Deuteronomy was full of verses about vengeance.

Vengeance is mine, and retribution,
In due time their foot will slip;
For the day of their calamity is near.

I whispered to Paul, inaudible to the drunks, "Back at the barn, you said you wanted to clear something up?"

He nodded. "Yeah. Obviously the only things you've heard about the resistance are government lies. They blame any kind of opposition on Jews or foreign agitators. And every five or six years they manufacture an outrage like Kansas City."

Four years ago, a bomb had exploded in City Market in downtown Kansas City. It killed seventeen people, mostly women and children. Internal Security arrested five "radicals" in connection with the bombing, one of whom confessed to the crime and apologized on TV. They hanged all five.

Paul leaned closer. "That was an Internal Security frame-up."

"How do you know?"

"None of our groups would target women and children. But it's obviously an effective way to convince folk to support the government and condemn resistance."

He was probably right. My pop had organized a family party for the execution broadcast.

"The so-called news are mostly lies," he continued. "They sprinkle in truth here and there to make the lies more believable, so you can't help but think maybe they are telling the truth about everything. Truth and lies become indistinguishable."

I caught Rachel's eyes. Her lips pressed together.

"I'm staying at the family farm," Paul said, barely audible. "Why don't you two come by tomorrow afternoon?"

Rachel nodded. "Sure."

"Don't tell anyone." He smiled. "I'll get you more drinks."

* * *

I picked up Rachel the next day and drove back the way I came. Paul's and Sarah's families lived less than a mile from me. The Turners and Wrights were the only blacks in the county with their own land, having moved here from Mississippi before the Depression. Like my family, they were barely scraping by, but it beat sharecropping or starvation-wage labor.

"You don't have to work?" I asked as we exited New Bethany.

Rachel, in a blue patterned dress and rose-red lipstick, shook her head. "I told Dad I wasn't feeling well and wanted to take the day off. He said he and Mom are worried about me. They have me seeing a therapist, you know."

I tried to keep one eye on the road and one on Rachel. "What did he say?"

"She. She works at the community hospital but comes by the house. I haven't told her anything about Jake's messages or changing the government, obviously, although I told her the war was wrong. She just nodded and said it's common to question the death of a loved one."

I wondered if she was crazy, if we both were. "Do you think therapy will help?"

"The whole world needs therapy. The whole world's crazy."

She had a point. I drove in silence until the next turn. "Your parents sure keep you on a leash."

"Tell me about it."

I swung onto a dirt track, entered a stretch of woods, and pulled up to the Turners' small two-story house. The windows were shuttered. Two cars and a faded red truck were parked outside. The truck belonged to the Turners. The cars I didn't recognize.

Mrs. Turner, a graying black woman in a simple green dress and bare feet, met us at the door. "Come on in."

The living room was dark, lit only by kerosene lamps. The floor creaked beneath my feet—raw lumber partly hidden by throw rugs that had been sewn together from old burlap feed bags and dyed blue. On the far end, Paul and Sarah rose from a sagging couch.

Paul shook our hands. His white fedora hung on a wall peg by the door. He didn't have his suit on either, just a long-sleeved shirt and tan slacks. His shirt was untucked and bulged slightly on the right side by the belt. Pistol, and not a peashooter. Where'd he get it?

Paul stiffened a little. He could tell I noticed the gun. He gestured to a pair of wooden chairs opposite the couch. "Please, have a seat."

His mother went up the stairs to the left. A yellowing curtain hung across the archway to the dining room. I smelled fresh-baked bread.

Rachel sat in one of the chairs but I remained standing. A pendulum swung beneath a plain-looking wall clock, ticking the seconds away. "Who else is here?" I asked.

"More people like you," Paul said.

"So what's up with you two?" Sarah asked before I could respond. "Why'd you run off after the show?"

I was probably in love with my dead brother's fiancée, but I couldn't say that. "We found out more about Jake."

I took the empty chair next to Rachel and told Sarah what we'd learned. Jake stood up when the war got too barbaric and they busted him for it. He planned to tell everyone back home what he saw, then he died and everything about it seemed damn suspicious.

"I've been thinking about it," Paul said. "Odds are good this intelligence officer had your brother killed."

"Someone should pay," I said. It was too great an injustice.

He nodded.

"Jake wants the wars ended," Rachel said.

Sarah raised an eyebrow. "Wants?"

Rachel kept her focus on Paul. "I was hoping you would know how to do that."

"Did you read the book I gave you?"

"*The Roots of Injustice*? Yes."

"Then you know the government uses the military to occupy foreign countries, to squeeze out corporate profits and prop up an egotistic delusion of manifest destiny. Thousands of Americans killed each year, not to mention the slaughter of others, but only the oligarchy benefits."

He reached beneath the couch and pulled out a large leather bag. He unzipped it and handed Rachel another book by Solomon Biafra, this one titled *Revolution*. No fake cover. "Can you get us some more dust jackets?"

She opened the book. "Sure."

"If people knew how badly the ruling elite screw them over," he said, "they'd take to the streets. You know before the coup, America had a semblance of democracy—one person, one vote. Unless you were black in the South. But instead of things getting better, they got a thousand times worse."

"We can vote," I said. "Well, *I* can't." I hadn't served in the military yet, which was required for full citizenship unless you managed some sort of deferral. I'd rather stay alive than vote, though, so maybe I'd run off to the Shawnee hills or Ozarks with Rachel once my draft number got called. We'd live in a cabin and hunt for food and have sex all night.

Paul kept talking. "You get one vote for serving in the military. But if you're rich, you can buy government shares at ten thousand dollars each. Do you know a single person who owns one of those shares?"

"A few of the downtown merchants," Rachel said. "Not my dad. He thought it was more important to spend the money on the store and the family."

"They modeled the 1936 Constitution on corporate law," Paul said, "where the more shares you own, the more votes you get for representatives and referendums. A hundred people at the top can cast more votes than the entire rest of the population. The inner circle comes from just a dozen families plus the military Chiefs of Staff and some church elders."

They'd glossed over this in school, saying it made sense that the more you invest in your country, the more say you should have in its future. And the leaders of finance and industry worked together for the good of the nation, steering it to prosperity and greatness.

"People put up with it," I said. Even my musician friends didn't talk about it much.

Paul leaned toward me. "The government throws workers enough bones to keep them on board. But mostly it's propaganda, fear, and blackmail that keeps them in power."

He turned back to Rachel. "Ending the wars would be part of the overall change. The troops themselves must rebel against their generals and fight for the people instead of against them. And it's not just America and its territories and client states where this needs to happen. The German Reich and Order of Europe, Greater Italy, the Japanese Empire and Asia Co-Prosperity Sphere, all must be brought down. Even the Pacific Commonwealth and the so-called neutral countries like Britain and Sweden are racist and quasi-fascist. And the Pan-Asian Soviet Union is more totalitarian than all of them. There's not a single free people on Earth. But there will be."

"There's no promised land out there," Sarah added, "except the one we make ourselves."

"How long will all this take?" Rachel asked.

"Not long once the groundwork is laid. But we have to set the foundation before we erect a new structure."

She leaned forward. "And what will this new structure look like?"

From his bag, he handed her a cardboard-bound book titled *Fields, Factories and Workshops,* by Peter Kropotkin. "*Roots of Injustice* describes the problem. This presents solutions. Dr. Biafra expands on it in *A Collaborative Future,* which I'll give you as soon as Sarah's done with it."

Did Paul get all his ideas from Solomon Biafra? He might as well be a Bible thumper.

Rachel dove into the new book.

"Don't let anyone see it, Paul said. "It's on the banned list."

"Everything interesting's on the banned list," she said, still studying the book.

I glanced at the door. What would happen if the cops discovered this? Or worse, Internal Security?

Paul turned to me. "You should read it too. It's about agricultural self-sufficiency, among other things." He waved his hands as he preached. "Kropotkin describes an economy that satisfies needs, not greed. A way of living based on cooperation, not competition. Local decision making, not top-down control by central governments and big businesses."

"Nice enough dream," I said.

"Reality, if we choose."

"You got enough people and guns to pull this off?" I wanted justice for my brother, but changing the whole world was way beyond our meager abilities.

"I told you there's an organization preparing for revolution."

Sarah nodded. "It's true."

Paul seemed to stare into my soul. "I didn't tell you lightly. Nor Rachel. I don't approach anyone until I'm absolutely sure I can trust them. My cousin vouched for you. And you play songs like *Land*, despite the risk."

"I vouched for Rachel too," Sarah said. "She's got a great sense of right and wrong."

Rachel blushed.

"Now before I tell you more," Paul said, "I need to know if you're in. Once you say yes, there's no going back."

I stood and waved Sarah over. "Can we talk in private?"

Paul frowned. "We can all talk together."

Sarah held up a hand and went outside with me. "Do you trust me, Ben?" she asked before I could open my mouth.

"What's that supposed to mean?"

"Exactly what I said. Paul came to me first and I'm an equal partner in everything he's doing."

"Why?"

"It'll make our lives mean something. We can turn things around. But I can't do it if you won't."

I sighed. I'd give it a chance.

We went back inside. Rachel and Paul were talking about Jake again. "We're here for your help," Rachel told him.

I tried to suppress my frustration. "Look, obviously we won't run to the cops. They're not exactly my friends. Just tell us what we're signing up for."

He nodded. "There's a movement. A lot of separate groups working in common cause. The movement has no name, and my group within it has no name. And within our group, there are many separate cells, each acting independently according to its particular geography and talents."

"Why doesn't it have a name?" I asked. "How are you supposed to know who you're with?"

"It's safer to be invisible. The original groups were all infiltrated and destroyed."

Rachel closed her book. "How do we fit in?"

Paul spread his hands. "I'm assembling a New Bethany cell. For safety, you won't have contact with any other cells. Even I don't know who's in them."

"Then how do you know there are any others?" I asked.

"We exchange coded messages and materials at drop sites. I know some of the codes, and where some of the drop sites are."

Rachel's face gleamed with excitement. "So how do we end the war in Cuba?"

"We will apply irresistible pressure." He stood. "But first, we have some formalities that we need to go over."

"Is this like joining the Moose Lodge?" I asked.

Paul's eyes narrowed. "This is deadly serious. Now, the movement, and therefore our group, and our local cell, have five simple rules." He held up a hand, fingers slightly apart. "That's it. Just five."

He folded his pinky down. "First, the government has informers everywhere. Tell no one about our existence. Say nothing about our meetings or actions."

Then he folded his ring ringer down. It had a silver band I hadn't noticed before. "Second, everything we do revolves around one thing: replacing the oligarchy with a free society."

He continued folding down fingers. "Third, potential members must be agreed on unanimously before we recruit them. Fourth, we take turns picking missions. Each person can propose a mission, and if the rest agree that it's doable, we do it. If we don't agree, the person can come up with a different plan."

He folded in his thumb, his hand now a fist. "Finally, there is one punishment for betrayal. Death."

I turned to Sarah. "Did you agree to all this?"

She nodded. "I did. You think you have it bad, try being poor and black. Then try being a poor black woman. Dr. Biafra, he's black, and his words can deliver us."

Like Moses to the Promised Land. Except he got divine help against Pharaoh's army.

Paul eyed me and Rachel, but especially me. "Now can you abide by these rules?"

I glanced at Rachel. "Yes," she said.

My two favorite people were in. My brother needed me. And I was no coward. "I'm in," I said, my stomach tight with anxiety.

Paul beamed. "Stay put. We'll be back." He motioned to Sarah and they exited through the archway curtain. Voices murmured beyond, and a door shut.

Rachel handed *Fields, Factories and Workshops* to me. She didn't act nervous at all—her eyes gleamed with excitement.

"I'd better not regret this," I said.

"We have inevitability on our side. But we'll be careful."

After a while, Paul thrust aside the curtain. Sarah followed him into the living room, followed by a burly unshaven man with a cowboy hat and tattooed forearms, and a young blond guy wearing a flat-topped cap.

Finally, a short brunette in jeans entered. Her, I knew. "Hi, Rachel. Ben."

"June," I said. Rachel stood and hugged her. They'd been classmates at New Bethany High, but then June went off to college somewhere. I'd seen her at a party a while back but she wasn't very attractive, kind of mousy and missing a couple of teeth, so I hadn't bothered asking what she'd been up to.

Just like something a snootie would do, and it wasn't like I was a movie star myself.

"Congratulations," Paul said. "You've been confirmed." He introduced the other two. The brawny guy was Amos. He smelled like cigarette smoke and had a powerful grip. The blond was Micah. He was a little chubby and had smooth, uncalloused hands.

"Is this everyone?" I asked.

"For now," Paul said. "But I meet a lot of people tending bar at the Deer Head and parties."

"I dare you to come up with a drink he doesn't know," June said.

Mrs. Turner came back down the stairs, said hello to everyone, and disappeared into the dining room. Drawers slid open and tableware clattered.

"Aren't you worried about holding illegal meetings in your parents' house?" I asked Paul.

Sarah spoke first. "This is our first meeting here. Last time we met in my family's equipment shed."

Paul nodded. "You can't see this house from the road. Besides, who can I trust more than family?" He pulled a handheld radio out of his pocket. "One of my brothers is watching the driveway."

He motioned for everyone to sit. He remained standing. "We now have seven active members, plus some auxiliaries and sympathizers."

I must have looked confused because he turned to me and said, "Everyone's level of engagement is different. Not everyone has to join a cell. They can provide information or help with logistics. They can stay home during parades. Boycott the big companies. Expose and shun informers. The key is to stop supporting the government."

"How many of these supporters are from your extended family?" I asked.

"Family's the logical place to start. And except out of fear, black folk have no reason to support the government."

"Hardly anyone does," Micah, the chubby blond guy, said. "Did you know babies are supposed to be euthanized if they're born with any sort of handicap?" His eyes narrowed. "Life should be sacred."

"The good news is," Paul continued, "the cell's large enough now to accomplish quite a bit. But for now, we need to act carefully. We should focus on building our local membership and developing our skill sets. At the moment, we have the advantage of stealth. Chicago may be a hotbed of radicalism, but places like New Bethany are unwatched."

Except for the local cops, he was probably right. I knew the county as well as anyone, but had never seen Internal Security investigators, nor anything more radical than the playing of old union songs.

"Next year," Paul said, "1984, is the fiftieth anniversary of the coup."

TV and radio announcers had proclaimed that next year's Liberation Day would be the biggest ever—fireworks, parades, and free barbecues the whole month of August.

"Hoover's crackdown in the Thirties and Forties was so overwhelming," he continued, "the movement has mostly focused on gathering strength, with enough resistance here and there to inspire people. But it's been decided to step things up, to spoil the regime's anniversary and show people it can be successfully challenged. The plan is to strike everywhere when the holiday begins, then follow with sustained blows. Like I said before, the government is already weak from corruption and rigidity and just needs a good kick."

I wasn't sure about the White House, but certainly the county government was corrupt. That didn't mean we stood a chance against sheriff's deputies, though. "What exactly will we do?" I asked him.

"That's for each cell to determine, as long as they fit into the overall campaign. Here in New Bethany, we're just starting. I think we should start a cleaning business or something like that, cover for our meetings and income for actions. A cleaning service will also give us access to businesses and rich people's homes."

Rachel frowned. "When are we going to bring our soldiers home?"

Sarah chuckled. "We haven't even done our first mission yet. We pick missions in order of joining. There's five people ahead of you."

Mrs. Turner entered. "Lunch is ready."

About time. I was starving. I led the pack into the dining room, which was as dark and barren as the living room. Ten rickety chairs crowded around a hand-built rectangular table. Seven chipped plates each held a baloney and cheese sandwich on thick-sliced bread, accompanied by a glass of ice tea.

Sitting next to me, Rachel didn't touch her food. "Can we make an exception?" she said after Mrs. Turner left.

Faces turned.

"Let's organize a rally against the military action in Cuba. Maybe it will catch on in other towns."

At the head of the table, Paul put down his sandwich. "As soon as we do something like that, the authorities will know we're organizing here and they'll launch an investigation. They'll photograph everyone at the rally and bring them in for interrogation."

Across from me, Amos spoke. "We should rob a bank. None of us have any money."

"Keep in mind the guards are heavily armed," Paul said. "A cleaning or maintenance business is a lot safer. It's my turn at the moment and I propose that we start such a business. We should also attend parties and other civic events and develop a mental list of who else we can recruit. Don't forget rules one and three, though—don't mention our cell, and everyone has to agree on potential members."

Rachel slapped the table with her hands. "For God's sake. Ben's right—this sounds like the Moose Lodge. Or one of my high school clubs."

I couldn't help but laugh.

Paul frowned at us. "We persist by being careful."

Sarah nodded. Rachel sighed.

Rachel was right. This movement had been around for God knows how long, but hadn't accomplished jack.

Paul crossed his arms. "If you want to survive in this business, you gotta be smart."

Chapter Eight

I wake tied to a pole and crossbeam with barbed wire, naked except for a moldy straw hat, arms stretched wide and bleeding from the wrists. In front of me, a bean field stretches toward a village of red-roofed houses and a white church with a bell tower on top.

A V-formation of black jets screeches overhead and passes over the village. Deep thuds shake my bones and the whole world catches fire.

A V-formation of Canada geese flies overhead. They're too high to hit.

Jake and I are in a duck blind, shotguns propped against the rough bench inside, dogs asleep at our feet. Rain pours down outside and drips from the edges of the grass-covered plywood roof.

I shiver from the cold. "I want to see how you died."

Jake squints. "No you don't."

"Yes I do."

Jake stands at attention in front of a desk. An officer sits behind it. It's Captain Tannin but his facial features won't register. "Corporal Adamson," he says.

I feel Jake's shame at getting busted back down to corporal. "Yes sir," he half-shouts.

"I hear you've been badmouthing me among the troops. Calling me a Nazi outhouse. Questioning our conduct of this war."

Most of them thought I was right, Jake tells me mentally.

"Germany is our ally," Captain Tannin says. "We learn a lot from them. They have a base on the moon. The freaking moon." He points at the unpainted wooden ceiling with exposed wires and ductwork.

I ask Jake who cares about the moon, but no one hears me.

The captain passes Jake a black leather bag with straps that are secured with oversize padlocks. "I have an assignment for you."

The padlocks seem ludicrous but I think I can pick them.

The real bag wasn't that big, Jake tells me.

I'm walking behind Jake on a dirt path through rolling hills of farmland and dense forest. The black bag is slung over his shoulder. He carries his rifle. Dark clouds swirl overhead. Thunderstorm coming. We should seek shelter.

The ground explodes beneath Jake. Smoke and dust fill my eyes. Waves of pain I can't feel.

The smoke clears. Jake's thrashing on his back. His legs are gone. He screams but no sound comes out. Just thoughts.

Help. Rachel. I'll never see you again. Ben, Pop, I'll never see you again.

I try to rush to my brother but can't.

He stops moving. I force my feet toward him but he's already dead.

I pull a hunting knife out of my belt sheath, cut the strap of the message bag, lift it away from Jake's body. A set of homemade lockpicks is in a jacket pocket. I wiggle a rake inside a padlock, but nothing happens. Hook pick and tension wrench. Not working. I remember the locks are ludicrous, don't belong. Cylinder turns and they all pop open.

There's a square piece of paper inside the message bag, nothing else. I pull it out. It's a photo of Jake lying on the dirt path with his legs blown off.

* * *

I met Rachel again the next day at the book store. Paul had warned us not to use the phone. You never knew when the government might be listening, and even harmless conversation could give something away. I much preferred seeing her in person anyway.

We climbed to the storage floor, Rachel leading.

I wondered if my dream was what had really happened to Jake, or just a story my mind puzzled together. Rachel would say it was Jake talking to me from beyond, telling me how he died. I decided not to further encourage her imagination by telling her about the dream. She had enough of her own to deal with.

Rachel directed me to the table in the center of the room and disappeared behind one of the overflowing book shelves. A book sat on the table, titled *Lives of the Christian Martyrs*. Not a good sign.

She returned clutching a sheet of paper and sat with me. "I wrote a pamphlet."

Block letters, neat as type, filled the sheet.

```
"Then Jesus said to him, 'Put your sword back into
its place. For all who take the sword will perish
by the sword.'" —Matthew 26:52
```

"Blessed are the peacemakers, for they shall be called sons of God." —Matthew 5:9

"Why'd you start with Bible quotes?" I asked Rachel.

"Everyone knows the Bible and most of them respect it. Just keep reading."

Thousands of American soldiers die overseas each year. Why?
Hundreds of thousands of foreign vassals die each year. Why?
Each generation of Americans is poorer than the last.
Each generation has fewer rights than the last.

These are the results of the illegal coup in 1934 that overthrew a democratically elected government and replaced it with a dictatorship by a cabal of corrupt elites. No longer do we have a government of the people, by the people, for the people. We have a government of the few, by the few, for the few. This government oppresses the people at home and abroad. America acts as an empire, sending soldiers overseas not to protect our borders from external aggressors, but to protect corporate profits, to enslave other people and steal their natural resources. And if some of these soldiers die in the process, the tyrants in the White House and on Wall Street shed not a tear.

"I know this is true," I said, "but most people will say things are better than they were before the change."

She drummed her fingers against the table. "Roosevelt had already started the work projects. Lindbergh just kept them going and took the credit. But government aid's practically non-existent now, just some token programs to keep people off the street. It's nothing compared to the costs of losing our freedom."

I returned to the pamphlet.

The Declaration of Independence, which used to be taught in schools, reads, "When a long train of abuses and usurpations evinces a design to reduce the people under absolute despotism, it is the people's right, it is their duty, to throw off such government."

I stiffened inside, but kept reading.

If you own shares in the government, even one, write your congressman and Senator and share your outrage.
If you are called to serve in the military, don't show up.
If you are in the military, refuse to serve abroad.
If you are in the police, serve the people.
If you hear government lies on your radio or television, turn them off.
Demand free and fair elections.
Refuse to participate in the sham of purchased votes.
Love thy neighbor and help one another.
Offer no support to the government or its corporate partners.
Without your support, the dictatorship will crumble and fall.
Peace and prosperity will follow for all.

Henry David Thoreau said, "Disobedience is the true foundation of liberty. The obedient must be slaves."
Let us no longer be willing slaves.

Rachel had a way with words. A way that would get us hanged for treason.

"I can convert it to a stencil and mimeograph it," she said. "Make lots of copies and distribute them anonymously, like in the newspaper racks. I'm writing something for our rally, too."

I froze. "What rally?"

"Jake was going to speak out. We have to take his place."

"I don't think he'd organize a rally. Probably just talk one on one."

She shook her head. "One on one keeps us divided. People draw strength and inspiration from being part of a community. It's why church services and football games are so well attended, and why the government holds parades and rallies, and makes kids join the Young Eagles."

I'd always skipped Young Eagle meetings, saying I had farm work to do but spending the time fishing.

"We have to tell people what we know," she said. "I'm doing this with or without you, Ben."

I wondered how, or if, my brother ever won any arguments with her. "What did Paul say about this?"

"I asked him again and he said I have to wait my turn, and even then, it's unlikely to be approved."

"Well, he's the professional revolutionary."

She leaned toward me, eyebrows knotted. "You said you were on my side. 'Forget that guy,' you told me."

"That was before we joined his group. What'll he do if we act on our own?"

"Nothing. We're not betraying the cell. And I'm happy to help them out, assuming they ever do anything. But Jake needs to move on, and we have to tell people the truth about the wars and the government. I thought Paul and his group would realize that and help, but I was wrong."

Rachel was as unstoppable as a hundred-car coal train. But maybe I could divert her. "Okay. But forget the pamphlet. If you tell people in writing to overthrow the government, Internal Security is obligated to lock you up, maybe hang you."

She took the pamphlet back and stared at it. "How would they know who wrote it?"

"New Bethany's small. They'll figure it out. And don't ask people to do things that will get them hurt. If you have to say anything, just talk about Jake and what he saw, and let people draw their own conclusions."

She looked up. "You're right, we have to be careful. But I can't live paralyzed and crushed into dust."

* * *

I barely recognized Rachel as she marched from behind her house and past the hydrangeas along the side. She wore a plain brown dress and flat shoes, and carried two paper shopping bags. Her black hair was bound beneath a bonnet, and she wore no makeup. Still beautiful, though—it didn't matter how she dressed.

I had my suit and tie on. At least the jacket warded off the October morning chill. "You look different," I said.

"That's the point."

It was Saturday, just after dawn, post-harvest season. Almost no one would be up. If they were, they'd be inside eating breakfast or watching TV. Even the cops would be asleep or drinking coffee.

"If we split up, we can cover more ground," she suggested.

"True, but missionaries always travel in pairs. And I want to make sure nothing happens to you."

We left my rusting truck in front of her house and strolled up the steps to her next-door neighbor's house.

New Bethany had a population of 5,400, not including farms like mine outside the city limits. Rachel planned to hit almost every single house and apartment—1,500 of them—in one day, and leave a flyer in their mailbox advertising the anti-war rally she'd planned. She wanted to skip only police and known informers, and there was no derailing her.

Rachel pulled a folded flyer out of her bag and slipped it in the mailbox next to the front door. This was technically illegal, but missionaries and other salespeople did it all the time. We couldn't afford stamps, and the Postal Service wouldn't deliver them anyway, they'd just hand them over to Internal Security.

"One down," she said as we returned to the sidewalk.

"Fifteen hundred more to go," I muttered. At least I'd talked her out of ringing doorbells. That would take way too long and be way too risky. Better to save the talking for the rally, where there'd be safety in numbers.

Inside Stories had a mimeograph machine, nothing fancy like the print shop, but functional enough for Rachel to print her flyers. The heading read, "WHY DID IT START? WHEN WILL IT END?" Beneath was a drawing of a graveyard, row after row of headstones and crosses. Then the words, "TOWN MEETING ABOUT OUR WAR IN CUBA. Come to the New Bethany Town Square, Sunday, October 16, at 12:30 P.M." Next week, after the churches let out.

The next house was small. Dog yips greeted us from behind the door. A middle-aged woman in a house dress and head shawl opened the door before we could retreat. I recognized her, but didn't know her name.

"Hi, Rachel." She eyed Rachel's bonnet. "When did you become a Millennialist?"

"Hi, Mrs. Chenier." Rachel handed her a flyer. "I'm not a Millennialist. I'm focused on Now Times, not the End Times. But I have been called, to help pull the world out of darkness."

Mrs. Chenier unfolded the paper and peered at it. "Is this an official town meeting?"

"It's an exercise in civic responsibility," Rachel said.

The woman bit her lip. "Okay, we'll try to come. Say hi to your parents for me."

Four houses later, we'd finished the first block. We glanced at our watches, hers dainty and silver, mine a grimy Army timepiece I'd borrowed from Grandpa. It had taken almost ten minutes.

"We'd better speed up," she said. "We'll have to split up, I'm sorry."

"Okay, let's do opposite sides of the street, though, so we can keep an eye on each other."

She smiled. "Good idea."

Cars drove by periodically, their occupants eying me suspiciously. I tried to ignore them.

After a while, I got hungry. And no sign of Rachel. I backtracked and found her several houses away, arguing with a heavyset man. Mr. Reilly, the local pesticide salesman.

I said hello to Mr. Reilly and pulled Rachel away. We'd been working all morning, but had covered less than a quarter of the town. "Come on, I've got a better idea."

"Reactionary jerk," she muttered as we strode down the street.

I steered her around the corner, toward Main Street. "I thought I was the hothead. We need to keep a low profile."

"Where can we reach practically everyone in town at one time?" I asked Rachel over hot dogs and sweet tea from a vending cart.

She shrugged.

"Hint—Friday night."

She exhaled and nodded. "Football game. We're at home against Gravelton."

"We can stick our flyers on people's cars."

"What about the guards?" she asked.

"We don't have to worry about the ones inside. Just Mr. Murphy, patrolling the lots. He's not even a real cop, just school security. If you have a few dollars, he's partial to shine."

Rachel unfastened her black leather purse and pulled out a small billfold. She didn't have much, but handed half of it to me, five dollars. "We can do the same thing tomorrow, flyer cars at churches. Although not everyone has a car."

True. Between the streetcars and everything being walking distance, you didn't need to plunk down money for a car if you lived in town.

"We don't have to contact everyone," I said. "Word will spread."

She didn't respond at first, then sighed. "I suppose so."

* * *

I arrived at New Bethany High School on the east end of town around seven on Friday, half an hour after kickoff. The sun had set and warmth fled with it. A paper bag on the passenger floor of my pickup contained a mason jar of moonshine from Mr. Haskins.

I pulled off Lindbergh Avenue into the north parking lot. It was full of cars—just about everyone went to the games. I meandered through the lot looking for Rachel, rolling down the creaky windows so I could see better.

Pole-mounted floodlights banished every suggestion of shadow. Beyond the chain link fence, the field was lit bright as day, but so were the bleachers and parking lots. The din of muddled voices reminded me of toad choruses during mating season.

A whistle blew. "Pass incomplete," the announcer said over the speakers.

My brother had played on the football team. Middle linebacker, varsity three years. He'd also been on the baseball team, wrestling team, and track team. Between that and his looks and confidence, it was no wonder Rachel fell for him.

I kept driving, taking the access road between the stadium and gym, into the west parking lot.

There she was. Rachel stood with a friend of hers from high school, Alyce, a blonde-haired girl with a pregnancy bulge. Rachel was dressed like a magazine model again—orange and white sweater, long skirt, checkered scarf.

I found an empty parking spot and hopped out, paper bag in hand.

Rachel crossed her arms when I approached. "You're late."

I glanced at the old watch I hadn't returned to Grandpa yet. "Only by five minutes." Actually, it was closer to ten.

The home stands erupted in loud cheering. A whistle. "Twenty-yard gain," the announcer said. "First down, New Bethany."

Rachel stared at the back of the wooden bleachers and bit her lip. Then she thrust a thick stack of printed paper at me. "Let's get started."

"Why's Alyce here?"

"She gave me a ride. She's going to help."

"Are you okay with that?" I asked her.

"Absolutely," Alyce said. "After what happened to Rachel? My husband hasn't finished his draft service and I'm not thrilled about him getting sent somewhere to die."

Rachel motioned us over to the nearest car, a beetle-like Ford Town Master. "Here's how we should place the flyers." She pulled the top flyer from her stack, folded it neatly in three, and slipped it beneath the driver-side windshield blades, oriented with the long edge perpendicular.

I groaned inside. "It would be quicker if we didn't fold them."

Alyce nodded. Rachel frowned. "Maybe you're right."

Mr. Murphy, the white-haired school security guard, shuffled toward us. "Why don't you get started," I told the girls. "I'll get Mr. Murphy's okay and hit the north lot."

I hurried over to the guard and tipped my hat to him. "Evening, Mr. Murphy."

He peered at me through thick glasses. He wore a light gray uniform with a black tie and tin badge, and county school board patches below the shoulders. "Benjamin Adamson. Haven't seen you around here for a while. You were one of the biggest troublemakers in school, from what I remember."

"Not even close." I'd skipped classes, spun some pranks, and got in some fights. But I never bullied anyone or sold drugs. The band room burglary and my public whipping had made me undeservedly infamous.

I passed the paper bag to Mr. Murphy. He looked inside.

"Quality product," I said. "Yours if you want it."

He opened the jar and took a swig. He grimaced and shook his head. "Woo-eee, that'll take the hair off a man's chest."

I tried not to envision his wrinkled chest. "You know Rachel and Alyce, right?" I thrust a thumb their way.

"Pretty as can be, both of them." His eyes narrowed. "What are you up to?"

I gave him one of the flyers. "We're advertising a town meeting on Sunday."

He studied the flyer. "Meeting about the war in Cuba? What's this all about?"

"It's about my brother. You knew Jake, right?"

He nodded. "Yeah. Damn shame he got kilt like that."

More cheering from the bleachers. Our whole family would go see Jake play, then we'd get ice cream, sometimes with Rachel along. We usually lost the game, but Jake always played well. Never missed a tackle.

Tears blurred my vision and I couldn't breathe. "We just want to talk about it," I choked out, my thoughts gone to weed.

Mr. Murphy shook his head and took another swig. "Go on, but be quick about it."

We finished all three lots, at least 300 cars, before halftime. The marching band began playing 'Onward, Victory!' Inside the fence, everyone stood at attention and faced the flag, right arms extended in salute. Required during all patriotic songs and the pledge of allegiance.

I extended my own salute their way, a middle finger. "Do you want to stay for the second half?" I asked Rachel.

"No, I need to write my speech for Sunday."

"But you've got all day Saturday."

"Look, I don't want to go in," she said. "I just can't do it."

I squeezed her hand. I understood.

Alyce waved goodbye and went to the ticket booth. I drove Rachel the half mile to her house.

She reached for the door handle as soon as we pulled up to the house. "See you Sunday."

We still had time to cancel the rally. No doubt someone would turn in one of our flyers to the police—the real police. But Rachel would never cancel. As I watched her walk up the front steps, I had a bad feeling, like watching black clouds swirl and funnel into a tornado.

* * *

I was chopping firewood behind the house when Sarah stomped toward me, a pained look on her face.

I put down the axe. She must have found out about the rally.

She pulled a crumpled piece of paper out of her coat pocket and unfolded it. It was our rally announcement. "You're not really going through with this, are you? Paul told Rachel it was a bad idea, and I thought you had more sense."

I sighed. "You know Rachel. She'll do it with or without me. At least she promised not to say anything inflammatory."

"Paul says—"

My stomach tensed. "I thought he was on our side. All this talk about changing things, and all he's willing to do is clean houses. Rachel needs me and Jake needs me. And Adamsons aren't cowards."

Sarah shook her head. "Why do you have to be so stubborn?" She didn't wait for an answer—not that I had one—and squeezed arms around me. "At least be careful."

Chapter Nine

The New Bethany Town Square was a small grassy space in front of the county courthouse. Main Street split into two here, running to either side of the square and the courthouse before recombining. To the south of the square, it ran past most of the stores. To the north, it passed the city and county police stations, then a stretch of newer buildings and houses.

The year after I was born, 1965, was the twentieth anniversary of retaking the Philippines from the Japs, forcing them into an armistice. Every town got a statue. In New Bethany, the government erected a marble Marine in the middle of the town square, rifle held high in triumph. It wasn't an ideal spot to call for an end to war, but it was the only public space in town.

Rachel lived only a few blocks from the square but I insisted on picking her up. The police would have seen the flyers by now, and might want to arrest her before we even started.

I was late again. Rachel stood on her front porch, wearing her funeral dress and tapping a foot. She carried a paper shopping bag in one hand, and scowled at me.

"Sorry I'm late." At Rachel's insistence, I'd put on my suit, and it took me forever to get the damn tie right. "Are you sure you want to do this? Talking to people one on one is a lot safer."

Her face tightened even more. "It's a little late to back out now. Besides, God blesses the righteous and Jake will be with us."

I led Rachel to the truck and opened the passenger door for her. "Let's get it over with, then."

I parked on Lincoln Street, just off Main, and we hopped out into chilly gloom. Dark clouds gathered in the west, threatening rain. I focused on the task—swung down the tailgate and pulled out the mike and amp I'd borrowed from Jesse, the band's bassist. He'd kill me if they got wet.

The amp had a power inverter so you could run it off a car battery. Together they weighed at least a hundred pounds, so I'd strapped them to a stand-up dolly. No mike stand, but I had enough to carry as it was. I handed Rachel the black microphone case and cables and she slipped them in her bag.

A couple dozen people were in the square, wearing coats over Sunday suits or dresses, the women's hats sprouting feathers of near-extinct birds. I recognized Alyce and maybe half the others.

Rachel's face fell. "I was expecting a lot more."

"Maybe they're afraid," I said. "Or it's the weather."

"Or they don't care. The weather is fine." She straightened. "We're early. More will come."

My stomach seized. Figures squatted or lay on rooftops around the square, pointing guns and cameras.

Atop the three-story law office building, a suited man held a long-lensed camera. Next to him, a man in black body armor braced a high-powered rifle on a tripod while another peered through binoculars. Opposite the courthouse, on the First Consolidated Bank roof, more of the same. On the east side of the square, city police aimed guns out the second-floor windows of the column-fronted City Hall.

The courthouse itself had a peaked roof. After the coup, the government had added a wooden bell tower on top, from which, I supposed, you could see the whole town. Beneath the purely decorative bell, half hidden by white columns, a dark-suited man stared at us through binoculars. A sheriff's deputy pointed a rifle with a fancy scope.

I'd never seen anything like it. Security for visiting politicians, sure, but nothing like this.

The clock on the bottom of the tower read 12:18. We had twelve minutes to prep or escape.

"Do you see the snipers?" I whispered to Rachel.

"Yes." Her voice quivered. "But we're not doing anything wrong. They're just trying to intimidate us."

She was probably right. They wouldn't actually shoot us. Or would they? We were easy targets, standing still in the open. They could take their time and go for a head shot.

Past the bank, I spotted Paul standing outside the New Bethany Diner, sipping soda or something from a jumbo-sized paper cup. No sign of the others. Not surprising since the group hadn't approved our rally. And it was better Sarah wasn't here—that would just add to my worries.

Rachel hugged Alyce and other people she recognized, then reached in her bag and pulled out my brother's portrait, the one that had been propped on his casket at the funeral. She leaned it against the base of the soldier statue.

Behind the picture glass, Jake smiled at me. I plugged the mike into the amp and clipped the amp to the car battery. I flipped a switch and the power light turned green. I tapped the mike, and the speaker thumped.

I wanted to hurry this up and waved Rachel over. I handed her the mike. "You're on." The battery would last at least an hour, but I doubted we would have that long.

Rachel examined her filigreed watch. "Let's let the crowd grow."

I glanced at mine. 12:30.

More people arrived. But half were cops—city police, county police, state police, and eight men wearing silver long-sleeved shirts, black pants, and matching ties. Their caps bore a perched eagle clutching a saber and whip. Internal Security.

New Bethany's gray-haired police chief paced back and forth, carrying a megaphone. The Internal Security troops stared at us, long batons and compact submachine guns fastened to their belts.

My knees shook. "Rachel, I've got a bad feeling. Really bad. We should go, right now."

She ignored me and tapped the microphone. "Hi everyone. If I could have your attention?"

People looked her way. Not counting enforcers, maybe three dozen stood in the park now, and an equal number beyond. Despite all his rhetoric, Paul was still among the cowardly, standing in front of the diner with his soda. The cops took positions around the perimeter, surrounding us.

"Most of you know me," Rachel said through the amp speaker, her voice unsteady. She'd skipped the pledge of allegiance mandatory at all public events. "My name is Rachel Tolson. I live a few blocks from here. You all either know or know of my fiancé, Jacob Adamson, who was killed in action about two months ago." She held up his photograph. "This is Jake. He was one of the finest men in New Bethany."

She pointed to me. "That's his brother Ben, he's here too."

I waved feebly. A dark-suited man took pictures.

"Jake died under suspicious circumstances," Rachel said. "He was going to speak out about what he saw. Soldiers killed by their own artillery. Civilians murdered for spitting. Children shot in the back for running away." She stopped and wiped away a tear. "Germany sent advisers who are teaching us how to be even more brutal, wiping out whole villages and putting children's heads on stakes."

Jaws dropped. Was she out of her mind?

"Why don't you shut up?" a man said. It was Mr. Reilly, the fat bastard who gave her a hard time while we were flyering. "The man died for his country. You're dishonoring our troops."

Eyes turned his way. Some of the cops nodded.

Rachel reddened and gripped the mike with both hands. "Jake's death was pointless. A tragedy." She swept her eyes around the square. "Our brave soldiers are dying in places like Cuba, Colombia, and the Philippines not to protect America from external aggressors, but to protect corporate profits. America was once a democracy. Now America acts as an empire, sending soldiers overseas to enslave other people and steal their natural resources."

Fuck. In the crowd, mouths opened and eyes darted. The police and Internal Security thugs pulled out their clubs and moved in.

Rachel either didn't notice or didn't care. "Our government is using our soldiers to oppress people just like you and me, decent people with families. Christian brothers and sisters. We—"

"Break it up," the police chief shouted over his megaphone. "This is an unauthorized assembly."

Cops moved through the crowd, shoving people away from the square and checking ID cards.

"Break it up."

Four silver shirts headed for Rachel. They fanned out and surrounded her. No way to escape.

"You have no right," Rachel said in the mic. "Let me speak."

I moved in front of her. Scanned my surroundings for anything that might make a decent weapon. Hitting a cop could get me ten years, but no way would I let anyone hurt her.

"We've got to bring our troops home," Rachel continued.

The nearest silver shirt, a burly-looking man with his club still belted, slipped brass knuckles on his hands. He rumbled toward me. I braced myself.

The thug swung at me. I swept my forearm and knocked his arm away. I kicked at his shin. The kick connected but didn't faze him.

"Ben!" Rachel cried out behind me.

The thug threw another punch, this one a blur.

The left side of my head exploded in pain. Everything went black.

Chapter Ten

I lie on a wide bed in a room wallpapered with flowers. I turn to face Rachel. She's lying on her side, eyes closed, smile on her face, bedsheet just short of exposing her nipples. We've been sleeping together for weeks now, and each night gets better. I edge closer and wrap an arm over her bare white shoulder.

Her emerald eyes flutter open and her ruby lips part. "How that he was caught up into paradise, and heard unspeakable words, which it is not lawful for a man to utter."

Behind her, on the far edge of the bed, my brother rises, head and torso bare. I can't see the bloody stumps, and don't want to. "I told you to protect Rachel," he croaks. "What have you done?"

I shouldn't be afraid. "I did what you wanted."

Rachel closes her eyes again and lies back against the pillow. Jake's eyes flash red. "You've got to fix this."

From someplace beyond, a woman screams. The air turns thick as liquid cement, crushing my chest. I fight for breath.

Darkness turns to gray, bringing the terror of wakefulness: a freezing concrete cell in the basement of the county courthouse. I was curled on the floor of the small cell, using my suit jacket as a blanket. A stainless-steel toilet was the room's only furniture. A fluorescent tube buzzed above.

I wasn't sure how long I'd been here, but my stomach knotted and nagged. The silver shirt thug had K.O.'d me and cuffed me while I was down. They'd dragged me and Rachel to separate rooms in the courthouse and I hadn't seen her since. An Internal Security officer, the oval-faced, dark-suited man who'd been watching from the bell tower, had claimed federal jurisdiction and told me I'd be charged with assaulting a national police officer. Even though I was the one attacked.

I heard muffled screams. Rachel's voice, somewhere nearby.

"Ben," she called, barely audible. "Please help me! Jake! Anyone, please!"

Every muscle clenched. Someone was trying to rape her.

The door had no handle. A small plastiglass window was the only portal to beyond. I sprang, smashing my shoulder against the door. It shuddered a little, but didn't give. "Stop!" I shouted as loud as I could. "Leave her alone!"

I kicked the door. It held. I kept kicking.

Rachel screamed again.

"Shut the fuck up," a man shouted.

I smacked my fist against the thick window. Pain set my knuckles afire and shot up my arm. The window showed no signs of damage.

"No, no, no!" Rachel's voice, loud.

"Stop!" I rammed the door again. It shuddered. Maybe a few more times and I could break the frame.

A white mist sprayed from a hole in the ceiling, filling the room with fog.

"Fuck you!" I ripped my shirt off, dunked it in the toilet, and wrapped it around my nose and mouth. It stank of urine. I smashed against the door again, then again. The room started to spin around me, but I willed myself to keep going.

The door opened. Two bulky men in city police uniforms and gas masks charged me with clubs raised, another two standing behind them.

I tried to dodge them and escape into the concrete hallway. Then I'd save Rachel.

A club bashed against my head. The pain brought exploding stars. I lost my balance and fell to the floor.

On my stomach, I lurched forward to block the doorway. A boot caught me in the ribs. "Rachel!" I shouted.

Blows rained down. I couldn't move. At least I'd disrupted the bastards, and maybe the ruckus would bring supervisors.

* * *

The next day, three silver shirts, led by Brass Knuckles, barged into my cell. They hog-tied me with iron shackles and short chains, and tossed me into the back of a long white van with grated windows. I ached too much to move, making the shackles excessive.

The van turned a couple of times, then hit a steady speed. Unable to rise from the metal floor, I couldn't see where we were going. What would happen next? What were they doing to Rachel? The pain made it hard to focus. Internal damage?

After two or three hours, we stopped. The back doors opened. Brass Knuckles and one of his companions pulled me out by the ankles and held me down against the asphalt driveway. A balding, grim-looking man in a white coat stepped forward.

"Where's Rachel?" I asked.

No one answered. The man injected a syringe into my arm. The world swam circles and faded away.

Rachel's angelic face emerges from gloom. She kisses me.

I'm in a maze of dark caverns lapped by inky waters. They extend into infinity. Echoing screams of the damned plead for help that will never come.

I woke strapped to a bed in a small concrete-walled room with a shuttered window and institutional fluorescents. I was wearing gray pajamas with 'H-132' stenciled on the front. A tube ran into my right arm from a clear plastic bag full of liquid. Machines made beeping noises. I felt groggy, but the pain had diminished.

The door opened and a matronly blonde-haired nurse entered, followed by a silver-shirted guard. "Yer 'wake," the woman said in a Kentucky accent.

"Where am I?"

She checked the machines, then undid my straps. "Time fer yer toilet visit." She pointed to a plastic curtain, presumably leading to a bathroom. "I'll help you git there."

Was she going to watch too? "Where am I? Where's Rachel?"

"Yer in the Illinois State Correctional Hospital," she said. "In Decatur."

Decatur was the dead center of the state, halfway between New Bethany and Chicago. "What about Rachel?"

"I'm sorry, hon, I don't know any Rachel."

"What the hell is a correctional hospital?"

She smiled. "We make you better, 'course." She helped me out of the bed as the guard stood by, looking bored.

* * *

I lay in bed a long time recovering from my injuries, which included cracked ribs and a bruised kidney. Doctors and nurses wandered in and out, always with a uniformed guard along.

None of them said they knew anything about Rachel, and they wouldn't let me call anyone.

I began to wither from boredom. I wrote songs in my head about sadistic cops getting their comeuppance. In my sleep, I wandered a dark underworld, searching for Rachel and Jake and finding only voiceless shadows cringing from distant screams.

After a while, I was well enough to sit up and walk, although they kept me strapped down unless a guard was present.

A mustached doctor, burly goon at his side, entered and stuck a syringe in my trapped arm. "You're being discharged."

About time. My eyes flickered and closed.

I woke on a smelly, stained mattress in a tiny windowless room, the only other furniture a steel toilet with no lid. I had no sheets or pillow, and was clad in pajamas with '418' on front and back. The air was freezing cold.

Two silver-shirted guards entered—a heavyset man carrying cuffs and chains, bald beneath his whip-clutching eagle cap, and an older guy holding a cattle prod. Panic drove away remnant wisps of fog and I scrambled to my feet, tensed for battle.

The guard with the cattle prod held up his free hand. "Siddown."

Baldy moved fast and flanked me. He grabbed my arms and snapped on handcuffs. He added thick ankle cuffs and a collar, connected with heavy steel chains. He clutched my right arm and led me out the door. Shocky followed.

The guards led me up two flights of stairs and down a hallway with white concrete walls, a white tiled floor, and fluorescent tubes on the ceiling. They stopped at a door with the number 4216 on it. Baldy knocked. "Delivery."

"Bring him in."

Inside, a lean man in a charcoal suit and black fedora sat behind a metal table, a pen, notepad, and open folder of papers lying in front. His close-cropped dark hair was streaked with gray. A microphone hung from the ceiling, and a reel-to-reel tape recorder perched on a shelf in the far corner, capstans rolling. Other than that, the walls were bare white concrete like everything else.

Baldy sat me on a narrow stool. Two spotlights shone in my face. He grabbed short chains from a ring on the floor and locked them to my ankle cuffs. "Prisoner's secure." Baldy and Shocky left the room.

I squinted and blinked until I could see past the glare of the lights. Across the table, the suited man peered at me. His irises were so dark, they merged with the pupils, gaping black portals to the end of the universe. "You are Benjamin Adamson of New Bethany, Illinois?"

I couldn't pull away from those eyes. "Yes."

"Special Agent Frank Lewison." He flashed a laminated badge—Department of Investigation, Internal Security Service. My skin froze. From what I'd heard, nobody ever returned whole from Internal Security interrogations, if they returned at all.

"I can tell by your reaction that you're guilty," Special Agent Lewison said in a calm voice.

"Guilty of what?"

"You've been charged with disturbing the peace, sedition, and assaulting a police officer."

The ridiculousness dispelled his hold over me. "He attacked me! I was just defending myself."

"You don't deny the other two charges?"

"I deny all the charges. I want an advocate."

Agent Lewison fixed his pitch-black eyes on me. Maybe I'd call him and his confederates Insects, short for Internal Security Thugs.

The Insect flipped through some papers stacked on the table. "Your family can hire a lawyer if they so choose."

"With what money? And do they know where I am?"

"Sounds like you should have kept clean."

My fists clenched.

He smirked at me. "Much bigger men than you have tried to break out of those chains. It's never happened." He studied his papers. "You're a violent man, Benjamin, and we're not taking any chances with you."

I almost laughed at his hypocrisy. "I've never started a fight in my life." I'd been scrawny as a kid, and generally peaceful, so I never went looking for fights. On the other hand, I didn't run from them either.

"Now, what is the nature of your relationship with Rachel Tolson?"

Good question. I decided on the most straightforward answer. "She was my brother's fiancée. Where is she?"

Lids shuttered the tops of his giant pupils. "I'm asking the questions here." He held up one of the flyers announcing the rally. "Do you admit helping distribute these materials the morning of Saturday, October 8, and the evening of Friday, October 14?"

"What's today's date anyway?" I had no idea.

The Insect sighed. "Look, I have a lot of interviews today. If we don't get through my list of questions in the allotted time, you can expect severe consequences."

I'd met a lot of assholes in my life, but this guy could be their pharaoh. "Can't you just tell me the date? I'll answer your questions then."

"November 4."

Holy shit. I've been here three weeks. "Does my pop know I'm here?"

"Your father was interviewed on..." He flipped a page. "October 18. Now, about the flyers you distributed?"

"Yes, I did that." No point lying about it, it wasn't a big deal.

He wrote something in his notepad and impaled me with his dark eyes. "And you provided the microphone, amplifier, and battery used by Miss Tolson on Sunday, October 16?"

"Yes." The Insects had watched me set them up.

"And you got them from..." He glanced at his printed notes. "Jesse Jones?"

"He's the bassist in my band. He didn't know anything about the rally or why I was borrowing his equipment." A lie.

"Really? He didn't ask what you wanted them for?"

"I said I wanted to practice with them." I had never borrowed them before, but it was all I could come up with.

"Are you a communist?"

The question was absurd. "No."

"Have you ever associated with any communists?" He kept asking stupid questions about communists and anarchists, then shifted gears. "You live with your father and grandfather?"

"Yes." Mother, sister, and brother all stolen by the Reaper. Two sisters if you counted the miscarriage that took my mother's life.

"You are currently unemployed?"

He hadn't mentioned Sarah or Paul. That probably meant only Rachel and I had been arrested. Things could be worse.

"Well?" His voice was hard.

"No, I help at the farm."

"And you were expelled from school? Never finished?"

My face tingled the way it always did when reminded of that. "Yes."

He flipped through his papers. "According to your records, you were a discipline problem in school. And you've been arrested four times on multiple charges. Off-season hunting, possession of alcohol as a minor, larceny by burglary, performing music at a public venue without a license, resisting arrest, and loitering."

"Yeah, I'm a real John Dillinger."

The Insect glared at me. "You know how many good-for-nothing punks I've seen in my career? I can tell right away when someone's born for prison. You fit the mold exactly."

Go fuck a porcupine, I wanted to say.

The Insect tapped his pen against the desk top. "Here's how this is going to work. You're too stupid and lazy to be of any concern to me. Miss Tolson, on the other hand, is a dangerous agitator."

From one of his papers, he read, "'America was once a democracy. Now America acts as an empire, sending soldiers overseas to enslave other people and steal their natural resources.'"

He fixed those dark portals on me. "That's seditious. Testify against her and we'll drop all the charges against you. There's a reasonable chance the Army will straighten you out and you'll become a model citizen."

"No way in hell." I would never betray Rachel.

He sighed. "I thought you'd say something like that. We'll correct your anti-social tendencies and then we'll revisit the matter." He gathered his papers together and rapped them against the desk until they were perfectly aligned.

My anger disappeared, replaced by sour-tasting dread. "I want to see an advocate," I managed. Didn't I have that right? Didn't he acknowledge it earlier?

The Insect slipped a hand under the desk and spoke in the microphone. "You can pick him up now." He glowered at me. "It's in your interest to reform quickly and learn to cooperate."

The door opened behind me. Baldy and Shocky entered.

"Room three," Agent Lewison told them. "Then transfer him to psychiatry."

Knees shaking, I rose from the stool. "You don't need—"

Shocky thrust his cattle prod against my neck, the pain jolting me and jerking my limbs. The stool toppled to the floor. Piss soaked my pajama pants and the stench of urine filled my nose. My skin flushed with embarrassment.

I heard Lewison say, "Did I tell you to do that?"

"Thought he needed some motivation," Shocky said.

"Well, get him out of here and come back and clean up that mess. It stinks in here now."

Baldy unfastened my ankle cuffs from the ring on the floor. "Move."

When we entered the hallway, Shocky cursed under his breath, something about assholes and fucking this and fucking that. They marched me to an elevator. Baldy hit the lowest button, B-3.

The elevator moved downward. "Are you really gonna clean that asshole's office?" Baldy asked the older guard.

"Fuck no. He can clean it himself. He's not my supervisor."

The doors opened into another white concrete hall. Screams echoed from hidden hells.

My feet wouldn't budge. An electric shock tore through my back, followed by another. I dropped to the elevator floor. The guards yanked me to my feet and dragged me down the hall.

"You're getting it extra bad for making us drag you," Baldy said. He knocked on a door. "Delivery." The door was marked '3.'

"Come in," someone said from the other side.

Inside the small room, an old man was strung up naked from the ceiling like a slaughtered cow. Cables ran from fixtures on the ceiling to the loops on his cuffs and collar. He didn't look conscious and might have been dead.

"I'll do whatever you want," I said, fingers shaking. Everyone ignored me. The two Insects inside the room, one burly and red-haired, the other skinny with a scarred forehead, lowered the naked man to the floor and unhooked the cables.

Baldy picked up a clipboard on a small table by the door. It had a pen attached with a string. He scrawled something on the clipboard.

"You're lucky," the scarred torturer told Baldy. "Normally there's a wait."

"Give this asshole the full works," Shocky said.

My bladder loosened again but it was already empty. "I didn't do anything."

The burly torturer glanced at a clock on the wall. "We got a shift change at twelve," he told Shocky, "which gives half an hour."

The scarred man pointed at the old victim lying on the floor, now semi-conscious and moaning. "Bring this one back to his cell, would you?"

"What's the number?"

"It's on the clipboard."

"133. Got it. We'll be back for 418 at noon." Baldy and Shocky left, dragging the old man.

The burly torturer picked up a long rubber truncheon. He approached me, then swung it violently at my head. I tried to raise my arms but the chains kept them pinned to my side. Blinding pain burst from my left temple and I fell hard.

The scarred torturer tied a smelly gag around my mouth and cut my pajamas away with a box cutter. I was too groggy to resist as the two men hooked the cables to my shackles and raised me about a foot above the floor. The wrist cuffs bit into my skin.

The burly man, truncheon in hand, stepped behind me. Air sped in and out of my nostrils and sweat trickled from my armpits.

Pain exploded in my back.

Rachel was their main target. Would they string her up like this?

Another blow. I choked on the rancid gag.

Poor Rachel. They'd show no mercy. Tears poured down my cheeks.

"Look at the little baby," the skinny one said. "He's crying."

The burly man behind me laughed, then hit me harder.

I shut my eyes. I'm going to kill these assholes. Every one of them.

Jake's face appears. He isn't wearing his army hat. *Stay strong, little brother.*

Brother, I think, this is all your fault.

Chapter Eleven

The Insects gave me new pajamas and left me alone in my cell, periodically bringing a plastic mug of water and a bowl of flavorless mush. I asked for a pillow and blanket, but the guards shocked me instead.

I had to lie on my stomach because of the pain. They wouldn't shut off the buzzing fluorescent tubes recessed in the ceiling, and I couldn't reach high enough to pull them out or smash them. The air grew even colder. At some point I managed a sort of half-sleep, not deep enough to dream, just snatches of unconsciousness between stretches of discomfort and dread.

After two or three days—I had no way to mark the time—the guards brought me to a new room, one floor higher. It was about the same size as the special agent's, but not so stark, with pale blue walls, bookcases, and potted plants. A saggy-jowled man with gray hair and circular eyeglasses peered at me from behind a desk with a portable tape recorder and open folder of papers.

The guards sat me in a thick wooden chair opposite this new interrogator. They kept my shackles on, but didn't fasten them to the floor. As soon as they left, the man depressed a red switch on the tape recorder and bared perfect teeth in a smile accompanied by probing eyes. "I'm Dr. Malluch. I'm a psychiatrist."

My thoughts flowed like sludge from lack of sleep and weeks of pain. "Why am I here? When can I write my pop?"

"After our session if you like. As for why you're here, your file suggests psychological issues that may need to be resolved."

How long would that take? "None of this is necessary. I didn't do anything wrong. Let me and Rachel go, and we won't cause any more trouble."

The Insect psychiatrist chuckled.

"What's so funny?"

"First you said you didn't do anything wrong and then you said you won't cause more trouble."

I should think before I talk. "When can I see an advocate?"

The psychiatrist ignored me and picked up a pen. "Now I'm going to ask you a series of questions as part of your initial evaluation, and I want you to answer yes or no. Please be honest or we won't obtain the proper results. And in case you're wondering, I'm trained to detect lies."

"And I can write my pop afterward?"

"If you answer the questions truthfully, yes."

A reasonable deal. "Go ahead, then."

I wouldn't mention my Jake dreams. Was a psychiatrist picking into Rachel's head too? If so, I hoped she had the sense to keep quiet about the matter.

"First question," he said. "Do you have difficulty trusting people?"

"Can I trust you?"

He sighed. "Yes or no, please."

I decided to give the psychiatrist the answers that would seem the most normal. "No."

He circled something on a sheet of paper. "Do you tend to avoid social relationships?"

"No." That was true, mostly.

"Do you prefer to be alone rather than in the company of others?"

"No." I did like to be alone in the woods or at a pond, though. It was peaceful.

"Do you believe you have more difficulty with relationships than the average person your age?"

"No." Although I had rotten luck keeping girlfriends.

"Are you impulsive or irritable at times? ... Do you ever lie to get what you want? ... Do you ever lie to avoid punishment?... Do you hate being told what to do?"

The questions went on and on. I answered no to most of them. Then he asked how much I drank, how often I got in fights, what I thought of the police, what I thought of the government...

The psychiatrist finally put his pen down. "Well, Benjamin. Do you remember I said I can tell when you're lying?"

How could he tell? I wasn't sure myself about all the answers. "Yeah."

"You promised not to lie, but you lied on over half the questions."

My heart started to quiver.

"But that's a part of your probable pathology." He scribbled something down. "We shall have to teach you to tell the truth."

Could I do a better job hiding my thoughts?

He shut off the tape recorder and his right hand reached beneath the desk. Baldy and Shocky entered.

"You can have the pen and paper when you start cooperating," the psychiatrist told me. He waved the guards forward. "Back to room three."

* * *

The Insects in Room 3 cursed at me for returning, and beat me even harder than before.

Baldy and Shocky hauled me back to the psychiatrist the next day. I could barely walk, aching from shoulders to calves, like I'd been hit by a freight train.

I had to find a way to end this hell. "I'll cooperate," I said.

Dr. Malluch folded his hands. "Let's try that last test again. This time, give me answers that are accurate."

I nodded. When he asked, "Do you have difficulty trusting people?" my answer became "yes." Being snitched on about taking the band instruments had taught me to be careful. A lot of other noes changed to yeses too.

After the test, he questioned me about my past. I answered as truthfully as I could without mentioning Paul's cell. I didn't want Sarah and her family brought here. I omitted Jake's visits too, and how Rachel and I felt compelled to continue his fight. I wiped all such thoughts from my mind, as if they were dreams vanishing forever beneath the tyranny of waking reality.

Finally, the psychiatrist passed me a ballpoint pen and lined paper. "You can write your family now. I'll make sure it's delivered."

During my first interrogation, Special Insect Lewison had said they interviewed my pop after they arrested me. Why couldn't he have asked where I was and tried to get me released? And Sarah, did she write me off too? That wasn't like her at all.

Maybe no one could reach me. Or maybe my pop needed some nudging. I wrote my address at the top of the paper, then,

Dear Pop & Grandpa,

The national police arrested me at the Town Square. I'm at the Illinois State Correctional Center in Decatur. I was injured but am recovering. I haven't been allowed to see an advocate, and they said you must hire one for me.

I am charged with disturbing the peace, sedition, and assaulting a police officer. All the charges are ~~bullshit~~ wrong. The cop threw the first punch and I was just defending myself. And I never said anything against the government. I didn't say anything at all actually. An advocate could clear things up.

Please hurry.
Ben

I folded the paper so only the address showed. "Do you have an envelope?"

Dr. Malluch unfolded my letter and read it. "Your wording is interesting. You sound quite convinced you are being persecuted."

"I'm just telling him where I am and what happened. You promised to deliver my letter. I'm holding you to that."

He put it aside. "I'll put it in the post box this evening. You can trust me."

Trust an Insect? Not likely, I thought.

The guards returned me to my cell. I lay on my stomach, too sore to do anything else, and wished I'd never been born.

* * *

Next morning, after a bowl of cold mush, Baldy and Shocky returned me to the psychiatrist's office. At least, I assumed it was morning. The lights never dimmed, and there were no windows, clocks, or differences in meals. But a government professional in his fifties or sixties would probably work normal hours.

"I mailed your letter," Dr. Malluch began after the guards left.

"Thanks."

He smiled. "You see, you can trust me. I'm here to help you."

Again with the 'you can trust me.'

"The youth are the backbone of our country," he said, "our source of national vigor. That's why we want to cure you and not just send you to a work camp the rest of your days. The nation cares about its youth."

He could fertilize all the corn in Illinois with that bullshit. The work camp threat kept me quiet, though.

The psychiatrist pressed the record button on his tape recorder and stabbed his pen against a sheet of paper. "Let's start with your relationship with Rachel Tolson. How would you describe it?"

I had to figure out where she was. Maybe I could take out Dr. Malluch before he summoned the guards, and grab his keys.

He stared at me. "Well?"

I shook off the daydream. "Like I told the other interrogator—"

"I'm not an interrogator. Like I said, I'm here to help you."

"She was my brother's fiancée and took his death pretty hard. If you're here to help me, where is she? Did you know the guards tried to rape her?" I hoped my outburst had stopped them.

"Which guards?"

"At the New Bethany courthouse." I recounted the story the best I could. Dr. Malluch took notes.

"Where is she now?" I asked. "Is she here?"

He sat for a moment, then said, "Yes, she was admitted here before you. She's one of my patients. She didn't say anything about an attempted rape. She hardly speaks at all."

"Is she okay? Is she being tortured too?" My toes clenched.

"'Torture' is such a negative term. We take only those steps necessary for the good of the patient, the good of society."

I almost laughed at the absurdity, but terror for Rachel overwhelmed it. "What are you doing to her?"

"I'm afraid I can't discuss her treatment with you. Patient confidentiality."

"When will she be released?"

The Insect leaned back in his chair. "First off, you've both been charged with serious crimes. From my perspective, she isn't competent to stand trial until she's been cured."

"Of what?"

He shook his head. "Again, patient confidentiality."

More absurdity. "How long till she gets out?"

He scribbled in his notepad. "Your concern for her is touching. Perhaps you're not hopeless after all."

"What do you mean by that?"

"We'll discuss that in a minute. Now tell me about your relationship with Rachel."

"Rachel and me grew up together. And we've been close since my brother died."

He scribbled some more. "I'll check into your rape accusations. If they're true, it's unacceptable. If you're lying..."

"Everything I said happened." My heart battered my rib cage. "What if it happens again? Can you keep her safe?"

He nodded. "We're professionals here, and have protocols to prevent violence."

I almost laughed. My body was covered with bruises.

"And she's in the women's wing," he continued.

Now I knew where she was. My anxiety eased a little.

Dr. Malluch leaned forward. "Let's talk about you. You have what's called antisocial personality disorder."

More bullshit.

He glanced at his notes. "You have difficulty conforming to social norms and following lawful behavior. You lie habitually. You are aggressive and angry. You shun work and the company of others."

"None of that's true. I'm in a band and play music for others. How is that antisocial?"

He gave one of his fake smiles and steepled his fingers. "Fortunately, your condition is curable. And you'll be happy to know, there are cures for Rachel's conditions too. You'll both be fine when your treatment is complete."

Chills ran up my spine. Would Rachel no longer be Rachel? Would my identity disappear too, with no ability to care?

Chapter Twelve

After more psychiatric interrogations, Baldy and Shocky hauled me into a small room, white concrete like everything else, metal table in the center with folding chairs on either side. A white-haired, crag-faced man sat at the far side of the table with an open binder and a folder stuffed with papers. He smelled like mothballs.

"Hello, Mr. Adamson," the old man said after the guards left. "I'm your advocate, Edgar Gamaliel." Staying seated, he extended a gnarled, brown-spotted hand.

I almost danced. Instead, I shuffled to the table, thrust out my bound wrists, and shook his hand. "So my pop got my letter?"

"Yes. I came as soon as I could. I believe the government acted with unnecessary harshness at the rally you were arrested at. I saw the whole thing from my office window." He pointed at a camera in a ceiling corner. "We're being recorded—keep that in mind as we talk. Me, I'm an old man with no family left and I don't care. You, that's a different story."

I didn't plan to say anything incriminating. I sat at the table. "Did you see that goon knock me out?"

He nodded with grim lips. "I did. It's not often an advocate has such first-hand knowledge."

"What happened after that?" I hoped my guess was right about the rest of Paul's cell not getting swept up.

"Internal Security questioned everyone. Only you and Miss Tolson were charged, though."

That confirmed it. Sarah was safe! I managed not to smile.

Mr. Gamaliel flipped through typed forms in his manila folder. "I understand you've been charged with three crimes?"

"So they say. I haven't seen a judge."

"I have copies of your paperwork here. It was filed in federal court, which is somewhat discouraging. Although if you ask me, the whole legal system is discouraging."

Some advocate. "They said they'd let me go if I testified against Rachel." I shook my head. "I told them no way, and now they're treating me for mental illness."

A cloud passed over his face.

"What is it?" I asked.

"By law, they can confine you until you're deemed successfully treated. In fact, once they start the process, you can't be released until they say you're cured. What did they say you have?"

"Antisocial personality disorder." I started to scoff, but it caught in my throat.

He wrote something in his notebook. "Don't take that diagnosis to heart," he said. "Internal Security psychiatrists are hardly objective. They categorize patients to 'prove' they need treatment and keep them out of the judicial system. It helps discredit them also. Then they make the patients more compliant and help the interrogators figure out how best to extract information and cooperation."

Was it safe for him to say that? He was old and still practicing law; he must know what he could get away with.

"Rachel's being treated too," I said. "But I don't know what for, or what they're doing to her."

Mr. Gamaliel turned to an earlier page in his notebook. "Miss Tolson's parents retained an advocate immediately after her arrest. James Greene, very capable."

Rachel had great parents. A little smothering, but they'd do anything for her.

Mr. Gamaliel continued. "I approached Mr. Greene since our cases are related. He's shown interest in a coordinated defense, so we'll be working together."

That sounded encouraging. "Can he get her out?"

He paused. "As you say, Miss Tolson is also under psychiatric care until she's deemed fit for trial, which could be months, years, or never. She was diagnosed with several disorders, including paranoid schizophrenia and obsessive-compulsive personality disorder."

My shoulders drooped. "What are those?"

"Paranoid schizophrenia means she can't tell what's real and what isn't." He stared at his notes. "According to her commitment forms, she suffers from hallucinations and paranoid delusions—"

"That's bullshit." She had her quirks, like all interesting people. But she was no loon.

He kept reading. "She believes her dead fiancé talks to her and wants her to overthrow the government."

She told them that? They must have really worked her over. What else did she say?

"I've known her almost my whole life," I said. "She's perfectly functional." I almost said normal, but Rachel overtopped most people like a tree in a hay field.

"I don't know her and I'm not a psychiatrist," he said, "so I can't speak to that."

"What's the other condition you mentioned?"

He scanned the page. "Obsessive–compulsive personality disorder. She's obsessed with her dead fiancé, to the exclusion of all else. She seeks to control everything around her. She feels compelled to be perfect at all times, from her appearance to her lettering."

Maybe they were onto something. I wouldn't say so out loud, though. "Can Mr. Greene get her out?"

"I'm afraid that once she's released from psychiatric care, the prosecution has a solid case for sedition. They found incriminating books at her family's store, and a pamphlet she wrote calling for revolution."

Despair drove off my upstart wisps of hope. Why did we think we could hide anything? Of course Internal Security would investigate an anti-war rally, and they must have seen every trick a million times. No wonder Paul was so skittish. We should have listened to him.

"The best Miss Tolson might hope for," he continued, "is some sort of plea bargain and reduced sentence, maybe probation since it's her first offense. She had a nervous breakdown during the interview, apparently. Mr. Greene had a hard time with it."

Poor Rachel. "Did you know she was attacked in the county courthouse?" I fought back tears and described what happened.

Mr. Gamaliel's face tightened. "I heard. Mr. Greene told me Miss Tolson wants to press charges of attempted rape against four jailers."

"Attempted?"

"Yes, apparently your commotion interrupted them before they could, uh, remove her pants. Afterward, Internal Security took custody and raised a fuss with the locals."

Lightness and relief washed through me. I'd accomplished something, maybe the best thing I'd ever done in my life. I could deal with anything now.

"Now let's discuss your situation," my advocate said. "First, we need to move you out of psychiatric care. Then hope for a reasonable judge."

My previous appearances before a judge had not gone well, but I didn't have a lawyer then.

Mr. Gamaliel placed a pen against blank paper. "Now, please tell me everything you remember about October 16. Every detail."

* * *

"You're moving," the sadistic Insect with the cattle prod said later that day. As always, the stocky bald guard was with him, bringing my chains.

"Where?"

"One of the loony wings."

Baldy put on the shackles and threw a cloth bag over my head. They led me out of the room and down four flights of stairs, probably below ground, the nether circles of the hive.

We entered a damp hallway. The sound of dripping water accompanied the muffled echoes of our footsteps. At one point, we approached another prisoner and guards trudging the opposite direction. I wanted to call out, forge a bond of solidarity with this invisible soul, but before I could think what to say, they passed.

We marched a long time, then climbed three sets of stairs. I managed not to stumble. One of the guards unlocked and opened a door. They shoved me inside and yanked the bag off my head.

My new room was a little bigger and had a narrow metal-framed bed with a sagging mattress. Like the old room, it had white concrete walls, a metal toilet, and no window.

"You're someone else's problem now," Shocky said.

No one brought dinner. But they shut the lights off after a while and it wasn't freezing. I climbed under the thin but clean blanket and fell asleep.

Sarah smiles at me. We're at the pond fishing. I have bluegills and a small bass on my stringer, the fish still alive in the water but staked to the bank. I may let the bass go so it can grow.

"About time you had a good dream," Sarah tells me.

"I'm dreaming?" I feel disappointment and irritation. I dig my boot heels into the muddy ground so I can stay here forever, but the sun fades and then the colors and then nothing remains but gloom.

* * *

The next morning, Dr. Malluch, carry case in hand, entered with two new guards. One, a wiry young man with tired eyes, carried a breakfast tray. The other, a husky man with curly red hair, clutched a set of lumpy gray clothes. And the obligatory cattle prod.

"Today is the first day of your treatment," the Insect doctor said.

I didn't like the sound of that. "Just let me go through the legal process."

"You have to be treated first."

The wiry guard placed the tray on the small table by the bed. It held a bowl of warm oatmeal, a cup of apple juice, and a pale blue pill. It smelled good, especially on an empty stomach, and I spooned down oatmeal as fast as I could.

"Take the pill," Dr. Malluch said.

"What is it?"

"It's a mood stabilizer. We're starting with a strong dose, and we'll gradually decrease it as your condition improves."

The Insects wanted people as uniform and uncomplaining as a crop of corn. "I'll take it later," I lied.

Dr. Malluch nodded at the guards. One grabbed my arms and pinned them behind my back. The other pried open my mouth and shoved the pill in my mouth. He lifted up my chin and patted my throat until the pill went down. Like I was a dog.

"Bastards," I said when they let me go.

The Insect doctor handed me the apple juice. I considered smacking it out of his hand, but didn't want to waste it.

"I spoke to Rachel," the doctor said.

"When is she being released?"

He ignored the question. "You were right about the attempted rape. But it won't happen here. As I said, men and women are segregated."

"Can I see her?"

Dr. Malluch peered at me. "What if I told you your obsession with Rachel is unhealthy?"

"I'm not obsessive. I thought I was just diagnosed as antisocial."

The husky red-haired guard threw the clothes—gray cotton long-sleeved shirt and pants—on the bed. Long pockets on the backs of the pants and shirt contained thick rectangular bumps and were buttoned shut. "Put these on."

"Why?"

"You'll be joining the ward population each day," Dr. Malluch said. "In the old days, the criminally insane could wander around hospitals unmonitored, and the violence was astounding. Fights, even murder, every day. Now we keep a close eye on all the patients and apply corrective measures whenever needed. It's part of their treatment too, to prepare them for re-entry into society."

Redhead brandished the cattle prod, so I put on my new clothes. The shirt had the number 326 on the front and back, in large fluorescent yellow. The clothes were thick and heavy, with metal disks on the inside, including two in the crotch. Wires ran through the fabric; presumably the pockets held batteries.

Dr. Malluch opened his carry case and removed a small metal box with switches, knobs and dials. He extended an antenna. "Decades of research have shown that aversion therapy is effective in treating behavioral disorders. Let me demonstrate." He flipped a switch and turned a knob to the right.

Searing pain ran through my legs and arms. I fell back against the bed.

He turned the knob back to the left. The pain stopped. "You're the antisocial one," I said.

"This is all part of the treatment. For both yourself and society. We can't very well have bad seeds disrupting society."

I didn't say anything, but bumped him up to the top of the kill list. I was too tired to dwell on it, though. I wanted to lie down and never get up.

The Insect doctor glanced at his watch. "Let's go."

The guards led me down the hallway, Dr. Malluch following with his control box. They opened a door into a gymnasium-sized room, full of men wearing lumpy gray uniforms like mine. The room was two stories tall. The upper half was ringed with windows with reflective glass. Light string music played over speakers in the ceiling, barely above audible.

I searched for Rachel, but saw only men. Over a hundred, all ages and races. Most sat on the white linoleum floor, backs against the wall. A few stood chatting with others in quiet tones, while others stared at the floor. The prisoners had dull, slack faces, like they'd given up on life. I felt that way myself, maybe from the pill they shoved down my throat.

"Good luck, Benjamin," Dr. Malluch said. He pointed at the opaque windows. "Do what you're told or you'll be shocked. The greater the infraction, the greater the punishment." He left, followed by the guards.

Prisoner eyes shifted my way. What were these people in for?

A white-haired old man offered a hand. "You're new. I'm Mortimer."

I shook his hand, which felt cold. "Ben. What goes on here?"

"Well, you missed breakfast and the morning lecture. Oh, and the roll call and Pledge of Allegiance."

"I had breakfast in my cell. They made me take a pill too."

"Ah, well, normally all our meals are in the cafeteria. They must not have your prescription there yet. They'll put it in your drinks once they do."

Not drinking would be harder to hide than spitting out pills. "What was the lecture about?" I didn't really care, but I was desperate for friendship.

He scratched his head, scattering dandruff flakes. "The usual. About taking responsibility for our lives, accepting God, and becoming model citizens. And obeying the rules, of course."

"Of course."

"So now we've got a little free time to use the toilets and reflect on how we can better ourselves. Exercise is next, then our daily shower, then lunch, followed by drills, breakout sessions, dinner, finally a movie if we're lucky, lectures if not."

"Sounds like a blast. How long you been here?"

"Since they built the place. Forty something years. So they tell me, anyway."

I saw myself as Mortimer decades from now and shivered.

"Your attention," a man said over the speakers. "It's time to proceed to the exercise area."

Patients/prisoners rose to their feet and ended their conversations. A dozen silver-shirted guards armed with cattle prods guided them to the other end of the room and lined them in neat, well-spaced rows. I joined the herd.

"Jumping jacks," the speaker voice said. "One and two and one and two and..."

I followed the voice's cadence, thinking this place made high school and its crushing conformity seem fun. Where was Rachel now? What was Sarah doing?

We did push-ups next, then sit-ups, then running in place... by the end, an hour of enforced fitness. Thanks to the beatings and weeks in bed, it exhausted me.

A door unlocked and the guards herded us into a white-tiled room. They made us take off our clothes and march single-file down a narrow corridor. Water sprayed from nozzles set in the ceiling. Past this, we were sprayed with a chemical-smelling foam, which the people ahead of me rubbed on their skin, forming a lather. The corridor made a U-turn, and more sprinklers rinsed off the soap. Just like one of those automatic car washes.

At the exit, we dried off and put our clothes back on. The guards ushered us into a cafeteria. Like the big exercise room, it had a high ceiling and reflective windows near the top. Slow piano music tinkled from overhead speakers.

Behind a laminated glass wall, a white-uniformed man ladled slop into plastic bowls. A second man passed the bowls through a small revolving door. They held a gray mush that smelled like overcooked corn, okra, and beans.

Beyond the mush dispenser, two men pulled numbered mugs off a rack of shelves and passed them through a second carousel. My mug had the number 326, same as my uniform. It had a purple liquid inside.

I followed the other inmates to a long table with benches, one of five. No one spoke, and no one touched their food.

I sat next to a thin black man with graying hair. "Why isn't anyone eating?" I asked.

He turned to me with tired eyes. "Have to wait for everyone to sit, then we pray, then we eat."

I sipped from the mug. Lukewarm and sugary with a vague grape taste. I wondered if they had put medication in it.

A mild shock ran through my skin. For sipping my drink?

"Number 326," a voice said over the ceiling speakers. "Not everyone is seated. Do not touch your food or drink until you are instructed to do so."

No way could I live here the rest of my life. Maybe I could make a rope out of my bedsheet and hang myself.

No, I just had to convince the Insect psychiatrist I was ready for release. Or at least a trial.

"What's in the mush?" I asked the graying man next to me.

He shrugged. "It tastes a little different from time to time, depending on what's in season. They say it's scientifically formulated to contain all the nutrients we need. Mighty decent of them if you ask me."

The last of the hundred or so inmates sat. "Let us pray," the ceiling voice said. "Thank you, Lord, for this food and drink. Thank you for this shelter over our head, for the kindly help of our doctors, and for allowing us to be born into the greatest country in history. We ask for your guidance as we strive to become better Christians and better citizens. Amen."

Mumbles of "Amen." Not from me. I dug in. The food was nearly tasteless.

"And now this news update," a radio-style voice announced over the speakers. "American troops report new battlefield successes in the Philippines, and have uncovered evidence that the Japanese Empire is supplying arms to the rebels..."

I tuned out the droning voice, playing bluegrass songs in my head. What would they do if I jumped on the table and started singing 'Solidarity Forever'?

"Air Force Colonel Matt Abram will be the first American on the moon," the loudspeakers continued. "He's completed his training at Germany's launch station in Southwest Africa and is scheduled for the next mission to Moon Base Asgard..."

When we finished eating, we lined up and set our bowls, spoons, and mugs on a conveyor belt that carried them through a small opening in the wall. Then we returned to the exercise room. The guards formed us up in drill lines, like Army recruits or a high school marching band, twenty-something ranks of four men each. They made sure everyone was perfectly in line.

"What are we doing now?" I asked the man next to me.

"We march in circles around the room."

"You're kidding."

A guard cuffed me in the ear. "No talking."

The speakers started playing *The Stars and Stripes Forever*. One of the more odious pieces by John Philip Sousa, the National Composer and my musical arch-enemy. The ranks marched forward. Except for me. I stepped out of line and extended both middle fingers to the windows, knowing I'd pay. "This torture I shall not bear," I shouted.

A few people chuckled. Then I paid the price.

Curled in remnant pain, I couldn't march with the others even if I wanted. The shock they gave me was a hundred times worse than the cattle prods, like being doused in gas and set on fire.

Worse, it was stupid of me to act out if I wanted them to release me. This was the wrong place to fight the government.

The hated music ended and I received a mild warning shock. "Number 326. Get up."

I stumbled to my feet. Two of the guards led me and a dozen others to a stack of plastic chairs, which we carried to one of the corners of the big room and arranged in a circle. Dr. Malluch, carry case in hand, joined us. He sat in one of the chairs, back against the wall, and opened his case. The two guards stood outside the circle, cattle prods in hand.

Dr. Malluch pulled out his tape recorder, placed it on the floor in front of his chair, and pressed the start button. He leaned down toward it. "Antisocial disorder breakout group, November 16, 1983. Dr. Thomas Malluch, facilitating."

He turned to me first. "Well now, Benjamin. I heard your first day is not going well."

"You can say that."

"You can go first, then. Tell us about your antisocial disorder. Why are you so angry all the time?"

I wasn't sure what to say. I was too tired to think.

"Go on," he said. "Be truthful. You won't be shocked as long as you're truthful."

"Why shouldn't I be angry? I'm trapped in the circles of hell for who knows how long, beaten and tortured for no reason. And the woman I love is stuck here too, and it breaks my heart." I met Dr. Malluch's glass-paned eyes. "I want to see Rachel."

"You're in love with her."

I was on a truth rampage. "Yes."

He leaned back. "Doesn't it feel good to admit it?"

I supposed it did. "So can I see her?"

"If both of you show signs of significant improvement, and there are no further discipline issues, then I'll see if I can arrange a meeting. How's that?"

My heart lightened, despite all the wiggle room he gave himself. "I'll do whatever it takes." Even march in circles to the martial cadences of The Soul Destroyer if necessary.

Dr. Malluch smiled. "See how easy things can be?" He wrote something on his note pad.

Dinner was the same as lunch, only with chunks of gristly meat in the mush. Afterwords, they returned us to the exercise room and sat us in rows. A big screen dropped down at the other end and the lights dimmed.

Triumphant march music played, full of trumpets and kettle drums. 'AN AMERICAN GIANT' appeared in screen-high letters. It panned up to reveal the Great Seal of the United States, a spread eagle with olive branches in one talon and arrows in the other.

The eagle turned its head to face us, flapped its wings, and morphed into the famous *Spirit of St. Louis* propeller plane. 'The Charles Lindbergh Story' appeared underneath.

My pop made the family watch this movie every year on Lindbergh's birthday. I closed my eyes, tired from all the punishment.

"The future of yesterday is today," a gristle-infused whisper informed me.

I opened my eyes. A short, round-faced man leaned toward me, his face urgent.

"That's President Clark," I said, still hoping to make a friend here. "This movie's about Lindbergh."

"What did he say?"

"'Peace is a virgin who dare not show her face without Strength, her father, for protection.'" The first quote that came to mind. I'd never won a Lindbergh quote competition in school, but I wasn't bad at them either, especially considering my indifference about the man.

The man nodded rapidly. "Yes, yes, now I remember. How about this? 'Living in dreams of yesterday, we find ourselves still dreaming of impossible future conquests.'"

"Yes, that's Lindbergh." I could see how he got the two confused. Clark's speeches tended to be muddled versions of The Master's.

The screen showed black and white family photos. "Lindbergh's father represented the Sixth District of Minnesota from 1907 to 1917," the narrator said, "and often discussed the nation's business with young Charles..."

Another quote came to me. "'The great industrial nations of the White race must band together against a pressing sea of Yellow, Black, and Brown.'"

And thus our alliances with Germany and Italy and colonization efforts in Latin America and the Pacific.

"'Using the science of eugenics,'" the short man said, "'we are guiding humanity into a New Golden Age.'"

"That's Clark again," I said. Or one of his speech writers. Lindbergh and Clark continued a long tradition of white supremacy in America and claimed it was scientific. But my high school science teacher said theories had to be supported by evidence. Sarah was black, but had more brains and talent than Lindbergh and Clark put together. White superiority falsified.

The man rubbed his chin, then thrust up an index finger. "'Is he alone, who has courage on his right hand and faith on his left hand?'"

I ransacked my brain. "'Is life so dear that we should blame men for dying in adventure? Is there a better way to die?'" Then I remembered Jake and lost all interest in the game.

The movie showed footage of Lindbergh's inauguration parade, thousands of Khaki Shirts saluting as his open-top limousine passed. They showed a close-up of Walter Waters, leader of the Bonus Army and then the Khaki Shirt Movement, saluting FDR's replacement. Waters was just a sergeant, but with the American Legion's help, led over a hundred thousand angry vets to seize the capital in return for overdue World War I bonuses and well-paid National Guard appointments.

Next to Waters, J. Edgar Hoover, who provided crucial inside information, and would be Director of Internal Security for four decades. William Dudley Pelley, generously funded by Nazi Germany, whose paramilitary Silver Legion assaulted communists, Jews, and union leaders, killing who knows how many.

Then Charles Coughlin, the radio priest with an audience in the millions. And Gerald Smith, leader of the Christian Nationalist Crusade. In return for policy influence, their speeches rallied national support.

Senator Huey Long, a key supporter before his assassination. Other politicians whose names I couldn't remember.

Finally, a group of bankers and industrialists, standing together in their black wool coats and top hats. It was their coup, and they still called the shots.

After the movie, guards led everyone back to their cells. They took my electroshock suit and I changed into my harmless pajamas.

It had been an awful day in an awful month in an awful year, but I had hope of seeing Rachel. I closed my eyes and pictured her beautiful face, then her laying with me and locking lips. I fell asleep before we got to the best part.

Chapter Thirteen

I was a model prisoner for long days afterward. I even marched to Sousa, although I protested by singing union tunes in my head.

I was constantly tired, and exercises made me dizzy. My mouth stayed dry as a desert no matter how much water I drank, and food wouldn't fill my stomach.

"Just some minor side effects of your drugs," Dr. Malluch told me. "Nothing to worry about. The good news is, your therapy seems to be working."

"I'm doing what you want so I can see Rachel." I reminded him about his promise every breakout session.

Maybe the doctors were helping, turning me into a different person. The Special Agent was right. I was a loser. Couldn't finish high school. Criminal record. No job. No money.

Obsessed with my dead brother's fiancée.

My pop always said I was lazy and selfish, and needed the Army to straighten me out. Army service would be easy after this. As long as they didn't send me someplace like Cuba.

* * *

After a while, two new guards, both of them burly and hard-eyed, entered my cell in the morning. Dr. Malluch followed. "Today's your day," he said.

"To see Rachel?"

"As promised. It takes time to cure antisocial disorders, but I'm pleased at your progress."

One of the guards tossed my shock clothes on the bed and I put them on. "Can I take a shower?"

The guard scowled. "It's not shower time yet. That's after exercises."

I hand-combed my hair and hoped Rachel would forgive my grubby appearance.

Dr. Malluch and the guards led me down a long corridor with small translucent panes of glass every five feet or so, then into a large octagonal room, cold and brightly lit. Like the exercise room and cafeteria, it had high ceilings and reflective windows in the top half of the walls.

Rachel sat on a plastic chair in the center of the room, wearing lumpy shock clothes like mine. Her skin glistened like wax, her hair looked matted, her eyes glassy and flat.

Our eyes met and she stirred to life. My heart pounded to drums, my head swam to fiddles. I left the jailers behind and headed for the dazzling woman I'd feared I'd never see again.

"You have fifteen minutes," Dr. Malluch blurted behind me.

Smiling, Rachel lurched to her feet. "Deerslayer." Her chair toppled backwards onto the floor.

Rachel. The guards, the psychiatrist, the unseen eyes above, all disappeared. "Rachel." I crashed against her and gripped her tight. "Rachel." We clutched each other, the only living souls in a netherworld of bleak pain.

Tears filled her eyes. "I'm so happy you're safe." She hugged me tighter.

I wasn't safe. And what about her? "Are you okay?"

She pulled back a little and shook her head. "I made a terrible mistake." Her green eyes held mine. "But it's so wonderful to see you. I feel like I've been entombed for decades and someone rolled a boulder aside and sunlight is flooding my eyes."

Dark thoughts invaded my mind. What if she'd been turned? What if this was a setup, a way for my captors to manipulate me?

No, that was ridiculous. Besides Sarah, Rachel was the one person I could rely on. She would never betray me. Never.

My lips pressed against hers. They were dry but warm. She didn't respond at first, then pressed back, wandering and exploring. She had morning breath but mine was probably worse.

It didn't matter. It was Rachel's breath, Rachel's lips, Rachel's tongue, all offered to me. Her fingers stroked my cheeks. I ran hands down her back and held her close. She smiled.

"Move apart," a voice said from the ceiling.

We didn't. We kept creating our own heaven and earth, light thrusting aside darkness.

Then her lips went limp and she pulled her head back. "All the things you did. You practically died on the cross for me. I didn't deserve it."

"I'd do anything for you. You know that." I kissed her again but she didn't kiss me back.

"Move apart," the ceiling voice repeated. Shocks jolted my arms and legs. I decided it wasn't pain. Poets and musicians wrote about electricity during a kiss. Thought becomes form.

Rachel shuddered and twitched. She gasped and stepped back. Her eyes darted to the guards, to the windows. "I was so naive."

"Did they hurt you?"

She nodded and her face clenched. Tears dripped from her eyes.

I should have found a way to stop her rally. I held her hands, which were dry and bone white. "I heard you told them about Jake's messages?"

I wanted to ask what else she confessed to, but our persecutors were listening. She was smart, though, and would find a way to signal what else she might have said. I hadn't heard anything about Paul or Sarah so she must not have mentioned them. Smart of them to keep their distance from the rally.

Rachel pulled her hands away and wiped her eyes. "I was so tired, and all drugged up. They got me to talk about Jake and his messages, how he needed closure to move on and I had to carry out his plan, to tell everyone what he saw and that we had to stop oppressing people overseas." She paused. "Obviously my grief therapy wasn't working very well."

Did she really think she'd been delusional, or was she just pretending?

She shifted on her feet and stepped close again. "I'm sorry I got you cast into this place. At least it's temporary. Promise you'll find me in the afterlife. We can all three of us be together."

Three? "Don't talk about death. We'll get out of here."

"They told me you're in love with me and that's why you ended up here, that I used you and you suffered the consequences."

They'd torn at her mind the way they did mine. "I do love you, Rachel. I helped you because I wanted to."

She gripped my hands, face granite, eyes serious. "Don't sacrifice yourself for me anymore." Her eyes drifted down. "It's sweet, and you're righteous, and I care about you, but... I don't think I can love you the same way you love me." Her voice dropped to a whisper. "I'm sorry. I'm still connected to Jake."

So she hadn't left that space yet. Why did I think I could take his place anyway?

Rachel kissed me on the nose, then gazed in my eyes. Hers welled with tears. "I wish things were different. I'm sorry I caused you such pain."

They shocked us again and we had to let go of each other.

How dare they? Despite the medications, my fists clenched. Something rose from the abyss inside me, something terrible. I forced the fingers back apart before it broke surface, not wanting to give the guards a reason to drag me away.

I feared the worst. "Did they say when they'll let you out?"

"You have to move on and forget about me," she said. "I confessed to everything in return for your release."

Panic rattled my bones. "Confessed?" Maybe she did give up Sarah and Paul.

"That the anti-war rally was all my idea and you could care less about it, you were just helping me because it was about your brother and you're in love with me."

"They didn't tell me anything about a release."

Her eyes widened. "What?"

"They tricked you." My vision blurred.

Rachel trembled and gasped. It looked like she might fall so I grabbed her arms.

She shook her head and sobbed. "I signed a paper saying I'm mentally ill, like the psychiatrists here said, and it drove me to say and do all kinds of crazy things I shouldn't have." Her arms jerked back and forth in my grip. "And they're probably right, only a crazy person talks to the dead and tries to fight the government." She shouted at the tinted windows. "Let Ben go! You promised!"

The guards approached. Black storm clouds boiled and swirled, hatred stronger than the wrath of the Almighty. "When are they letting you out?" I screamed.

She started bawling. "Never."

They tricked us and now Rachel was stuck here forever. Weeks of suppressed anger burst out of their cage.

My body moved on its own like I was observing some mad beast intent on murder. My arms grasped the nearest Insect and my teeth clamped down on his nose.

He screamed. Salty blood ran past my lips and over my tongue.

Acetylene hot shocks seared my skin. My teeth clenched together and something slipped over my tongue toward my throat.

The screaming grew louder. My lips spit out a piece of cartilage that used to be a nose.

An alarm sounded. Someone tackled my body and tried to pin it to the floor, but my arms and legs writhed and battered. Fists connected with faces.

Rachel screamed. The shocks wouldn't stop. I smelled burning flesh. My vision narrowed into smaller and smaller circles.

Something hard hit the side of my head and my limbs stopped thrashing. A needle pricked my neck and the room faded into nothingness.

Chapter Fourteen

I woke feeling dull pain all over. My mouth felt like dry cotton. I was strapped to a bed, naked, in a bright room full of medical equipment. A short middle-aged man with a neat mustache and white coat peered at me through round glasses. "You've been out a while."

"What happened?" I had done something awful, from which there was no return, but my memories were vague shapes in a fog.

"You don't remember?"

"I was talking to Rachel. Is she okay?"

"Miss Tolson wasn't injured, if that's what you mean." He shook his head. "Certainly she'll never see you in the same light again."

The fog began to lift. The taste of blood, the feel of human flesh slick against my tongue... "The medicine, the torture..."

The real trigger was Rachel condemning herself on my behalf, probably for nothing. After what I did, certainly for nothing.

"You bit a man's nose off," the man said. "In all my years of practice, I have never seen such a thing, such an act of psychotic barbarism. Dr. Malluch is being placed on leave for his incompetence. And we can no longer allow you to mix with others."

A bored-looking young man in a white uniform painted gel on the backs of metal disks and stuck them to my skin—feet, forehead, and everywhere in between. Wires ran from the disks to a console near the bed.

I strained against the leather straps but without effect.

"Don't bother," the assistant said. "No one's ever broken those straps."

"Can you sew it back on?" I asked the doctor. "The nose?"

"Yes, they took him to surgery, but there will be scarring. And he'll have to be reassigned."

The assistant wiped my left inner elbow with an alcohol swab. He unlocked a cabinet and moved things around. The doctor, meanwhile, fiddled with knobs on the console.

"What are you doing?" I asked.

They ignored me. The assistant returned with a syringe and plunged a clear liquid into my arm vein.

"That will help activate your nociceptors," the doctor said from the console. "Your pain receptors. They'll go into overdrive as soon as we apply a current."

More torture. Judging by the amount of effort, this would be the worst yet. "You're sick sons of bitches, you know that?"

The doctor laughed. "I do love the irony of your statement."

The assistant injected another drug. "And this will block the production of enkephalin," he said. "That's one of your pain regulators." He glanced back at the doctor, probably for approval. The doctor nodded.

The assistant forced a black rubber ball into my mouth and secured it with straps. Then he strapped a cloth over my eyes. Nothing I could do but wait now.

"Your past punishments were unfortunately insufficient," the doctor's voice said. "I think your new regimen should do the trick, though. And if we still don't see any progress, there's always surgery. In fact, there's a good chance we'll do that anyway and send you to Repurpose Section."

I wasn't sure exactly what he meant, but it had to be bad. I'd kowtow to Dr. Malluch and maybe they'd let me go, eventually. I had to see my advocate! And Rachel, was there still a way to get her out?

Sudden pain tore through my skin and muscles, unbelievably worse than the cattle prods or shock suits. My skin seared from electric whips. My arms and legs shook and twisted, the bones threatening to shatter. My eyes bulged, like only the cloth was keeping them from popping out of the sockets. I plunged deep into an eternal lake of fire.

* * *

I woke in my cell. They kept me confined there, bringing meals and drinks spiked with something that dulled my mind more each day.

"From now on," my new doctor, the short man with the neat mustache and round glasses said, "you go to the pain room for every infraction."

I violated none of his rules, but he sent me there anyway when I asked to see my advocate. After that, I stopped talking entirely, and only ate my food because the guards threatened me. I thought constantly about killing myself but couldn't muster the strength to try. My spirit sank through layers of muck and stone, miles beneath any possibility of escape, leaving behind an empty husk.

At some point, my original guards, Shocky and Baldy, entered my cell with shackles and chains. I didn't have the energy to care where we were going.

They led me back to the interrogation room. Special Agent Lewison, the charcoal-suited Insect with the demonic eyes, sat behind the metal table.

As before, the guards plopped me on the narrow stool in front of the table, and chained me to the floor. I turned away from the spotlights and said nothing.

Special Insect Lewison leaned toward me and snapped his fingers at eye level. I tried to focus. Why was I back here?

He opened a folder and wrote something on a sheet of paper, then fixed his dark eyes on me again. "Are you proud of yourself?"

Was he serious?

"I asked you a question," he said in rigid tones.

"Just shoot me and get it over with."

He sniffed. "That would waste a perfectly good bullet. And however many years of labor we can squeeze out of you before your body gives out." He paused, but I had nothing to say.

"It was stupid of Dr. Malluch to let you visit Miss Tolson," he continued. "I would never have allowed it. But you're under my jurisdiction again."

The psychiatrists must have given up on me.

Lewison leaned back in his chair. "I haven't quite decided what to do with you, Benjamin. You're of no importance and no one gives a Monday morning shit about you. I'd have released you a long time ago if you'd cooperated instead of being a gum-headed jackass. And you were making decent progress in the psych ward until you went berserk and bit that guard's nose off."

"You tricked us," I managed.

"I didn't do anything. Miss Tolson confessed of her own free will."

Bullshit. I kept quiet, though.

The Insect flipped through his folder and read, "U.S. Criminal Code, current edition, Chapter 2, Section 201(b). Assault on a sworn officer of the United States, where bodily injury is inflicted, is subject to imprisonment with hard labor for a minimum of ten years."

Everyone knew that.

He fixed his black eyes on me. "Since you maimed the officer in question, and are a repeat offender, it's quite likely you'll receive a life sentence."

I'd force them to kill me somehow. Why live without hope?

"As for Miss Tolson," he said, "she can't be released until her treatment is complete, and then she faces a life sentence at hard labor for sedition."

I saw Rachel years from now, her beauty and mind gone, weather-beaten and hunch-backed, shoveling dirt and rocks with blistered, bleeding hands. "Please let her go. She's learned her lesson."

"Frankly," he said, "given the depths of Miss Tolson's delusions and the violence you've exhibited, Repurpose Section is the most likely option for the two of you."

My new psychiatrist, who'd never given his name, had mentioned that too. "What's that?"

"It's for people who can only be reformed through brain surgery. Then we find useful labor for the part of you that remains."

My lungs stopped working and a drumbeat of blood pounded my inner ears. "Please. If you let Rachel go, I'll do whatever you want."

He shook his head. "She gave us the same offer for you. Her offer was worth a lot more."

"You didn't even honor it."

"I intended to. But you still have to be treated for your psychiatric condition. And after what you did to that guard, well..." He flipped his hands up.

I'd been so close to release. Didn't matter. No way could I live outside knowing Rachel would suffer and die here.

The Insect interrogator leaned forward. "But here's the wrinkle. Why I took time for you today. I think you and Miss Tolson were lying when you claimed to act alone."

The statement might have startled me into unconscious betrayal, but the medications helped for once, keeping my reactions sluggish. "What do you mean?"

"Southern Illinois was always a quiet area before Miss Tolson's outburst," he said. "There was the occasional hooliganism from bored teens or career criminals like yourself, but that was about it. No economic sabotage or messages of agitation."

"Economic sabotage?"

"A lumber company office in Vienna was set on fire." Vienna was a small town in the Shawnee Hills with an officially mispronounced name.

"Following that, all sorts of hand-painted signs went up along roads." He examined a typewritten page. "'Stop cutting down our forests,' 'Stop polluting our streams.'" His dark eyes returned to me. "Crap like that."

It was news to me. I shrugged.

"We think Miss Tolson either started something or she's a part of something."

I shook my head. "Rachel just didn't want anyone else to die like Jake. I was her only partner."

The Insect studied me but I was telling the truth. Rachel and I organized the rally by ourselves, and I hadn't heard anything about burning down a lumber office or putting up signs.

He opened his folder and passed a flyer across the table. A photo of my face was below the header. Next to it, Rachel's face pre-captivity, at its loveliest.

FREE BENJAMIN ADAMSON AND RACHEL TOLSON!

They were arrested on October 16 for questioning Jacob Adamson's wasteful death as part of the occupation of Cuba. They have been denied a trial and access to their advocates and are being held incommunicado, under false psychiatric pretenses, at the Illinois State Correctional Hospital in Decatur. This violates basic human rights and long-standing legal precedence, dating back to the original U.S. Constitution and Declaration of Independence.

Please write and call ISCH Chief Administrator Dexter Mitchum, Governor Wiley Bonenfant, Rep. Alfred Caldwell, and Sen. Clinton Storm, and ask that Benjamin and Rachel be allowed to meet with their advocates and contest their trumped-up charges in court.

Addresses and phone numbers followed.

I blinked and stared at the flyer. I almost smiled. Someone out there cared about me. Sarah?

"Who wrote this?" Agent Lewison asked.

I didn't respond, hypnotized by the word "FREE."

His face clenched. "This is your only chance to make yourself useful. Who wrote this? Who put up those signs?"

"How would I know? I've been stuck in here."

"All this flyer has done is make things worse for you. The state can't possibly release you now, it would set a precedent of weakness. And do you really think anyone gives a shit about you? We haven't received a single call on your behalf."

Maybe one of Rachel's friends, like Alyce, made the flyers. "Did anyone call about Rachel?"

Lewison pounded a finger against the paper. "Besides, the entire premise of this flyer is ridiculous. Not only are we acting within the law, we ARE the law."

The Insect didn't answer my question. "Not everyone has phones," I said, "or can afford long distance. Did you get any letters?"

He waved a finger over the desk. "Do you see any letters here?"

Just his folder of notes and official forms. Which didn't prove anything, not after the way they tricked Rachel. Truth from prisoners, lies from captors.

"Let me ask you something," he said. "What if I pulled some strings and got you released?"

"What about Rachel?"

He pulled a blank sheet of paper out of his folder and slid it across the desk. He tossed a ballpoint pen. It bounced and skidded and stopped just short of the edge. "Give me five names. Just five, and your future will look a lot better. Rachel's too."

I didn't trust him, couldn't trust anyone here. He did think I was dumb—might as well play that up. "Names of who?"

Lewison leaned forward and gritted his teeth. "Subversives."

"I don't know any subversives."

"Then you have no value and I might as well send you and Miss Tolson to Repurpose Section."

Part of me wanted to take the pen and write 'Santa Claus,' a blatant communist. Or 'Jesus of Nazareth' for throwing out the money changers and condemning the rich. The stakes were way too high, though. I had to sacrifice someone.

Lewison narrowed his pitch-dark eyes. "If you won't cooperate, maybe Rachel will tell me what I need to know. How do you think she'll react to the special pain regimen you're on?"

My knees betrayed me and rattled like maracas. "She already told you everything. Don't hurt her anymore."

"Last chance," he said. "America has enough trouble with external enemies and there's simply no tolerance for internal sabotage. We've got to work together. And these saboteurs have made things worse for you and Rachel. That was probably their intent, to sacrifice the two of you to further their cause. You can repent for the mistakes you made. Do the right thing for everyone, and give us the information we need to stop these criminals. Then you and Rachel can go free."

Rachel freed? My voice bypassed my brain. "I don't have any names now. But let us go for real, and I'll be your spy. I'll get you some names."

What the hell was I doing?

His eyebrows raised. Then he leaned back and shook his head. "I can't let you two roam free without anything in return. You should have taken my offer." He reached under the desk.

I'd tried even the unthinkable, but there was no way out.

The door opened. Shocky and Baldy entered.

"Take Mr. Adamson back to his cell," Lewison told them. "Then bring Rachel Tolson here. But bring her to the pain center first."

Chapter Fifteen

"I pledge allegiance to the United States of America, President Clark, and our Captains of Industry, to worship God with all my heart, and uphold the principles of duty, morality, and hard work."

Chanting words I didn't believe, right arm extended toward the flag in salute, was better than being shocked. I pretended my middle finger had recruited its neighbors, a five-fold 'screw you.' Fuck every one of you evil bastards for what you're doing to Rachel and me.

The surge of secret hatred felt good. Normally my moods alternated between despair and panic about Rachel in the pain room and maybe giving up Sarah and her family.

I'd been assigned to yet another psychiatrist, declared cured of 'explosive rage disorder' as long as I took my new medicine, and sent back to the gymnasium, back with other psych prisoners arranged in neat rows. Above the American flag on the wall and ringing the entire perimeter, invisible guards watched from behind reflective glass, ready to activate our shock suits at the slightest infraction.

"Fuck President Clark," a soft voice spoke behind me. I peered over my shoulder. It was the short, round-faced man I'd traded Lindbergh quotes with.

I knew better than to say anything, so I turned around and waited for the pre-breakfast lecture. The floor guards watched me with alert eyes, hands on their cattle prods.

"Man is man," the ceiling speakers proclaimed, "when he casts off selfish material pleasure and contributes to history and the growth of the Nation..."

I settled into a half hour of mind manure and played Pale Moon Rising songs in my head, visualizing my fingers on the guitar frets. Too bad Rachel missed our last show. Would there ever be another chance?

After breakfast, during our free hour, Round Face asked me, "Where have you been? Why are the guards so skittish around you?"

I wasn't sure I wanted to talk to anyone, but maybe it would keep me from going genuinely crazy. "I got in a fight with some guards and sent one of them to surgery."

I still couldn't believe I bit a man's nose off, and preferred no one knew about it.

Round Face pursed his lips. "I'm sure he deserved it."

"Hey, I never caught your name."

"Enos."

"Ben."

We didn't shake hands since that would draw extra attention from the windows. We talked about our lives before captivity. Enos said he'd taught history in high school, and was arrested for anti-American agitation.

"I was just telling my students the facts," he said. "Lindbergh brought us out of the Depression, made sure everyone had jobs, and built up our infrastructure, but Clark hasn't accomplished anything."

I was skeptical. Enos hadn't acted subversive before, and was taking a lot of chances confiding in me, especially with all the eyes watching us.

Best to play along, though, and not say anything incriminating myself.

* * *

After a few days, the guards returned me to the interrogator's office. Special Insect Lewison flipped through typewritten pages in a folder while I sat on the stool in front of his desk, shackled to the floor.

Did he have Rachel tortured as badly as me? Did she give anyone up? Best not to ask—he used our worries against us.

Perhaps reading my thoughts, the Insect slid paper and a pen toward me. "Write down five subversive things you've heard in the psych ward. Quotes are best, and make sure you write down who said it."

A test. Which was hopeful—he was still interested in me. If I passed, he might let me out to trade for Rachel.

Which meant I would forfeit the last shreds of my soul. There was no creature lower than the betrayer. Dante had reserved his deepest circle of hell for treachery.

I picked up the pen. My hand shook, and I had to concentrate on each letter.

"Fuck President Clark." -Enos (I don't know his last name but he is Prisoner #117)

Three other quotes—summaries actually—were from Enos and one from a younger man named Carl. I shouldn't have fingered Enos, but there was a good chance the Insects planted him to test me. Carl was an asshole and even so, I only mentioned his complaints about the shitty food.

The Insect read my betrayals and set the paper aside. "Good work, Benjamin. You know, your father's a patriot. Your brother was a patriot. It's time for you to follow their lead, to put away childish things, wouldn't you say?"

I nodded reflexively.

Jake spoke to me for the first time in weeks. *He must not know how I changed.*

It was nice to hear my brother's voice again, imaginary or not.

Lewison fixed his dark eyes on me. "Do you love your country, Benjamin?"

I loved the land—the fields, the woods, the ponds. I loved playing bluegrass with my friends. I loved Rachel. And Sarah. And even Pop and Grandpa. "Yes."

The Insect stared at me. "You should. You were lucky to be born here. America is unique among nations, the biblical City upon a Hill, and we have a special place in history. God has chosen us to transform the world, to enlighten and unite all peoples."

I kept quiet.

"Together, as Americans, we fulfill the Will of History. And this gives meaning to our lives. Do you understand?"

I nodded. They'd claimed this a million times in school.

"History is written through conflict and it is our duty as Americans to strive together, so we may triumph and fulfill our destiny. Some of this conflict is external, against nations on the wrong side of history. But we have enemies within as well."

His black eyes glittered. "Most of these are agents for foreign powers. Others, the anarchists for example, are clinically insane, driven by brain disorders to kill and destroy. They commit atrocities like the market bombing in Kansas City, going all the way back to Haymarket in the last century. They attack society and hurt people just for the sake of doing it."

Paul had claimed Internal Security set off the Kansas City bomb as a provocation. One of the two was a liar or dupe.

Agent Lewison folded his hands. "So you see, Benjamin, how even you are needed."

Don't believe a word the Insects say, Jake told me. *But do what's necessary to free Rachel.*

Enos was gone when I returned to the psych ward. He didn't return. Carl was denied food and water for three days for complaining about the meals.

I hoped Enos was a plant or a fellow snitch. As for Carl, he seemed destined for trouble.

After two more betrayal sessions with Agent Lewison, my captors moved me to a new room with a comfortable bed, dresser, desk, and TV. It had a wash basin next to the toilet. Best of all, it had a window. The window had bars, but I could see down into a concrete courtyard where guards gathered to smoke. It was surrounded by four story red brick buildings with tiled roofs and tall smokestacks.

Rachel was in one of those buildings. I hoped she was okay.

The door opened and my latest guards entered with breakfast. No chains or shock suits. And a real breakfast—hard-boiled eggs, toast with jam, a banana, and grapefruit juice. No pills.

I dove into the food, the best thing I'd eaten in months. After I finished, the guards returned. They led me down hallways and into a small room with a bullet-proof glass divider in the middle.

Special Insect Lewison sat at a metal table on the other side. In front of him were folders, an open briefcase, and a small TV set wired through the wall. On my side of the plastiglass, a wooden chair faced the table.

"Please sit, Mr. Adamson," he said.

My guards left the room. A lock clicked.

I sat in the chair and thought about ponds in summer, calming my mind. The plastiglass had a circle of pencil-sized holes at face height. Beneath that was a small revolving door.

Lewison folded his Insect hands. "I trust your new accommodations are an improvement?"

"It was a low bar, but yeah."

"Good. I'm pleased with your progress. You need training, though. You'll have two weeks to learn everything you need to know. Clandestine service training normally lasts a year, but we have an accelerated program for rapid deployment that covers the essentials."

I nodded. I could do that.

"As soon as you're prepped and pass the tests," he continued, "we're releasing you."

The thought of freedom nearly gave me a woody. And if the agent was sending me out to spy, it meant Rachel hadn't given anyone up.

Of course not, Jake said. *She's strong and she cares about people. She confessed for your sake, didn't she?*

"Are you releasing Rachel too?" I asked Lewison.

"As soon as you give us five names with enough evidence to bring charges." He turned the TV so I could see the black and white screen. On it, Rachel sat on a bed in a room like mine, reading a paperback. She wore pajamas with the number 296 on them. No visible bruises, but her face sagged and her fingers gripped the book like claws. The Insects had hurt her.

"You seem to have a stunted sense of self-preservation," Lewison said in even tones. "But you do care about Miss Tolson. Rachel. She'll bear the burden of any infraction, and that burden will be harsher than you can imagine."

Beatings. Electrocution. Repurpose Section. Other things I hadn't been told about yet.

"On the other hand," he said, "the more you cooperate, the better things will be for both of you. As you can see, we've given her a nice room like yours, and plenty of books to read."

I did know five people I could trade for Rachel. Unfortunately, one was Sarah. I could no more betray her than I could Rachel. And betrayal in general was the ugliest thing a person could do.

Lewison placed a small note card on the revolving door tray and spun it to my side. It read, P.O. Box 1819, Champaign, Illinois 61820.

Champaign was fifty miles away. Did he live there? Did he do some of his work there?

"Memorize that address," he said. "That's where you'll mail your reports. You'll be tested before you leave to make sure you remember it, along with everything else we tell you."

"So I just send you stuff in the mail?" That didn't seem top secret.

"You won't write a return address. And as long as you stamp it and don't enclose cash, no one will open it. Except me, obviously."

He pulled a tiny rectangular camera out of the open briefcase and held it next to the plastiglass. The camera was connected by wire to a plastic bulb. "This is one of your tools to gather information. You'll take photos of people, preferably doing something incriminating, and documents. It's winter so we'll put it in a coat."

He raised the camera. "This will go inside the lining. Only the lens will be visible, and it will be disguised as a button." He squeezed the bulb. "This goes in your pocket. When you press the pocket, it will send a signal to the camera and snap a photo. You'll get a chance to practice before you leave."

"And what if someone asks me where I got the jacket?"

"You were given money when you got out and you bought it in town because it was cold. I'll write a story for you to memorize."

He put the camera back in the briefcase and brought out a small tape recorder. "This will also go inside your jacket. It can record up to two hours of audio per tape. It's voice-activated, and won't record when it's quiet."

I'd had plenty of experience fiddling with my bandmate Jesse's 4-track. "How's the sound quality?"

"Good enough. Now, your job is to find the lumber company arsonists and any other subversives active in southern Illinois. It should be easy, since at least some of them know you and Miss Tolson. Probably they're friends of yours. Maybe even family."

My stomach hardened. "You expect me to turn in friends and family?"

"If you want Rachel released, yes." He leaned forward. "Look, I know it's hard. I don't expect you to turn in your father or grandfather. Judging from the field interviews, they're loyal Americans. But I know Rachel is more important to you than anyone else in your life, so it's a reasonable trade. And you'll be serving your country. You should be proud."

I wasn't sure how I felt about Paul, and didn't really know his other recruits. I sort of knew June, she'd gone to my school, one of Rachel's friends. But Amos and Micah were strangers.

So it was mostly the weasel factor I had to overcome, plus finding some sap to stand in for Sarah. I'd hate myself the rest of my life, and would probably end up curled around a still in some cold woodlot till my liver gave out or I froze to death.

"I'm in," I said. "And if I do this, you'll let Rachel go?"

How could I trust him? Did I have a choice?

The Insect placed a sheet of paper against the plastiglass. It was an order of release, with *Rachel Tolson* penned over the first blank line. "All I have to do is sign it."

I'd go along for now and see what happened. Planning wasn't one of my stronger talents. "I'm yours. What else do I need to know?"

"A lot. Equipment is the least of your concerns. You need to be creative and courageous. You need an accurate memory. And you have to be able to fool and manipulate people. There's more, a lot more, but one thing at a time."

Fool and manipulate people. This guy was probably a master. "You can teach me all this?"

"We have experts in each subject who will provide instruction." He passed a book titled *A Field Guide to Lies and Liars* through the revolving door. "Read this today. It's mostly photos, facial expressions and body postures to look for. We'll go over it tomorrow, then the more you practice, the better you'll get."

He passed two more books through, both short. One was titled *Memory Tricks*. The other, *Memory Games*. "Read *Memory Tricks* and play the games. They're fun, actually."

I tried to remember actual fun. Fishing. Hunting. Dancing. Playing music. Most of the times, with Sarah. If I turned in Paul, or anyone else in the cell, the Insects would torture them till they broke. Like Rachel and me. One of them might give up Sarah. Being poor and black, even if she hadn't hurt anyone, they'd hang her.

Chapter Sixteen

By the end of rapid training, I knew all sorts of mnemonic tricks and could remember long sequences of names and numbers. I could focus on individual conversations in a crowded room, while pretending not to. I could decipher facial and body expressions, knowing better now what to look for, and control my own—I hoped. I could pick a lock with a bobby pin, a skill I hadn't used since high school, now improved by theory and expert tutelage.

Thanks to Special Agent Lewison and his crew of experts, I could lie, cheat, and steal, and get away with it. I was ready for government work.

Lewison visited my room for the first time. He was flanked by two younger men, also wearing charcoal suits and black fedoras. One of them laid two garment bags on the bed. Then he reached in a jacket pocket and handed me an envelope.

The envelope contained ten crisp ten-dollar bills and a bus ticket back to New Bethany, which included local transfers on both ends. "I guess this is it," I said.

Lewison fixed his dark eyes on me. "I have to admit I'm impressed how well you mastered the skill set."

Just because I didn't finish school didn't mean I was stupid.

"Being a criminal gave you a head start," he added.

Asshole couldn't say anything decent about me. I suppressed my anger. "I'm not a criminal."

"Not anymore, I hope. You remember everything we talked about?"

I nodded, then unzipped the garment bags. One held my suit, the one I'd worn to the rally, along with my wallet and other clothes. I slipped the money into the wallet, easily the most it had ever seen. The other bag contained a black wool trenchcoat. I still couldn't believe it was winter. I'd missed the harvest.

"You bought the coat at a thrift shop in Decatur," Lewison said. "You don't remember the name of the shop, but it was near a bar you spent half a day at." He showed me photos of a seedy bar to memorize.

I examined the trenchcoat. It matched my suit, but wasn't overly fancy, with plastic buttons and no embroidery. The button holes were frayed. The camera lens lay behind the lapel button hole, which was torn slightly open. There was no matching button on the other side, just some loose threads, but the mike was hidden there. As long as I kept the lapel open, they were invisible.

"Anyone I can rendezvous with?" I asked. "For possible leads?" Maybe I could expose the Insects' informers once Rachel was freed. Everyone knew about Darren and Will and Candy, but there had to be others.

"What do you mean?"

"I mean coordinate with the other informers, so I can finish quicker."

He frowned. "You're on your own. Don't tell anyone you're working for me. That's non-negotiable."

That might confirm the theory that informers worked independently so no one knew who was a rat and who wasn't. Even informers had to beware. Just as likely, there was no one else in New Bethany he could rely on. Or they worked for competing agents or agencies.

Lewison held out his hand. I shook it. It felt like a normal hand, not cold and chitinous.

"Good luck," he said. "Rachel's counting on you."

"How's she doing? Can I see her in person?" The black and white monitor screen had no sound, no touch, no bonding of souls.

Lewison's lips pressed together, as if the request irritated him. "She's in the female section, and your last visit put a guard in the hospital. You can see her when you complete your mission and she's released. Then you can spend the rest of your lives together."

I put on my suit and the trenchcoat. Two silver-shirted guards led me down a series of hallways to an austere lobby with plastiglass front doors and an Internal Security Service seal on the wall, a bird of prey with outstretched talons. The doors unlocked with a buzz and a click. I hurried through, not looking back.

The cold air outside made me shiver. To either side, the Internal Security Center and attached Correctional Hospital stretched into the distance, four stories of red brick with tall chimneys wheezing smoke into a gloomy sky. If there was a boundary between the interrogation center and psychiatric hospital, it wasn't clear. Ahead, a concrete bunker guarded the gate of a tall electric fence topped with razor wire.

"Bus stop's down the driveway, right where it meets the road," the older of the two guards said as they escorted me to the bunker.

I didn't thank him.

The guards opened the gate for me. A two-lane road lay ahead, fronted by a glass bus shelter. Four men and two women, all wearing hats and coats, sat there or stood outside, smoking cigarettes and talking quietly.

The sign on the shelter said 'Local', with three numbers below. I was supposed to take the Number 6 into town and get off at the main bus terminal, then wait for an intercity that would take me home. I should have had my advocate pick me up, but I hadn't seen him in weeks. For all I knew, my case had been dropped long ago.

My bus—long and silver with red, white, and blue trim—arrived with a creaking of brakes. I boarded after the others and gave the driver my pass into town.

The bus was more than half full, mostly men. None wore uniforms, but cops and hospital staff in New Bethany changed in locker rooms. I wanted to ask, any of you bastards torture people for a living? What would I do if one of them said yes?

I took a seat up front, near the door. I had to focus on freeing Rachel. Revenge could come later.

The bus stopped several times at prison gates, factories, parking lots, and a train depot. Passengers hopped on and off. I'd been confined in a small part of a huge complex, probably thousands of employees and tens of thousands of inmates. Beyond one of the high double fences, slack-faced prisoners labored in the cold, loading and unloading trucks, their movements slow and stiff, like marionettes jerked by palsied hands. Repurpose Section?

A man sat next to me. Thirtyish, pale skin, sunken eyes in a long face, narrow nose. He wore a heavy coat and a felt fedora. He ignored me and rummaged through his pockets.

The bus departed a razor-topped double gate flanked by watch towers. The long-faced man shot a middle finger toward the window, then turned back to me. "I could kill for a smoke."

He was too desperate-looking for a doctor or guard. "Is that what got you here?" I asked.

He laughed, which turned into a cough. He extended a hand. Small scabs dotted the back. "Auto theft. Never hurt a fly. Name's Aaron."

I shook his hand. "Ben."

"So, smoke?"

I held out empty palms. He sighed.

The bus drove onto a four-lane highway, passed brown, stubble-strewn fields, then entered Decatur. 'Welcome to Decatur,' the roadside sign said. 'Pride of the Prairie. Population 100,616.' Twenty times bigger than New Bethany. As for prairie, there wasn't much left of that—it had all been plowed and planted.

We passed three billboards illustrating Love of God, Love of Country, and Love of Duty; then miles of warehouses, depots, and factories. These gave way to small wooden cottages, and we turned onto a city street. Tall blocky buildings loomed in the distance.

Downtown Decatur was crowded, and we inched from stop to stop, brick and concrete buildings all around. I spotted the bus terminal, a long, high mass of concrete with a Lindbergh statue plopped in front. We turned there and pulled into a covered lot next to several other buses parked diagonally.

I headed straight for the men's room, then into a brightly lit café with plastic tables and chairs. It was past lunch time, so I bought a hot dog and chips at the counter and splurged for a Coke.

I sat at one of the empty tables and started eating. Aaron appeared and eased into the chair next to me, a cheeseburger, can of beer, and pack of smokes on his tray. "Thought you were a local," he said. "But you're a migrant like me."

"Not a migrant. Headed home." I hoped he hadn't seen how much money I had in my wallet.

He popped open the beer and took a swig. "Decatur's my home but I've got to move on. Police say I'm not welcome anymore."

"Sore times."

He downed more beer, ignoring the burger.

"Where'd you get the beer?"

"Next door, at the news stand. They've got all kinds of travel necessities there." He lit a cigarette and offered me one.

"No thanks. Don't smoke." I did intend to buy a beer or two though.

He leaned toward me. "Can you use your bus pass any time?"

"Why do you ask?" The answer was yes, of course.

"I need a hand with something. I'll make it worth your while."

He smiled but my guard went up immediately. I could probably take him—he was pretty scrawny—but no doubt he had friends around somewhere.

I must not have disguised my suspicion because he said, "I got money. I ain't gonna try to take yours." He lowered his voice to a whisper. "I just need to pick up some supplies and I've been banned from the local drug store. I'll give you the money for it, and a free high afterward." He leaned back. "What do you say?"

"What are you talking about?"

"Smash. I can cook but I need the ingredients. You can have some when we're done."

A Smash addict. Or a dealer. That explained a lot. I glanced around. No one was paying attention.

I examined Aaron. His eyes and hands didn't show any signs of lying. Should I try it? I needed something a lot more powerful than beer. I was about to go down as the Judas of New Bethany.

"If you try to roll me," I said, "I'll break your neck."

"Quit being so goddamn paranoid." He retrieved a pen and notepad from a coat pocket and wrote down a list. He tore off the page and passed it to me.

Cough syrup with codeine, 5 x 1-pint bottles. Ephedrine, 3 x 100-count bottles. Iodine. Rubbing alcohol. The list went on.

"I'll get the acetone and match books at the hardware store, and the rest they'll have at the kitchen."

"Kitchen?"

"I know a woman with a full setup, and she keeps it clean. She'll let us use it in exchange for a cut."

"How much will this stuff cost?"

Aaron took off his right shoe and pulled up the insole. He handed me $100 in tens and twenties. "That should do it."

As I stuffed the bills in my pocket, keeping them far from my nose, a thought occurred. Maybe I could turn this guy and four others into "revolutionaries." People who didn't know Sarah who I could trade for Rachel. It was scummy, but better than the alternative.

Aaron led me to the drug store, two blocks from the bus station. I grabbed a shopping cart and started filling it. I added drinks and snacks.

The checkout girl gave me a funny expression as she rang up all the cough syrup and ephedrine. I looked pretty dapper in my suit, though, and had learned how to disguise lies.

I leaned toward her and raised my eyebrows. "First my little sister got sick, then everyone else. I'm probably next." I kept eye contact half the time, examining the increasing cash register total the rest of the time, and as I made up details, gestured with my hands.

"I hope everyone feels better soon," she said as she handed me the receipt, which totaled more than I'd expected.

I met Aaron down the block at the streetcar stop. I gave him some of the bags and the receipt. "I went over. Do you have another ten?"

He peered at the receipt. "I didn't say buy snacks. That's on you."

The streetcar arrived. We got off at a neighborhood of small white houses with unkempt lawns. It looked deserted, but most of the houses had Christmas lights on the front and manger scenes in the yard. I'd forgotten all about Christmas. It was ten days from now.

We hiked into the neighborhood. The bags grew heavy. Near the end of the street, Aaron cut between two houses and knocked on an aluminum back door with a small curtained window.

Inside, a dog barked and growled. A baby started crying. The curtain parted and a woman, her face shadowed, stared at us.

The curtain closed. "Git," a female voice said, and the barking stopped.

The door opened. The woman was blonde, indeterminate age, baggy eyes, wearing a long-sleeved blouse and loose pants. "Aaron Little," she said, eyes darting. She focused on our bags and smiled with tobacco-stained teeth.

"Out at last," Aaron said. "Can we come in?"

She jerked a thumb toward me. "Who's this?"

"This is Ben. He's cool."

She opened the door and waved us into a tiny room with a washer and dryer and piles of dirty clothes. The baby screams grew louder. "This is Edna," Aaron said once she shut the door behind us.

I put out a hand. "Nice to meet you."

She hesitated, then shook my hand. She had scabs on the back like Aaron. "Yeah."

"Ben did the buying," Aaron said.

"Just got released," I said. It still seemed weird, being able to go wherever I wanted.

Edna's eyebrows raised. "What were you in for?"

I started to spin a story in my head about a bar fight, but it would be better to tell the truth, more or less. Everyone in New Bethany would know about the rally fiasco and the news could have spread. I'd see where these two stood. "My brother was killed in Cuba—"

"Sorry about that."

"And it drove me nuts, him dying for sugar companies. I helped organize an anti-war rally and the government hauled me in."

I examined their faces. Aaron peered at me but didn't say anything.

Edna shook her head. "But they let you go?"

"I got sixty days and some awful beatings." I fixed on their eyes, hoping to look sincere. "Now I'm even more pissed off. This country needs a revolution."

She smiled. "Follow me, Karl Marx. We can talk later."

She led us through a messy kitchen and dining room and into a living room that stank of cigarette smoke and chemicals, the air hot and dry. No Christmas tree. A German shepherd poked its ears up and rose from the floor, growling.

"Shut up, Kaiser," Edna shouted. The dog obeyed.

Behind Kaiser, a girl in a faded house dress sat on a tattered sofa, cradling a crying baby. The girl looked my age, with thin lips and limp straw-colored hair, but with smooth cheeks and a delicate nose.

"That's my sister Talitha," Edna said.

Talitha glared at us.

"Sorry if we woke your baby," I said.

Her face softened a little.

A pink bow fastened the crying baby's light brown hair. She wore a matching pullover with faded stains on it. She reminded me of my cousins when they were born, or my little sister Abby, who I still missed, almost as much as Ma and Jake.

Talitha's brow furrowed. "Are you okay?"

I must have drifted. Embarrassed, I asked, "What's your baby's name?"

"Ladonna. She's usually pretty quiet."

I went over, met Ladonna's eyes and waved. She stared back and stopped crying. "Ladonna," I sang softly, "hello. Ladonna, hello. I'm Ben, hello. I'm Ben, hello."

Eyes wide, her mouth opened into a smile. Too young to criticize crappy lyrics.

Talitha smiled too. "She doesn't normally like strangers."

"Okay," Edna said behind me. "We've got work to do." She waved Aaron and I past the living room and down wooden steps into a poorly-lit, semi-finished basement. At the opposite end, she gripped a mostly empty floor-to-ceiling bookcase. She pushed it to the right on hidden wheels, revealing a wooden door.

She'd make a believable spy. I just had to get her to talk about overthrowing the government. I could hit my quota right here in Decatur, and no one in New Bethany would ever know what I'd done.

Edna unlocked the door and switched on fluorescent lights and a vent fan. We entered a room with a table and chairs, wooden work benches, shelves full of chemicals, and a stove. It stank of gasoline and iodine. Pots, bottles, funnels, and syringes covered every surface, like a chemistry class with makeshift equipment.

"Let's see what you've got," she said. She cleared space on the table and we dumped out our bags.

She counted the cough syrup bottles and tapped her chin. "You are a godsend, Aaron. I'm flat broke and so are my customers."

"You need more customers, not to mention a little business sense." Aaron clapped his hands. "Let's get cooking." He removed his coat and hung it on a wall peg. He turned to me. "It'll get hot in here, might want to strip down a little."

I took off my trenchcoat and suit jacket, which meant I wouldn't be able to access the camera and tape recorder. I turned on the recorder as I placed the coat on a peg. "Uh, need any help?" I couldn't even make moonshine, though, and this looked way more complicated.

Aaron threw the ephedrine bottles and a grinding mortar in a ceramic bowl. "You can grind up the pills for starters."

I sat at the table, facing the others, and dumped out the pills. "How many doses will this make?"

"Forty to fifty." He turned on a stove burner and poured paint thinner into a pot, then added the cough syrup and began stirring. Even with the ventilation fan, the fumes made my head swim.

Edna joined Aaron at the stove, measuring acid into a glass jar. "So how are you planning to fix the world, Ben?" she said as she worked.

"I was hoping you could help. I don't know anyone here."

"Everyone I know's just trying to get by."

It only took a few minutes to grind the pills into a powder. "Done."

Aaron took the powder. "You got enough RP?" he asked Edna.

"Yeah, I've got a good recovery rate. But I could always use more, it's a pain to make."

Aaron turned to me and pointed to a pile of match boxes, each holding fifty matchbooks. "Tear the striker strips off all the matchbooks and put them in this pot." He placed a large ceramic pot on the table.

"Why?"

Edna huffed. "It takes like a second per match book."

"It's for red phosphorus," Aaron said. "It's a reagent."

"Where'd you learn how to do this?" I asked.

"Edna knew the guy who invented it."

Edna sighed, then waved off the compliment. "Aaron's just as good. He was a pharm tech before he got caught stealing and sent to prison."

I said to Aaron, "I thought you were sent away for auto theft."

"Had to change professions. I'm blacklisted from pharmacy jobs."

I got to work, but wasn't up to Edna's speed standards. Back at the stove and adjacent counter, Aaron and Edna mixed and filtered the contents of various pots and bottles. The stench grew unbearable.

"I heard there's no laws against making this," I said.

Edna answered without turning her head. "Not important enough for the government to care about."

"Why aren't the churches yelling about it?"

"None of their flock use it, I guess. Not like alcohol—and the government doesn't care about that either."

Maybe drugs and alcohol were considered release valves. I stopped tearing match books. "People need hope in their lives. There's gotta be others out there trying to fix things."

"If I wanted to hear preaching," Edna said over her shoulder, "I'd go to church. Now shut up and let me focus."

How was Paul so good at recruiting people? They must have to be the right people for starters.

By the wall clock, we worked almost four hours. The finished Smash was a murky yellow liquid with an acrid stink. Edna funneled it into a brown glass bottle and dipped four syringes in hydrogen peroxide. She smiled and her fingers twitched. "Show time."

We turned everything off and went back upstairs. It was dark outside and the blinds were shut. Edna shooed the dog away.

Talitha had washed and brushed her long blonde hair since earlier, and changed into a white blouse and light blue skirt. She looked pretty.

She carried her baby out of the room and returned alone, plopping down on the sofa. She grinned, showing perfect teeth. "I was trying to quit again, but whatever."

"You say that all the time," Edna said. "Then you threaten to kill me if I take you seriously."

"Well after today I'm lowering the dosages till I'm off."

Edna drew smoky liquid into the four syringes and handed them out. "I'll deflower the virgin," she told Aaron, smirking.

Talitha didn't wait. She lay back on the sofa and hiked up her long skirt, revealing pale calves and thighs spotted with red bumps. A shame—she had nice legs.

She pinched her left inner thigh, stuck the needle in, and pushed in the plunger. She sank against the cushions and her eyes rolled back.

Aaron sat on the stained carpet and injected an ankle vein.

Edna directed me to a cushioned chair, and knelt next to me. "I'm giving you a half dose, that's all you'll need. Too much will make you sick. Roll up your sleeve."

I did, although I wasn't sure I wanted to go through with this.

"Make a fist."

My arm veins popped up from the skin.

"Nice veins." She swabbed my inner elbow with rubbing alcohol and inserted the needle. She drew the plunger back a little. Blood leaked into the syringe. "That's to make sure you hit the vein. If you miss, you'll ruin the rush and fuck up your arm."

I started to say 'wait,' but she pushed in the plunger, all the way to the bottom.

"Unclench your fist." She pulled out the syringe and strode to another chair to do herself.

A rocket took off in my head and exploded into a chainsaw orgasm. My heart pounded like it would explode. My scalp tingled, then pinpricks rushed through the rest of my body, all the way to my fingertips and toes. Heat flushed my face. Webs of lightning wove cotton candy dreams, wrapping the room in warm bliss. I sailed through the air and landed in dizzy heaven.

All the bad things in the world vanished, back to the underworld. If only Rachel were here too. Then it would be perfect.

Beneath the warm coziness, vague nausea began to stir.

* * *

After a couple of hours, I started feeling normal again. Still high, but not lost to the world. The feeling of nausea disappeared.

Aaron lit a cigarette. "So, what do you think?"

"You're right that alcohol doesn't compare." No wonder people liked it so much. "I was afraid I'd throw up, though."

"That's normal the first time. Nothing to worry about."

Edna took a cigarette from Aaron. "Why don't you two crash here tonight?"

I didn't feel like returning to the bus station and wasn't sure how to get there anyway. "Alright, but I need to head out in the morning." Maybe I'd find some people to recruit back home, and I had to see my family and friends.

Talitha leaned toward me. "Where you from, Ben?"

"New Bethany."

"Never heard of it."

"It's down south."

She kept asking questions and my whole life story spilled out, incoherent bits at a time. I didn't say anything about spying for Lewison, though, or messages from my dead brother.

Edna yawned. She exchanged glances and smoke clouds with Aaron, then turned and strolled down the hall. Aaron winked at me and followed her.

The baby started crying in the adjacent room and Talitha left too. I lay down on the smelly sofa and wished Edna and Aaron had been more willing revolutionaries.

The radiators pinged and clanked. A bed creaked in a distant room, followed by moans and muffled dirty talk. I put a cushion over my head to drown it out.

A hand grabbed my foot and shook it. I threw the cushion off my face.

Talitha stood there. She glanced away and blushed, then gazed in my eyes. "Ladonna's asleep now. How you feeling?"

The high had mostly worn off. "Fine."

"Um... can I sit with you?" She rocked on her feet and picked at her thumb. The bed was still creaking in the other room.

I sat up and made room for Talitha on the sofa. She smiled and eased down next to me. She wasn't knockout beautiful like Rachel, but she was definitely pretty and definitely interested in me. I remembered Rachel's words, "I don't think I can love you the same way you love me."

"I'm glad you stayed over," Talitha said, and edged closer.

Ah, what the hell. I kissed her. We escalated to tongue exchange right away. She tasted like toothpaste. Her hand ran up my leg and cupped my crotch. I returned the favor, slipping fingers beneath her panties.

She made little moaning noises, then rose from the couch. She led me by the hand to her bedroom, just past the living room.

The bedroom was small, and crowded by a double bed, chestnut wardrobe, cluttered vanity, and a crib that looked like a jail cell, where the baby was sleeping. Talitha slipped out of her clothes, saying nothing, eyes on me as I undressed.

My bruises had disappeared, thankfully. I tried not to focus on Talitha's leg and arm sores. Other than that, she had a nice body—trim but curvy. My heart pounded. "You have any condoms?"

She shook her head. "All out. I have an IUD though."

Which was no help if she had the clap. Oh well. I climbed in the bed with her. She wasn't Rachel, but I needed to get laid more than anything in the world. Needed to feel less broken.

"If you come first," she said, "I'll kill you." She didn't smile.

"Ladies first, I always say."

"And don't wake Ladonna."

She lay back and closed her eyes and made me do all the work, which was boring. This wasn't one of those encounters I'd reminisce about later in life.

She started breathing faster. Finally she shuddered, and smiled at last.

Death averted. I shut my eyes, escaping the cursed world. I kept going and going, treading a tightrope the Insects couldn't reach with their grasping claws and devouring mandibles. Summer sun warmed my skin and meadowlarks whistled flute-like pitches. Time disappeared.

I finally lost control and exploded out of the trance. When I caught my breath, guilt washed in and turned everything sour.

What the hell was wrong with me?

"Thanks for the bonus orgasms," Talitha whispered as I collapsed beside her.

I hadn't noticed.

She squeezed against me and wouldn't let go.

Chapter Seventeen

Barefoot and clad in gray prisoner pajamas, Rachel and I sprint down a concrete hallway.

Run. Run. The hallway doesn't end.

The thing behind us, shadowed and hulking with huge compound eyes and daggered mantis arms, draws closer and closer. I'm exhausted and so is Rachel, but we can't stop. The monster behind us will never tire and never give up.

Rachel gasps for breath and slows, about to drop. The thing closes within pouncing distance. I'm terrified, but plant aching feet, turn and rush it.

"Run, Rachel!"

I'm strapped on a gurney in a familiar room full of medical equipment. Electrodes are fastened to my naked body. The giant mantis steps out of darkness and peers at me with bulbous thousand-faceted eyes, antennae swiveling above.

Searing pain tears through my body. I scream and scream but no sound emerges. The mantis clicks its mandibles and hisses through its legs.

A hand pushes my shoulder. "Hey, wake up!"

Talitha. I'm in her bed.

"You were thrashing around in your sleep." She looked concerned.

Overwhelmed by shame, I didn't respond, and buried my head in her arms.

* * *

Talitha got up at dawn to breast feed her baby, not bothering to put on clothes.

"How old is she?" I asked, guessing between six months and a year.

Talitha turned and smiled, baby fixed to her left nipple. "Ten months. Any day now she'll say her first word." She stuck her face near Ladonna's. "Mama. I'm Mama."

She looked at me. "Ladonna can't get Smash through breast milk, in case you're wondering."

"Father around?" I asked, knowing the answer. Mine were the only men's clothes in the room.

Her smile disappeared. "Good riddance is all I can say."

I found the shower and scrubbed thoroughly. And remembered my burdens—betray five people so Rachel could go free. I wished I could raise an army, free all the prisoners, and cleanse the world of Insects.

When I returned to the bedroom for my clothes, Talitha had a white robe on and Ladonna was back in her crib. Talitha held up two syringes. "Good morning, sweetheart," she half-sang.

Sweetheart? She barely knew me.

She patted the bed and I sat. I wasn't sure I wanted more Smash, but it would be rude to turn down a gift that was such a pain in the ass to make. And it drove away the Insect horrors. I decided not to object as Talitha injected me, then herself.

The rush was as powerful as before, like the world's highest roller coaster plunging into the embrace of angels. After the rush, we lay on the bed together, lost in bliss, her sapphire eyes gazing into mine. No stomach objections this time.

"What were you dreaming about last night?" she asked.

"Another nightmare. I have them all the time. The Insects—the government—tortured me for months. I feel like a part of me died."

She held me and stroked my hair and asked about all I went through in prison and why I was there. I minimized the details, but said the government and banks were run by monsters and people deserved better.

"I know, sweetie," she said. "I try not to think about it."

In me, beneath the Smash bliss and the day-to-day shit of survival, the monsters had excavated a cyclopean underground lake of anger. The lake was too enormous to forget, but between the bliss and Talitha's warm body, I could ignore it for now.

Someone knocked on the door. I still felt a little muddled.

Talitha sat up and half-shouted, "Go away."

Aaron entered, ignoring Talitha and frowning at me. "I thought you were going back to New Bethany today."

"That was the plan. But I'm not sure now." Even if I couldn't recruit Aaron or Edna, there must be thousands of other possibilities in a city this size. Maybe even some real revolutionaries. It was worth trying.

Talitha ran a hand along my right arm. "Stay here with me."

Aaron stood at the foot of the bed. "Does New Bethany have Smash users?"

"Yeah," I said. "Why?"

"I'd like to go with you."

"What? Why?"

"I told you, the police told me to leave. If I don't, they'll lock me up for good. I don't know where else to go." His eyes darted. "Maybe you could help me set up there? And I thought we could be partners. In this revolution thing."

"What? You didn't seem the least bit interested yesterday."

"That was yesterday. I thought about all you said, and you're right."

He looked sincere. One down, four to go.

I eyed Talitha, who was growing more beautiful by the hour. I had to keep her out of Lewison's net. A baby needed her.

"I do have to go," I said. "My family—"

She fixed lidded eyes on me. "Ladonna and I are your family. And Edna. We need you. You're nice. I never meet anyone nice."

Alarm bells sounded through the bliss. No one moved that fast.

"And you're so brave," she continued, "standing up to the government. You're the bravest person I've ever met."

Hardly. "I'll come back," I lied.

"I'll join your revolution."

"You will?" I didn't want that. I had to sacrifice someone, but not her.

"I wanna be a part."

"You can't," Aaron told her.

"Yeah," I said, "you have a baby to take care of."

Her eyes widened. "Then go, get out!" She threw herself face down against the pillows. "You ruined my high."

Aaron led me out of the room. I looked back and it broke my heart to see Talitha sad. She was so nice. So beautiful. I was so happy around her. I wanted to marry her.

But I'd probably never see her again.

* * *

It was a two-hour wait for the next bus to New Bethany. I kept thinking about Talitha. Part of me wanted to run back and disappear in her arms.

But ice cold sober now, it all seemed a Smash mirage. I actually thought about marrying some druggie I just met? Rachel was who I cared about, and I had to focus on freeing her.

"It's a four-hour bus trip," Aaron said. "I can fix you something to make it more bearable."

"No thanks." It wouldn't be the same without Talitha to share it with. And I had enough troubles without getting addicted to Smash. "Where's the nearest liquor store?" The news stand only had beer.

Aaron led me to a state-licensed liquor shop and I splurged for a pint bottle of real Kentucky bourbon. In the store's grungy bathroom, I rewound my tape recorder, not wanting to implicate Talitha and Edna.

"Lemme give you some advice," Aaron said on the way back to the bus station. "Forget about Talitha. She's not as nice as you think she is."

"Leave me alone, okay?"

She was a lot nicer than anyone else I'd met up here.

I drank the whole bottle on the way to New Bethany, and fell asleep watching the empty fields roll by, stretching to the overcast horizon.

Someone shook me awake. "We're here," Aaron said. It was dark outside.

We stumbled out into the cold. New Bethany's bus station, in the center of town, was a lot smaller than Decatur's, with no stores or cafes. I was starving, but too nauseous to eat.

First, I had to ditch Aaron so I could visit the farm, the Tolsons, and Sarah. "I know the perfect place for you," I said.

"Oh?"

"Yeah, you can't stay with me, my pop doesn't take to strangers."

We took the streetcar up to Lindbergh Avenue, an east-west state road that ran along the north side of town, then took another streetcar west. Aaron told me about his life growing up in Indianapolis, the youngest of three brothers and a sister.

"Sometimes I wonder if I dreamed the whole thing," he said.

We got off at The Concrete Arms, a run-down apartment complex on the edge of town. It had three buildings facing a common parking lot, each one nine stories of unpainted concrete, small windows, and flimsy balconies. The government built it in the Forties to house workers for a cement factory that went bust within a year of opening. Now, since rent was so cheap, it was full of people down on their luck.

"This place has plenty of rooms," I said. "They've got furnished efficiencies with utilities for $30 a week." A day and half of work at minimum wage.

"That's pretty cheap."

"Yeah, it's privately owned but the government subsidizes the rent. And if you're unemployed, the state will pay you to do construction work and pick up trash. Minimum wage but better than starving."

He nodded. "They do that in Decatur, too. Looks bad to have people living on the streets."

"I'll come by in a few days. Got a lot to take care of first." An understatement.

Chapter Eighteen

I hitched a ride home in the back of a pickup driven by a young couple passing through to Carbondale. I slapped the cab window when I spotted the mailbox and red reflector marking the farm entrance, hopped out as soon as they stopped, and thanked the smiling couple.

Someone had put up a hand-lettered 'Trespassers will be shot on sight' sign. I strode down the long dirt driveway toward the weather-beaten two-story house I hadn't seen for two months.

The lights were on inside. No Christmas decorations, but we hadn't done that since Ma died. I smelled wood smoke as I approached the unlit porch, reminding me of family gatherings and Sunday chicken dinners.

The door was unlocked. In the living room, Pop, Grandpa, and my Uncle Floyd sat in front of the cast iron wood stove embedded in the fireplace, half-empty mason jars of moonshine in their hands. Pop and Grandpa were in their usual spots—stuffed armchairs draped by old quilts. Floyd slouched on the tattered sofa beneath yellowing framed photos of Adamsons long in the grave. The three turned and stared at me with unshaven faces, Pop's stubble grayer than I remembered.

"Ben! My boy!" Pop got up and hugged me, something he almost never did. "They let you out. No thanks to that worthless lawyer, I assume."

Shaking his head and grinning, Grandpa grasped my hand. "Welcome home. It's the best Christmas present we could ask for."

"Thanks," I said. "It was rough."

"You missed the soybean harvest and wheat planting," Pop said, his smile fading. "Had to hire a couple of deadbeats from Concrete Arms to fill in."

"Believe me, I wish I'd been here."

Pop shook his head and pointed at a letter on the coffee table. "Bank foreclosed."

"I thought you paid them off."

"That was three payments ago. We didn't get enough for the soybeans, just like the corn, and we're busted now. Paying that lawyer didn't help."

"Can't you sell the tractor or something?" I asked.

"Son, I already missed payments on that. And I hocked everything else after the drought two years ago. The only reason we have anything is 'cause the bank lets us. Now they're calling in their loans. I hear they already got a buyer, gonna put up houses."

"Why would anyone buy a house out here?"

His lips pursed like he wanted to spit. "It's some kind of retirement village. They're trying to move old folk out of the cities to make room for hotels or shopping centers or some scam like that. Anyway, we ain't leaving. This is Adamson land, and ain't no way some greedy Chicago bank's taking it from us. Probably the Jews behind it all."

More Lindbergh crap. "Pop, the Jews were all expelled in the Forties."

Still sitting, Floyd, his eyes red-rimmed from years of alcohol abuse, sipped from his glass jar and met my eyes. "You're a damn fine shot, boy. You're back in the nick of time."

"In time for what?" I hoped he was just mouthing drunk talk.

"Whadda ya think? Throw back them Pinkertons or whoever else the bank sends."

"Are you kidding? The government near killed me just for helping Rachel speak about my brother. What do you think they'll do if we shoot someone?"

"No one's shooting no one," Pop said. "But we ain't letting the bank throw us out either."

Floyd glared at me and scoffed. "You're a coward, that's your problem."

After all I'd been through, he dared call me a coward?

I knocked the mason jar out of his hand, soaking the sofa and throw pillows with strong-smelling alcohol. I hauled him to his feet. "Say that again, you goddamn loser. I dare you."

I didn't wait for Floyd to answer, and threw him back against the sofa. He landed in a heap.

"Stop that!" My Aunt Eunice stood at the base of the stairs in her nightie.

Pop waved his hands. "Floyd's kin too. Hold your fight."

"We've got to stick together," Grandpa said.

"Floyd ain't kin," I said. "Not as far as I'm concerned." I eyed Aunt Eunice. "Wish you'd divorce the skunk. Find someone who'll make your life better, not worse."

I stomped out the back door and went to the kennel. There I'd get a decent welcoming.

* * *

Next day, after a quiet family breakfast of fried eggs and toast, I wrote a letter to Special Agent Lewison and addressed it to the P.O. box in Champaign.

I'm making progress. I found one revolutionary and think he can lead me to more. But I can't focus on my work because the bank's trying to take my family's farm. It's your fault because you locked me up and I wasn't around to help, and they had to offer up scarce money to an advocate. Please stop this injustice before we get evicted. You know from your interviews my family are patriots.

Maybe an exaggeration that my arrest was the cause, but I had to say something. Five generations my family lived here. I provided more details and fished around for a stamp.

I wondered if Paul or Sarah could help. Neither of their families had telephones. I stole the last mason jar of moonshine in the kitchen and hopped in the truck.

First stop, the Wright farm. Sarah's family had a raw-looking two-story house like the Turners, but with a covered porch in front. Like my family's, but without a screen.

Sarah's gray-haired grandma, who'd filled my childhood with stories of indentured servitude and lynchings in the South, sat in a rocking chair by the door, wrapped in a thick blanket against the chilly December air. "Well how you do, Ben?"

I waved since she had this aversion to handshakes. Didn't like touching anyone who wasn't kin.

"Doing fine," I said. "Ain't it cold to be sitting on the porch?"

"Naw, they say refrigeration makes the meat last longer."

I nodded. Kind of made sense.

"'Sides," she said, "real cold ain't got here yet."

"Sarah 'round?"

"Naw, she ain't been here fo' days. She workin' this job in town, y' know, and ain't got a car t' go back an' forth."

"Where's it at?"

She scrunched her face wrinkles into deep furrows. "Don't rightly know. She never told us the particulars."

Sarah's two older brothers, Abe and George, came out of the house, but they didn't know where she was either, just that she had a cleaning job and worked a lot.

"Paul work there too?" He'd mentioned starting a cleaning business as an excuse to get together, to access businesses and houses, and bring in some money.

Abe nodded. "And Mary."

Paul's younger sister. He must have recruited her too.

I didn't want Sarah's grandma to scold me, so motioned the brothers inside before passing around the jar of shine. It was mid-morning, but winters were relatively quiet on farms, a relaxing change from the sixteen-hour days the rest of the year. I only took a couple of sips and let Sarah's brothers have the rest.

My next stop, the Turner farm, was just up the road. Paul had moved out two months ago, his mother told me. About the time I was arrested.

"Where's he at?"

Her hand gripped the doorknob. "Why you wanna know?"

Did she think I was a spy for the government now, planning to turn him in? Was that why he moved out?

I fought the surge of panic. "I'm trying to reach Sarah. Her brother said she's doing cleaning work with Paul."

Her face relaxed a little but she didn't let go of the doorknob. "You want me to tell him you stopped by?"

"He still tending bar at the Deer Head?"

"I reckon so. It's good money."

"I'll catch up with him there."

She nodded and shut the door.

Why was I hunting down Paul and Sarah? What if the Insects tortured me again? Or worse, tortured Rachel in front of me? I might give them up. They'd hang. And Rachel and I would pay for not telling earlier.

The less I knew about what Sarah and Paul were up to, the better.

Then again, they might be my only chance at five names.

Next stop was the Tolsons, to ask about Rachel's legal defense and tell her family she was doing okay, at least for now.

Mr. Tolson answered the door. He stared at me. "So they let you out." Like Mrs. Turner, he kept one hand on the doorknob, not inviting me in.

"Yeah."

His bushy eyebrows knotted and lips compressed beneath his mustache. "Where's Rachel, then? Why didn't they let her out?"

"I don't know," I lied. "The government's mad about some things she said."

He stabbed a finger at me. "It's your fault she was arrested."

"What?" The rally had been Rachel's idea, not mine. I tried to stop it.

"The whole family's under investigation, and they closed our store."

"Why? What for?"

"Illegal books."

Maybe Lewison could fix that. Another letter to write.

Mr. Tolson's eyes narrowed. "You and your brother, I wish Rachel had never gotten mixed up with you." He started to close the door.

"Wait, I came over to talk. Tell you how she's doing."

He reopened the door. "You've seen her?"

"Yeah. She's doing okay." Relatively speaking, I didn't add.

He leaned forward, eyebrows raising. Warm air and a faint odor of burning coal leaked past him. "When did you see her last?"

"Just a few days ago. I raised dust about wanting to see her before I left, and they showed her on a TV screen." Not quite the truth, but close. "She seems healthy." As well as could be expected for someone who'd been tortured.

I described her cell, how she had a decent bed and shelves of books. "I saw her in person too, about a month ago."

I didn't mention her glassy eyes and shock suit, or my going berserk and biting a guard's nose off.

Mr. Tolson stared at me, as if expecting more.

"How's her case going?" I asked.

He rubbed a thumb against his mustache. "They put her in so-called psychiatric care and she can't enter the legal system until her so-called doctor allows it."

Yep. "And there's no way to fight it?"

"Mr. Greene is doing his best." His voice trailed off.

* * *

My advocate's office was across the street from the county courthouse. Convenient location. I climbed creaky wooden stairs to the top floor and opened a door labeled "E. Gamaliel, Adv."

An elderly woman looked up from a crossword puzzle on her desk. "Yes? May I help you?"

"I'm here to see my advocate, Mr. Gamaliel."

"Is he expecting you?"

The door past the desk opened. My mothball-smelling advocate smiled and shook my hand. "Mr. Adamson. You've been released?"

I nodded.

He motioned me inside. "Please, come in."

His office was dusty and crowded with books. He pointed to a leather chair. It made crackling noises when I sat.

Mr. Gamaliel sat behind his desk, which was covered with stacked papers. "So they let you out of psychiatric care?"

"Yeah, I played nice for two months and they decided I was cured." Not a complete lie.

"Great! I knew they didn't have a tenable legal case against you. The Internal Security officer threw the first punch." He smiled again. "You must be happy to be free."

There are no free people, I wanted to say. Especially when they're obligated to bleat out their fellows.

"What I'm here to see you about," I said instead, "was if you can help fight First Consolidated Bank. They want to throw us off our land." I gave him the details.

He sighed and folded his hands on the desk top. "That's a sad situation. But unfortunately, from what you describe, the bank's within its legal rights."

Pop was right. This guy was useless. Or maybe the legal system was useless. "There must be something. What if I brought over our bank records and letters?"

Mr. Gamaliel swept a finger around the dusty office. "Mr. Adamson, how much do you think rent costs for an office near the courthouse? Not to mention electricity and a legal assistant?"

I shrugged. "I just know farm expenses. But I get your point. I'll pay you as soon as I get some money together."

"Your father still owes fees and expenses for your arrest case. At our last meeting, he was verbally abusive, and even demanded his deposit back."

"Well, you didn't do anything for me."

He flipped his palms up. "That's not true. I prepared a case for trial. But once you entered psychiatric care, there was nothing I could do. It's a loophole in the law, as I explained during our consultation." He straightened in his chair. "I'll tell you what—you all settle the balance to my break even point, and we can open a new case."

I might as well wait for a dump truck full of manure to pass through the eye of a needle.

* * *

Even though Mr. Tolson had blamed Rachel's problems on me and Jake, I wrote Agent Lewison another letter, asking him to re-open the family's bookstore.

Then I volunteered my services to Pop, who told me to set traps for intruders. It was a waste of time, but I did it anyway. I didn't have time to dig pits, but set out foothold traps and made some snares.

I found deer tracks in our wood lot, a whole herd. Maybe I could fit in some hunting before I got run out of town or killed in Pop's war.

Chapter Nineteen

The next day, I drove to the Concrete Arms to check on Aaron. I asked around and found him in the courtyard, chatting with a couple of shabby-looking tenants.

I pulled him aside. "Making friends?"

"I've met all the addicts."

"How many is that?"

"Close to fifty, most of them living here or squatting."

A lot more than I'd expected. "Where do they get their money?" The county was near dormant during the winter, and panhandling would get you sent to a labor camp to learn the value of work.

He shrugged. "Maintenance work. Odd jobs. Maybe some stealing."

"Not much to steal around here. Except land of course."

He raised an eyebrow and continued. "Some of the tenants have kitchens set up, but their purity's crap and they don't filter out the contaminants. This town needs a professional touch."

"Good thing you're here, I guess."

He paused before answering. "So how's the revolution coming?"

My jaw tensed. "It's not just the government that's the problem. Bank's planning to take our farm. And Pop won't leave."

He squinted at me. "And that's what you think we should be working on?"

Maybe I could solve all my problems at once. "What do you think about recruiting an army to help him stay?"

Aaron's eyebrows raised. "You got anyone in particular in mind?"

"Just you so far. But we can find more here."

"And what do you want them to do?"

I thought a second. "First, we need a defensive force to man the farm perimeter, keep the Sheriff's Office or Pinkertons from evicting us. Then we take the fight to the enemy. Picket the bank. If that fails, we escalate." What I really wanted to do was blow it up, but how would I get away with it?

The tenants he'd been chatting with disappeared. Aaron gestured toward the front door of the nearest building. "Why don't you meet some of the locals?"

"Sure."

He pulled open the creaking door. It was my first time inside. The lobby and stairwell beyond stank of piss and vomit. An 'out of order' sign was taped to the elevator.

Aaron led me up nine flights of stairs to the top floor. He knocked on the first door.

The peephole in the door darkened. "Yeah?" a man's voice said.

"Aaron."

Bolts slid and the door opened. A young black man I'd seen somewhere before peered at us. "Who's this?"

"Ben. He's with me."

"New Bethany, fifth generation," I said.

He smiled and shook my hand. "Melvin."

We followed Melvin inside. The dingy room stank of chemicals, like Edna's lab, and sweat, and worse things, things my nostrils refused to identify. A middle-aged black woman stirred a pot on a stove burner. A balding, stubbled white man poured liquid from a plastic bottle into a funnel. A wheat-haired boy in his teens tore strikers off match books. And a young woman with dark hair sat motionless in a chair, head down against her chest.

Aaron introduced me. The black woman was Esther. The balding man was Thomas. The blond boy was Joel. And the brunette, who couldn't be nudged awake, was Charity.

Another man lay unmoving on a filthy mattress in the corner. Pus dripped from his pants cuff. One of his bare feet had fiery red lines running along the skin and a large blackened abscess in the middle. He seemed to be the source of the most objectionable of the smells.

I pointed at him. "You should take that man to a hospital."

"Steve? Doesn't want to go," Esther said from the stove. "And it's his apartment."

Aaron met my eyes. "We can drop him off if you want."

"Well, yeah."

"I'll teach them how to cook properly," Aaron said.

Esther turned and wagged a finger. "Don't need no uppity white man from up north tellin' me how to cook."

"Your product sucks," he said. He turned back to me. "It only takes them an hour to make, but that's 'cause they skip some of the steps." He pointed at Steve. "It's no wonder Smash has a bad rep around here. These people are poisoning themselves. The other kitchens are just as bad."

I knelt by the sick man on the mattress. He smelled like rotting meat. I fought not to puke. "Hey, we're taking you to the hospital."

He fixed blank eyes on me. "I need a hit. My leg, it's hurting again."

I didn't want to see where the pus was coming from. I really didn't. But it was the only way to know how bad off he was. I pulled up his pants leg.

Past the ankle, the skin was black and leathery. A little further, the calf disappeared, reduced to red oozing pulp and yellow-white bone. Plump maggots crawled over the bone and buried their heads in the rippling pulp. The stink of rotting flesh burrowed down my nose and tore at my innards. I threw up all over the floor.

"You asshole," someone said.

I kept throwing up, each taste of bile making me sicker, until there was nothing left to lose.

* * *

Aaron and I carried the rotting man down the stairs, leaving a trail of squirming maggots in our wake. I dry heaved every few seconds. We threw him in the back of my pickup and shut the gate.

"He must have missed the vein," Aaron said as I drove in town to the community hospital. "And ignored it."

We dropped him off outside the hospital, but didn't stick around.

"I'll move the people out of his apartment," Aaron said on the way back.

"Why don't you get them off Smash too while you're at it." I had more grist for nightmares now and wasn't sure if the stink would wash out of my clothes.

"Not possible," he said. "I know from experience. Best thing to do is provide a safe product and make sure it's used right."

"I quit."

"You only did it twice. It takes a week or so to get hooked."

I pulled into the Concrete Arms parking lot, thinking about Talitha and wondering if we'd ever see each other again. If we did, I'd convince her to quit Smash.

"I'll straighten things out here." Aaron opened the passenger door with a rusty creak.

"Keep a watch for potential revolutionaries," I said before he got out. "I'll be back."

He turned to me. "How will I know?"

"Steer eyes on anyone who criticizes the government. If they're high or drunk, they're more likely to open up. But be careful. The government pays informers, so these apartments are probably full of them."

The funny thing about informers, I'd heard, was they mostly turned in other informers. They worked independently, and in a quiet place like New Bethany, the most suspicious people were the ones spying on others.

* * *

I returned to the farm and grabbed my old Remington rifle. I'd never missed deer season and wouldn't start now. I filled the eight-round tube magazine, released Bandit and the other dogs from the kennel, and headed for the woods.

Our wood lot was twenty acres, mostly pecan, persimmon, and maple trees, and ran along a small creek. I left the dogs at one end and climbed into the tree stand at the other. I pulled the bolt up and back to load a cartridge into the chamber, ran the bolt home, and checked my point of aim. When all was set, I blew a whistle.

I heard barking, coming closer. A few minutes later, a doe bounded into view, following a trail through the understory. Behind her followed two fawns and two yearlings, a male and female.

I aimed at the yearling buck, its rudimentary antlers curving inward at the top, and pretended it was Lewison. Holding my breath, I squeezed the trigger.

The rifle gave a loud crack and kicked against my shoulder. I hit the yearling between the eyes. It crashed to the ground. No suffering, unlike what Lewison deserved.

I loaded the next round, swiveled the rifle, and aimed at the other yearling's heart-lung section, all in a couple of seconds.

Another bang and it dropped. "Take that, Malluch."

I let the doe and her fawns run off. Mostly to carry on the herd, but also, there was something sacred about motherhood. Only a fiend killed mothers.

* * *

I processed the venison, and the next day, hunted a neighbor's farm. I took down a seven-point buck, two years old I reckoned, and split the meat with the land owners.

Christmas was less than a week away. I wanted Rachel released by then. Probably we wouldn't have to worry about the bank until after New Year's, but still I planned one solution for both.

Hoping for better luck this time, and no rotting flesh, I returned to the Concrete Arms. Aaron stood in the parking lot, talking to a couple of shabby-looking men. He ditched them and strode over.

"Come on in," he said, grinning.

We entered the center building. "I'm head chef of the Concrete Arms now," Aaron said as we started climbing stairs.

"Congratulations." At least his product, if he was telling the truth, would be safer.

"It's the first step toward a business empire."

That's all he seemed to care about. "Did you try to recruit anyone?"

"I laid the groundwork. You can pitch them."

The elevators were still broken, naturally. We climbed all the way to the top again, nine flights of stairs. "Top floor's best for cooking," Aaron said. "No one above to complain about the smell. And no one else wants to live this high up."

He knocked on one of the wooden doors. A Latina woman let us into a corner apartment that stank of iodine. The same people from the rotting man's apartment were in the living room—Melvin, the young black man; Esther, the older black woman; Thomas, the balding white man; Joel, the teenage blond boy; and Charity, the girl with black hair. Half were nodded out on chairs or the floor. The other half gazed at me with lidded eyes.

I stood in the center of the room. No way could these sad sacks fight off Pinkertons. "Anyone know how Steve's doing?"

I got no response other than shrugs.

I switched on my hidden tape recorder. What if some of these people were informers? The government paid, and a devil's deal could keep you from jail.

A hardcore Insect like Lewison wouldn't trust a druggie. Local cops would probably take anyone, though. Regardless, I was just following orders. It would only matter if someone cut into my quota.

I clapped my hands to get the sad sacks' attention. "Listen. How would you all like to change the world? Make it better?"

No one showed the slightest sign of interest. But at least that meant none were informers. "Okay," I announced. "My friend Aaron here is really helping you out."

"It's true," Aaron said. "I've tripled the purity and cut out the contaminants. All while keeping prices reasonable."

"We need something in return," I said. "I'll even throw in some codeine, so you can cook some freebies."

Everyone gaped at me, even the semi-conscious ones.

"I need you to clean up and distribute some flyers around town. It'll only take a couple of hours."

"What sort of flyers?" Charity asked. She had a festering sore on her left arm.

"To ask people to call the First Consolidated Bank and tell them not to take my family farm away." I talked about growing up on the farm, and how I was scared my pop would get himself killed if we didn't stop the eviction process.

"I'm with you," Melvin said. "Righteous cause, and sounds easy 'nuff."

Most of the others jumped in, voices slurred. "Me too." "Sure." "Yeah, why not?"

"Won't we get in trouble?" Charity asked. "This couple got arrested a few months ago for rousing people 'gainst the war in Cuba."

Charity wasn't at the rally and didn't go to my school, but word must have spread. "That was me and my friend Rachel," I admitted, and told them how my brother was killed in Cuba and we raised questions. "They let me go, though."

Aaron stared at me. I'd told him about the rally when we met, but never mentioned Rachel.

"They let you go, but not your friend?" he asked.

Uh oh. "She did all the talking. She got mad and criticized the government, so she has to go to trial."

He sighed, seeming to buy it. "Sorry about that."

"Long as we keep criticism of the government to ourselves," I told Charity, "they won't arrest us."

She nodded.

"Do you know if they caught the people who set that lumber office on fire and put up those roadside signs?" This was risky, in case Paul's cell was involved, but I could record over the responses if I had to. Vienna was over an hour from New Bethany, though, so it was probably someone else.

Charity looked confused. "Huh?"

"My uncle told me about it," I lied. I added details and studied everyone's faces, but no eyes widened with recognition.

I captured everyone with the hidden camera, and asked for names and life stories. Most were drifters. None had family who cared. Their lives seemed miserable.

In jail, at least they'd kick Smash and live longer. Then I remembered the beatings, the hellfire shocks, the hopelessness. They haunted my dreams, and the sight of electrical outlets gave me jitters.

I'd beg Lewison to go easy on them.

Chapter Twenty

That afternoon, after recruiting more addicts, I express-mailed a status report to Lewison's P.O. box, along with a cassette and a roll of film.

I wrote that I'd met thirteen people plotting acts of civil disobedience. I had six on tape complaining how corrupt the government was. And there was Aaron, who schemed to create a drug empire. I had surpassed the Insect's commandments, and Rachel should be released in time to join her family for Christmas.

Would Lewison buy it? They weren't legitimate revolutionaries, but quite likely he had quotas to fill too, and I was giving him almost three times what he'd asked for.

Lewison liked to spout official crap like fulfilling the Will of History and smiting enemies who lurked everywhere. But he was probably an expert liar, and who knew what he really thought? His hair was graying, but he hadn't advanced beyond Special Agent. Maybe he was angling for a higher position, but hadn't filled his quotas. Or maybe being a creepy-eyed asshole held him back.

I wasn't sure how the Insect hive worked, but city and county cops cared more about padding their wallets than anything else. If I gave Lewison a lot of arrests, he'd look good and maybe move up the hierarchy. Maybe that's what he really wanted.

I'd have to hope I was right. I couldn't find the people who'd burned down the lumber office or put up the road signs, not without traipsing around the Shawnee Hills where I didn't know anyone. As for the flyer, that had to be Sarah, maybe with Paul's help on the wording. I'd have to claim failure there too.

Next, I sat in my room and composed a flyer. I didn't have Rachel's penmanship and it took several tries before everything was centered and it looked presentable.

The First Consolidated Bank is stealing our land!

The Adamson Farm in New Bethany has been family-owned for five generations but greedy bankers are trying to seize it so they can build houses there.

Please help stop this by calling or writing the
bank (number and address below) and tell them not
to kick the Adamsons off their land!

This is not an isolated incident. The banks think
they can take whatever they want. Farms are being
seized everywhere you look. This must stop. We the
people have rights to our land! Stop the theft!

The bottom line instructed where to call and write, and what to say.
With luck, enough people would follow through to shame the bank into
backing down.

And the language, even though it didn't criticize the government
directly, sounded revolutionary. If it wasn't enough, we could picket outside
the county courthouse.

Late that night, downtown deserted, I picked the back door lock of the
print shop on Main Street. With a little experimenting, I figured out the
photostat machine, and printed flyers until it ran out of ink.

* * *

Around 9:00 the next morning, Aaron and I assembled the gathered
troops, twelve newly bathed addicts with winter coats and hats to keep warm
and conceal their injection sores.

How would Jake handle this as a squad leader?

*Everyone's taught from birth to follow orders. Just plan out your strategy and give
clear instructions that are easy to follow.*

I gave each volunteer a hundred or so flyers and showed them a map of
New Bethany, divided by pen into sections. "You each have a specific
territory. Place a flyer in each mailbox until you either run out of flyers or
houses."

Once my troops knew their assignments, I dropped them off in their
territories. I drove back and forth, observing the troops and giving an
encouraging shout whenever I spotted someone sitting on a curb. "Keep
going, my family's farm depends on it! And everyone else being screwed by
the banks!"

After a while, cops started picking them up. Then a cruiser pulled me
over.

I recognized the two cops who exited the car, Joe Wilson and Scott
Collins. They'd gone to my high school and lucked into hometown
government jobs after their Army service. They hadn't bleached their hair

and weren't as bad as that asshole Lance Ferguson. They weren't exactly friendly, either.

Joe waved one of my flyers. "Is this your doing?"

How to answer? "It's a collaboration."

"Why don't you follow us to the station?" Scott said. "Unless you want us to arrest you here and impound your truck."

"No need for that. I'll follow you."

To get the addicts to Lewison, I had to get arrested, then confess to working for the Insects. The problem was, I wasn't exactly following Lewison's orders. My recruits weren't his targets. But if he was anything like the local cops, that shouldn't matter.

Before I turned the ignition key, I prayed silently, the first time since Ma died. Even in the pain room I hadn't prayed.

God, if you're up there, part the clouds for once in my life. Please convince Agent Lewison to release Rachel.

Silence.

The city police station was a small brick building just north of the county courthouse. I followed Joe and Scott through the revolving plastiglass door. Inside, beyond the metal detector, policemen escorted two of my addict recruits toward the holding cells.

The metal detector at the entrance beeped when I entered. The blue-uniformed entrance guard searched me and found my miniature camera and tape recorder.

"What's this for?" he asked. Joe and Scott stared at it too.

I whispered, "I'm working for Internal Security."

They stared at me. "You?" Scott asked. "An informer?"

My face tingled and my stomach churned. "I'm not an informer, I'm an investigator. Call Special Agent Lewison in the Decatur office."

What would Jake think about this? What about Sarah?

You're not working for the enemy. You're working to save Rachel.

The cops moved me to a basement cell by myself and tossed me a blanket. "Just sit tight," Scott said. "We have to type our reports, then we'll call this Agent Lewison."

"Maybe we should work together," I volunteered.

New Bethany police probably wouldn't know or care about the timber office arson or road signs. The Shawnee Hills were practically in Kentucky. But they might have other leads, in case Lewison rejected my addict army. And maybe I'd find out if they knew anything about Paul's cell.

Scott crossed his arms. "What do you mean?"

"Are you investigating any subversive activities or people? Do you have any leads?"

"Even if we did, we wouldn't be able to tell you."

* * *

The unlatching of my cell door woke me. Two silver-shirted Insects entered, Joe and Scott following. One of the Insects pulled out handcuffs. "You're being transferred. You're going with the other prisoners so we don't blow your cover."

I let them cuff me and throw a canvas bag over my head. I panicked when it cut off my vision, but forced myself under control.

They led me upstairs and outside into the cold, then up some steps into a vehicle, configured like a bus. They chained me to a metal seat.

I heard footsteps approach along the aisle. "Where you taking us?" Melvin's voice said.

"Shut up," a man growled.

"My arm hurts," Charity said in strained tones.

"Shut up."

The engine turned over and we started moving. I should be damned to the lowest circle of hell for betraying thirteen people and condemning them to the Insect hive. But my heart seized every time I thought about Rachel alone in a prison cell, either dying there or going insane. This was her only chance for freedom.

I hoped the Insects would let the addicts go once they realized they were harmless. Aaron, though, would be nailed to the cross. How could I have done that to him?

Chapter Twenty-One

When the Insects finally pulled my hood off and uncuffed me, I was in a familiar room with a thick plastiglass divider in the middle. I sat there for a long time.

Finally, Lewison entered the other side. He fixed his black eyes on me through the plastiglass and shook his head. "Nice try."

Not a promising start. "They're revolutionaries. Did you listen to the tape?"

"I told you I wanted the people responsible for the sabotage and the signs. These are drug addicts you recruited and deployed yourself."

"The folks who made the signs aren't in New Bethany. I asked—you can hear some of the replies on the tape."

"How many people did you ask? How hard did you look?"

"As hard as I could without people figuring out I was a snitch." Mostly true. I cast my line again. "Aaron volunteered. He was my co-organizer." Shame radiated from my cheeks. "Go easy on him, though. No one deserves what I went through."

The Insect sighed. "Tell you what. As a reward for your effort, I'll see if I can re-open the Tolsons' book store."

A start. Maybe this wasn't hopeless.

"Their store will require regular inspections," he continued, "to make sure they only carry acceptable materials. But if they comply, there's no reason to keep it closed. It's the only bookstore in your town."

"And my farm? It's all we've got."

His lips pressed together. After a moment, he said, "That's a trickier case. It's purely a private matter, out of government jurisdiction."

No such thing.

"Best I can do," he said, "is not have your family arrested in connection with your flyers."

Asshole. "They didn't know anything about it. It was all me."

He gave me a raised eyebrows know-it-all look. "You see what happens when you don't think things through? If you focused on the greater good, helping America instead of just thinking about yourself, you'd make your situation better instead of worse."

My whole plan had been idiotic—Lewison was too different from the cops in New Bethany, more sold on ideology than schemes to get ahead. I nodded gravely and hoped he'd buy it.

"What about Rachel?" I asked.

"Still waiting for five insurrectionists worth trading for."

My stomach tightened. "I gave you thirteen."

He leaned forward, face tense. "You seem to be under the mistaken impression this is a negotiation. I have four aces, Benjamin, and you've got a seven high. Do you want me to haul you back in here, this time for good?"

I shook my head.

"Do you know what will happen to Rachel if you don't cooperate? An anti-American agitator diagnosed with mental conditions?"

I remembered the slack-faced prisoners I saw loading trucks, moving like wind-up toys. Would they really turn someone as smart as Rachel into a mindless drone?

They would, Jake's voice told me. *Insects have no sense of morality.*

My throat closed up and I had to force out a response. "I'm trying. Can you at least give me partial credit?"

"For those jokers? I don't think so, and I warned you this wasn't a negotiation."

My mind froze, then I asked, "Can I see her?"

Lewison fiddled with the television monitor on his desk and turned the screen to face me. Rachel lay on the bed of her cell, face in her pillow. Tired or despondent. She was alive, at least.

"I mean, talk to her," I said.

"You can talk to her all you want once she's released."

"Can't she at least see her family for Christmas? She looks really depressed, and her family is too. Have some heart."

He exhaled. "That's fair enough. It's one of the most important times of the year, and her family should see she's being well treated. If they want to come up here, I'll arrange a visit."

Two minor victories in a landscape of defeats. But Rachel wasn't an inch closer to escaping this hell.

Lewison scribbled in his notepad.

"I need more money," I said. "It wasn't cheap recruiting all those people."

"Of course." He passed an envelope through the revolving window. "I was expecting such a request."

The envelope contained $200 and a bus voucher home. He'd given me a raise.

"I'm giving you another chance," he said. "Get it right this time."

* * *

The guards escorted me to the front gate without a word. The sky was cold and gray and threatened snow.

I took the #3 bus to Decatur. No Aaron this time. They were probably working him over. Too bad—I kind of liked him even if he did spoil things with Talitha.

Talitha. I should see her. I promised I'd return. I didn't think I actually would, but here I was in Decatur again. Maybe she'd make me feel better.

You definitely need a girl who's not Rachel, Jake's voice sounded in my inner ears. *But a drug addict? Come on.*

Talitha's nice. We like each other. And I can search for revolutionaries here, fill Lewison's quota without endangering Sarah.

You should find another way.

How?

I walked to the drug store and picked out some food and a box of condoms. I didn't buy any Smash supplies.

Like last time, Edna's German shepherd, Kaiser, barked threats when I knocked on their back door. Edna peeked through the window, then opened the door, lit cigarette in hand.

"Well, if it ain't Karl Marx." She motioned me inside the cramped laundry room, then bolted the door behind me. "Thought you split."

"I did, but I'm back now." I let Kaiser sniff my hand, which seemed to satisfy him.

"Where's Aaron?"

I shrugged and tried to conjure a believable lie.

Edna eyed my paper bag and spoke before I could. "You bring anything?"

"Some food."

She snorted and led me into the living room and its ingrained stench of cigarette butts and iodine. Talitha, wearing a long white dress, was sitting on the sofa next to a mustached man about Edna's age. Ladonna, cute as ever, was wrapped in a blanket against the arm rest.

Talitha stared at me with glassy eyes. "Ben?"

"I told you I'd come back." I waved at Ladonna, who grinned.

The mustached man turned lidded eyes toward Talitha and jerked a thumb my way. "Who's that?"

She stood, a little unsteady, then crossed the room and hugged me. "You came back for me?"

"I missed you." I did.

"I can't believe it."

Edna stubbed out her cigarette in an overflowing ashtray and led the man out of the room. "You've had your fun, Ray. But you'd better leave."

"Who the hell's that?" I asked Talitha. I heard the back door unlatch, followed by muttered voices.

Talitha fidgeted and avoided eye contact. "Ray? One of my sister's old boyfriends. He kinda has a thing for me and I was feeling down. Forget it, he's harmless."

My stomach hardened. "You move on quick."

She looked down and bit her lip.

I had serious problems to deal with and didn't have time for jealousy. "It's not like we made any kind of agreement, though."

Talitha closed the distance and pressed her cheek against mine. "If you stay, I'll be faithful to you."

Solidarity. I could do that. "Likewise. Though to be honest, I don't know what you see in me."

"You're good. You care about people. Not just about yourself."

Most folk, Pop for example, would disagree with that. On the other hand, there were Sarah and Rachel and Jake's opinions. And now Talitha's.

"You're also cute," she whispered. "And you made me come three times."

Her blue eyes met mine and my heart thundered. We kissed and everything else fell away.

Footsteps sounded behind me. Edna. "I sent Ray home," she said. "He's a reliable customer but that's about it. Mind if you tell me what's going on?"

Talitha backed out of our embrace but held onto my hand. "Do you mind watching Ladonna a while?" she asked her sister. "I'll make it up to you."

Edna sighed. "Sure."

Talitha led me into her bedroom. We stripped off our clothes and latched together. This time, neither of us closed our eyes.

Talitha and I held each other after we finished, sharing the warmth of our bodies. "I'm so happy you came back," she said.

She meant it, I could tell. We were a couple, or at least that stage right before. Aaron was wrong about her.

With chunks of my soul burned away by the Insects and with Talitha adding new chunks, I felt different about Rachel now. Her safety was still my top priority, and I loved her profoundly, but the element of desperate lust was gone. I had been childish, chasing after my dead brother's fiancée, hoping someday she'd feel the same way.

Talitha sat up. "Stay here. I have to check on Ladonna and I'll come back with a present." She threw on her dress, not bothering with undergarments.

I fell asleep in the bed, but Talitha's voice, more singsong than usual, woke me before any nightmares encroached. "Wake up, sweetie!"

Her present was predictable—two syringes part-filled with smoky yellow liquid.

"I thought you were quitting," I said.

"Not in the winter. Winters are too bleak around here. Smash is the only thing that keeps me sane."

She was right about bleakness and how it gnawed sanity away. "Well, since you already prepped them..."

According to Aaron, it took a week to get hooked. Nothing happened last time I stopped. And Edna's product wasn't full of contaminants.

Talitha stuck a needle into one of my leg veins. "Less noticeable there. And you shouldn't hit the same vein over and over or it'll sink." She pulled the plunger back a little, drawing in blood, then pushed it all the way in.

Nothing at first, then a torrent of electricity and heat and crazy ecstasy, turning to bliss and the embrace of angels. Talitha did herself and settled next to me, breathing heavily.

We lay together a while, enraptured by the rush and inner sun, then Talitha pulled off her dress and straddled me. All the hidden wonderful things in the universe sallied forth into my head. "I love you," I said, words bypassing any kind of filter.

"This is what heaven must be like," she whispered. "I wanna be like this forever."

What are you doing?

Jake. I couldn't ignore him. Beyond this bed, beyond this haze and pleasure, was Rachel. And Jake. And thuggery, poverty, death.

No heaven on earth.

The whole world damned beneath hobnailed jackboots.

The room darkened. I put on my pants and opened the curtains to check the weather. Outside, illuminated by street lamps and Christmas lights, white powder sprinkled down and stuck to the street. Like magic.

Talitha came up behind me and wrapped arms around my chest, her nipples rubbing against my back. She rested her chin on my shoulder. "Together forever?"

"I'd like that."

Once I freed Rachel, if I could keep the bank from taking the farm, Talitha, Ladonna, and Edna could move to New Bethany. They'd have to quit Smash, but we could live a peaceful, joyful life, free of Insects. I'd marry Talitha and we'd have kids of our own. I'd teach them how to farm and fish and hunt, like Pop taught me and Grandpa taught him.

The powder turned to a heavy deluge of thick white clumps. We watched the snow bury the world for a while, then closed the curtain and returned to the bed.

* * *

It was still snowing the next day, and no one plowed the street. I decided to stay in Decatur and visit Rachel on Christmas. Then I needed to find five revolutionaries to betray.

Edna cooked Smash. Talitha and I helped, and made food. We did everything together, like my pop and ma used to. I filled the coal furnace in the basement. I learned how to hold Ladonna, made mush for her, and played games with her. Talitha taught me how to hit myself so we could synchronize our rushes.

Best of all was the sex. Broken and desperate on our own, we fit together in just the right way to make one whole being.

As I lay spent on Talitha's bed, pressed against her beautiful naked body, Jake's voice returned.

What are you doing? You need to focus on Rachel, Pop, and saving the farm.

I know. I will. But like Lewison said, I need to think things through. And Talitha's my future, beyond all that.

Smash won't help you think.

It's temporary. Can't I taste a little fun before my spirit returns to the underworld?

Talitha nudged me. "Tell me more about your revolution."

It wasn't my revolution. I doubted there was a revolution at all.

"America used to be a democracy," I said. I told her how different it was now, how we were little more than slaves but there were revolutionaries who wanted to live free or die trying. I talked about my brother's rebellion and death, but didn't mention Sarah or Paul or their cell.

I told Talitha how I organized people to pass out flyers to save my family's farm. I told her about Rachel's rally and how we were arrested and tortured. My hands shook as memories wormed past the Smash bliss.

"I should have done more," I said. "Stopped Rachel from going to that rally. Stopped her the first time she said Jake wanted justice."

Talitha looked confused, so I told her about our visions.

"Is everyone weird down there?"

I thought about it. "Maybe we're more in touch than city folk."

She snuggled against me, her skin warm as a fireplace. "As long as you're here for me, I'm here for you. Does your brother's fiancée have an advocate?"

"Yeah, who's been no help. The Insects—"

"Insects?"

"Internal Security thugs. They made Rachel a psych patient, outside the legal system. I wish I could break her out somehow."

Her eyes widened. "Out of the correctional center? Which has an army of guards?"

"Yeah, it's impossible. And even if she escaped, she'd have to run the rest of her life. And her family would be persecuted."

Talitha nodded.

"Maybe I could kidnap someone, this asshole Lewison for example, and demand an exchange. Same problem afterward, though. We'd have to hide and our families would suffer."

I slid out of bed and peeked past the curtains. Bloated snowflakes tumbled down outside, cars and shrubs now amorphous white mounds.

Decatur was a big city, at least compared to New Bethany. It must have a revolutionary cell. Maybe they could help me. Or I could trade them for Rachel. Or both.

How could I find them? According to Paul, the cells exchanged coded messages. But where were the drop sites? What were the codes?

I threw on my clothes.

"Where are you going?" Talitha asked.

I tossed her the dress lying on the floor. "Let's talk to Edna."

Edna was passed out on the living room couch. I nudged her ankle. "Edna. Can we talk a minute?"

She didn't move except to extend a middle finger.

I sat on a cushioned chair near her head. "Have you met anyone else who talked about revolution?"

Edna's head rotated to face me, her eyes half lidded. "You're the first. Now quit bothering me." Her eyes closed.

No leads. I could distribute flyers, see who nodded in agreement. Or looked like they had something to hide. Survival of the fittest through five decades of Internal Security seek and obliterate meant actual revolutionaries might be more afraid of entrapment than interested in recruitment.

"What do you do for Christmas?" I asked Talitha. They didn't have a tree or lights.

She looked down. "Since mom went to prison, not much."

"I was wondering…"

"She worked as an accountant. Took some money and got caught. They sent her to a work camp in Nebraska and won't allow visitors." Tears filled her eyes and started to drip. "Dad… Dad left us when I was six. Mom had some boyfriends after that, but never remarried."

Poor girl. I wiped her tears away with my fingers. "I should get you a present. But I have no idea what."

"Let's go shopping. I have a little money left from my job."

"What do you do?"

"Bicycle courier, before it got icy. I was thinking of hocking the bike, but then I'll be even more of a loser."

I held her hands. "Don't put yourself down. Life is hard enough as it is."

Advice for myself as well as her.

Once the city finally plowed the roads, we took the bus to Main Street, which had full-size department stores. The sidewalks were crowded with last-minute shoppers bundled against the cold.

First, I bought a pack of unlined paper and a black marking pen to make flyers. Then, tinsel and a wreath. I bought Talitha a silk dress on consignment. She bought me a shirt and her sister a necklace.

"We should make eggnog," I said as we carried our bags of loot to the next stop.

Talitha shook her head. "You can't drink on Smash. It'll stop your heart."

Scary. We bought cough syrup and ephedrine instead, and a chicken for Christmas dinner.

Back at the house, I penned a flyer based on Rachel's pamphlet, the one we never printed but Internal Security found anyway. I couldn't remember her literary quotes, but remembered lines like 'without your support, the dictatorship will crumble and fall.'

"We have a government of the few, by the few, for the few," Talitha read.

I laughed inside. I could inspire people to fight the government, and the Insects wouldn't jail me because I'd say I was just fishing.

Then again, I still had to meet my quota.

"You should write something about the cost of food," Talitha said. "And electricity, coal, phone service. Everything's expensive. My gramma, rest her soul, said the government used to make the companies charge affordable rates."

"Yeah, my grandpa said that too. That was back when they cared what people thought."

She frowned. "You know who Father Coughlin was, right?"

"Shill for Lindbergh and the coup."

"Gramma used to listen to his radio broadcasts before he got taken off the air, and said he preached on and on against the bankers, especially in the early days."

"Probably why the government took him off the air. Twined snakes, that's what we've got."

"Huh?"

"The banks and government, twined snakes. Add the churches and you have three. An unholy trinity." Thoughts began churning. The New Testament was full of admonitions against the rich, like 'you can't serve God and money.' But money was all the banks and conglomerates cared about. And what about the government? They said everyone was supposed to work together for the good of the nation. Some people, like Lewison, actually seemed to believe that.

Clouded fragments swirled, the precursors to an idea—a way to destroy the beast altogether. Could I not only free Rachel, but avenge Jake's murder and more?

After dinner we all got high. I led Talitha and Edna in Christmas carols. Then I sang some Pale Moon Rising songs, wishing I had my guitar. What was Sarah doing for Christmas? I hadn't seen her for months.

Edna took me aside when I got tired of singing. "I have to say, it's fun having you here. Just don't hurt my sister. She really likes you and she's not the strongest person in the world."

"Talitha keeps me going," I said. "No way could I hurt her."

Which made my situation even more difficult.

Chapter Twenty-Two

In a shadowed room, Rachel lies on her prison bed, face down, unmoving. I watch her from a window above and take notes.

Behind me, giant insects stare with compound eyes and hiss through daggered legs. Huge mandibles click and gnash.

'This is a dream,' I try to write in my notebook. My hands shake so much, the lettering's impossible to read.

I put down the notebook and tap on the glass. No response.

Dr. Malluch appears next to me. His circular eyeglasses are opaque and smeared with blood. "She won't eat. I don't think she'll last much longer."

* * *

In the pre-dawn darkness, I kissed Talitha awake. She stretched and pressed her nude body against mine.

"I have to see Rachel on Christmas," I said.

Her eyes narrowed. "Why?"

"I told you all we went through. I want her to know I'm trying to help her get out."

She studied me. "Are you in love with her?"

My feelings for Rachel were profound, but too complex to articulate. "She's family. But I don't love anyone the way I love you." Which was true.

"You're a sweetie." She kissed me. "I wanna go with you, though."

"It's not a place you should go near. The circles of hell breach the surface there. I won't be long."

Her face tightened. "I'm going."

Why was everyone so stubborn all the time? I went back to sleep.

Barking woke me. Kaiser, in the other room. Dressed in a nightie, Talitha was brushing Ladonna's fine hair. She glanced at the bedside table, which had two filled syringes on top.

I heard Edna's voice, too muffled to make out the words. Then a man spoke.

Talitha pulled a leather bag from underneath the crib mattress, unzipped it, slipped the syringes inside, and returned the bag back to its hiding place.

Someone knocked on the bedroom door. "Who is it?" Talitha said.

The door opened. It was Aaron.

Holy shit, they let him go! If Lewison wasn't going to credit me, that was a downright fair thing to do.

"I thought I'd find you here," he said.

"Do you mind?" I didn't have any clothes on.

"Come out when you're decent. So to speak."

I wanted to know why the Insects released him, and what happened to the others. But thoughts of Smash buried all else. As soon as Aaron left, I exchanged glances with Talitha. She retrieved her leather bag, placed Ladonna back in her crib, and we got high.

We lay in bed for a while, gazing in each other's eyes, then made love, lingering and exploring and joining. After the bliss tapered off, we showered together and changed and went to the kitchen to make lunch. No sign of Aaron or Edna—they were probably in the basement cooking.

I was right, because after we ate, they exited the stairwell. "I made you sandwiches," Talitha told them.

"Thanks," Edna said.

I addressed Aaron. "So they let you out too?"

"They're letting the whole crew out, except the ones with medical issues, and busing them back to New Bethany. You're going too, I assume?"

"I've got a ticket. But I'm staying here."

Talitha squeezed my hand. Aaron rolled his eyes at us. "Young love. There's not a drug on earth that dulls the brain more."

"You're a cynical son of a bastard," Edna told him.

"So are you, that's why I like you." He turned to me again. "It's the Smash, you know. You're new in the world, so let me explain. You get high with a girl and have sex with her, you think there's this bond. But it's an illusion."

My jaw tightened. "What the scat-munch do you know about it?"

Talitha glared at him. "You're just jealous 'cause we're happy."

Maybe my happiness was just a surface layer but I planned to hold onto it.

Aaron held up a hand. "Don't mean to offend. Just trying to help." He leaned closer. "We have to go. The revolution's down south, not in Decatur."

I showed him my flyer. "I'm gonna make copies and distribute them here. Got any suggestions for spots?"

Aaron's eyes widened. "Are you soft in the head? This is Internal Security's state headquarters. No one's stupid enough to be a revolutionary here."

Edna nodded. "He's probably right. Aaron's a smart guy."

Unlike me, apparently.

"There are three of us right here that can fight the revolution," Talitha said. "Four if Edna's willing."

"I'm not," she said. "And I don't want any foolish talk like that in my house."

"Amen, my practical temptress," Aaron said. He stared at me. "They exiled me, remember? Decatur cops pick me up for anything, or even see me around, they'll lock me up for good."

"Stay through Christmas," Edna told him. "We'll keep the blinds shut."

Aaron smiled. His eyes took us all in and he held up a dark brown bottle. "Merry Christmas, everyone. Who's up?"

* * *

"Do you have a phone?" I asked Edna once I was coherent again.

"Are you kidding? At thirty dollars a month plus surcharges for calls outside the county? Talitha makes a dollar per package, which doesn't add up to much."

"About ten dollars a day," Talitha said. "And then the government and church give me some aid for Ladonna. She passed the eugenics tests, otherwise I'd get zippo."

Edna kept talking. "Besides, I heard the microphones are on all the time and the government can hear everything in the room."

Smart of her to be careful. "I have to call the Tolsons," I said. "Rachel's parents." I hadn't forgotten the number.

"There's a payphone at the grocer's," Talitha said. "It's only a couple of blocks."

Bundled against the cold, Talitha and I trudged glove in glove to the glass phone booth. We crowded inside, protected from the wind.

The first minute cost 65 cents, then a quarter per minute afterward. I had enough for six minutes. I'd have to watch my words since the Tolsons were likely being monitored.

"Tolson residence," one of Rachel's sisters answered. "Serena speaking."

"This is Ben—"

"Ben? Oh."

"Are you visiting Rachel?"

"Um, yeah, uh, tomorrow afternoon. Except Jimmy, he's not feeling well. He's staying with a babysitter." She chuckled.

I turned to Talitha. "Are the buses running tomorrow?"

She shook her head. "Everything's shut."

I spoke in the handset again. "Can you give me a ride?"

"Hold on, let me get dad."

"Please deposit 25 cents," a mechanical voice said.

I dropped a quarter into the bulky iron phone box. "Hello?"

Silence on the other end.

Fifty cents later, Mr. Tolson spoke, "Hello Ben."

"Hi, I was wondering if you could pick me up in Decatur tomorrow on the way to see Rachel."

"You want to see Rachel?"

"I want to see that she's okay, and let her know I'm doing everything I can to get her released."

"Why are you in Decatur?"

"Long story and I'm on a pay phone."

"How long have you been there?"

"Three days. I got arrested again, for trying to save the farm. I'll tell you when you get here."

"And you're in prison?"

"No, they released me. I'm staying at someone's house."

"Please deposit 25 cents," the phone insisted. I dropped in more change.

"Have you been in touch with your family?" Mr. Tolson asked.

My hands shook. "Why? Did something happen?"

"Where do you want me to pick you up tomorrow?"

I didn't want to give out Talitha and Edna's address over the phone. "Mid-Decatur Food Market, out front." I gave the cross streets. "What time?"

"I'd say, be ready between two and three."

"I'll be there."

"I'm sorry I was rude to you when you came over. I know you think the world of Rachel."

That was a turnaround. "I do. Hey, did you get to re-open your store?"

"Yes, they told me on Friday, after they said we could see Rachel. How did you know?"

"I gotta go. See you tomorrow."

I went in the store and got more change. Then I dialed home.

The number was disconnected. Shit!

"What's wrong, sweetie?" Talitha asked on the way back to the house.

"Something bad happened back home. I think we've been evicted." I fought to hold back the tears. "I should have been there. Five generations we've lived there. I thought you and me, we could marry and our kids could be six."

She gripped my hand. "Oh, Ben."

At the house, Edna and Aaron stared at me but I didn't want to talk to them. We went straight to the bedroom and I buried my face against Talitha as she held me.

"We can go down and see if we can help," she said. "Aaron can stay here and look after Edna."

* * *

Christmas in a strange town, without my family. I missed Sarah too—she always made me laugh, and never let anyone push her around.

Talitha trimmed my hair and washed my clothes. She put on the lavender silk dress I'd bought her, looking magazine-beautiful in it. At ten till two, we threw on our coats and hats, said goodbye to Ladonna and Edna, and trudged through the snow to the food market.

The store was shuttered and the parking lot empty. Talitha and I stood in the semi-sheltered doorway, huddled against each other for warmth. "We should have had them pick us up at the house," she said, teeth chattering.

"Didn't want to give out your address over the phone. This is bad enough."

At 2:30, the Tolsons still hadn't arrived. But fifteen minutes later, their blocky white passenger van pulled up. We hurried inside to escape the cold, and took the remaining seats in the back.

I introduced Mr. and Mrs. Tolson, their younger daughters, Serena and Samantha, and their middle-aged lawyer, Mr. Greene. "This is my girlfriend, Talitha."

Samantha turned to Serena, sitting next to her in the middle bench. "Ben has a girlfriend in Decatur?"

I ignored them and addressed Rachel's dad as he put the van in drive. "Mr. Tolson, what happened back home? The phone's disconnected."

He kept his eyes forward and pulled onto the road. "Let's discuss it afterward. We're running late."

Mr. Greene directed Mr. Tolson to one of the correctional center parking lots, fronting a long brick building, four stories tall, coal-stinking smoke billowing out of tall chimneys. A sign at the entrance read "Decatur Correctional Hospital," and underneath, "Women's Wing."

Silver-shirted guards checked us in, and escorted us to a room with a thick plastiglass divider. On the other side, guards brought in Rachel, clad in gray pajamas. No cuffs. She looked healthy and her hair was brushed, but her eyes blinked a lot.

"You have half an hour," one of the guards said.

Rachel ran to the circle of speaking holes in the plastiglass, tears streaming down her cheeks. "You came! I've missed you all so much!"

I don't think I'd ever seen her so happy. We all wished her a Merry Christmas.

Her emerald eyes widened when she spotted me in the back. "Ben?"

I waved, but had to wait my turn. Her family spoke to her, then Mr. Greene. "Miss Tolson, I want you to know I'm still working on your case. I have a number of affidavits stating that you are of sound mind and should not be held here against your will. How are you being treated?"

"Better than before."

The guard glanced at his watch. "Five minutes."

Mr. Greene finished. I edged to the front. "Hi Rachel."

"They let you out?"

"Yeah."

"After what you did to that guard?"

Talitha spoke behind me. "What did you do?"

I half-turned my head. "It was self-defense. I'll tell you later." Some of it, anyway.

"That's Ben's girlfriend," Serena threw out. "She lives here. In Decatur, I mean."

Rachel looked surprised. "Oh."

We weren't here to discuss Talitha. "They gave me the special treatment," I said, "scientifically enhanced pain."

Rachel nodded and her lips twitched. She'd been in the hellfire room too. I fought not to cry.

"I'm out now," I said. "And I'll get you out, promise."

She placed her hands against the transparent wall. "How?"

I pressed my hands against hers, wishing I could dissolve the two inches of intervening plastic and glass. "I'm still working it out, but I'll find a way."

Her eyes met mine with trust I didn't deserve—yet. "I know you will." She smiled again and my heart ached that she was trapped on the other side of that barrier.

When we returned to the van, I asked Mr. Tolson, "Before we go, can you please tell me what happened to the farm?"

He fidgeted. "I'm sorry I didn't tell you on the phone. I should have."

Just say it! "What?"

"Your father's dead."

"*What?*"

"I'm sorry."

Talitha gripped my arm. Mrs. Tolson mumbled some sort of apology. Mr. Tolson resumed, "Mr. Greene heard from your attorney, Mr. Gamaliel. He, uh, knows the facts more directly."

Mr. Greene folded his black-gloved hands. "I'm sorry, Ben."

My hands shook, then my knees. "What are you talking about?"

"Well," he said, "I guess you know the First Consolidated Bank foreclosed and took possession of the farm and all its assets."

"I saw the letter." Did my pop refuse to leave, and get shot?

"The bank sent the sheriff and two of his deputies to enforce the eviction order."

"During the holidays?"

"It was because of those flyers you distributed. They decided to act before any kind of public outcry made it more difficult."

My ears throbbed, like a cadence of underwater bass drums. My throat squeezed shut, making it hard to breathe. I'd fucked up again, worse than ever.

Mr. Greene avoided my eyes. "Your father, grandfather, aunt, and uncle were at the house, and wouldn't leave. There was some arguing and a scuffle, and according to the police report, your father punched the sheriff in the nose."

And the sheriff shot him? I waited for Mr. Greene to finish.

"The deputies placed your father in cuffs," he said. "Your grandfather too. Your Uncle Floyd, though... according to everyone there, he ran upstairs and started shooting a rifle from one of the windows."

Shit, shit, shit! I should have been there.

"Unfortunately," the lawyer said, "your uncle was drunk and not much of a shot."

The Tolsons inched away.

"He missed the sheriff and hit your father in the head. He died right away, most likely."

My knees gave out and I lost my balance. Talitha grabbed me, but we both fell hard. The back of my head smacked against the icy asphalt.

Talitha held me on the way back, and gave directions to her house. People spoke to me, but none of it registered.

Chapter Twenty-Three

I collapsed in Talitha's bed. She lay next to me, eyes moist. "I'm so sorry, sweetie."

She held me a while, then got up. "I have to feed Ladonna. But I'll be back, okay?"

No answer came to me, and she left.

Jake? I thought. It's your turn to take care of Pop now. I ruined everything. I killed Pop and lost the farm. Maybe I'll join you soon.

You can't. You still have to take care of Rachel. Nothing's your fault, it's the bank's and the government's. You didn't kill anyone. And I still need your help.

Everything I touch turns to shit.

No, look how happy you've made Talitha. Don't give up.

Someone shook my foot. I'd drifted off.

Talitha stood by the bed, still wearing the silk dress, biting her lip. Beyond, Ladonna lay in her crib.

"Look, I can't bear any more bad news," I said, "so don't tell me."

"You're going to leave me when Rachel gets out, aren't you."

My toes clenched the shoe insoles. "She doesn't feel that way about me. I can't deal with this. Just leave me alone."

She looked down and pressed her thumbs together. "I understand why you'd be so attracted to someone as beautiful as Rachel."

What good was a girlfriend who piled on like this? "My pop's dead. My whole family's gone. Don't you care?"

"Of course I care, sweetie." Talitha joined me on the bed and draped her arms around me. "I'm sorry, I'm just scared all the time. I can't help it. Ladonna depends on me but I'm such a terrible mother."

My remnants of self-control vanished. "It's fucking Christmas and…" Tears burst from my eyes. I had a ma and pop and brother and sister and we were happy once and now they were all gone forever. I was all alone.

Talitha sniffled and stroked my back as I trembled and cried.

"I'm so sorry," she said. "I wish things were better."

The outburst slowed. I wasn't alone.

I wiped the tears away. "How much Smash do we have?" I couldn't deal with non-stop pain anymore. I just couldn't.

She rubbed my shoulder. "Lots."

"Can we...?"

"Of course. And we still have that chicken to cook." She sat up and pulled me out of bed. "Come spend Christmas with me."

* * *

Time disappeared in a haze of Smash. I didn't want to pass the threshold into addiction, but it was the only way I could function. As soon as the bliss wore off, darkness and dread replaced it, the permanently gray Illinois winter settling into my soul. And guilt, the worst of the lot, making me want to scream and stab myself with a kitchen knife. Talitha never questioned, never lectured, just shot up with me and kept me going.

"Are we going down to New Bethany for the funeral?" Talitha asked over mac and cheese she made everyone for lunch.

My aunts would try to organize something. "You're coming?"

She squeezed my arm. "Of course, sweetie."

I still had a bus ticket, but how would Talitha get down there? "I'm broke again. And I don't have a place to live." I addressed Edna and Aaron, "Do you have money we could borrow?"

Edna scoffed. "Do I look like a bank? I don't remember the last time I had spare money."

"I could steal a car," Aaron said. "We can all go."

Edna shook her head. "I've got responsibilities here. People expect me to cook for them, provide a decent product, and that's how I get by. I can't up and leave. Besides, there's Ladonna and Kaiser to take care of."

"Okay, you stay here," Aaron said, "and get some friends to stay with you and help out. I'll bring Ben down to New Bethany."

"And Talitha and Ladonna," I said.

"Sure, them too."

Something about Aaron irritated me. Like Paul. Maybe the problem was mine. They were go-getters and I wasn't, at least not by nature.

"How hard is it to steal a car?" I'd never tried it, other than sneaking off with one of the farm trucks.

"All you have to do is find one that's unlocked and hot wire it. Done it a hundred times." He didn't seem a bit nervous about the idea, even though it had landed him in prison.

Talitha retrieved a dusty suitcase from the attic and brought it into the bedroom. We started packing. I didn't have much. I definitely needed more clothes.

She pulled her leather bag out from under the crib mattress. "We should stock up."

I followed her to Edna's room, where Aaron was also packing. "We need at least a week's supply of Smash," Talitha told him.

"We have enough codeine for one more batch," he said, "then we'll have to stop by the Concrete Arms. You're welcome to stay at my place there, plenty of room."

Yuck. But if I wanted to recruit anyone, my aunts lived too far away.

Edna and Aaron went down to the basement. Talitha hocked her bicycle and bought diapers and snacks. She looked depressed when she got back.

"We've got enough cash now, but I can't work as a courier anymore. I'll never get ahead. We're always barely surviving."

"Know the feeling." Of course, she could always save money by quitting drugs or working somewhere else, but that would be a hypocritical thing to say. "If it helps, we can plant a garden in the spring and grow our own food. Raise chickens too. Our own little farm."

We played with Ladonna a while, then got high and lay together on the living room sofa. Clothes on—I wasn't up for sex anymore.

* * *

Someone knocked on the front door and Kaiser barked. Talitha and I shared a glance. Usually Edna answered the door, but she was downstairs cooking.

"I'll get it," Talitha said. She stumbled to the door and peered through the peephole. "It's a black couple." She shouted against the door, "Who is it?"

"Is Ben there?" It sounded like Sarah.

Sarah! I staggered to my feet. "Let her in, she's my best friend." What the hell was she doing here? She must have talked to the Tolsons.

Talitha opened the door. Sarah, wearing a brown button-down coat and snug hat with ear flaps, walked in and smiled at me. Wavy locks of hair cascaded past the hat, like she'd decided to become a glamour model. Paul, white fedora on, followed her in and shut the door behind him.

Sarah sniffed the air. "You're fucking kidding me."

"What?" I asked.

"How long have you been on Smash?"

It was that obvious? The high was mostly gone. Or was it the smell from the basement?

"You don't know what I've been through," I said. "You have no idea."

"This is your best friend?" Talitha asked me.

Sarah looked her up and down. "You must be the famous Decatur girlfriend."

Talitha blinked. "Famous?"

Sarah's eyes narrowed and she clenched a fist. "If you got him hooked on Smash, I swear I will kick your ass."

Edna and Aaron came up from the basement and eyeballed Sarah and Paul. "Can I help you?" Edna asked.

Sarah's nose wrinkled. "Yeah, I'm here to pick my friend up. He's got a funeral to go to."

"When is it?" I asked.

"Your Aunt Joanna is organizing it," she said, "which means no one has any idea."

And who would pay for it? Pop didn't have life insurance—said it cost too much.

I stumbled into Sarah's arms. She smelled like coconut oil.

"I'm sorry, Ben," she said, holding me tight. "Your pop had his faults, but you don't deserve all this grief."

He was kind of an asshole, I had to admit, but that was mostly after Ma died and the joy fell out of his life. Now it didn't matter.

"You've got a car?" I asked.

"I do," Paul said.

Memories intruded. "Where were you when the Insects arrested us and beat the shit out of me?"

He squinted. "Insects?"

"I'm so sorry," Sarah said, still holding me.

Talitha, Edna, and Aaron were staring at us. My stomach clenched and the remaining haze vanished. I couldn't let anyone know about Paul's cell.

Sarah met my eyes and ushered me onto the sofa.

Talitha sat on my other side and held my hand. She told Sarah, "I'm taking care of him. We love each other."

I nodded in agreement.

"Wow," Sarah said. "Congratulations, I guess."

"What happened to my grandpa?" I asked. "I heard he got arrested too?"

"Yeah, he's in county lockup for assault and non-payment of debts. Your Uncle Floyd, uh..."

"Offed himself," Paul said.

I felt unexpectedly sad for him, poor pathetic drunk. You couldn't live with something like killing your brother-in-law and destroying your family.

"Somehow he got hold of a razor blade," Paul said, "and the deputies left him alone in his cell a whole day. Slit his throat and bled out."

"Okay, that's enough," Talitha said.

"Why don't you two settle a bit," Edna told Sarah and Paul. "I've got water and tea."

Paul sat in a chair. "Tea, thank you."

Sarah waved away the offer.

Edna went into the kitchen and Aaron took the other chair. He regarded Sarah and Paul. "Are you revolutionaries with Ben?"

Paul's eyes widened. "Excuse me?"

"I am too," Aaron said.

Talitha leaned forward. "Me too."

Sarah pinched my side, hard.

I managed not to panic. "Sarah's my best friend from New Bethany. And Paul's her cousin. They're not even close to revolutionaries."

Talitha snuggled against me. "Can I still come with you?"

"Yes, yes, we're all going, same as before, only now we have a ride."

Paul stared at me with narrowed eyes.

Chapter Twenty-Four

Paul had a small white sedan that ran on ethanol, which was a lot cheaper than diesel or gasoline, and didn't need rationing coupons. We filled the trunk, mostly with baby stuff. Paul, Sarah, and Aaron crammed in the front bench, Talitha and I in the back, with a makeshift baby seat for Ladonna.

We couldn't pick up anything decent on the radio, so Sarah sang some Pale Moon Rising tunes. She tried to convince me to join in, but I wasn't in the mood.

As the sun set over frozen fields, I ran through my options. I could let Rachel rot a week or two more, and try to find trades when I returned to Decatur. If the prospects there were as dismal as Aaron and Edna thought, I could head up to Chicago where the fish swam dense. From what my family said about Chicago, though, I'd likely end up with a knife in my back. Final choice, I could turn in Paul's crew and find a way to spare Sarah. Then I'd leave town and never return.

What would Jake do? What would Rachel do? They'd never snitch on Paul. He and his movement were trying to change the system and end the war that killed my brother. Lewison was on the other side, the side that needed to go.

Up front, Aaron asked Sarah and Paul a lot of questions, like "How long have you known Ben?" and "What do you do for a living?"

Sarah did all the talking, telling harmless stories about growing up in New Bethany, about farming, fishing, and music. "Our county ain't the most exciting place on earth, but Ben's got a knack for livening things up."

"You too," I said. "So what's up with the glamour hair?"

She yanked off her snug hat and ran fingers through the thick locks. "Like it? I'm a townie now."

"It'll take getting used to. But it looks good."

"It'd better. It's a pain in the ass." She turned to Aaron. "So what about you? What's your story?"

"Former pharmacy tech," he said. "Currently unemployed. Got in some trouble with the law and need to relocate."

Sarah turned around to face me. "Mostly I'm interested in how my best friend turned into a damn drughead."

"I'm not a drughead," I said. "It's just to get me through... Remember I was drunk for three days after Jake's funeral?"

She nodded. "How long will this last?"

I started to tell Sarah what I'd been through, but started crying instead.

Talitha reached over the baby seat and held my hand. "Oh, sweetie."

Embarrassed, I forced myself under control.

Sarah told Talitha, "Well you *seem* for real. Mind if I ask, whose baby that is?"

"Mine."

Sarah rolled her eyes. "Of course. I mean who's the father?"

"Shitty ex-boyfriend. When I told him I was pregnant, he said I should take rat poison to kill it. I started throwing shit at him and he took off. Never came back."

She hadn't told me the rat poison story. No wonder she thought I was nice, compared to that psycho.

"You weren't doing drugs while you were pregnant, were you?" Sarah asked.

"I was clean most of the time. My doctor moved me into a women's center, run by Catholic Charities, so I'd have a healthy baby."

"And I guess since you're white, the government gives you vouchers for medicine, food, diapers...?"

"It isn't much. But the women's center's still helping me. And the church down the street. It's a good deal, an hour a week listening to the preacher and they give you a box of food after."

"And she works as a courier," I said.

Sarah's eyes stayed on Talitha. "I'm curious why you latched on to Ben. He's a nice guy, but he's poor as sand, he's no sugar daddy."

Talitha reddened in anger. "We love each other, you nosy cunt. Why don't you back off?"

I'd never seen Talitha so mad. Ladonna started to cry. Paul gripped the steering wheel and Aaron stared at the empty fields.

Sarah held up her hands. "Sorry. No one ever accused me of being tactful. I just wanna make sure my best friend doesn't get hurt."

I leaned forward. "That's enough, Sarah. If you can't tell she's good then you're dense."

"You're one to talk, sticking Smash in your veins." She watched Talitha try to comfort Ladonna. "I'll shut up now."

* * *

Paul dropped Aaron off at the Concrete Arms parking lot.

"Coming in?" Aaron asked.

"We'll be back tomorrow," Paul said.

"Where are Talitha and me staying, then?" I asked when we pulled out.

"Micah's."

"Who's Micah?" Talitha asked.

"Friend of ours," I said. One of Paul's recruits, the chubby blond guy.

Paul turned onto the state road—Lindbergh Avenue once you entered city limits—and headed east into town. "He lives with his fiancée," he said. "They're interns at the community hospital."

I wish I'd known that when we dumped off the guy with the rotting leg.

"They have a guest room," he continued.

"And we can stay there?"

"As long as you behave, I'll make it work." He turned left on Chestnut Street, which went past the medical buildings. Rachel's house was four blocks in the opposite direction.

Sarah turned around and glared at us. "No Smash in his house, got it?"

"I need to quit anyway," I said.

Talitha eyed me and pressed her lips together. Then she stared out the window at the small, red brick hospital. It would have all kinds of drugs. We could score a year's worth of codeine, even morphine, if we pulled off a heist.

I buried the idea. "Can we stop by the farm?"

Sarah's eyebrows raised. "We're almost at Micah's. Besides, there's a Pinkerton living at your house."

My whole body clenched. How could this happen? "A bank thug living in my house?"

"To keep anyone from coming back, I guess." She gave me a look of sympathy.

"What about our stuff?"

Paul answered first. "Bank will probably auction what they can and haul the rest to the dump."

"How can they..." Five generations of Adamsons all gone, nothing left.

"Standard procedure," he said. "Banks want every dollar they can swindle."

Despair turned to rage at the injustice. "Fuck those scat-munchers. It's our house, our stuff. I need a gun."

Sarah threw up a hand. "Whoa, cowboy. Let's think before you rush in there and get killed."

"I'm a good shot. You know that."

"Arrested and hung, then."

She was right. I needed a workable plan. And maybe my aunts had already moved our belongings out.

Paul parked on a gravel pad in front of a small prefab house at the north end of Chestnut Street. "Here we are."

A red compact car, which I'd seen at the Turner farm, sat to the right. The house still had Christmas lights and a wreath up. The curtains were closed.

Paul got out and knocked on the door. Sarah and I followed.

Micah, thinner than last time we met, opened the door. "Paul. Sarah. Ben. Come in."

I waited for Talitha, who carried Ladonna.

Their living room was tidy but small, with a varnished wood floor, paisley sofa and matching chairs. Past the living room were a dining nook and doorways leading left and right. No television, no radio.

A chubby woman with curly brown hair rose from the sofa. "Hello."

"I have a favor to ask," Paul asked.

Micah answered first. "Yes?"

"You know Ben's house was stolen by the bank—"

Micah scanned me head to toe. "And you need a place to stay?"

"Not long," I said, trying to keep calm. "Just a few days."

I introduced Talitha and Ladonna. Micah introduced the chubby woman—his fiancée, Beth. She cooed over Ladonna and bonded with Talitha right away.

Micah showed us to their guest room. It was cramped, and with the crib assembled, we had to move the dresser into the hall.

"Sorry it's a little small," Beth said.

I shrugged. It was a palace compared to prison.

Talitha turned toward the wall and started nursing Ladonna. "It's kind of you to put us up," she said over her shoulder.

Beth escorted me back to the living room, where the others stood talking. "You guys don't have a radio?" I asked. Music had power like nothing else to make life semi-tolerable.

Micah shook his head. "Radio and TV are just propaganda outlets."

I started to tell him about the St. Louis station that never repeated the same song more than once a month, but Paul intervened and shook Micah's hand. "We'll see you tomorrow morning." He turned to Beth. "Maybe you could take Talitha and Ladonna over to the hospital tomorrow morning for a checkup."

"Do you have a way to get people off Smash?" Sarah asked.

Beth and Micah looked alarmed.

"Talitha and Ben," Sarah said. "They're tame, don't worry. But they'll live longer if they kick their habit."

I shook my head, but she was probably right.

"I'll see what I can do," Beth said.

Paul and Sarah left, and Talitha settled Ladonna in her crib.

"Phone's off limits," Micah told me.

I eyed the bulky black phone hanging at the dining nook entrance. The handset cord hung loose, not plugged into the base. "How come?"

"Only reason we have a phone is because the hospital requires it. But you never know when the government's listening in, and they keep records of who calls who. We only plug the handset in when the phone rings, so they can't activate the microphone when we're not using it."

"Fair enough." There were plenty of pay phones around.

Beth fixed leftovers for us to eat. A terrible craving arose as we sat at the small dining table, like my chest had grown hollow and something was clawing to get out. Talitha kept fidgeting and licking her lips.

We hurried through the food. "I've got to check on Ladonna," Talitha said.

"It's been a long day," I added, knees shaking. "I promise I'll be better company tomorrow."

Beth and Micah squinted at us. Then Beth said, "Okay, see you in the morning."

We hurried to the bedroom, trying to be discreet but afraid we weren't. Talitha zipped open her leather bag.

"My body's clenching all over," I said. "I think I'm gonna be sick."

"Oh, sweetie," Talitha said. Her lips trembled and she sniffled. "I'm so sorry." She filled a syringe and motioned for me to sit on the bed. "Make a fist. I'll hit you, you're shaking too much."

My fingers were trembling. Hers were too, but she was more used to this than me.

"This is the ultimate show of love, right here," she said. "Taking care of your lover before yourself."

She injected me first. I hoped Sarah wouldn't find out.

Chapter Twenty-Five

Talitha and I woke before dawn and got high before anyone could interrupt us. We held each other a while. Then she had to feed Ladonna.

"You can take the first shower," I told her.

As soon as I heard water running, I pulled the camera and tape recorder out of my coat, wrapped them in a dirty shirt, and hid them behind the wardrobe. If Paul spotted them he'd cite rule number five and kill me, maybe Talitha too.

Would he? Was he capable of murder? He was serious and dogmatic, and I didn't aim to tempt him.

Beth served corn flakes for breakfast. Afterward, she walked Talitha and Ladonna to the hospital for checkups and any missing vaccinations.

Paul and Sarah arrived soon after, at half past eight.

"I have to be at the hospital by nine," Micah said.

"Not a worry," Paul said. "This won't take long." He turned to me and pointed at the paisley sofa. "Have a seat."

I sat, wondering where this was going. Paul and Sarah pulled chairs close to me. Still standing, Micah winced. "Don't scratch the floor."

Sarah rolled her eyes but apologized.

"Are you well rested?" Paul asked me.

"Yeah. I should go see my aunts, see what the arrangements are."

"I'll give you a ride wherever you need to go."

Sarah stared at me. "Are you high now?"

The haze had mostly worn off. "No."

"Good," she said.

Paul steepled his fingers. "I don't know what to think of you."

"What do you mean?"

"You and Rachel, organizing that rally. I'm disappointed by your naïveté, but impressed by your initiative."

My fists clenched at the memory of Paul sipping a drink while the Insects attacked. "You could have helped."

"You didn't follow the rules, and didn't listen to me."

"They tried to rape Rachel and they tortured us, worse than you can possibly imagine, and..." I lost control—again—and started crying.

Sarah moved next to me on the sofa and rubbed my shoulder. "I'm sorry I wasn't there."

"I told the others to stay away," Paul said. "So they wouldn't get caught."

My tears wouldn't stop. "Evil fucking sadists... Rachel..."

Paul sighed. "I am sorry about what happened. You're out now and we'll find a way to help Rachel."

"We flyered the town for your release," Sarah said. "Maybe it helped."

All it did was aggravate Lewison's surliness, but I'd keep that to myself. I wiped my eyes with a shirt sleeve. "Thanks."

"You'd do the same for me."

I squeezed her hand. "They decided Rachel was the only one worth keeping. We have to get her out."

"Why did you raise an army of drugheads?" Paul asked.

I gave him half the truth. "I was trying to save the farm. Which didn't work." Like everything I tried.

"I could have told you that. But again, impressive initiative and organizing, especially without Rachel in charge."

My muscles tightened again. "What's that supposed to mean?"

"She strikes me as more of a self-starter."

The nerve of that soda-sipping asshole! "Screw you."

Paul tensed. "I was a little surprised the feds let you out the first time. But even more surprised the second time."

I hoped he wouldn't search our bedroom. "They let everyone go. We didn't say anything against the government. And it was the holidays."

"Well I'm glad you're out, Ben," Sarah said.

"Where have you been?" I asked. "I stopped by your house."

"I got the message. We've been busy."

I remembered Paul's plans to recruit others and start a cleaning business. "Tending bar? Cleaning houses?"

"Both and a lot more," he said.

"Never thought I'd have to clean houses for uppity white women," Sarah said. "But like Paul says, it's income, a reason to meet, and access to all kinds of places."

"How does Micah fit in?" I asked. "And June? And what's his name, the big guy?"

I wondered if I should 'fess up about my deal with Lewison. I could be a double agent—get Rachel out, but work for the resistance.

Micah answered, "Always good to have a doctor on call. And someone with access to supplies."

"Since she's white, June owns the business," Sarah said. "On paper, anyway. American Cleaners and Fixers." She grinned.

Clever name. Probably her idea.

"Mary and I are maids," she continued, "Amos is the handyman, and Paul does the driving."

"Enough," Paul said. He reached into his jacket and pulled out a pistol, a .45 ACP M1911A1. Army issue, heavy stopping power for a handgun.

I tensed but didn't panic, probably thanks to the Smash remnants.

Sarah's eyes widened. "What—?"

"Not here," Micah said.

Paul ignored them and pointed the pistol in my general direction, although not directly at me. "Now Ben—"

"Don't point that at me." Good thing I hid the spy gear.

His gun didn't waver. "Remember what I said the penalty was for betrayal?"

Now my muscles did want to tremble. No way would I mention Lewison now. "What are you talking about?"

"You know too much. And you brought in all these unreliable people. Talitha. Aaron."

"They don't know anything about you. Neither does the government. I didn't talk."

"And with you on Smash, you're even more unreliable. I have no idea what to do with you."

"Well you're not shooting him," Sarah told him. "There's no one I trust more, and that includes you. Now put that damn gun away."

Paul frowned at her. Sarah crossed her arms and narrowed her eyes.

He holstered his gun. "I'd better not regret this. Alright, Ben, are you still with the program?"

Huge relief. "You promised to help Rachel. Get her out of that hellhole and I'll do anything." My jaw tensed. "And some people need to pay for what they've done."

"I'm with you," Sarah said.

The relief grew, tinged with guilt. I squeezed Sarah's hand again. "I was wondering why so many people support the regime, and how to change that."

"It's mostly fear," Paul said. "By demonstrating widespread resistance, we remove that fear. It has to be successful resistance, though, not a disaster like your rally."

Not that again. I glared at Paul and he leaned back in his chair like he wanted to apologize but thought it might show weakness.

"Why do the churches support the government and banks?" I asked. "Why would someone like Father Coughlin, who preached against bankers, support a coup led by them?"

Paul folded his hands. "The business leaders stayed in the background, pulling the strings. Coughlin opposed the bankers but supported the coup since he hated Roosevelt and Jews, and loved Lindbergh and the sound of his own voice."

Sarah shook her head. "Any preacher with self-respect should be telling their flock to resist. But none of them do, at least around here."

Micah stood. "I have to go to work."

He left and Paul offered to shuttle me around. "You dress well for a farm boy," he said on the way to the car.

I hated wearing a suit, but didn't have much else. "Just following your lead. But yeah, I need my clothes."

I hopped in the back of his car, Paul and Sarah in front. We stopped at a pay phone and I called my Aunt Joanna, who lived on her husband's farm in the next county.

"I'm headed over today," I said. "Is Aunt Eunice there?"

"Yeah," Joanna said, "and your Aunt Sybil. Eunice isn't talking to anyone. She's taken a vow of silence. Too bad she didn't do that thirty years ago."

"I wanted to know, what did you grab from the house? Like letters and photos. And my guns and guitar."

"Nothing."

My throat tightened. "Nothing?"

"They wouldn't even let us have the scrapbooks. Sheriff Johnson said it was a crime scene, and then the bank would hold an auction. He said our family brought this on ourselves, attacking him and his men."

After all our suffering, they had to pile on? "Call my advocate. Maybe he can help."

"We don't even have money for the funeral. How are we supposed to pay some lawyer?"

I slammed the receiver down, then picked it up again and smashed it against the phone housing over and over. Pay phones were tough, though, and nothing broke.

When I could finally speak, I gave Paul directions. Half an hour west, toward Missouri.

* * *

I didn't say anything on the way back to New Bethany, still trying to absorb it all. My pop was dead and the bank had seized the farm, the house, and all our belongings. They wouldn't even let us have the family photos or my brother's trophies—everything had to be inventoried for auction. Aunt Sybil said the sheriff shot our three dogs, murdered them in their pen. I'd bawled like a newborn at that, embarrassing myself in front of everyone.

The only positive news was, Aunt Joanna's in-laws had raised bail money for Grandpa. He'd be released soon, and there was talk of a plea bargain.

About ten minutes from New Bethany, Paul turned into a wooded driveway. "Could you get out of the car, please?"

My skin turned cold. "Why?"

"So I can access the seat. I have something for you."

I relaxed. "Oh."

We all got out. Paul pulled up the back seat and reached inside. He passed me a small pamphlet titled *On Leadership* by Dr. Solomon Biafra. Inside, the text was written in small type with narrow margins.

"Ben," he said, "I'm putting you in charge of Aaron and Talitha and all the other people you recruited. At this point, they can't know anything about our cell or movement. But they can play a role as a separate cell that you lead."

"I thought we didn't have leaders."

"It's not that we don't have leaders. It's that everyone's a leader. But you have experience and these others don't."

Last time I'd recruited people, Lewison rejected them. But maybe we could frame others who deserved time in prison, like bankers, corrupt cops, and Pinkertons.

Paul pulled out bundles of paperbacks secured by rubber bands. *The Roots of Injustice* and *Revolution* by Solomon Biafra. *Capital* by Karl Marx. *Fields, Factories and Workshops*, by Peter Kropotkin. And *Anarchism and Other Essays*, by Emma Goldman.

"I'd like you to read all these," he said, "and your recruits to read them, once you trust them."

"Why?"

"It makes clear what we're fighting for, and how we hope to transform the world."

Sarah gave a smile of pride. "Dr. Biafra was his mentor."

That explained all the Biafra books.

Paul dumped the books in a paper grocery bag. "I'm a doer, not a thinker. These are some of the thinkers, and they point the way. Once you know the way, you can walk it. Dr. Biafra teaches that although we're constrained by the world we're born in, we're each responsible for everything we think or do within the limits of those constraints—every action, every inaction."

"Tell me something," I asked as he returned to the driver's seat. "Wouldn't a guy like Solomon Biafra be watched by the Insects?"

"He works through intermediaries. I never actually got to meet him in person." Paul started the ignition and drove to the Concrete Arms.

"They should tear this place down," Sarah said as we parked. "Ain't right for people to live like a bunch of termites."

Paul scoffed. "Half of Chicago lives in apartment buildings. Nothing wrong with living near other people."

"I'm with Sarah," I said as we got out. "I'd never live in a place like this."

Carrying the bag of forbidden books, I led them up to Aaron's apartment on the top floor of Building C, the one on the west. He answered the door and let us in.

Someone had smashed a rectangular hole into the adjacent apartment and a man in denims was installing an unpainted door frame. Three familiar faces were cooking Smash—Melvin, the young black man; Esther, the older black woman; and Joel, the blond teenager. All three glared at me, like they wanted to kill me.

"Welcome to the capital of my future empire," Aaron said. He introduced Paul and Sarah to his crew.

"This place is a dump," Sarah said. "And smells awful. How do you all live like this?"

No one answered her. "How many people did the cops pick up?" I asked Aaron. "Did they all get released?"

His eyes shifted up. "Including you and me, there were fourteen of us flyering. They picked up everyone but Festus, who ran off before he got spotted. They bused us all to Decatur for questioning, which lasted three days, long enough for everyone to go through withdrawals. Everyone but you, lucky bastard."

"That's because I was clean."

"They released seven, including me and you, and gave us bus tickets back. The other half are still in Decatur, supposedly getting hospital treatment. Everyone's mad at you."

My chest tightened with guilt. "I'm sorry," I told everyone.

"I went through four days of hell thanks to you," Melvin said.

"Sorry," I repeated.

My vision clouded with tears. "The whole thing backfired. The bank took my farm and my pop got shot in the head. He's dead and my whole family's gone and we lost everything we own."

I wiped my eyes, embarrassed.

Everyone looked down. "Sorry." "Sorry about that." "Beast of a deal, brother."

My skin flushed with anger. "The banks, I fucking hate 'em. They're not doing you any favors either. You know, the most dangerous animals are ones that are cornered with nowhere to go. That's us. We've got nothing to lose by fighting."

I passed out the books, feeling like a real revolutionary instead of a turncoat. "Read these. We'll discuss them afterward, then pass them on to others."

I turned to Paul but he didn't say anything. I handed him a copy of *Revolution* to mark him a newbie also. "You should read this too."

I was craving by this point, and took Aaron aside. "Can you spare a hit?" I whispered.

"For you, sure."

"Do you have any clean needles?"

"There's a bag of points and bottles of hype in the bathroom."

I assumed *hype* meant hydrogen peroxide. "Can you take Paul and Sarah on a tour? They're not really revolutionary material, but they'll give me crap if they see me, you know…"

"Sure. Help yourself to whatever you want." Aaron joined Sarah and Paul. "Let me show you around."

Paul, ever the recruiter, went along, and Sarah seemed glad to escape.

I searched Aaron's room and found a small bottle of Smash, enough for three or four hits. He did say to help myself. I took the bottle down the hallway to the bathroom, locked the door, and shot up.

I must have overdone it, because my heart banged like it might explode. I started to panic, then the buzzsaw swept through my nerves, followed by the cocoon of bliss. I lay on the floor, the dirt and hair-strewn linoleum a sweet embrace I disappeared on.

Pounding on the door woke me up. I crawled to the doorknob and pawed at it until the lock turned and the door opened.

Joel stood there. "I gotta use the bathroom."

"Yeah, yeah." I couldn't stand up, and crawled into the hallway.

Joel went into the bathroom and I lay against the wall.

Someone shook me awake. Joel again. "You overdosed. You need to get up and keep moving."

He marched me up and down the short hallway. No Sousa at least. And no one watching. I had a hard time keeping my balance. I started feeling sick and rushed to the toilet. I threw up again and again.

Aaron returned with Sarah and Paul. They glared at me.

"You got the brains of a dirt clod," Sarah said.

* * *

Back in the car, Paul shook his head. "I've seen more than my share of addicts and alcoholics. Chicago is full of them. But I'm not working with one. It's too dangerous. You need to quit, and wean your recruits off too."

"You wouldn't be in this mess if it weren't for that Decatur girl," Sarah said.

It took me a while to process their words. "You never like any of my girlfriends," I told Sarah.

"That's not true. 'Course, flings is a better term for them."

"Talitha's not just a fling." We loved each other.

"You and Talitha are tight," Paul said. "I don't think you should ditch her. I think you should help each other get clean."

Sarah agreed.

They were right, of course. "I'm quitting as of now," I promised. "I threw up for half an hour. Not fun."

Sarah crossed her arms. "Well look who just applied to Northwestern."

My eyes wanted to close, but I had work to do. "Can you give me a lift to my farm?" I asked Paul.

Sarah spoke first. "You're high as Moonbase Asgard and you want to take on a Pinkerton?"

"It's my house."

Paul's eyebrows raised. "Remember the rules? It's not your turn for an op."

"Not an op. I just wanna get my family's stuff before they auction or burn it."

He didn't respond.

"I have guns there. Two rifles and a shotgun. And lots of ammo."

"Think they'll still be there?" he asked.

"They're locked in a cabinet, so maybe. We can sneak in after dark." The high would wear off by then.

Paul kept driving and I fell asleep.

A hand nudged me. "We're here." Sarah's voice. "Wake up."

We'd arrived at Micah's house. As I fumbled the car door open, Paul told me, "See you at eleven."

The front door was unlocked. Talitha sat on the living room sofa, Ladonna on a towel next to her. Beth sat in one of the chairs.

Talitha peered at me funny but smiled. "Hi sweetie."

I sat next to her and kissed her soft lips. "I love you so much."

"I love you too." Her eyes told me she knew I was high.

"Tests go okay?" I asked.

Beth spoke first. "Results won't be back for another few days. But Ladonna is underweight and underactive, and was behind on her immunizations."

Talitha picked up her baby. "She seems fine to me."

"I'm concerned about you as well," Beth said. "And Ben, I'd like to run some tests on you also."

Concern poked through the Smash coziness. "What kind of tests?"

"Hepatitis for starters."

Chapter Twenty-Six

Paul and Sarah showed up at eleven as promised. We gathered some gear and drove to the farm shortly before midnight. My Smash high had worn off, replaced by fury at the bank and their lackeys.

"Can I borrow your gun?" I asked Paul on the way. "Just in case?" Not that I was any good with a pistol.

"You can grab your own gun if they're still there. And don't worry, I'll take care of the Pinkerton. They're the biggest scum on earth."

"What do you mean 'take care of'? Can't we lock him in a closet if he's awake?"

"We'll see what circumstances dictate."

We turned onto the county road that went past my farm. Ours was the only car. Even during the day it didn't have much traffic.

I spotted our porch light across bare fields, a hundred yards in from the road. "Cut the headlights," I said.

Paul followed my instructions, and darkness turned darker. Patches of stars peeked through openings in the clouds.

"Slow down and turn when I say. There's a mailbox and a red reflector." You couldn't see the reflector without headlights, but the mailbox stood out.

We pulled onto the long dirt driveway, which didn't have a gate, just that stupid 'Trespassers will be shot on sight' sign. When we neared the house, I told Paul to coast to a stop.

We slipped on our wool ski masks and glove liners, hopped out of the car, and walked the rest of the way. The glove liners were too thin for this cold, but we wouldn't be outside long. Paul had cut one of the tips off to free his trigger finger, and carried his .45 by his side.

Except for the porch, all the lights were off. My family's two trucks were parked out front, plus a black sedan I didn't recognize.

Quietly, I led Paul and Sarah to the mud room in back. The door was bolted.

The adjacent kitchen window didn't have a lock, though. I'd snuck through before and could do it quietly. I looked inside, and didn't see or hear anyone. I slid open the window, moved the trays of dead herbs aside, and scurried through.

I opened the back door for Sarah and Paul. The gun cabinet in the mud room was locked and I didn't have a key. I peeled off my gloves and pulled my makeshift tension wrench and picks, fashioned from bobby pins, out of a jacket pocket. It was a simple four pin lock, one I'd mastered in middle school, and took me only a few seconds to open.

Sarah started to say something, but I put a finger over my lips. I pulled out my Remington rifle and filled the magazine. I passed the shotgun to Sarah, and the other rifle, an ancient Winchester, to Paul, along with boxes of shells. Paul propped the rifle against the wall by the door, sticking with his pistol.

Couldn't blame him—have to go with what you're comfortable with. I motioned for them to follow me. We kept our masks on.

The ground floor was deserted. "Can we go?" Sarah whispered.

I shook my head. There was a lot I wanted, mostly upstairs. And I didn't want the Pinkerton sneaking up on us or calling for help. We had to nab him first, tie him up and gag him.

Rolling my feet over the hidden support beams, I crept up the stairs. They creaked behind me. Paul—I hadn't warned him how to step quietly.

I held up a hand, then heard bedsprings rasp. I continued up the stairs and peeked into the dark hallway.

The door to Grandpa's room, the biggest bedroom, eased open. Shit—what do I do?

Behind me, the stairs creaked again as Paul climbed the rest of the way. For a revolutionary, he was an awful burglar.

I raised my rifle and breathed deeply to calm my racing heart.

A man's outline appeared in the bedroom doorway. He flicked on the hall light. It caught me like a deer in a spotlight. A bulky man stood at the far end of the hall in his underwear, pointing a .38 Special revolver at me.

We fired at the same time. A red hole appeared in the man's hairy chest. A searing pain ripped my left shoulder.

The Pinkerton stumbled backward, smacked his head against the wall, and slid to the floor, leaving a bright red slick.

Fuck. My hands dropped the rifle and clutched my shoulder, which streamed blood. Lots of blood.

From the bedroom, a woman screamed.

Paul ran past me. He shot the prone Pinkerton in the head, then rushed into the bedroom. I heard more screams, then two more shots.

Sarah ran up the stairs with the shotgun. Paul emerged from the bedroom, his face rigid. He checked the other rooms.

Sarah knelt beside me and put the shotgun down. "You okay? Oh. Stupid question."

"There's a first aid kit in the bathroom," I said. My shoulder hurt like hell, but I picked up the rifle and scurried into the bathroom. Sarah followed.

I started to pull the medical box out of the towel closet, but Sarah grabbed it from my trembling fingers. "Let me get that."

She helped pull off my coat, shirt, and undershirt, which were soaked with blood. My whole arm ached now, not just the shoulder. She pressed gauze against the holes on both sides, which turned the pain into blinding waves of fire. I gritted my teeth and snorted air through my nose, and remembered the Insects' pain had been much, much worse.

"Sorry," she said. "Gotta stop this bleeding. Hold the gauze, would you?"

I tried to keep them in place with my left hand, wondering who the woman in the bedroom was. Paul had murdered her.

Sarah squeezed antibiotic cream on the back of two compress dressings and rubbed them together. "Take the gauze off."

I did, and she taped the dressings over the holes. She wrapped a thick bandage around my shoulder, fastening it with safety pins. "That should hold till we get to a doctor."

Paul peered into the bathroom. "No one else here. You okay?"

"No, I'm not okay. I just got shot."

"Don't be a baby. It was a low-power round through the shoulder. You'll be fine."

Sarah made a huffing noise. Beneath her ski mask, she was probably scowling at her cousin for being a dickhead.

"I'll get a clean shirt," she told me, and rushed out.

"Good job," Paul told me. "You didn't freeze. You fired on reflex, at center mass. I'm impressed."

"Who was the woman?" I asked Paul. "Did you kill her?"

"I had to. Witness. The Pinkerton was dying—you hit him in the chest with a deer rifle. Probably ruptured his heart. I just finished him off. Sometimes it takes a while for someone to die and they can do a lot of damage in the meantime."

Paul sure thought nothing of killing people. "We've got masks on," I said. "No need to commit murder."

"Couldn't take the chance. No time to reflect in battle. As you know."

Battle? "Was the woman armed or did you shoot her in cold blood?"

He fixed hard eyes on me. "I told you when you joined, we have to take this business seriously. I had to kill dozens of people in Army Intelligence."

Army Intelligence? My brother's nemesis. The bastards who might have killed him. "You never said you were in Army Intelligence."

"I was a sergeant following orders. They stuck me on a retribution crew in Mindanao. We picked up and interrogated anyone suspected of aiding the resistance. Anyone who killed an American, we killed their whole family and burned down their house. Orders from the top."

"You're everything Jake couldn't abide," I said.

He didn't blink. "I got out as soon as I could. I realized my family back home, other black folk, even poor white folk, were as oppressed as the Filipinos. I was on the wrong damn side. I learned about Dr. Biafra and sought him out."

I wasn't in the mood for his life story. "I'll be the main suspect in a double homicide. They'll hang me."

"Well, let's make sure they don't find the bodies."

Sarah returned with a flannel shirt, one of mine, and helped me put it on.

"Let's take the first aid kit," I suggested.

She nodded, then turned to Paul. "Better get started cleaning this shit up."

"Good thing you're a professional," he said.

"I expect you to do most of the work," she responded, voice tense. "It's your mess."

Sarah and Paul wrapped the bodies in bedsheets and cleaned up the blood. They put the bodies in the trunk of the Pinkerton's car.

According to her ID card, the woman was Veronica Burns, age 24. She wore a wedding ring, but the photo of a smiling man in her purse didn't match the Pinkerton. Nor did the Pinkerton's wallet photos contain her. They must have found my house a convenient rendezvous spot for an affair.

"This actually works in our favor," Paul said. "If the Pinkertons find the bullet holes and spray luminol around, they'll know people were shot. But as long as we just take your rifle, and leave everything else, a jealous husband will be the prime suspect."

I wasn't going to leave what I came for. "And what if he has an alibi?"

"Maybe he does, maybe he doesn't. If—"

"We need to get Ben to Micah," Sarah interrupted.

Paul shook his head. "Have to clean up first. He'll be fine."

I thought so too. The bandages had stopped the bleeding. Besides, I had packing to do.

I stuffed clothes, photo albums, and Jake's sports medals into suitcases and boxes. With the pain in my shoulder, I couldn't lift my left arm, so it was slow going.

"Let's just cover our tracks and get distant," Sarah told me. "We should set the house on fire."

"No way. I'm not burning my house down. And I'm not getting shot for nothing."

Sarah shook her head. "Even when shot, you got to be a damn stubborn fool?"

"Would you want your family erased from existence?"

Sarah gave in and sped things up, loading everything into Paul's car.

"My truck will hold more," I suggested as I brought my guitar.

"Someone might notice it."

We finished packing and cleaning about an hour before dawn. Paul recovered all five bullets, even the one from my rifle, which had punched through the wall into Grandpa's room and ricocheted into a corner.

"I'll take care of the bodies and the Pinkerton car," Paul said.

"The reservoir's a good dumping place," I said. "It's an old quarry, deep. Hardly anyone goes there in winter. And if there's any ice, it won't be thick yet."

"My thought too. Sarah, drop Ben off at Micah's, then pick me up at the reservoir."

On the way to Micah's, I decided I could never confess to working for Lewison. Paul had murdered an unarmed bystander. He'd shoot me too.

Maybe I should turn him in. If I turned in his whole cell, Lewison would let Rachel go. Assuming he hadn't been lying.

But how could I do it without risking Sarah? Even if I didn't mention her, the Insects would assume she was involved. She was constantly in Paul's company.

I could warn her and give her time to flee. But she'd never do it. Stand your ground, stand by your friends, that was Sarah.

Chapter Twenty-Seven

Sarah dropped me off at Micah's. I took the two suitcases—I'd need new clothes.

The door was locked. I went to the side window of the master bedroom and tapped on the glass.

The heavy curtains parted. Micah's round face peered at me. He pointed toward the back of the house.

The back door opened as I arrived. Wearing pajama pants and a heavy jacket, Micah stared at my blood-stained trenchcoat. "What's going on?"

My body craved Smash and my shoulder burned in pain. I edged past him into the laundry room and closed the door. "I was shot. Can you help?"

"Go into the bathroom, sit in the tub, and take your clothes off."

"All of them?"

"Wherever you were shot." He went into his bedroom.

In the guest room, Ladonna started crying.

I followed Micah's instructions. The bandage leaked red, but at least it wasn't a torrent anymore.

Micah entered the pastel-themed bathroom with Beth, who rubbed her eyes, then shook her head.

Talitha peered in, wearing her white robe and holding Ladonna. Her jaw dropped. "Oh, sweetie, what happened?"

"Got shot. The shoulder, could have been worse. And my coat probably absorbed some of the energy."

Beth unwrapped Sarah's bandage and peeled off the back compress. I couldn't see her reaction but she inhaled sharply. "I've never treated a gunshot," she said behind me. "Can you do it, Micah?"

Micah gave me a reassuring look. "I was an Army corpsman before they sent me to medical school. I can patch a gunshot."

"The army sent you to medical school?"

"Sure, in exchange for twenty years in the Reserves."

"Does Paul know?"

"Of course. Half the doctors in the country are in the Reserves." He peered at my shoulder. "What kind of weapon?"

".38 Special."

"I'm going to have to clean the cavity, assess the damage, and look for bullet fragments."

I assumed that would make my current pain seem like nothing. "Can you do something about the pain?"

"On it." Beth left the room.

"How'd you get shot?" Talitha asked me.

"Let's save the questions for later," Micah said. "Could you wait in the living room and give us some space here?"

Talitha frowned and left.

Beth returned with a leather bag and pulled out a clear bottle. "We've been stockpiling supplies. At least we're not selling on the black market like some other doctors I could mention."

She filled a syringe from the bottle and injected my arm. "This should help with the pain. I stocked up with morphine today to help transition you and your girlfriend off Smash."

The pain and anxiety disappeared beneath a warm rush and tingling skin, then a pleasant fuzz. Vaguely like Smash.

Micah unscrewed the shower head and attached a metal hose. He ran water through the bullet hole, then poked and probed it. It felt uncomfortable but not intolerable. "You're lucky," he said. "Normal round, low power, went through the muscle. No fragments I can see. Missed the subclavian artery and the brachial plexus."

He pulled more things out of the medical bag. "I'm going to clean the wound and sew you up. You'll have trouble moving your arm for a while, I'm afraid."

When Micah finished, the window drapes were glowing with morning light. Beth gave me a bottle of antibiotics and the liquid morphine.

I sat on the living room sofa with Talitha and the interrogation began. I couldn't focus, and kept nodding off. I told them everything that happened, though.

"Paul killed two people?" Micah asked.

"He didn't want any witnesses."

"Jesus Christ," Beth said. "What the hell is wrong with you all?"

"Ask your fiancé," I said. "The military turns people into killers." Even my brother until his conscience said enough.

"I never killed anyone," Micah said. "And combat is mostly self-defense, and defending your buddies, and following orders. It's not the same as murder."

"From what I know about Army intelligence, Paul was a professional murderer."

Beth folded her arms. "You can't stay here."

Micah shook his head. "He's got to stay long enough to recover."

"And what about us? Aiding and abetting a double murder?"

"Wasn't my doing," I said. Although it was my idea to break in the house.

"We're all in this together," Micah said. "The other things we did, minor though they seemed, and even conspiring together, fall under the Sedition Act. Ten years in a labor camp, minimum."

Beth's lower lip quivered. "I barely did anything."

"Let's not panic," Micah said. He patted my wrist. "You should rest for now."

Talitha examined the bottle of morphine. "I'll take care of him."

Beth frowned. "Ten milligrams orally every four hours as needed. Mix it with water. I had to inject him so Micah could treat the wound, but that shouldn't be necessary from here on."

"You said this morphine was for us?" Talitha asked.

"Yes, it's a lot safer than Smash. You ought to go completely clean, but in the interim, you can at least attenuate your risks."

I wasn't sure what attenuate meant, but didn't want to sound stupid by asking.

Talitha and I retreated to our bedroom. "Drinking this gift would be wasteful," she said, and filled a syringe. "And if she says ten, I say twenty." She injected an ankle vein, then lay back on the bed. Her eyes rolled upward. "Damn, that's good."

I lay on the bed with her, my pain and panic submerged but not completely gone.

She sighed. "I can't believe people died because you wanted a photo album or two."

"I thought we'd lock the Pinkerton in a closet. None of us knew about the woman."

"The police will catch you. They won't stop looking."

"Paul hid the bodies."

Talitha whispered in my ear, "You didn't kill anyone. Worst comes to worst, you can turn in Paul for the murders."

"He'll be hanged," I whispered back. "Sarah, they'll hang her too."

"Better them than you."

"No way. Besides, I shot someone. That's life in prison. I'd rather die than go back there."

She looked away. "Everything was perfect before they showed up."

"I'll talk to Paul. Make an agreement that if one of us gets caught, no matter what, we won't mention Sarah."

Talitha gripped me. "Don't put them before you. I don't wanna lose you."

I drifted off and fell asleep.

* * *

Micah and Beth returned after dark. Sarah came by too, parking Paul's sedan behind the house.

I unloaded my guns, ammo, guitar, and fishing gear. And my brother's high school letter jacket, with *Jake* embroidered on the front. It was covered with patches from all the different teams he'd played on.

The family photos and other keepsakes, I'd give to my aunts and grandpa. In case my aunt's house was being watched, Sarah drove me to an abandoned barn near the county line. We stashed the boxes inside.

At a gas station, I called my Aunt Joanna. Pinkertons couldn't tap phone lines and it was unlikely they'd enlist federal help this soon.

"Yeah?" It sounded like my nephew Matt.

"It's Ben. Put your mom on the phone."

After a pause, Aunt Joanna answered. "How are you, Ben?"

I'd practiced my lie. "I took some things from the house, some of the family history. No one was there to stop me. But if the bank notices, I'll be the main suspect."

Her voice rose. "What are you saying?"

"I take it no one's come by looking for me?"

"Not that I know of."

"Can you pick up the stuff?" I told her where I'd hidden the boxes. "Tonight?"

"Tonight? Well…"

"Please, I went to a lot of trouble."

"Okay, okay," she said. "You're coming to the funeral, right?"

"When is it?"

"The coroner's office hasn't released the body yet, so I'm not sure."

Still? Maybe they were short-staffed during the holidays. "Well, put a notice in the paper so everyone knows, okay?"

"Good idea. What should I do if the police show up looking for you?"

I refrained from smacking the phone against my head. "Say you haven't heard from me and have no idea where I am."

* * *

I woke with vague recollections of Jake crawling through the snow, trailing blood from his stumps. Pop yelling at me for not helping. Rachel trapped in a big goldfish bowl filling with water, trying to shout but no words coming out.

My shoulder throbbed, getting worse by the minute. I shot up with morphine, not a lot, only enough to dull the pain. "Make me one too, sweetie," Talitha called from the bed.

Normally I would have lain in bed with her afterward. But I had to get the cell focused on Rachel. I threw on my winter clothes from the house—camouflage wool blend jacket and pants, lined cap with ear flaps, and snow boots. I slid my hunting knife into my belt sheath, just in case.

According to Beth, American Cleaners and Fixers was on Lindbergh Avenue, five blocks west of Chestnut Street. I had passed by several times, but never noticed a sign.

I kissed Talitha goodbye and exited the back door into the cold. Behind the house was a thirty-acre woodlot owned by an absentee family. It was a miracle these trees hadn't been cut down, although they'd been hunted clean of wildlife. I took a shortcut west through the woods, then southwest along the tree-lined railroad track, invisible from roads or houses.

The cleaning business was in a low brick building sandwiched between the railroad and Lindbergh Avenue, next to an abandoned general store. I knocked quietly on the back door.

A hulking red-haired man in his thirties, wearing a cowboy hat, opened the door. Amos. He'd shaved since our last meeting, back when I joined the cell.

"Well if it isn't Ben," he said. "Come in."

I entered a concrete-floored room with exposed wiring and ductwork, full of cardboard boxes, machine parts, and shelves of tools and chemicals. Messy for a cleaning company. It smelled like bleach and burning coal.

Amos shut the door and slid the bolts home. He led me down a dim hallway, bare bulbs struggling to throw back the darkness. He pointed a thumb at the first door on the right. "I have a cot in there. Wife and kids left me when I lost my job, then the bank took the house."

Sadness weighed down my limbs and I wished I'd taken more morphine. "Know the feeling," I said.

We kept walking, passing more doors. "Kitchen. June's office. Bathroom. Conference room. I set them all up, took what I could from my house."

The hallway opened into a spacious room, brightly lit by fluorescent tubes. The front wall was mostly glass, half-obscured by vertical blinds. In the middle of the room, Paul scanned a newspaper at a desk with a telephone and a paper calendar. Sarah slept on an old sofa wedged in one corner. Paul's younger sister Mary sat in a tattered chair, doing her nails.

Paul asked me, "Did Micah tell you where to find us?"

"I would have found it anyway. How many American Cleaners and Fixers are there in New Bethany?"

He tipped his white fedora at me.

On the sofa, Sarah stirred and blinked. "Deerslayer."

"Sarah Sahara, star of the era." My callback to our childhood name game made her smile.

Mary waved at me. "Hi, Ben."

"You joined too."

She nodded. "I used to work for Spotless Office Cleaning, but the owner's a racist asshole."

Sarah sat up. "She stole some of their clientele. Helped get us started."

"So what brings you here?" Paul asked me.

"We have to free Rachel."

Paul raised an eyebrow. "Any suggestions?"

I could turn in his cell. But there had to be another way. "My first idea was to break her out, but—"

His eyes widened. "Out of a state facility? We'd need trained commandos with armored vehicles or a helicopter."

"And then she'd be pursued the rest of her life, and her whole family persecuted. She'd turn herself in rather than see them suffer." A possible solution flashed into my head. "This Internal Security interrogator, Special Agent Lewison. He has the power to release her. I wonder if we could blackmail him."

"About what?"

"I don't know yet. Lewison works in Decatur and I think he lives in Champaign. That's where we have to look."

If he commuted that far—about an hour drive—he must have family there. It was hard to imagine Lewison with a wife and kids, but Insects had to reproduce somehow.

Paul smiled. "Okay. Beth and Mary are ahead of you in the queue though."

"Everyone else went?"

Sarah responded first. "Paul started the cleaning business. Mine was to free your ass from prison—"

"You're the best."

She smirked. "Don't you forget it. We fit Micah in and redistributed some medical supplies. Then Amos had us burn down the office of the logging company that fired him."

It was them!

"Purely spiteful," Sarah continued, "but June was all for it and convinced the rest of us. She's a nature lover—kind of like you, except she doesn't hunt or fish. She got kicked out of college for organizing protests against strip mining."

"I'm guessing the 'Save Nature' signs were her idea?"

Paul squinted. "How did you know about that?"

Careless of me! I decided to tell the truth. "Lewison told me while he waved Sarah's petition in my face. He wanted to know who was behind it. I told him I had no idea, which was true."

Paul chewed his lip. "Who did he suspect was involved?"

More truth. "He thinks there's some sort of rebellious conspiracy in southern Illinois that Rachel's either a part of, or inspired. He decided I was just a stooge."

"What do you think Rachel told him?"

"Nothing, or you'd have been arrested by now. That's how you know I stayed quiet too."

He nodded. "You and Rachel, I knew I chose right."

"Speaking of, Rachel and I joined before Beth and Mary. It's my turn for a mission."

"Yes," Paul said, "but you went ahead and did things on your own."

Not that again. "Come on—"

"Tell you what. We've already planned our next two missions. We'll do those, and by then maybe you'll have a solid plan for us to follow. So far, you've only got a vague idea."

True. We couldn't blackmail Lewison until we knew his vulnerabilities. "What are these next two missions, and when are we getting them out of the way?"

Paul leaned back in his chair. "We'll discuss it later."

* * *

The Concrete Arms was a five-minute walk from American Cleaners and Fixers. Aaron wasn't in his apartment, although his cooking staff was. An elderly black woman sat facing the window.

"Anything interesting out there?" I asked.

She gave me a toothless smile. "Jus' keepin' an eye on things."

I turned to the others. "Where's Aaron?"

Shrugs and dunno's.

"I'll wait for him."

I snuck into his bedroom—it didn't have a lock—but didn't see any Smash bottles. Either he hid them or took them with him.

He'd added a small wooden table and chair since my last visit. The five illicit paperbacks I gave him lay on the table. In front of the chair, a ballpoint pen rested on a pile of blank paper. Behind it were a stack of envelopes and a roll of stamps. Who was he writing, and why?

I heard the apartment door open, and scurried back into the hallway. A second later, Aaron peeked in from the living room, draped in his heavy coat.

I calmed myself before speaking. "Well there you are."

He strode into the hallway and eyeballed my jacket. "Switched to camo."

"I hate suits." I changed the subject. "How's the reading going?" Not that I had made much progress.

"Where'd you get the books?"

I hadn't invented a cover story. "You can find anything if you search enough. They're inspirational, don't you think?"

"You can't buy Biafra in a book store, or is it different down here?"

"You know who he is?"

"I've heard of him, he's from Chicago. He's old as buried coal, on oxygen, never leaves his apartment. Rumor is, he works for the government now."

Chills rippled across my skin. "What are you talking about?"

"He's setting people up to betray themselves."

That couldn't be true, could it? "How do you know all this?"

Aaron froze for a second. "You hear all kinds of things in prison. Didn't you?"

"Biafra wrote books about revolution. Why would he work for the government?"

"The ISS can break anyone given enough time or the right levers."

Probably true. They broke me and Rachel. "And how's he supposed to betray anyone if he's a dying recluse?"

Aaron shrugged. "Just telling you what I heard. Maybe he has intermediaries."

That meant Paul could be a government agent too. Or was being duped.

But why would Lewison want me to find this group in southern Illinois if he had Paul? No, Paul was probably genuine. Regardless, I'd be careful. I trusted Rachel and Sarah. And Talitha. Everyone else—Aaron included—I had to watch.

Aaron motioned me into the living room. "So where are you staying?" he asked.

"At my aunt's," I lied.

"How'd you get here?"

"You're full of questions. I hitched a ride."

He filled a syringe with yellowish liquid and transfixed me with serpent eyes. "Want some?"

My shoulder ached again. The morphine had worn off and I'd been without Smash since last night. "No thanks," I said regardless. "I'm trying to quit."

He gave me a skeptical nod.

"Pinkertons in the parking lot," the old woman by the window said.

Looking for me? Who else?

I must have given my shock away because Aaron stared at me and said, "They here for you?"

"What do they want?" Maybe I was just being paranoid.

He raised an eyebrow. "You tell me. I heard they came yesterday too."

Fuck! I shoved my head past the old woman and peered out the window. A black sedan like the one at my house was parked in the courtyard. Two men in gray suits and black fedoras stood next to it, talking to Melvin. That weaselly bastard!

"Is there a back way out?" I asked the woman.

"Why, yes. Of course." Her words came painfully slow. "There's stairs at the ends of the hallways. Oh, yes, and the middle. There's doors at the bottom. Four per wing, I believe…"

I lost patience. "Thanks." I headed for the apartment door.

Aaron scowled at me. "You gonna tell me what this is about?"

"Later." He didn't act like he was working with the Pinkertons, but Melvin was part of his crew, and there was probably a reward for me. Sarah, Rachel, Talitha, trust no one else.

I sprinted to the stairwell at the end of the hall, ignoring staring faces. I ran down the stairs, two or more steps at a time, crashing outstretched arms against rails and walls and jolting my injured shoulder with pain. I didn't have time to care, though.

The stairwell doors had faded black numbers in the center. I went down the nine flights as fast as I could. Heart pounding, I exited into the ground hallway and pushed open a thick door that faced away from the courtyard.

A chubby man in a wool coat and black felt fedora stood a few feet from the door, a photograph-sized piece of paper in one gloved hand. He stared at me and glanced at the paper. "Benjamin Adamson?"

"Never heard of him." I bolted for the woods across the street, a belt of skeletal trees along the unnamed creek north of town.

"Adamson! Stop or I'll shoot!"

Pinkertons weren't real cops. They couldn't shoot someone in the back without getting in trouble. Not without prior permission, anyway.

Heavy footsteps pounded after me. I picked up speed.

"He came out the back," a voice wheezed well behind me, presumably into a walkie-talkie. "Running for the woods."

I stuck to the plan, ran across the road, left Chubby behind. They must not have expected me, or were short-staffed, because I made it to the trees.

Snow covered the ground and made my boot prints obvious. And with leaves off, you could see all the way through the narrow strip—it was only four to five trees wide. The creek was incised from old ditching and land clearing, a good three feet below the banks. The water was ankle deep and ice cold; only a determined flow kept it from freezing solid.

I'd played hide and seek plenty of times as a kid. I clambered up the opposite bank, keeping tree trunks between me and the Concrete Arms. I ran out the other side of the trees, then walked backward through my tracks back to the stream.

I scuttled down the creek on my hands and feet, the icy water stinging my fingers and soaking my socks. Chubby shouted from the road, probably waiting for his companions on the other side of the apartments.

I was in my element. No way would city boys catch up, and I wouldn't leave any tracks.

But I couldn't go to my father's funeral now, or see my aunts again. I'd be hunted the rest of my life.

Chapter Twenty-Eight

I made it back to Micah and Beth's house with no one following. My shoulder howled in agony from my bear crawl down the stream, and my hands and feet burned from the frigid water. Frostbite? Hopefully not—I was only in the stream a few minutes and had been moving the whole time.

The back door was locked and the curtains drawn. I rapped on the door, then the dining room window, but no one answered. I pulled my makeshift lock picks out of a coat pocket and opened the back door.

In our room, Talitha's old suitcase lay open on the bed, her clothes and toiletries packed inside. She was leaving? The crib was still assembled. Where was she? Ladonna was gone too.

I peeled off my wet clothes. I rubbed my fingers and toes back to life, then changed into denims and a checkered fleece.

I searched the nightstand drawer for the morphine. Had to get rid of this pain. I couldn't find it, and rummaged through the suitcase.

Talitha's leather bag lay beneath the clothes. The Smash and morphine were inside. Why had she packed everything? I stared at the bottles and gave in to the Smash. Talitha was right, it was better than morphine.

I hit my left wrist and lay back against the pillows. A freight train pounded through my head and left me in shattered bliss.

* * *

The bedroom door opened. I wasn't sure how much time had passed, but I was still a little high. Talitha entered, holding Ladonna. Her eyes were red and moist.

"What's wrong?" I asked.

"Some test results came back. Ladonna's got a bad liver. And I have hepatitis." She started crying.

I held her and cursed God for the sadist he was. "They, they're treatable, right?"

She pushed me away and pointed at the bottles and syringe on the nightstand. "You were rooting through my stuff."

Anger forced its way through the haze and sympathy. "You were getting ready to leave me and take all the drugs!"

"I wouldn't leave without you. How could you say that? But Beth wants us out of her house."

Beth entered the room and frowned at us.

"What's wrong with Ladonna?" I asked her. "And Talitha?"

"Our lab finished the initial tests. Ladonna has a malfunctioning liver. I'm not sure why yet, but it's serious. Talitha has asymptomatic early-stage hepatitis B. You probably have it too. Unprotected sex. Unfortunately, there's no treatment."

Words wouldn't come, only the feeling of more crushing weight.

"I came back to the house," Beth continued, "and brought them to the hospital for more tests. Unfortunately, my supervisor saw us and yelled at me because your girlfriend doesn't have any insurance or money. He said we aren't a charity operation."

"What the hell?"

"You should go back to Decatur. She has a doctor there, and the hospital's a lot bigger."

"You can't treat them here?"

"No."

Talitha wiped her tears away. "I don't wanna be here anyway."

If I returned to Decatur, I could figure out how to blackmail Lewison. My life in New Bethany was over. "I can come with you."

"Can I talk to Ben alone?" Talitha shooed Beth out of the room and shut the door.

Talitha reached behind the wardrobe and pulled out my shirt with the betrayal gear wrapped inside. My heart stopped.

"Is this yours?" she asked me. "I heard it fall on the floor while I was taking my clothes off the hangers." She unfolded the shirt on the bed and held up the tiny camera. "Is this a camera? What's the rest of it?"

My first instinct was to lie, as Lewison trained me. Tell her it was someone else's, maybe Micah's. Or tell her I was using it for the revolution.

I decided on the truth. "Yes, it's a camera and a voice-activated tape recorder. They're mine, but I haven't used them since we got here."

She poked at the tape recorder. "Used on who? Where'd you get it? It's not the kind of stuff you buy at a department store."

I hesitated.

"Ben? I have enough problems, please tell me."

Fear mixed with guilt. "I'm afraid you'll hate me. Which I deserve. Internal Security gave it to me. I have to turn in five agitators so they'll release Rachel."

Her jaw dropped. "What? I thought you were this wild jacks revolutionary and I felt bad Ladonna and I were holding you back."

She shouldn't think that. "You're the best thing that—"

"You're just another informer? Turning in your friends and family?" Her voice rose and she tugged at her hair. "What did you tell them about me? About my sister? Will they arrest me now?"

I tried to wave her volume down. "No, I'd never betray you—"

Beth opened the door. She stared at us, then the camera and tape recorder. "What's that?" She didn't wait for me to answer. "Do you work for the government?"

"I'm on your side. But we'll stop gumming your life. Can you give us a ride to Decatur?" We couldn't take a bus; the Pinkertons would surely be watching. And with Ladonna along, it was too cold to stand by the road with our thumbs out.

Beth turned and strode away. I followed her into the living room. The handset was missing from the phone.

"Micah," she said. "Micah has the keys. I'll, uh, I'll be back." She hurried out the front door.

I had a bad feeling. But she wouldn't go to the cops, and her fiancé seemed harmless. Nevertheless, I packed in a hurry, then loaded my shotgun. If Micah gave us trouble, I'd take his car and get us the hell out of here.

* * *

Standing in the hallway with my shotgun, I heard the front door open and close. I peeked around the corner and spotted Micah with a 9 mm pistol in his hand. He saw me too.

I pushed the safety off and stepped into the living room, shotgun aimed at his head. "Drop the pistol."

He hesitated.

I fought to keep my hands from trembling. "You know a lot about gunshot wounds. What do you think 12-gauge steel shot will do to your head at close range?"

His eyes darted to the right. Reinforcements? I heard the back door open. Should I shoot Micah and swing the barrel around?

I couldn't pull the trigger, but I backed into the dining room so I could cover both Micah and the kitchen, which led to the laundry room and back door.

Paul edged into the kitchen doorway, pistol in hand. Behind him came Amos and Sarah, carrying rifles. Paul and Amos aimed at me. Sarah pointed her barrel down and away.

"Put down the gun," Paul growled at me.

I was up against a seasoned killer but he'd likely execute me if I gave in. "No way. I'll shoot Micah unless you put down yours."

"Where's your girlfriend?" His voice was cold.

I wish she'd stayed in Decatur. I wish she'd never met me. "Talitha's not involved."

"Check the guest room," Micah shouted.

Paul met my eyes. I glared back, trying to disguise my fear. "No way am I letting you past me."

Keeping his pistol on me, he shouted over his shoulder, "Sarah, go get Talitha."

She stared at him. "Excuse me?"

"This is all a mistake," I yelled.

Paul kept talking to Sarah. "Ben'll shoot me, but he won't shoot you."

She shook her head. "Oh, leave the poor girl alone. She's about as dangerous as a three-legged bunny."

"Go get her. At least make sure she's not sneaking out the window."

Sarah grumbled and entered the dining room, rifle still held down. She glared at me and licked her lips. "I don't know what the fuck's up with you. I can't believe you'd betray me." Her face sagged. "But I ain't gonna shoot your girlfriend so don't shoot me, okay?"

I met her eyes, trying to communicate that I was the same Ben she'd grown up with. "Go around Micah, not between us." My voice sounded feeble. "I didn't betray you."

Sarah detoured around him, shaking her head and mumbling. Knowing her, she was probably praying.

I kept my gun trained on Micah. I wished I could aim at Paul, who was the bigger threat, but he'd shoot well before I got the barrel around, and it was unlikely he'd miss.

Sarah returned from the hallway. "Talitha's in the bedroom. I told her to stay put."

Still pointing his pistol, Paul impaled me with determined eyes. "Put down your gun or you die, then your girlfriend. Just like the Pinkerton and his floozy. You've got three guns aimed at you and you know how it's going to go down."

I'd doomed myself, but worse, I'd doomed Talitha and Ladonna. My fingers oozed clammy sweat onto the shotgun. *Breathe. Don't panic.*

Standing in front of the hallway, Sarah exhaled. "Okay, morons. Let's everyone lower our guns and talk like reasonable people."

Paul didn't budge. "You first," he told me.

"Hell no. You think I can trust you?"

I tried to gauge what would happen if I swung the barrel at him. I'd probably take three bullets. Unless they hit me in the head, I'd get a shot off before I died. With luck, I could take out Paul. But once I died, they'd kill Talitha even if Sarah objected. And without my help, Rachel was doomed.

"Ben's bluffing," Micah said, his voice as tense as mine. "He'd have shot me already if he was going to do it."

"Ever heard of dead man's trigger?" I said. "Someone shoots me and the trigger pulls." I had no reason to think that was true, but Paul was apparently unwilling to sacrifice his doctor comrade, and it sounded good.

"This is bullshit," Sarah said. She pointed her rifle at Paul. "Put your gun down."

He blinked. "What are you doing? I'm family."

"Put down the goddamn gun." She looked serious.

With a sniff, he lowered his pistol and laid it on the floor. "I thought we were on the same side."

"Then give me some credit." Sarah swung the barrel toward me. "Now you, dipshit."

She wouldn't shoot me. She was just taking charge, which was fine by me. "Don't let your psycho cousin kill Talitha. She's got a baby, for God's sake."

"No one's getting killed here," she said.

I pushed the safety in and gently lowered my shotgun to the floor. I put up my hands. "Okay, Sarah, we've been best friends our whole lives. I trust you."

"Now go sit down," she told me. "I'm going to get your girlfriend and we're gonna talk this through."

I sat on the couch, surprised I hadn't shit myself. Sarah brought Talitha in, clutching Ladonna. Talitha's eyes were red-rimmed from crying.

Sarah steered her to the couch next to me. I edged over and reached an arm over Talitha's shoulder, but she shrugged it off and looked away, trembling.

Sarah and Paul pulled up chairs. Amos and Micah remained standing, holding their guns, barrels down at least.

Now what? The danger was far from over.

"You're an informer for the government, aren't you," Micah began.

"They don't know anything about you," I said.

Faces relaxed a little.

Might as well tell the truth. "Agent Lewison, the one in charge of my case and Rachel's, let me out of prison so I could spy for him. He said if I gave him evidence to arrest five subversives, he'd release Rachel."

Paul shook his head. "I should have known. Should have figured it out."

"What have you given him so far?" Micah asked.

"I recruited a bunch of addicts at Concrete Arms and had them put out flyers. To save the farm. I was trying to do two things at once."

"And they were all arrested?"

I nodded. "Yeah, but released. Lewison said they weren't worth anything and didn't count toward my obligation."

Surprising he didn't imprison them anyway, though.

Talitha stared at me like I was a wife-beating lowlife. "That was slimy."

I wouldn't blame her if she ditched me. "I know. But I knew they wouldn't get in real trouble, and maybe they'd kick their addictions."

Talitha told the others, "I don't wanna be mixed up in this. Can I go?"

"No one's going anywhere," Paul said, "until we sort this out."

"Please," she said, "let me and Ladonna go."

Sarah scowled. "Would you quit? Seriously."

"If you check the tape," I told Paul, "you'll see it's blank." I hadn't used it since mailing my last report.

He paused before answering. "Maybe you already handed it in."

I wanted to punch him in the face even though I'd earned his ire. "I wish I'd handed something in. Rachel confessed so they'd set me free—and for nothing. I'm her only hope now." My limbs grew heavy. "She doesn't deserve life in prison." Or worse. "She was just trying to help Jake, help his legacy, and make things better."

Paul nodded. "I know. You and Rachel, victims like you, are exactly why I've dedicated my life to this struggle. So you know how much your betrayal hurts me?"

"I didn't betray you. But you sure butt-fucked me, killing those two people in my house. The Pinkertons are after me. They'll never give up, the police either."

"What do you mean, after you?"

"They must have cleared the husband. And I'm the next logical suspect."

Sarah bit her lip and Paul's eyebrows knotted.

I told them how the detectives showed up at the Concrete Arms and chased me, but that I lost them, at least temporarily. "And Aaron had some interesting things to say about your mentor, Dr. Biafra."

Paul was quiet a couple of seconds, then asked, "Like what?"

"That he's a government stooge."

Paul's jaw dropped, then he shook his head. "That's absurd. Where did he get that?"

"Someone in prison, he told me."

"Sounds like we need a little talk with Aaron. He's nosy, that's for sure. If he weren't a Smash head, I'd think he was a spy. Then again, you're a Smash head and you're a spy."

He might be right about Aaron, considering the envelopes and stamps I found. And that Lewison let him go.

Micah shuffled his feet. "What do we do with them?"

"They know too much," Paul said.

"Let Talitha go," I said, my voice cracking. I didn't want to live anyway, I just wanted Rachel and Talitha safe.

Talitha clasped her hands in prayer to Paul. "I won't say anything. I'll help you. Anything, whatever you want."

"The burden falls on you two," he said. "The code is clear about betrayal. But I need to know more."

"Let's bring Aaron in," I said, guts clenched in desperation, "and sort this out."

* * *

Once my nerves had calmed a little, I wrote Aaron a brief letter.

Dear Aaron,

Sorry I had to run. Melvin sold me out to the Pinkertons. I'm not sure what to do now.

Meet me at the cement factory across the street, inside the main building at 8 PM tonight. You'll need a flashlight. Tell no one.

Your comrade,
Ben

p.s. bring some you know what.

I handed the letter to Paul and asked him to drop it in the mail slot for Aaron's apartment. Then I went to the bedroom, where Talitha had retreated.

Talitha was sitting on the bed and rocking Ladonna in her arms. She refused to look at me.

I sat next to her. "I won't work for the government. I'll find another way. I won't turn in any real revolutionaries."

She glanced at me, then refocused on Ladonna. "You absolutely won't turn in me or my sister?"

"Of course not."
"What about Micah and Beth and the others?"
"Them either." Closing off my options.
We sat in silence. My shoulder started aching again. "I need a hit," I said.
She pinched her lips together. "Help yourself."
As I rooted for her leather bag, she said, "Make me one too."

Chapter Twenty-Nine

At 7:30 the next night—New Year's Eve—Micah drove Paul, Amos, and me to the cement plant. Sarah and Beth stayed at the house with Talitha. My meeting with Aaron was at eight, but we needed to get in position first.

Paul carried his pistol, Amos his rifle. I was unarmed—they didn't trust me with a gun. Paul let me plant the microphone and camera in my trenchcoat, though, agreeing it was a good idea to record the meeting.

The old cement factory loomed six stories high in the frozen darkness, massive cylindrical silos on one end, colossal building on the other, all the lower windows broken out. Snow drifted down. It was already ankle-deep.

We entered one of the open doorways of the main building—someone stole the metal doors before I was born—and entered an immense open area, the ceiling sixty-some feet above. Snow blew through the broken windows and formed piles below, but otherwise it was dry inside. I'd almost had sex here once in high school, this girl Lily I'd been trading smooches with. Unfortunately, a bat swooped over our heads just as I was unhooking her bra. Lily had shrieked and run off.

We switched on the flashlights we'd brought from American Cleaners and Fixers. Toilet roll tubes duct-taped to the ends focused the beams and made them less visible from outside. I led Paul and Amos over dusty debris to a cluster of giant rusty vats, each one ten feet high. "Hide here." I pointed to an open section of floor just beyond. "I'll greet Aaron there. I'll cough when the time's right, then you jump out and say 'hands up'."

"Decent plan," Paul said. His eyes narrowed. "No funny stuff."

"It's too cold to be funny," I said out of reflex, and shut off my flashlight. The others turned theirs off, too.

Just before eight, a beam of light stabbed through the darkness from the northeast entrance, which faced the Concrete Arms. I switched on my flashlight and waved it, making an obvious target.

A figure in a heavy coat and fedora entered, sweeping a flashlight toward me. A second figure followed, also bundled up, but with no light.

Shit. Aaron was supposed to come alone.

The figures approached. The first man was Aaron. The second was that blond-haired teenager, Joel, one of my recruits the police arrested. He held a black crowbar in his right hand. And he probably hated me as much as that weasel Melvin did.

"I told you to come alone," I told Aaron.

"We can trust him," Aaron said. He looked sober.

"Yeah," Joel said, equally sober.

"Who else did you tell about this meeting?" I asked Aaron. "I told you Melvin is a stooge. He might not be the only one."

Aaron smiled briefly. "Melvin's no longer able to turn anyone in."

"He suffered a tragic fall from the roof," Joel said. "Nine stories. Splat."

"The cops found a half-empty jar of moonshine where he fell from," Aaron said. "Alcohol's a killer." He smiled again.

Damn. "Well that's one problem solved."

"What is it you wanted to talk about?" Aaron asked.

I coughed.

Paul and Amos stepped out from behind the huge vats, guns in hand. "Not a word," Paul said.

Aaron's jaw dropped and he stared at me. I snatched the flashlight out of his hand and pointed it in his face so he couldn't see.

"Put your damn hands up, both of you." I swiveled the light toward Joel. "And you, drop the crowbar." I jerked a thumb toward Paul. "No talking or that man shoots you. Comes naturally to him."

They hesitated, then put up their hands. Still holding the crowbar, Joel squinted at me, obviously confused. "What the hell's going on?"

Amos pointed his rifle at Joel's face. "He said drop the damn crowbar."

He did. I winced as it clanged against the concrete floor and echoed off the cavernous walls.

I circled behind Aaron and pulled off his heavy coat.

"What are you doing?" he asked.

I examined the coat. It had a hidden camera and tape recorder, which was running. Sure enough, he was an Insect spy like me. Disappointing. I also found two capped syringes of yellowish liquid, presumably Smash. Like I'd requested in my note.

Aaron's eyes widened, then he blinked some sort of rapid pattern at me, like Morse code. Too bad I'd skipped so many Young Eagle meetings and never learned Morse code.

I draped his coat over my shoulder. He shivered, his underlying sweater not enough protection from the frigid air.

I jumped straight in. "Are you working for Agent Lewison?"

His mouth dropped again. "No."

"Then why else would you have the same spy gear he gave me? Why else would you be writing secret letters?"

Everyone stared at me. Aaron sputtered, "You're saying you work... You're admitting that to your partners here."

Hopefully that would draw him out, thinking we were all on the same side. "I don't appreciate being lied to." Ironic but true. "You just happened to board the bus when Lewison let me out, and just happened to enter my life."

"They let me out of prison, you saw it yourself."

"Why did he send two agents?" Maybe I was just bait.

"Why is your friend pointing a gun at me? That's what I want to know."

Paul inched his gun barrel closer. "The thing about guns," he said, "is that we get to ask the questions, not you."

Silence.

"I wouldn't have trusted a stranger in New Bethany," I said, partly to get a reaction and partly to fill in Paul. "But in Decatur, where I didn't know anyone, I'd be looking for someone to trust. You made sure I returned to New Bethany, you helped organize people, and when the cops arrested us, the Insects released you almost as fast as me. Probably released the others too as part of your crew. And you got me addicted to Smash, probably to control me."

Although Aaron was an addict too. Did Lewison know?

Aaron snorted. "You got yourself addicted, you paranoid son of a bitch. I'm telling the truth, I don't work for Lewison. But we're on the same side. Now can I have my coat back? It's freezing."

Paul held up a hand. "Enough." He waved his pistol. "Both of you, on the floor, face down."

Aaron and Joel stretched out on the dirty floor. Paul pulled handcuffs out of a jacket pocket and slapped them on Joel's wrists. "These were for Aaron, but you seem more of a fighter."

Paul caught my eyes. "Let's smooth their edges. Especially Joel."

I pulled a small bottle of morphine and syringe out of a coat pocket. Micah's suggestion, make our captive drowsy and high. I'd only brought one point so they'd have to share.

I filled the syringe to 20 units and injected Aaron's neck vein. He was a careful guy and less likely to be diseased than Joel. I gave Joel more, enough so he'd nod out.

Paul slid a black cloth bag over Aaron's head. "Leave that on."

I transferred the syringes from Aaron's coat pockets to mine, then draped the coat over Joel's head. I lifted him to his feet.

Paul lifted Aaron. "Let's go."

We led the two to the doorway. Paul aimed his flashlight tube toward Micah's car across the street, a barely visible outline through the falling snow, and switched it on and off three times.

Micah's car started. He kept the lights off and drove into the parking lot. Less than halfway in, the wheels started spinning in the snow.

Fuck.

Micah tried reversing, but the car wouldn't move. Just what we needed.

I exchanged glances with Paul. We'd have to help, but what about the prisoners?

He pointed to the car. "You two go help. I'll keep an eye on these two." He spoke in Aaron's ear. "Any funny business and I shoot you in the head."

Amos slung his rifle and we hurried to the car. Micah rolled down the window. "I've got chains on the tires, but it's too deep."

We braced ourselves against the hood and started pushing. I wasn't especially strong, but Amos was built like a bull, and we got it moving again.

Paul brought the prisoners. We threw Aaron in the trunk, Joel in the backseat. Micah headed into town, hands trembling on the steering wheel. "Hope no one saw us."

* * *

Micah drove past American Cleaners and Fixers—we didn't want Aaron to see our headquarters—and turned right on Pine Street. He pulled into the empty, snow-blanketed parking lot of the New Bethany Church of the Revelation, a peaked-roof structure erected around the time I was born. All the lights were out.

We'd scouted the place beforehand. The side door had a simple spring lock, easily shunted with a plastic shim. I opened it again and we ushered our hooded prisoners inside, then down a flight of stairs to a basement conference room. I'd left a portable heater on, and it was nice and warm inside.

Amos and Micah took guard positions upstairs. I shut the conference room door and switched on the lights. Paul seated Aaron and Joel at the long table and pulled off their makeshift hoods. He left Joel's handcuffs on, although it wasn't necessary—the boy couldn't keep his eyes open.

Paul and I sat opposite the prisoners. I started my tape recorder again.

"Where are we?" Aaron asked, his words slow, eyes glazed, pupils pinpoints.

I needed some medicine myself. My shoulder ached, and was bound to get worse.

"You're here to enlighten us," Paul said. "Only the truth shall set you free."

Aaron blinked. "Are you with Internal Security too?"

Paul leaned forward. "I'm asking the questions."

I jumped in. Only way I could keep Aaron alive was to keep him fooled. "Yes, he's with Internal Security. Chicago office."

Aaron peered at Paul. "I didn't know they hired blacks. I thought you were just one of Ben's friends."

"I didn't know either at first," I said before Paul could respond. "But he said he joined when he got out of Army Intelligence."

Aaron turned rigid. "Why am I here?"

"He's down here investigating leads," I said. "He won't tell me what. But he wants to know what we're up to."

Paul exhaled and nodded. "That's right. And don't you dare blow my cover if you value your future."

"He gave me the same warning," I said, then changed the subject. "You knew I worked for Lewison?"

"Of course," Aaron said.

"But you don't work for him? Who do you work for?"

"Sidney. Sidney Gray. He's my handler."

Paul leaned forward with knotted eyebrows. Anxious to take control. I folded my hands and he asked, "He works for Internal Security too?"

"Yeah." Aaron turned back to me. "You'd like him. Feel sorry you got stuck with Lewison. What I hear, he's an insecure, snotty son-of-a-bitch. He's had a nest of bugs up his ass since he got passed up for promotion. At least that's what Sidney says."

That confirmed my guess that Lewison had a low rank for his age. And implied dissension among the Insects. Just like high school—full of ambition, backstabbing, and pettiness.

"Sidney's a chum," Aaron continued. "Debriefs me over beers."

My jaw tightened. "Why didn't you tell me this earlier? I feel like a damn fool."

"Orders from the Chief, Sidney said. Follow your trail and step up if you falter or trip."

"How long you been working for him?"

His forehead furrowed. "Couple of years. He pulled me out of prison—when I got nabbed for dealing stolen painkillers—and offered me a deal. I'd have been there for life otherwise."

Familiar story. Except in my case, I did nothing to deserve it, except maybe not trying hard enough to stop Rachel's rally.

"Like I told you," he continued, "there's slim pickings in Decatur, though."

"Why'd he let you get re-arrested for auto theft?" I asked.

"A ruse. Part of my cover." His eyes began to close.

Paul took control, snapping fingers to wake him. "How many handlers are there, and how many informers do they have?"

Aaron peered at him. "Why do you want to know that?"

Paul smacked the table with his palm, startling Aaron and even causing Joel to stir. "Answer the question. You're watching Ben and I'm watching you."

Aaron licked his lips. "Several case officers at Decatur. Don't know exactly how many. Most double as interrogators, and they each have their own network. There's also psychiatrists and support staff."

Memories of Dr. Malluch and his sadistic colleagues made my legs twitch. "How do the psychs fit in?" I asked, trying to keep my voice from trembling.

"Diagnoses, profiles... And Sidney told me they've perfected the science of breaking people."

They broke me and Rachel. We didn't mention the cell, but otherwise we gave in. And the person I used to be, the farm kid who spent his days fishing and playing guitar, had died. Some of me lay in a grave with Jake, some in a morgue cooler with Pop, and the rest had been electrocuted into vapor.

Paul retook the initiative. "How many informers?"

Aaron shrugged. "No idea."

"Are there any other networks in New Bethany?"

"No, I don't think so. You don't have one?"

"Ben was going to be my first recruit," Paul said. "But he was already taken."

Paul's pretty good at this, I admitted to myself.

"We're the first, it seems," Aaron said. "Federal, anyway. This town's gotta be the least important place in the country."

I tensed at the insult but didn't say anything.

"Five thousand people?" he continued. "No bases, no industry to speak of? They wouldn't have bothered if it weren't for Rachel Tolson. I'm glad to be here, though."

"Why's that?" I asked.

"It's like owning a franchise. And Sidney provided a comfortable allowance."

"So you enjoy this work?"

"Beats lockup."

Anything beat lockup. "Me," I said, "I've got no choice. I have to turn in five revolutionaries for Lewison to free Rachel."

"How many do you have so far?"

Apparently zero. "Lewison's standards are too high. I brought him thirteen people, but he wouldn't give credit for a single one." I wished I could strangle the bastard. I condemned those poor saps to the Insect hell for nothing.

Paul drummed fingers against the table. He leaned toward Aaron. "How do Edna and Talitha fit in?"

I interrupted. "They don't."

Paul narrowed his eyes at me. "I asked Aaron."

"Edna and I," Aaron said, "we have this on-off thing, but it doesn't involve ISS or this fake revolution."

My hands gripped the table before I could stop them. "Fake revolution?"

He shrugged. "There's other Rachels out there. We know that from the logging office fire and the roadside signs, things like that. But you and I have been doing all the recruiting here. We haven't found anyone already involved. Extrapolate to the rest of the country, and I bet most of the people who think they're fighting some sort of revolution are actually in a government net. Waiting to get scooped up or used, like you."

The world turned even bleaker. What if he was right?

Paul drummed his fingers faster, like he was thinking the same thing.

Aaron's head tilted down to his chest. Paul woke him, then asked, "What have you reported back to Agent Gray?"

Aaron scratched his arm. "Not much to say. There's the Biafra books, but that's just Ben conning people." He waved a hand. "This whole meeting is stupid. Here we are, a bunch of government birdies each singing their own song, not hearing the others."

Aaron had no idea Paul was a real revolutionary, if I could call him that, but he'd figure it out if we botched this.

"You're right," I said. "We need to work together." I wasn't sure where I was going with this, but it would be a waste to kill him if he could help free Rachel or get the Pinkertons off my back.

"I thought we were," he said.

"First thing, I've got this problem with the Pinkertons."

"I saw. But you didn't tell me why."

I wouldn't mention the missing Pinkerton agent. I presumed they hadn't found the body or there'd be a big uproar. "I told you about the bank taking our farm. They wouldn't even let us have our stuff, so I broke in and took some of it."

"Good for you," Aaron said.

"Can you help?"

"How?"

"I don't know, have our handlers tell them to back off?"

"Pinkertons are private," he said. "They don't have to listen to ISS if they don't want to."

"I thought everyone had to."

He paused. "Pinkertons have to obey the law, but they're outside the chain of command and the owner's part of the inner circle."

Future bait for my hook. "Second thing," I said, "I need five people of value. Lewison doesn't care about addicts. I was thinking, there's some corrupt sons of bitches in this town." Like the bank manager and sheriff. "Corruption and selfishness undermine national unity. Lewison's all about national unity, fulfilling the Will of History together. "

Paul's mouth opened but he didn't say anything.

"I've been wondering about the bank here," I continued. "First Consolidated. They're evil as hell, and with the Pinkertons, they have their own private army."

Evidence of corruption would be easy. But I'd probably have to plant something to meet Lewison's standards.

"So you think we should investigate them?" Aaron asked.

"Among others."

Aaron turned to Paul. "What do you think?"

"Sounds like you're on to something."

Thankfully playing along, at least for now.

Paul continued, "Not a word to Gray or anyone else about me or our meeting, got it?"

"Why not?" Aaron asked.

"To be successful, covert operations have to be compartmentalized. Didn't they teach you that?"

"Let's keep your handler on the sidelines for now," I told Aaron. "I need those five names. Paul's going to help me, can't you help too?"

Aaron nodded. "Sure. I sympathize."

"We need to hurry," I said. "Lewison's not very patient." Once he gave up on me, they'd carve out Rachel's brain, at least the part that made her Rachel.

* * *

I returned Aaron's coat, keeping his spy gear and syringes. Paul placed bags over Aaron and Joel's heads, and we dropped them back off at the cement factory.

"We have to be careful about Aaron," Paul said as we pulled away. "We can't trust him."

I didn't respond, too worried about how to get Lewison five names before someone killed me.

As we headed back to Micah's, Paul said, "First sign of trouble, I'm taking him out. I'll make it look like an accident."

I assumed that was directed at me too.

Talitha embraced me when we entered the house. She looked high, with droopy eyes. "I was worried you wouldn't come back."

Had she forgiven me? Even though I didn't deserve it? I kissed her, but she didn't kiss back. Which answered my question.

"Did you see Aaron?" she asked.

I had to tell her. "He's a spy for the government."

Paul threw up his hands.

"They should know," I said.

Sarah shook her head. "Figures."

Talitha stared at me. "A spy like you?"

"No, he's a professional. He snitches for a living, although I think he prefers dealing Smash."

"But I've known him over a year. He and Edna are practically a couple."

Paul pointed at the couch. "Ben, Talitha, sit." As if we were dogs. We followed his instruction, though—not important enough to argue about. Sarah and Beth took chairs. Paul and Micah remained standing.

Paul described how Aaron admitted working for an Internal Security agent. He glared at Talitha. "You can't tell anyone any of this. Nothing about Aaron, about Ben, and especially about the rest of us."

She shrank against the back of the sofa. "I won't."

"I think Aaron can help us," I announced, hoping for allies. "He thinks Paul works for the Insects too. I want to go after the bank and sheriff, make them pay for taking my farm and killing my pop."

Talitha nodded. The others looked skeptical.

"How do you plan to sell that to your handler?" Paul asked.

"He's not my handler," I said. "He's my extortionist. I'll find a way."

Beth folded her hands together. "Talitha should go back to Decatur so Ladonna can get the care she needs."

"We need to keep an eye on her," Paul said. "She knows too much."

Talitha's lips trembled. "I won't say anything to anyone. I just wanna go home."

I looked at the others. "We're all equal, right? Let's put it to a vote. Who thinks Talitha should be allowed to save her baby?"

Paul scowled. "Biased wording."

"Okay," Sarah said. "Raise your hand if you think we should let Talitha go home."

Beth, Sarah, and I raised our hands. Micah followed.

Paul shook his head and stabbed a finger at Talitha. "If you betray us, someone will shoot you in the head. That's how it works."

Talitha flinched. "I'd never do that."

I half rose from the couch. "We're all on the same side. No need to keep threatening us." I sat back and told Talitha, "I'll join you as soon as I can. Two weeks, tops." A lofty goal, but I'd try. Every day Rachel sat in prison was a day lost from her life.

Beth rubbed her forehead. "I could drive her, but it's too late now. Maybe tomorrow—it's a holiday and I'm not on call."

I met Talitha's glazed eyes, then addressed the others. "We'll see you in the morning, then." I escorted her to our bedroom.

Inside, I removed the two syringes from Aaron's jacket. "Present from Aaron."

Talitha's grin nearly cleaved her face in half. "Nice. I was afraid we'd run out." Then her face fell. She picked up Ladonna and rocked her into coos. "Here I am, about to get high when my poor baby's sick."

I kissed Talitha's forehead, then her baby's. "Decatur's twenty times bigger than New Bethany. I bet their hospitals can fix anything."

She sighed, then smiled. "Remember how happy we were together at Christmas?"

"Until I heard about my pop?"

"Yeah." She massaged the back of my hand. "Let's forget the rest of the world. At least tonight."

I nodded in agreement, although the world was like a runaway fever with bone-grinding pain, not something easy to forget.

"You and me," Talitha said, face coming alive. "It's New Year's Eve, and I wanna party. It's supposed to be the funnest night of the year."

New Year's. Normally I brought my guitar to a party, jammed with Sarah and the others, got drunk, occasionally got lucky. Sometimes I remembered the whole night, sometimes not.

Talitha settled Ladonna back in her crib and threw arms around me. "I'm still mad at you, but you're my boyfriend and we should be happy tonight."

We made love, got Smashed, made love again, got Smashed again. It was the best New Year's since Adam met Eve, before an Insect tricked them into betrayal.

Voices murmured in the living room, but whatever they were saying didn't matter.

* * *

Someone banged on the bedroom door. Morning light filtered through the curtains. "Time to go," Beth's voice insisted through the door.

Everyone else was gone. While Talitha fed Ladonna, I disassembled the crib.

Talitha kissed me afterward. "Happy 1984."

I couldn't think of anything to be happy about. "You can take the morphine bottle."

"What about your shoulder?"

"Beth said she stocked up." I rooted through my inner pockets and gave her most of my money too. I could always sell my fishing gear and guitar if I got desperate.

Maybe they could help throw off the Pinkertons. "Can you mail some letters on the way?"

Talitha's forehead wrinkled. "What for?"

"Let some people know what's going on, and make it seem like I left town. Send from Springfield if you can." It was the state capital and wouldn't be far out of their way.

She asked Beth, who agreed, and gave me envelopes and stamps.

I addressed the first letter to my aunts and the rest of the extended family, saying the Pinkertons were after me for repatriating our family belongings. I had to split town and wouldn't be able to see my pop buried. I told them to call Preacher Bill and explain what happened to Pop and our farm and ask if he'd help with the funeral. My military service would start soon, I wrote. Maybe I'd volunteer for the Navy, which was a lot safer than the Army. I could make it a career—I didn't have any other options. Or I could hop off the boat and live in sunny Tahiti, fishing in the surf all day.

My second letter was to my advocate, Mr. Gamaliel. I asked him to help my aunts get the farm back, and said we were all being harassed by Pinkertons. Could he help somehow? We could pay him in land—he could have one of the farm fields.

I addressed my final letter to Earl Brogan, New Bethany branch manager of First Consolidated Bank. I demanded the return of our family farm, and warned, "I've got friends in the government, if you know what I mean." I doubted the threat would work, but it might drive a wedge, and maybe they'd call off their thugs.

Beth and Talitha loaded the car, then came back in to fetch Ladonna and say goodbyes. I handed Talitha the letters, and we embraced.

"You promise," she said, "only two weeks?"

My family and farm gone, I had no reason to stay in New Bethany any longer than I had to. "Yeah. And I'll write."

She scribbled her Decatur address on a piece of paper. "Don't forget about me."

"I can't. I love you." I kissed Talitha, then kissed Ladonna's forehead. "And you too, cutie pie."

"We love you too," Talitha said. She shuffled out the door with Ladonna.

I stared out the window and watched Beth drive away with my last remnants of happiness.

* * *

Talitha was gone. At least that meant I could focus on Rachel and Jake. I returned to the bedroom, sat on the bed, and switched off the lamp.

I dreamed about them almost every night. Some visions I could remember better than others, but they always meant something. Whether Jake was communicating from beyond, as Rachel believed, or his memories were prodding dormant sections of my brain, I needed his help. I wasn't strong enough or smart enough to get through this alone.

I had a hard time clearing my head. I kept seeing Talitha in the passenger seat of Micah's car as it pulled away. And my pop's brains blown out. Guns aimed at me. Paul shooting helpless people in the head. Police pulling the Pinkerton car out of the reservoir and releasing a bulletin for my arrest.

Morphine would help, put me in a dream state, but I didn't have any more. I let all the anxious thoughts play themselves out, until only my breath remained. I shut my eyes. "Jake," I whispered. "Tell me what to do."

In the darkness, indistinct shapes organize into silhouettes of the bed, wardrobe, dresser, and walls. Jake stands before me, shadows lifting, lettered jacket over broad shoulders, close-cropped hair, stubble-free cheeks and chiseled jaw.

"What should I do?" I ask him.

You've got to clean up, for starters.

Not the answer I expected.

You're trying to run a race with hobbles on.

You're right. And then what?

You're camouflaged. The Insects don't think much of you. Don't let them guess otherwise. Set out traps and wait in ambush.

Hulking mantis creatures step on spring traps. Steel jaws fly together and clamp chitinous legs to deep-rooted trees. From my perch midway up an ancient oak, I raise my Remington and shoot the abominations between their bulbous compound eyes. They topple, one after another. Rachel lies beyond, wrapped tight in a sticky cocoon. I draw my knife and leap to the ground.

The combine crawls over the field, knifing, threshing, consuming everything in its path, faceless men in black suits and silk top hats at the steering wheel. I rise from my hiding spot in the corn and jab a crowbar into the engine. Metal grinds and snaps and gray smoke pours out and the machine shudders and halts.

Someone knocked on the door. "Are you okay?" Beth's voice.

I opened my eyes to shadows. "Yeah, yeah." I turned on the light and the bedroom reappeared.

Beth entered, a frown on her face. "Are you leaving too?"

"Help me go straight," I asked.

Chapter Thirty

As time crawled forward, my chest hollowed out, body and soul one gaping cavity. My bones ached and muscles cramped. Beth added small doses of morphine to cups of water, enough to smooth the edges and stop the shakes. But I craved the rush and bliss of Smash.

At night, the full horror of existence hit me in the face. Bone-white tendrils of dread poked from the sweaty bedsheets and wormed through my head. My life was over. It had never been anything but pointless. You're born into salted fields, eke out a brief, stunted existence, and die shriveled and forgotten.

Jake shot the child in Cuba, over and over. An explosion blew him in half, over and over. Talitha smiled and called me sweetie. Then disappeared forever, into the arms of a grizzled man who morphed into skeletal Death. Hulking insects strapped Rachel to a gurney and plunged drills into her brain. Trapped in waking nightmare, I couldn't sleep, but couldn't get up.

Once I started screaming, Beth gave me pills to put me under.

Sarah came over and stayed with me. I had trouble following her words, but she swabbed my forehead with a cold washcloth, changed my sheets, and fed me soup.

When I was a little more coherent, she brought her fiddle over and handed me my guitar. We sat in living room chairs and tuned our instruments.

"We shouldn't play any Pale Moon Rising songs," she said. "In case someone hears."

"Then what?"

"Something cheery." She launched into 'Ragtime Annie.'

The guitar part was easy compared to the fiddle lead, but I struggled through it anyway—it had been too long. Sarah was nice and didn't give me the stink eye, but when we finished, she said, "Let's try that again."

Second time went a lot better. "'Whiskey Before Breakfast'?" I suggested afterward.

She chuckled. "I don't recommend it. You don't wanna end up like Mr. Haskins."

"Why not? He's happy and does what he wants."

When Sarah was elsewhere, I wrote love letters to Talitha, although I couldn't give a return address. My hand shook, making my bad handwriting worse.

I asked for more morphine, but Beth would only give me the bare minimum, not enough to get high.

"You'd get a lot sicker quitting outright," she said. "It might even kill you. But if I give you any more, your system won't clean."

Jake and I conversed frequently. Even after death he was a talker.

I'm glad you found a replacement for Rachel. It was creepy, you trying to replace me.

Rachel's smart and brave and beautiful. Nothing to do with you.

You never were any good at self-control.

You should never have left her and re-enlisted. That's the stupidest thing anyone in our family's ever done, and we've done a lot of stupid things.

I know. Forgive me. I hope Rachel will forgive me.

You're in my head. I have to forgive you.

I closed my eyes and pretended Talitha was in bed with me and we lived in my farmhouse and there were no banks or Insects or Pinkertons.

* * *

When we weren't playing music, Sarah and I read from the books Paul had brought from Chicago.

"When Rachel and me first joined up," I told her, "Paul said there'd be a big attack this August, to disrupt the 50th anniversary celebrations."

"Yep."

"Is our cell taking part in that?"

"Everyone is. We haven't decided the particulars yet, though."

Or maybe she wasn't supposed to tell me. "What if it's a setup? Aaron said Biafra's working for the government."

She huffed. "And you believe a word that man says? Besides, the cells are all independent. No one knows what we'll do. Hell, we don't even know yet."

Smash cravings amplified my anxieties. "August is eight months away. Rachel should be the priority now. I don't know how much time she has."

Sarah reached over and patted my knee. "I'm working on it."

* * *

Someone rapped on my bedroom door. Sarah entered before I could respond. Paul followed her, carrying a typewriter and stack of white paper. He set them on the small desk in my room. "Happy 1984."

I sat up. My sheets were soaked with sweat again. "That was days ago. And I've got nothing to be happy about."

"You look like shit, that's for sure."

I hadn't shaved since Talitha left, and didn't have much energy or appetite. At least the hollowness and cravings were less desperate now, like I'd settled into acceptance, and Beth's pills helped me sleep.

Sarah sat on the foot of the bed, squeaking the springs. "Here's something that might make you happy. We're postponing Beth and Mary's missions and we'll find a way to help Rachel."

My fatigue disappeared. I squeezed her hand. "You are the best."

Sarah smiled but Paul didn't. He adjusted the brim of his fedora. "There's too much scrutiny from Internal Security and Pinkertons now, so we decided to stay quiet a couple of months. And see if we can get them to leave. We can't let them interfere with the 50th anniversary campaign."

I threw aside the damp sheets and swung my legs onto the floor. "You'll help Rachel, though? Like you promised?" My nose started to run, one of my countless withdrawal symptoms.

Paul stayed still as a statue. "That was a promise to a comrade, not a government snitch."

I wiped my nose with a handkerchief. "I never snitched on you. I'm on your side. Didn't I prove that with Aaron?"

"Maybe."

Sarah interrupted. "Okay, enough. I trust Ben, and we've already decided we want Rachel freed."

Paul shifted on his feet. "Yes, we did. But it's a lot more difficult and complicated than anything else we've done so far. We'll have to agree on each facet, probably split up the work. And we can't get caught, that would make all our efforts pointless."

"We won't," I said. "Let's get started." I'd promised Talitha I'd been done in two weeks—stupidly optimistic of me—and had already wasted nearly half of that. And Lewison wasn't exactly patient; the longer I took, the more likely he'd give up and have Rachel lobotomized.

I sat at the typewriter to give myself something less panicky to think about. It was black and silver and tinged with rust. "What's this for?"

"There's one for Aaron too," Paul said. "June bought them. Old, but they still work."

He fed in a sheet of paper and turned the roller. "Both typewriters have quirks. Yours skips a space sometimes. Aaron's has misaligned 'd' and 's' keys. June bent the type bars with needlenose pliers so they're slightly above the other letters. It will help identify his typewriter later."

I glanced over my shoulder at him. "In case we want to type something that can be pointed to Aaron?"

"June said we'll need a copy of something he wrote so we can duplicate his typing style too. So we'll give him a typing book to practice with, and keep his discarded exercises."

I hoped Paul didn't plan to set me up the same way. "And why would he switch to a typewriter?"

"I'll tell him orders from above. Reports have to be typed from now on. Easier to read."

I tapped a key, printing a question mark on the paper. "I've never used one of these before."

"Beth can teach you."

I turned the desk chair so I could see Sarah too. It scraped against the wooden floor. "You're positive Dr. Biafra is on the narrow?" I asked Paul.

"Yes. You know Sarah and trust her. She trusts me, and I trust Solomon. Therefore, you should trust Solomon."

Sarah raised a thumb.

Those were a lot of links that had to be solid, but on the other hand, I had no reason to trust the Insects. They sowed suspicion of Biafra, manufactured atrocities like the Kansas City bombing, and got people to inform and spy on each other.

We could be sneaky too, only without committing mass murder. "I think one of Internal Security's strategies is to spark internal war amongst the resistance," I said.

"That is apparent," Paul said.

"Then why don't we do the same, create internal war among the elite? Unravel the threads that hold them together?" Something I'd been thinking about for a while.

He rubbed his chin. "We have a game plan already. But what you said—how would we do it?"

I thought back to twined snakes and *The Charles Lindbergh Story*. "The coup was carried out by politicians and paramilitary troops, organized and financed by rich industrialists and bankers, and supported by church leaders like Charles Coughlin and Gerald Smith. Those are still the three corners of the oligarchy—State, Business, and Church. What cracks between them can we pry open?"

Sarah gave me her 'I'm impressed' smile, which I'd only seen a handful of times the past nineteen years. "Jesus said it himself, 'It's easier for a camel to go through the eye of a needle than for a rich person to enter the kingdom of God.'"

"Yeah, and he threw the money changers out of the temple and called them thieves," I said. "Why do Christians support the bankers then?"

"Religion is a distraction," Paul said. "Always has been. Religious dogma keeps the elite in power, keeps the downtrodden from fighting injustice. If they turn the other cheek, their brainwashers say, everything will be perfect in some fairy-tale afterlife."

Sarah shook her head as he spoke, then stared at him. "I pray you see the light before it's too late."

Paul huffed but otherwise ignored her. "I'm still working on Sarah," he told me, "but you strike me as a fellow skeptic."

"Let's just say if there's a God," I responded, "he hasn't done me any favors."

Paul picked up my copy of *The Roots of Injustice* and held it like a secular Bible. "Religion is exploited by the powerful. Groups like the Dominionists say our leaders are blessed by God and everyone else should obey, like in medieval times."

The Dominionists supposedly had a lot of influence with the elite, but they were only one church of many. "I still think we can turn these groups against each other," I said. "You still have access to books or a printing press, right?"

"Why?"

"Can you get some anti-Christian books? Like about using witchcraft or devil worship to get ahead in business?" I had never seen any such books, but one of my Sunday school instructors insisted there were dangerous people out there who followed Satan.

Still sitting on the bed, Sarah scowled and leaned forward. "How's that supposed to help anything?"

I scooted my chair closer and tried to explain. "We can plant evidence of Satanism and drug dealing that implicates Sheriff Johnson and First Consolidated Bank."

Paul's lips nearly formed a smile. "Revenge, huh?"

"The evidence doesn't have to be strong enough to hold up in court, only in public opinion. Especially the opinion of zealous churchies. New Bethany isn't Chicago."

"I know," he said. "I grew up here."

"People talk. Tell someone a story, and before long, everyone in town knows it."

Sarah nodded. "They sure love to gossip at my church."

I remembered her complaining how ladies at First African Baptist had asked her mother why Sarah spent so much time hanging around white boys, whom she couldn't marry.

"Is there anyone you can pass information to, without them mentioning your name?" I asked her.

Her forehead furrowed. "Keeping my name out will be the hard part, but I can think of some folk."

"We have to reach white folk too." They were the majority by ten to one and there wasn't much socializing between blacks and whites.

"There's also the barn circuit," she said. "We know all the musicians and fans."

"Yeah. And Preacher Bill's church ladies, if I can find a go-between." They gossiped more than anyone. I turned to Paul. "And maybe you could drop some hints at the bar."

"The Deer Head's a deputy hangout, you know. I have to be cautious."

"We just need some gentle conversation nudges," I said. "Like when you were recruiting me and Rachel, only less obvious."

"I'd have to be a lot more subtle. You were already open then, and just needed a little structure."

"We're still on your side," I reminded him again.

This was only the first phase of my plan to free Rachel and bring down my family's persecutors, a plan still partly shrouded in mist. I had to be careful, though—anger the Insects while they still had Rachel, and they'd scoop out her brain.

* * *

Once Beth taught me how to use the typewriter, I tapped out a letter to Lewison. I made a lot of mistakes but didn't correct them, to maintain his unimpressed opinion of me.

```
Dear Special Agent Lewison,

Got a typewriter.  Takes longer but easier to read
and more oficial  looking.

I  have  news.  Your  coleague  Agent  Gray  sent  an
informer  also.  His name is Aaron Little.  I thought
he was a subverive and turned him in to you, along
with  all  those  other  people  who  you  should  have
released  Rachel  for,  but  realy  he  works  for  Agent
Gray.  Maybe  you  know  this.  His  job  is  to  spy  on  me
```

and try and take credit for any subversive that we find.We can work together though. He is very good at manipulation.

Lastly, I have some tro uble with the Pinkerton Dtective Agency and maybe county police. As I told you in my last letter, the First Consolidated Bank took my family farm and my father was killed when the sheriff and deputies came to throw everyone out. His death was an accident but it shouldnt have happened.

Heres the new info. The bank would not let me and my aunts have our family belo ngings even though there ours. So I went into the house and took some things. There was no one there to stop me and its my stuff so why not? I went to meet with Aaron and some Pinkertons chased me. They work for the bank and so does Sheriff Johnson and his deputies.
I cannot carry out my duties with Pinkertons and sheriff chasing me. And I cant go to my pops funeral if they come make a mess. Can you tell them to back off and leave me alone?

Your faithful servant,
Benjamin Adamson

* * *

I was in the kitchen chopping potatoes and carrots for dinner when I heard the front door unlatch. My fingers gripped the knife even though it was probably Micah or Beth.

"Just me." Micah entered the kitchen—I'd guessed right. He had his white doctor's coat on and was carrying his leather briefcase. "What are you making?"

"Stew. Enough for everyone." I laid the knife on the cutting board.

Micah pulled a manila folder out of his briefcase. "Can I borrow your tape recorder?"

"Why?" My nose started running again and I wiped it with a damp handkerchief.

"Paul told me about your plan to drive wedges between the churches, banks and government. I can start the process."

"How?"

He slid some glossy color photos out of the folder and arranged them on the counter. It was the man Aaron and I had dropped off at the hospital. His calf was rotted away, maggots crawling over blackened flesh and oozing red pulp and exposed bone. Remembering the stink nearly made me heave.

"We amputated the leg," Micah said, "but he's going to die anyway. His internal organs are failing. I'm going to give copies to the *Bugle* and the local churches, and talk to them about the drug scourge in town. I thought I'd record the conversations—maybe someone will criticize the government."

"Good idea. Don't say anything about Aaron, though. Or me."

"Who should I say is responsible?"

"The addicts are making it themselves, but the government isn't doing anything to stop it, and the pharmaceutical and chemical industries are hauling in money selling the ingredients. There's no incentive to do anything." This was all true as far as I could tell.

"What about Aaron being a government agent, recruiting addicts to spy on people?"

I did want to reveal that at some point, but the time wasn't ripe yet. "Let's save that for later."

I went into the living room, Micah following, and lifted his wool overcoat off the hat stand. I tucked my tape recorder and microphone inside, and showed him how to use it.

"I'm taking the day off tomorrow," he said. "Wish me luck."

Hard to believe this was the same guy who'd pointed a gun at me. "Remember," I said, "it's a lot easier to say you don't know the answer to a question than try to make up a lie."

He nodded, but sweat beaded on his forehead.

* * *

The next night, while I was in bed re-reading *On Leadership*, Micah returned my tape recorder. He grinned. "June made copies of the tapes. Paul's listening to them."

"What did they say?" I asked.

"There was a lot of disgust. And questions why the government hadn't banned the sale of the ingredients. The Methodist pastor thought we should treat the addicts. The Dominionist wanted to send them all to work camps." He sighed. "Nothing blatantly seditious, though."

I played the tapes on the recorder. Micah's voice sounded tinny through the pinhead-sized speaker.

"That's the most disgusting thing I've ever seen," the newspaper editor said. "We can't print a photo like that."

As I was listening, the back door opened and closed. Sarah entered the bedroom. "Thought you'd find this of interest." She unfolded two flyers and tossed them on the bed.

One had a photograph of the dead Pinkerton detective, with the name Everett Sherman beneath. The other had a picture of the dead woman, Veronica Burns. There was a $10,000 reward for their whereabouts.

Shit! "Where'd you find these?"

"A man in a gray suit was passing them out at the grocery store and talking to people. I acted busy and only mildly curious."

"This man, was he a Pinkerton?"

Her eyes dropped into a 'duh' expression. "Wasn't the milkman."

Probably their families were frantic by now. "I wish Paul hadn't killed them."

She looked down and sighed. "Me too."

The bodies were well hidden for now, beneath twenty feet of murky water and a layer of ice. But once the temperature warmed, people would start fishing and boating in the reservoir again. Would someone find the car, maybe snag it with a hook?

* * *

Paul arrived with a duffel bag, heavy by the grimace on his face. He set it on the bedroom floor and unzipped it. "Here's your witchcraft books."

"Where'd you get them?"

"Dropped at a cache upstate. I don't know who does the printing and I don't want to know."

I wondered where his supply drop was, but he'd never tell me if I asked. I emptied the duffel bag, finding dozens of books, mostly duplicates.

The first, a short pamphlet, was titled *Inno A Satana (Hymn to Satan)*. The left column of text was in some foreign language, the right column in English.

"Nineteenth century Italian poem," Paul said, "a toast to Satan."

Sounded as illegal as you could get. I picked up one of the thicker books, *Principles and Practices of Black Magic*.

"That's mostly about communicating with demons," he said.

"Do people actually use it?"

He shrugged. "It does seem stupid, but we're a superstitious country."

Would he say the same thing about Rachel's ghost book? My back stiffened. Paul shouldn't be so arrogant.

There were only two copies of *The Grand Grimoire*, a thick hardcover book with occult symbols on the front. They looked used.

"That's an old one," he said. "Dates to 1522. It contains instructions to summon Lucifer, then tells you how you can offer your soul in exchange for favors like wealth or power."

Perfect! "Did you read it?"

"I just skimmed the books to see what we had."

The last book was bound in leather, with a strap holding it shut. No title.

"That's the *Necronomicon*. It describes long-lost gods called the Old Ones, and how to summon them."

"And then what happens?"

He chuckled. "Nothing. All this stuff is bunk."

"There's life after death," I said, feeling Jake was watching. "So maybe the rest of it's also true. Why would so many people believe in God all through history if there was nothing to it?"

Paul sighed. "Tell you what. You believe in the supernatural if you want. But ask yourself this—why would an all-powerful, all-loving God permit his chosen people to be exterminated?"

Good question. The American Jews had been exiled to Canada, but in Europe they had disappeared. Millions of people in the 1930's, zero now, with no official explanation. The sheer scale of it turned my skin cold.

God or no God, I had things to do. I had to make my targets seem so repulsive, and the reaction so threatening, Lewison would have to make arrests. I opened *The Grand Grimoire* and began reading.

Chapter Thirty-One

After a week of hell, my body was Smash-free. I felt like a different being, one I'd never been before. It was like I'd been beaten senseless and burned at the stake, but emerged from the flames as a disinterred essence of supernatural energy.

My rebirth was precarious—one iodine whiff, one sight of a filled syringe, might plummet me into groveling like a starving dog. Best to avoid the Concrete Arms.

I'd promised Talitha two weeks. One week left. I washed and shaved, then joined Sarah, Paul, and Mary at American Cleaners. They were loading mops, buckets, and other supplies into the trunk of Paul's car.

"Can I come with you?" I asked. "To search for evidence we can use?"

Paul examined my face, then nodded. "Absolutely."

"You'll have to help clean too," Sarah said.

I'd never been good at cleaning. I fished for a reaction. "That's women's work."

She scowled. "How about I show you how a woman can knock you out?"

I laughed to let her know I was kidding. Sarah stuck her tongue out.

We parked in the small side lot of the American Eagle Insurance office, a two-story brick building on upper Main Street. Sarah flipped through a big key ring and unlocked the front door.

We entered a reception area for customers. No surveillance cameras, but it wasn't a bank or police station. Paul and I slipped on surgical gloves so we wouldn't leave fingerprints.

Past the reception area, rows of wooden desks faced forward in a large room, with a glass-fronted supervisor's office behind. Typewriters, adding machines, and file racks covered the desk tops. Tall black file cabinets ran along the walls.

"Where's the manager's office?" I asked.

Sarah pointed to a stairwell. "Upstairs." She handed the key ring to Paul and passed me an extendable-handled feather duster. "Don't forget to clean."

A wide hallway ran the length of the second floor, flanked by wooden doors. The manager's office was on a corner facing Main Street. Paul unlocked it.

A brown leather sofa hugged one wall, with file cabinets opposite. A secretary's desk sat in the middle. Behind, a second door led to the inner office, with an imposing varnished desk and wood-paneled walls. The heavy blinds were drawn.

The desk drawers and file cabinets were locked, and we didn't have keys. They were easy to pick, though, needing only a couple of bent paper clips and a few seconds of jiggling.

I rifled through the hanging folders in the secretary's office. Mostly blank forms. The faint whine of a vacuum cleaner sounded from below.

"Greedy bastards," Paul remarked from the inner office.

I joined him. "What?"

Sitting in the manager's plush leather chair, desk drawers open, Paul handed me an official-looking document. "This is from the New York home office. Performance review guidelines. It emphasizes growth, earnings, and profitability, and doesn't say anything about helping people who have suffered losses."

"Grandpa always said they were crooks."

Paul pointed to a table full of technical terms. "They set a goal to deny at least 30% of claims. Anyone who wants to get ahead in this company has to deny claims, using whatever excuse they can come up with."

I returned to the file cabinets and finally found something—a carbon copy of a letter from the insurance manager to Sheriff Johnson, complaining that one of his deputies was helping people fabricate auto damage claims. There was no follow-up.

I called Paul over. "Everyone knows how corrupt the local cops are, but here's some evidence. There's no record about how the matter was settled."

"The Sheriff's Office probably promised the manager a cut. This is good—we can add our own material, and people will believe it."

Bingo.

Paul sat at the secretary's desk. "How about this—the cops killed your Uncle Floyd."

"You mean directly?"

"We don't have to change how it happened. He was left alone in his cell with a razor blade. Almost certainly provided by the cops, along with a threat of torture and life in a labor camp."

"Worst possible threat for Floyd," I acknowledged. "No booze and a lifetime of hard labor."

"I bet they didn't want a trial. Bad publicity, what the sheriff did to your family."

My shoulders collapsed at the reminder. I didn't think Sheriff Johnson cared what anyone without money thought, but maybe Paul was right.

Farmers were a defensive lot, protective of their land and families, and might support someone against Johnson next election.

Paul fed a blank insurance form into the secretary's typewriter and started punching keys. "Here's what you're going to discover and reveal to others—your Uncle Floyd apparently named Sheriff Johnson his life insurance beneficiary."

"Why would he do that?"

He stopped typing and tapped his chin. "Threat of torture? How about this—$10,000 to his wife, $20,000 to Sheriff Johnson, and the sheriff would cover the policy fees and kick half his cut to the insurance company to let it slide."

"You missed your calling as a scam artist."

Paul didn't smile. "I'll backdate the application a year before Floyd's death—the sheriff and insurance manager would want it to pass muster." He finished typing up the form and passed it to me. "Can you forge your uncle's signature?"

I only vaguely remembered what it looked like. "I'll scribble it like he's drunk."

Using my left hand, which I didn't normally write with, I scrawled some practice signatures, then wrote *Floyd Bailey* on the insurance form.

Sarah came upstairs with more evidence of insurance fraud, committed both by the company and clients. "A lot of cheats in this town."

We photocopied anything useful, then put everything away and re-locked the cabinets. Paul and I cleaned the upstairs rooms, mostly emptying the trash and mopping. Sarah and Mary finished cleaning downstairs. Before we left, Paul filled a carry bag with blank insurance forms and stationery with the company name on top. "In case we want to write anything else."

* * *

We didn't find anything useful at my church or Sarah's—nothing potentially seditious. Paul thought the Southern Illinois Baptist Association, a regional support group, might hold more promise. They had a one-story building on the east side of town, across the street from a paving company that was shut for the winter.

I didn't see anything of interest inside the Association building, which housed a meeting room, kitchen, and office. But as Sarah and Mary cleaned, Paul searched their files and smiled. He sat at the office typewriter and fed in official stationery. "I have an idea."

"What's that?"

"According to their files, the Baptist Association sponsors missions abroad. Some of these, I suspect, include smuggling."

"Smuggling ... what?"

Below the fedora, his eyebrows dropped into lecture mode. "People. For decades now, churches have been smuggling Christians out of Japanese territory and the Soviet Union, wherever they're persecuted."

Paul knew a lot, I had to admit. "Can they smuggle people out of America?" I'd never heard of anyone trying, but maybe he had.

He stared at me. "If you're referring to yourself and Rachel, there's ways to avoid the police. But there's no place on Earth that's free at the moment."

Except my fishing pond. But that was an illusion.

He hadn't explained his idea yet. "What are you typing?" I asked.

Paul kept his eyes on the paper. "I'm writing letters that will point to a conspiracy. The Southern Illinois Baptist Association is sponsoring missions to Malaysia, one of the many involuntary parts of the Japanese Empire."

"That's in the files?"

He glared at me and sighed. "I'm making it up. But you and Aaron will break in here and look through the mission files, find it and be utterly astonished."

My face flushed. Even if this campaign was my idea, I was still just a dumb farm kid. "So the Insects will think the local Baptists are subversives?"

"Yes, and the more religious leaders they arrest, the bigger the backlash."

My shoulders rose. This might work after all! I shouldn't have felt stupid; Paul was using his talents to implement my plan. We were all working together, and maybe we'd succeed.

Paul kept typing. "According to these documents you'll stumble upon, in return for Japan releasing Christians from prison, the Japanese government wants reports on conditions inside the U.S."

"And the Association agrees, I take it?"

He nodded. "God's flock comes before government bureaucrats."

I'd let Aaron find it. And I could trade some of the names to Lewison.

My stomach tightened. If I went through with this, innocent people would suffer the wrath of the Insects. I wasn't any better than them. I never had been, had I?

Was anyone pure or virtuous? Was it even possible in a world like this?

* * *

The next night, Paul and I parked near the *New Bethany Bugle* building, our next target. It was located on Main Street, across from the Tolson's book store. Dressed in dark clothes, we snuck through the mostly unlit alley between Main Street and Locust Street, keeping to the shadows, not using our flashlights.

The *Bugle* building was dark inside—no one ever worked late there. The back door was secured with a deadbolt. We slipped on our surgical gloves

I'd spent a couple of hours with Amos's tools to construct better lock picks. With shears, pliers, and a hose clamp, I'd shaped tension wrenches, feeler picks, and rakes a lot stronger than bent bobby pins or paper clips.

Still, the lock was a bastard. The easy method, raking the pins while keeping tension on the tumbler, didn't work. The holes were too precisely machined and none of the pins caught.

"Maybe there's another way in?" Paul said behind me.

"Shut up and keep an eye out." I peeled off my gloves, which dulled my sense of touch. I pocketed the rake and pulled out a feeler pick. I probed the pins until I found one a little stiffer than the others. I lifted until I felt a slight click. The pin was aligned with the cylinder shaft, and as long as I kept pressure with the tension wrench, I could move to the next one.

Once all the pins were set, the tension wrench rotated the tumbler. The door opened and I put my gloves back on. Paul congratulated me with two fingers to his forehead.

Micah had scoped out the newspaper office pretty well while pitching the drug scourge story. The next issue was posted in the back room of the ground floor on blue and white layout boards. The room had no windows, so we switched on the lights.

The lead story read 'Car accident hurts two.' The rest of the front page contained the usual government press releases about economic growth and military victories, and a photo of President Clark smiling and holding a baby. The other pages were dominated by ads, with sports, weather, and notices sprinkled in. Nothing about the missing Pinkerton or his bedmate. And no sign of Micah's drug abuse story.

Glancing at the layout boards, Paul said, "Hard to believe there used to be independent media in this country."

He untaped the word search puzzle from its place on the fifth page. He made a photocopy and passed it to me along with a pair of scissors. "Cut out the letters we need, would you?"

Hurrying but trying to be careful, I cut out nine letters from the word search copy and handed them to Paul. He glued them over letters on the original, almost mimicking Rachel's flair for precision. Once complete, the letters NATASLIAH took up two thirds of the bottom row.

Paul photocopied our modified word search and taped it to the layout board where the original had been. It looked authentic.

He stood back and crossed his arms. "Hail Satan. Think anyone will notice?"

"Only one person has to notice it," I said, "then they'll tell everyone else." It wouldn't be the newspaper editor, he took the puzzles and ads for granted.

"We could plant some stories while we're here. Or change some of the wording."

"Guarantee the staff would notice that."

He nodded. "You're probably right."

"We could place some cryptic ads, though."

Paul poked around and found some ad forms and stationery.

"Let's get out of here," I suggested. We'd been here long enough.

* * *

Next morning, I prepared a classified. I picked the 'Meetings' category and wrote, 'The New Bethany Success Circle will hold a special meeting this Saturday.'

At two lines, it cost a dollar, which I stuffed in the envelope with the ad form. June dropped it in the mail.

Then, wearing masks and gloves, Paul and I snuck into the manicured backyard of Earl Brogan, New Bethany branch manager of First Consolidated Bank. We stuck to paths cleared of snow. The Brogans had a big two-story white house with Roman columns in the front and a glass-paned walkway that connected to a four-car garage. Fruits of blood money.

Sarah had asked to come too, but I'd insisted it was too dangerous, and the more people along, the greater our chance of getting caught. The real reason was, if Sarah was arrested, I'd seize up and break.

Paul and I had staked the place out. The Earl was at the bank, and his wife had left for her biweekly bridge game with three other well-to-do housewives. Their four kids had moved out, married or in college. The Brogans already had housecleaning services, but it was just as well—American Cleaners and Fixers wouldn't be suspected for anything we did.

The back door was locked. Deadbolt, but it looked like a standard hardware store model.

I slipped my tension wrench in the back lock and a dog started barking. The rake pick dropped from my other hand. The barks weren't the yaps of a poodle or terrier, more like something with big teeth.

I picked up my tools, feeling embarrassed. What kind of dog was it? Was it trained to kill? The back windows were obscured by white curtains.

A Doberman Pinscher thrust his head through the curtains by the door and barked at me through the window, ears back, teeth bared. He—or she—meant business.

Paul whispered behind me, "Maybe we should go."

My fear diminished. A family, even a banker's family, wouldn't keep a truly psychotic dog in the house. "Nah. Once we enter, I'll talk to the dog, get him to settle down. I grew up with dogs. Unless they've been abused, they're as friendly as animals get. And that includes humans."

Paul didn't respond.

"Keep an eye out, would you?" I said.

"What do you think I'm doing?"

The lock turned and I opened the door, entering a dining room with a polished table and cut-glass chandelier.

The Doberman—a he—thrust his head up to me, shouting in dog language that I had five seconds to live. "No," I said firmly, averting my eyes from his.

He didn't attack.

I motioned Paul inside. The Doberman barked at him as he entered.

"Stay calm," I told Paul, and shut the door. Beyond the dining room, an open door led to a kitchen, and a wide archway framed a living room with plush sofas and a fireplace. Even with a dog, the house smelled like lavender air freshener.

"Nice dog," I told the Doberman. "Good dog."

I glanced at Paul. "Start looking around."

He kept an eye on the dog and skirted toward the stairs at the far end of the living room.

I sang to the dog to keep his attention. "Hey little doggie, what's your name? Don't need to bark, let's play a game..."

Not my finest effort, but dogs didn't know much English. "Would you like a treat?"

His tail nub wagged. All dogs seemed to know the word 'treat.'

I sidled into the kitchen and opened the refrigerator. It was stuffed with food. Hopefully the Brogans wouldn't miss a little. I tossed the dog a slice of ham. He grabbed it from the floor and gulped it down, then stared at me for more.

I had a slice myself, then threw him another. "Hurry up, Paul," I called. I tore off pieces of ham and threw them across the kitchen, one at a time, to keep the Doberman busy.

We were developing a rapport when the dog rushed into the living room and started barking. Paul?

No, a face at the front window, a middle-aged woman's, peering past the half-open curtains. The dog leaned against the window and barked fiercely. The woman stumbled backward and retreated.

Did she see me? Her eyes hadn't locked on me—probably focused on the dog.

Regardless, we had to leave. And we hadn't accomplished anything. I rushed to the stairs, unlatched a waist-high dog gate, and strode up to the second-floor hallway. The walls were covered by silver-framed family photos. No sign of Paul.

"Hey, there's someone outside," I called. "We should go."

Paul leaned out a doorway at the far end of the hall. "Who?"

I peeked out the hall window at my end. A woman in a blue coat, her back to me, hurried down the paved walkway to the street.

"Probably a neighbor," I said. "Either the dog scared her off or she's going to call the police." I hoped not the latter.

"We don't have much time, then. Bring your camera in here."

I entered a study with big curtained windows and a Persian carpet. Silver-framed photographs, books on business strategy, and trophies—mostly gilded men swinging tennis rackets—lined shelves behind a walnut-wood desk and a big leather chair. Below the book shelves, matching drawers with brass knobs were open.

Paul pointed at stacks of papers neatly arranged on the desk top. "Can you photograph all these?"

"Are you kidding? Why?"

"They're bank statements and phone records. I bet some of it's useful."

I doubted we would be so lucky, but maybe we could stretch something into a conspiracy, like if the Earl called pay phones or withdrew a lot of cash.

I peeked out the window, but didn't see any police cars. Yet, anyway. I faced my hidden camera lens toward the documents and started taking pictures.

Paul held up a monogrammed handkerchief with the letters *E. B.* monogrammed on them. "This could be useful. Found it in the master bedroom."

Maybe a little obvious as planted evidence, but we weren't trying to fool detectives, just churchies.

One of the portraits on the shelves caught my eye. Earl Brogan and Sheriff Johnson shaking hands. Brogan was one of the sheriff's chief backers, coordinating enough rich people, ones with a lot of voting shares, to keep Johnson in office. There were photos of the Earl with Congressman Caldwell and the mayor, too.

I photographed them all, then flipped through the bank records until I found pages listing checks to the sheriff's election fund. Thousands of dollars over the past couple of years. Considering Sheriff Johnson ran unopposed the last two elections, none of it was needed. I took more photos, feeling more anxious with each click.

"Let's go," I said. We put everything back and dashed down the stairs.

* * *

The Smith farm wasn't far from mine. And like my family's, it had been seized by First Consolidated Bank. The perfect spot to set up a fake Satanic ritual.

We'd argued for hours when planning this. Amos had proposed an elaborate scheme to steal police uniforms and cars, photograph them at the barn, and leave boot prints and hair samples from our targets. I'd told him that was a crazy waste of time and would probably get us caught. The others had agreed, and instead, we'd bought surplus snow boots, same type as the Sheriff's Office used.

Our entire cell, even Beth, piled into three cars, all of them "borrowed," and drove to the Smith Farm at night. We entered the weather-beaten barn, switched on our flashlights, and traced a pentagram. Sarah placed half-burnt candles all around. Micah spilled blood along the pentagram and poured some in the middle.

I set up an altar behind the pentagram—a small table covered with a black cloth, with a painted cow skull hung above.

The others painted Satanic symbols all over the barn interior. Paul dropped Brogan's monogrammed handkerchief.

Last, we placed a locked trunk against the wall. It contained copies of *The Grand Grimoire, Principles and Practices of Black Magic, Hymn to Satan,* and the *Necronomicon.* It also held a flask filled with human blood from the hospital, a hunting knife crusted with blood, a vial of Smash, and syringes. Or so they told me—I'd stayed far away while they packed it.

Sarah grimaced. "I'm gonna do my best to forget I took part in this."

I wished I could observe the reactions of the churchies who discovered our display. I also wished I could unlock the trunk and inject that Smash into my veins.

You can't, Jake reminded me.

I know.

I hurried away.

Chapter Thirty-Two

The morning after the Smith barn setup, I awaited Aaron inside the cavernous main room of the abandoned cement factory. I couldn't free Rachel or take down my family's destroyers without him. The Insects were more likely to believe him than me. And maybe he could do something about the Pinkertons.

Overcast sunlight dribbled through the broken windows and divided the dead building into bands of dark gray and blackness. I was alone this time, with only the dust and cold to keep me company. I'd brought my hunting knife, sheathed beneath my wool trenchcoat, in case of trouble.

Two silhouettes entered, exhaling plumes of fog and sweeping flashlight beams back and forth. Aaron and Joel, presumably. I slipped behind rusting machinery and switched on my tape recorder.

Once the figures drew closer, dim window light revealed the narrow, sunken-eyed face of Aaron and the cherubic young face of Joel. Aaron carried only a flashlight, but Joel had his crowbar. I stepped out of shadow and aimed my flashlight in his eyes to disrupt his vision.

"I didn't say anything about inviting him," I told Aaron, my muscles tense.

"You didn't say he couldn't come either."

True. Next time I'd be more specific. My note, which Sarah had dropped in Aaron's mail slot, just listed the time and place.

"I'm alone," I said.

Aaron's eyes darted. He waved Joel toward the empty water tanks. "Check the place out. Make sure there's no one else."

Joel nodded and left us.

Aaron shivered despite his overcoat and gloves. "It's cold in here."

"You're from upstate," I said. "Aren't you used to it?"

"I try to stay indoors in the winter. So why am I here?"

Perfect cue for my first request. "We can't meet at your place until you get the Pinkertons off my back."

"I told you before, they're outside the chain of command."

I spoke quietly. "You can spread a rumor—that the Pinkertons are spying on the Sheriff's Office."

"Why would they do that?"

I shrugged. "Let your listeners speculate. You're new here, how would you know?"

"And who did I hear this from? Why would they tell me? Why would I pass it along?"

This was getting frustrating. "You're a spy, you can come up with something."

"And how is this supposed to help?"

"Concrete Arms is full of informers, so you can channel the rumor to the sheriff. Sheriff Johnson has never liked the Pinkertons, says law enforcement is the business of police. Said it in public, even."

"It's a territory thing, I assume?"

I'd hooked him. "You got it. Competition. The Pinkerton Detective Agency has to make a profit, but the local cops have their own money schemes. Ask around, the cops shake people down—" Like Bully-Boy Ferguson robbing me outside the Tolson house.

"I've heard that," Aaron said.

"And they work for banks, like Pinkertons but with the force of law. The sheriff's office serves eviction notices for First Consolidated Bank."

"Like at your farm."

"Yeah." Barbed wire tightened around my heart. "But the bank also hires Pinkertons—as guards, for snooping, and who knows what else."

"Like to track you down for stealing things from your house?"

"It wasn't stealing."

"You'd think that would be a police matter."

"Except I didn't break the law. It's my house, my stuff." Maybe not according to the bank—a paper proclamation Aaron didn't need to know, and in any case, a thin charade over vicious premeditated thievery.

Joel's boots crunched over broken glass in the darkness behind me. At least I assumed it was Joel. Aaron waved him off and reached into a coat pocket. He unfolded two sheets of paper. The missing person flyers.

Shit! I tried not to react.

He passed me the flyers. "How does this fit in? Pinkertons were distributing them."

I examined the notices like I'd never seen them before. "I don't know, they don't look familiar. But I could use $20,000 if you have any leads."

He took back the flyers. "We can work together on it and split the money."

"As soon as I get Lewison five names and he releases Rachel. Then I'd be happy to." I returned to the matter I needed Aaron for. "Sheriff Johnson doesn't like the Pinkertons and vice-versa. It's only natural the Pinkertons would try to dig up dirt on the sheriff, to use as ammunition. If we channel rumors about that to the sheriff, he'll activate his own informer network. We keep the rumors going, maybe he'll evict the Pinkertons from the county."

Unlikely, I thought, but the more distrust between my enemies, and the more evidence for Lewison, the better. "And you can figure out who the informers on both sides are. We can't afford any more Melvins screwing things up."

Aaron nodded. "Okay, makes sense. So that's why we're meeting?"

"Part of it. I need to know also, if you've found any subversives yet."

"It would help if you gave my recorder and camera back."

"I will." Maybe. "But you don't need them to look for targets."

His shoulders drooped a little. "I've been putting my infrastructure together."

In other words, focusing on his drug empire.

He straightened. "I went by the Deer Head Saloon. Only bar in your whole redneck county."

I let the insult slide. "Yeah, New Bethany's dry, but the Deer Head's outside city limits. Sheriff Johnson's part owner."

"Busy guy. Anyway, guess who I saw there! Your friend Paul, tending bar."

"Yeah, it's to supplement his stipend." I congratulated myself on the misdirect.

He sniffed. "It's the perfect job for a government spy. He must hear everyone's life stories. I should open a bar somewhere once I save enough. Maybe I could get Gray to pay for it."

He'd taken control of the conversation again. I didn't have time for his empire dreams. "I've been poking around," I said. "Remember I said, when the sheriff came to evict my family, my Uncle Floyd shot my pop by accident?"

Aaron's eyes drifted down. "Yeah." For an Insect spy, he looked sympathetic.

"They stuck Floyd in a cell at the courthouse, and he ended up with his throat slit."

"Yeah, I remember Paul saying that at Edna's. I really did think Paul was just a friend of yours."

"Acquaintance. I was only eight when he joined the Army, so I never really knew him like I know Sarah." I steered the conversation back on track. "About Floyd, I'd been wondering, how did he get hold of a razor? Then I heard the sheriff netted $10,000 out of it."

Aaron raised a skeptical eyebrow.

"This is real." I repeated the story that Paul and I had concocted. "I heard from this woman that Sheriff Johnson arranged a life insurance policy on my uncle, with Aunt Eunice as one beneficiary, but himself as the other. I didn't believe it, so I broke into the insurance office to find out for myself." I paused. "Don't tell anyone I did that."

"Of course not." He looked sincere, but he was a trained liar. "Gray told me you were a skilled burglar."

"You must know everything about me."

"Enough to know we're a lot alike."

I hoped not. From beneath my coat, I pulled out a manila envelope full of photocopied documents and passed Aaron a copy of the policy Paul had typed up. "I found this."

He trained his flashlight on it and stared. "Insurance isn't my thing."

I led him through the policy. "Ten thousand to Aunt Eunice, twenty to the sheriff—"

He squinted. "I thought you said he only got ten."

"That's because he split his twenty with the insurance company, to pay them off. It was a three-way split, except if my aunt got anything, she's kept it secret from me. 'Course, she hasn't spoken one word to me since I got back."

Aaron peered at the papers. "Looks like the policy was taken out a year ago."

"Probably backdated. The whole thing's a fraud." I breezed past the irony. "I don't know if my uncle cooperated so my aunt would inherit some money, or if the sheriff just forged his signature."

I pulled more documents out of the folder. "I found lots more while searching the office." I went over the company guidelines to deny claims and the deputy's auto insurance scam. "There's more here, look it over." I gave him the folder. "The insurance company, the bank, the sheriff's office, the Pinkertons, they're all corrupt as the devil."

Aaron exhaled fog. "And this seemed like such a harmless little town. So why are you showing this to me? What do you want me to do with it?"

I'd let him run with it. "I don't know. I thought since you have a lot more experience as a spy, you could tell me."

"Well, we're looking for anti-government activity, and sure, there's fraud here, but it's a little outside our scope."

"Isn't fraud a form of economic sabotage? It undermines national unity. And you can't tell me Lewison and Gray would turn down potential arrests."

He pressed his lips together and expelled vapor from his nostrils. "Yeah, maybe. We're talking important people though. Semi-important, anyway. They won't arrest a sheriff unless he's a Soviet spy or something. Tell you what, I'll send your folder to Gray and ask how to proceed."

"If anyone's arrested, I want credit. I need five people to get Rachel out."

"Yeah, yeah, you'll get your five, I know how obsessed you are with that girl."

"Also, that's my only copy. Can you make copies? There's a print shop on Main Street."

He nodded. "Sure."

The Insects might wave off the insurance scams. But more evidence would follow, weaving a web of conspiracies they would have to act against.

* * *

That night, Paul drove Sarah and I to Mr. Haskins's place. He hated the sheriff and preachers as much as anyone, and was one of our best bets to spread rumors.

Mr. Haskins owned about a hundred acres of forest northeast of New Bethany, the largest stand in the county aside from the reservoir park. He sold firewood and hunting leases, but most of his money came from distilling moonshine. He couldn't legally charge, but it was understood if you didn't make an appropriate donation, you wouldn't get more in the future.

We pulled off the narrow county road onto a rutted dirt track through leafless oak and hickory trees. Someone, probably Mr. Haskins, had plowed it. The car bounced over potholes but the tire chains kept us from skidding on the hard-packed snow. Paul slowed to a crawl regardless.

"Should have brought a truck," I said from the back seat.

Paul didn't respond, focusing on the twin beams clawing a path through the darkness. We pulled into a clearing with sheds and an old log cabin. Light from kerosene lanterns flickered in the cabin's two small windows.

Sarah and I got out while Paul stayed in the car, lights off but engine running and heater on. I smelled wood smoke from the cabin.

The front door creaked open and Mr. Haskins, wearing a fur-lined jacket and a crumpled felt hat, strode onto the covered porch with a shotgun. He aimed it at my chest. "You got five seconds to state your business."

I froze, then remembered it was just Mr. Haskins. "Relax. It's Ben and Sarah."

He lowered the shotgun barrel and grinned, his remaining bottom teeth poking up like sentries. "Didn't recognize you, too dark out here."

"Anyone else here?" I asked.

"Just me and General Grump."

His old tomcat.

"Come on in," he said. "Been a while. Hope you brought your guitar and fiddle." He shuffled back inside.

I exchanged glances with Sarah. Opportunity missed.

"Next time, I promise," I said as we followed him into the front room. Heat radiated from the cast iron stove in one corner. Mr. Haskins shooed General Grump off the quilt-covered sofa and gestured for us to sit.

"Drink?" He scratched his grizzled chin and grabbed two small glasses off one of the shelves by the kitchen entryway.

Buying moonshine was my cover. "That's why we're here."

We sat on the sagging sofa and he brought us glasses half-full of pure-smelling moonshine—no solvent odor.

I held mine up. "Better days." Toasts were supposed to be patriotic but Mr. Haskins didn't like the government any better than we did.

He dragged a wooden chair up to the sofa and clinked his glass against ours. I only took a small sip but it still burned my tongue and mule-kicked all the way down. Smooth but extra-strong. Next to me, Sarah grimaced, but didn't cough.

"My special reserve," he said, licking chapped lips. "100% heart, plus some secret steps. Interested?"

I pulled $50 out of my pocket, courtesy of American Cleaners and Fixers. "Can we get it at the regular price?"

Mr. Haskins squinted and scratched his chin. He took the money, opened a cabinet, and brought us four jugs. Two had "SR" penned on the cap.

"Two Special Reserve, two regular," he said. "Only condition—you bring your instruments over some time and we play the demons away."

"You got it," Sarah said.

I took another sip. "Deputies and church ladies still bugging you?"

"I'm paid up with the sheriff, and the churchies don't dare step on my property." He cursed the teetotalers for a while, saying Jesus turned water into wine and got everyone drunk, then switched topics. "Heard about your pop. Awful sorry."

I thought he'd know. News spread in our county like a fire through bone-dry grass. "Thanks." I drew from my well of anger. "The bank and sheriff took our farm and killed my pop—I thought it was greed, but it was more than that."

"What do you mean?"

"They're in a cult. Sheriff Johnson, some of his deputies, Earl Brogan, Mr. Bell the *Bugle* publisher, some others. They meet at the Smith farm, one of the families they evicted, and now at our farm. Supposedly they're places where mystic energy converges."

Sarah glanced at me with a suppressed smile. She and Mary had started spreading vague rumors about cults and secret lairs, mostly by recounting snippets of supposed gossip in front of kids. They'd also dropped a couple of *Hymn to Satan* pamphlets in trash cans on the chance someone would find one.

"Quite a tale," Mr. Haskins said.

"You gotta promise not to tell anyone this next part," I said, knowing he'd repeat it anyway.

"'Course."

"I snuck on the farm to get some family stuff back, and there was a circle of blood on the floor, and weird markings. I grabbed what I could and took off."

His bloodshot eyes widened.

"People need to know this," Sarah said. "We can't have Satanists running the county. No wonder they're making everyone's lives miserable."

"Yeah, maybe you should tell people," I said, "but please don't let anyone know you saw us. I'm trying to lay low. Say you heard it from someone else."

Mr. Haskins clapped me on the shoulder. "Barn circuit, we stick together."

* * *

Next morning, June brought a copy of the *New Bethany Bugle* into the cleaning office. "Paper's out." She opened it to the word search. The letters NATASLIAH took up two thirds of the bottom row.

I laughed and gave everyone a thumbs-up.

"Question now," Paul said, displaying a rare smile, "who will notice?"

"Someone will," I said. "You can bet it'll be a big joke in the schools. Then give it a day, everyone will know about it."

They printed our cryptic ad too. But no sign of Micah's drug scourge story.

"Should Micah complain?" I asked. He never came to the cleaning office—would be too suspicious.

"Waste of time," Paul said. "What I've noticed—Micah too—is that drug and alcohol use increases each year. Same with crime and suicide. But the media's only allowed to say how great everything is."

"We can work this," I said. "Have Micah visit the church pastors and talk about the Smash outbreak. Show them the rotting leg photos, say the paper wouldn't print the story because it was too embarrassing."

Paul nodded. "Good idea, although Micah will want to be careful what he says. Let's go to his place and work up a pitch."

* * *

June brought me a suit, fake mustache, and large wire-rimmed glasses, and dropped me off at the St. Lazarus Catholic Church, three blocks east of the courthouse. The priest, Father Campbell, a young transplant from Iowa, heard confessions most mornings. According to June, a self-professed 'lapsed Catholic,' you entered a box where no one could see you and only the priest could hear you.

June had delivered her fake confession the day before, and had arrived early enough to duct tape Aaron's voice recorder beneath the chair in the priest's booth. Disguising her voice, she told the priest she was having an affair with this well-to-do man, whose name she couldn't reveal. She said she found robes and a Satanic pamphlet in his closet, and instructions on how to communicate with some creature named Baal. She said she wanted to leave him, but was scared. The priest said absolutely she should leave him, and adultery was a sin. With a shaking voice, according to June, he'd asked for permission to discuss the presence of Satanists with his superiors, which she'd granted.

Amos had gone later that morning and confessed that he worked as a private detective and had killed someone. He said was afraid he'd go to hell now. The priest told him murder was a mortal sin, but if it was in the line of duty, that was different. Amos replied that he'd been paid to do it, and the priest had said he'd have to talk to the bishop about it, and he should come back.

Now it was my turn. I'd never been inside St. Lazarus. It was much more ornate and medieval than New Bethany Baptist, with a high arched ceiling, stained glass windows, statues of saints, and burning candles. It smelled of dusky incense.

In a dim hallway behind the altar, the confession booth was carved from lacquered oak, with a door in the middle and red velvet curtains on either side. One of the curtains parted and a middle-aged woman exited, fondling turquoise-colored rosary beads. I turned to study a rack of pamphlets until she left, then strode to the confessional. I pushed aside the curtain and entered a small cubicle, closing it behind me.

Inside the dark compartment, a lacework grille, with small perforations in the shape of a cross, served as a window to the priest, currently closed off by a wooden panel. There was a padded board below the grill. I knelt on it and started my tape recorder, in case someone found Aaron's recorder before we could retrieve it.

The panel behind the grille slid to the right, revealing the silhouette of a man, presumably Father Campbell. He coughed, then said, "Welcome. What do you wish to confess?"

I deepened my voice, as I'd practiced. "I've seen evil things. And done some evil things."

"What sort of evil things?" the silhouette asked. "You must confess your sins to be absolved of them."

I had to seem nervous. "This is all confidential, right? You don't report what you hear?"

"Besides myself, only God will hear what you say."

"Just making sure." I paused, as if gathering courage. "I'm a law officer for the county. But... okay. We do things we shouldn't. We set up scams, like helping drivers get insurance money in exchange for a cut. We help the bank take houses and farms, again for money. We accept bribes to let people off—not just driving offenses, but for anything. Sheriff Johnson and some of his men—not me—are involved in drugs and who knows what else—anything that'll make them rich."

"I see," the priest said, sounding not entirely surprised. "And you are involved in some of these offenses?"

"Not the really bad stuff. But I've accepted money and generally look the other way."

I paused again. "The main reason I've come to you, well, is Sheriff Johnson, some of the deputies, the bank manager, and some others are in some sort of cult. I've heard some talking, and did a little follow-up. They meet at the Smith farm, one of the families they evicted, and sometimes the Adamson farm. Something about places of energy. I thought you should know—it gives me the creeps and the church might want to look into it."

The priest made the sign of the cross. "I'm glad you came to me. May I have your permission to discuss these matters with my superiors? Leaving out your specifics?"

"Yes, but don't mention me or that I work for the sheriff. I have a family."

"You are protected here. But you must do penance. You must reject Satan and all his works."

"I do. I want to tread the right path. That's why I'm here."

"Pray the rosary and act of contrition for each of your sins. Now, repeat after me." He led me through some prayers, ending with, "I absolve you from your sins in the name of the Father, and of the Son, and of the Holy Spirit."

My shoulders shrank inward and I was thankful to be sheltered in darkness. I'd lied to a priest, which wasn't a huge deal in the scheme of things. But I was also exposing him to the wrath of the Insects, which no one deserved, except the Insects performing the wrath.

* * *

Jake, Rachel, Sarah, and I are sitting on the front porch of the farmhouse. I strum the chords to 'Land' on my guitar. They echo through the air, spreading like radio waves.

Paul sits down with a shiny guitar and starts playing 'Sweet Home Chicago.'

Now one and one is two
Two and two is four
Better watch your step
Or I'll shoot you to the floor.

Those aren't the real lyrics. Jake picks up his guitar and Paul fades away.

Four and four is eight
Eight and eight is sixteen
Look here little brother
And learn from what I've seen.

A bright flash washes out my vision. A fiery mushroom cloud rises over New Bethany. Oh my God. I can't breathe. We're trading nukes with the Japs and they've hit New Bethany. The shock wave will arrive soon—we've gotta get out of here.

"Time to wake up."

I was in Beth and Micah's guest bedroom. No Talitha. The overhead light was on. Beth stood by the light switch, wearing her white doctor's coat.

"What is it?" I asked her.

"You said to wake you when we came home for lunch."

"Oh, yeah. No alarm clock." I had a lot of night work coming up and was stocking up on sleep, but I needed to make some phone calls.

We ate sandwiches, then Micah gave me a ride to a phone booth in the south part of town. While he waited in the car, I thumbed through the thin directory chained to the bulky black phone and looked up New Bethany Baptist Church.

I dropped in a quarter, dialed the number, and put my lips against a toilet paper tube to disguise my voice, deepening and echoing it.

"Hello?" Preacher Bill's slick voice.

"Preacher Bill?"

"Yes. How may I help you?"

"I'm one of your congregants. I'm calling because—"

"I'm sorry, I'm having a hard time understanding you."

I spoke slower, enunciating my words carefully. "I'm one of your congregants. We must have a bad connection." Paul had said Internal Security could listen in whenever they wanted, although they didn't have the manpower unless they were working a case. "Maybe the government screwed up the line."

"Why, uh, why don't you come to the church then?"

"I can't, I'm working double shifts. But listen, I found this Satanic poem in my son's room."

"I, I've heard about those. I'm trying to get to the bottom of it."

"Well, you need to do something about it. Shit—sorry—I need to go. I'm straightening out my son—don't spare the rod, Proverbs says—"

Preacher Bill threw in an "Amen."

"But you need to rout Satan's minions and re-Christianize our county," I finished.

I hung up and Micah drove me to another phone, from which I called thirty New Bethany houses and workplaces, randomly picked from the directory. I hung up after the second ring, before I lost my quarter. The Insects didn't need to ring a phone to listen in, but that wasn't widely known, and when people realized how widespread the two-ring calls were, it would bring out the paranoia most folk developed from birth but tried to suppress. The more paranoid people were, the more likely they'd fall for our conspiracies.

I decided to call the same people later on from a different phone. At least the ones I could remember. Maybe not everyone would react, but some would.

* * *

That night, I drove Aaron to the Southern Illinois Baptist Association building in a stolen black sedan—the closest I could find to a Pinkerton car. We wore masks and gloves. I parked behind the Association building and picked the lock of the back door.

"You're good at that," Aaron said once we were inside. "Sure is helpful having a burglar on the team."

I led him into the office. We shut the blinds and switched on our flashlights.

I'd told Aaron—and this was true—that the Association sponsored missions abroad, most people's only opportunity to interact with foreigners. Other than shooting at them, I didn't add. I'd suggested searching the Association's files for any possible connections in enemy countries. Aaron had been skeptical at first, and I'd agreed, but said we might as well look— that was our job. I even returned his camera, although I said I'd deployed his tape recorder and hadn't retrieved it yet.

The file cabinets and desks were all locked, but the locks only had three pins and were simple to pick. Aaron found a ledger in a desk drawer and started taking pictures. I flipped through hanging folders in one of the cabinets without planted evidence.

"Anything interesting?" I asked over my shoulder, hoping Aaron wouldn't give up too quickly.

"Lists of donors and payees."

Aaron finished photographing the ledger and put it back. "You haven't told me where you're staying."

He still hadn't found our planted Malaysia conspiracy. "Outside," I said, "here and there. Can't stay with my aunt thanks to the Pinkertons."

His eyebrows raised with suspicion. "Isn't it too cold for that?"

"I practically grew up outside. All I need is a tent, heavy blankets, and a fire."

He frowned, apparently buying my story. "And what if we get a blizzard? You've gotta find something better."

"Lots of empty cabins and sheds in the winter."

"What about Talitha? She's not exactly the outdoors type."

"I sent her back to Decatur. She's got a baby, I don't want her involved. Just hurry up, okay?"

In one of the file cabinets, Aaron found missionary applications, reports, and hundreds of letters. "Here we go. I can't photograph all of them, we'll have to sort through them."

"Someone has to keep watch. Just look for trouble countries and forget the rest for now."

I returned to the main room and stared out the front windows. No one pulled up and only a few cars drove down the narrow road at all.

Aaron had to find our evidence on his own. But what if he didn't? How would I get him to keep searching without raising suspicions?

After half an hour or so, Aaron motioned me back in the office. He clutched Paul's fake documents in one hand. "These bastards are trading information to the Empire of Japan."

I feigned surprise. "What?"

"They're sponsoring missions to Malaysia, part of the Japanese Empire. They're meeting with officials and getting Christians released from jail."

"And?"

"In exchange, they're reporting on conditions inside the U.S."

I examined the documents and turned my surprise into enthusiasm. "I hope you have film left."

He grinned. "I've got extra cartridges."

I patted him on the back. "Chicken and dumplings." Pop's favorite saying when something actually went well.

Aaron photographed everything. We duct-taped my voice-activated tape recorder underneath the office desk, and left. I would return later that night and take all the fake documents so no one else would see them.

Rachel's freedom was still beyond the visible horizon, but I was finally making progress.

Chapter Thirty-Three

My promised two weeks expired the next day, but my operation wasn't close to finished. I wrote Talitha.

Things are taking longer than expected. Very sorry. I'll be there soon. Love, Ben.

June retrieved Aaron's tape recorder at St. Lazarus. Sitting on my cot in American Cleaners and Fixers, I listened to recorded confessions and took notes. Lots of lapsed faith—I wasn't the only skeptic in town—and some tales of infidelity, but nothing that would interest Lewison.

Sarah barged in. "Smoke on the horizon." She grinned.

I followed her to the big front window, joining Paul and June. In the distance, a plume of gray smoke billowed upward. The Smith farm was in that direction, about that far away. "Would be nice to take a look."

"We can't show interest," Paul said. "Cops will be on their way."

That night, I switched out the tape at the Baptist Association. When I returned to the cleaners, I stuck the used tape in Aaron's recorder, ran a patch cord to a 4-track mixing deck Sarah had borrowed from another band, and played it through a portable stereo in June's office. I turned down the treble and boosted the mid-range to improve the voice resolution.

The tape began with idle chitchat. No introductions. I heard at least six different voices, including Preacher Bill from my church and Pastor Jedediah, the youngish head of the Baptist Association.

Pastor Jedediah talked fast but loud. He led the gathered in prayer, then the group talked about the Satanic altar at the Smith barn, going over everything they'd seen.

"Why'd you have to burn the place?" a slow, drawly voice said. "I didn't get to see it."

"The fewer to see the devil's work, the better," Preacher Bill said. "It'll trouble our county no more."

"Praise the Lord," a woman said.

"Who's E.B.?" a nasally voice asked. "This handkerchief you brought back?"

"Must be Earl Brogan," Pastor Jedediah said. "Manager at First Consolidated Bank. That's all I can figure."

"Who the tarnation else carries monogrammed handkerchiefs?" a deep voice asked.

"I can't believe he'd be involved in something like this," the nasally voice said.

"You cannot serve God and money, Matthew tells us," Pastor Jedediah said.

At last, something worth reporting?

"The Dominionists say you can," the drawly voice said.

"That's because they think ends justify the means," the woman said.

"And the sheriff?" came the nasally voice. "Sure, there are rumors about insurance scams and shaking people down, but..."

"And who do you think led Sheriff Johnson down the path of corruption?" Preacher Bill said. "Who is the ultimate source of corruption in men's souls?"

"So what do we do about it?" Jedediah asked.

"I've written Congressman Caldwell," the deep voice said. "He's a godly man. He'll help."

"Obviously this town needs prayer," Preacher Bill responded.

"Father Campbell is addressing it in Sunday's sermon," Pastor Jedediah said.

"So am I," Preacher Bill said. "May our Lord Jesus guide my thoughts."

"Satan's minions in our town," Pastor Jedediah said, "something all the churches must unite around. Even the Negro ones."

"Nothing can withstand the power of prayer," Preacher Bill said.

I laughed—the sickly laugh of a condemned man at the gallows.

"How about a prayer rally at the courthouse?" the deep voice said. "Demonstrate that while man's law can be corrupted, God's can't."

They went on for another hour, but said nothing Lewison would consider blatantly seditious.

We'd have to prod them some more.

* * *

I was getting sick of skulking around New Bethany, unable to show my face. When I mentioned it to the others, Paul said, "You need a disguise. I'll see what I can find."

June took our available tape recorder to St. Lazarus to record Father Campbell's sermon.

"Some useful material," she said when she returned to the cleaners. "I recorded the sermon and some conversations afterward. Left out the rote stuff."

Father Campbell spoke for twenty minutes against official abuse and corruption, and how Satan's influence had to be recognized and stopped.

After mass, once the other parishioners had left, June approached the priest. "Powerful sermon, Father Campbell."

"Thank you. And you are?"

"I went to church here growing up and I've rediscovered my faith."

"Wonderful!"

"One of my friends," June continued, "said there's a Satanic cult, a real one, in New Bethany. You think that's true? I guess it shouldn't be surprising, given the level of corruption here."

"I've heard it from multiple sources," Father Campbell said, "that yes, there is a clique that's rejected God in favor of Satan and promises of worldly power."

"Really?"

"Did you hear about the Satanic masses at the old Smith barn?"

"My friend told me, yes—on one of the properties the bank took over. But someone burned it down."

"I wrote the bishop and he came in person, with specialists. We visited the site to bless it and remove the stain."

"Scary," June said. "Thanks. But don't you think these Satanists will just find someplace else to carry out their blasphemies?"

"Not around here if I can help it."

June's voice rose. "What they start stealing babies to sacrifice?"

"I promise... I promise it won't come to that."

I copied the tape and erased June's conversation from the original. I typed a report for Lewison and enclosed the amended original tape in a padded envelope as evidence of anti-government activity. I added,

```
It's common knowledge the Catholic Church is loyal
to the Pope in Vatican City, not the President in
Washington. Father Campbell and his associates are
dangerous.
```

* * *

Except for Micah and Beth, the cell held regular meetings in the windowless conference room of American Cleaners and Fixers. Paul brought back news from his bartending gig that Preacher Bill had led a posse to my farm, seeking to cleanse the second hotspot of devil worship. Suit-wearing men with guns had chased them off before they even got down the driveway.

"Good news," I said. "I'm guessing the men in suits were Pinkertons."

Paul nodded. "Fair assessment."

"How many in the posse?"

"Didn't get a number. But the preachers are planning a visit to Concrete Arms next. Hope to turn the town addicts and drunks toward God."

Our work was paying off. "Do you know when?"

Paul shook his head.

"Let's see if we can find out." I'd have to warn Aaron and set up a confrontation.

The mayor and city police refused to get involved, except to tell people to stay calm. Not surprising. Mayor White never did much of anything besides ribbon-cuttings and riding in parades.

Unfortunately though, Sheriff Johnson fought back, visiting the town pastors and the newspaper office. He visited Brother Jedediah at the Baptist Association too. I listened to the recording.

"There's talk around town about me," the sheriff said in his gravelly voice. "Being a devil worshiper. I want you to know, right now, that's complete nonsense. I'm as God-fearing a Christian as anyone else, and so are my deputies."

"Well, that's good to hear," Brother Jedediah said.

"I won't stand for smears of my good character."

"You belong to a church?"

"First Methodist," the sheriff said.

"And you attend every Sunday?"

"I go when my duties allow it. I have to uphold the law seven days a week."

"God's law supersedes that of men. You should attend church every Sunday and study the Bible daily."

I heard a chair scrape. "Tell you what. I'll commit to that. Church every Sunday and I'll crack open a Bible." He sounded insincere even on the recording.

I typed a letter to Lewison, saying he should bring in Brother Jedediah. He thought God's law should supersede the government. Which explained what Aaron had found at the Baptist Association, that freeing Christians was worth providing secrets to the Japanese Empire.

* * *

Time to stoke the fires. I called the Sheriff's Office from a pay phone and told the receptionist, "I've got some information for the sheriff. I would dearly like him to stay in office—he's a mighty reasonable guy—but Preacher Bill and Father Campbell are trying to replace him, either next election or sooner. They concocted some bullshit about a Satanic conspiracy and they'll get their own candidate in unless you do something."

Next, I called the county courthouse and told the receptionist that a bunch of Jesus nuts were planning to take over the building. I called the First Consolidated Bank and said I'd heard Preacher Bill bragged about burning down the Smith barn.

Sarah and Mary discussed the impending courthouse takeover in front of kids who knew Will Coulter's kids. Being unusually motivated for an informer, Coulter would most likely find out and pass the information to the police. But Sarah and Mary would just be two colored ladies, if they were mentioned at all.

Chapter Thirty-Four

In the darkness before dawn, I tromped across a snowy field of weed stalks to an abandoned trailer circled by barren trees. The back door had no lock—not surprising. Once inside, I switched on my flashlight and swung the beam around, avoiding the grimy windows. Mice scurried for cover. Other than that, the trailer was mostly empty except a tattered sofa and wooden table.

The property, which was too small to make a living farming, had been abandoned for years. I wasn't sure what happened to the owners. Moved away, looking for work? Killed overseas? Sent to a labor camp?

I switched off the flashlight and sat on the sofa, throwing a cloud of dust and mildew into the still air. The old factory was a better spot for a rendezvous, but with Pinkertons on the prowl, it was safer to change locations.

Aaron arrived an hour after sunrise, sniffing the musty interior. Joel entered behind him, carrying his crowbar. Ever the faithful guard dog.

"It's freezing in here," Aaron said after stomping the snow off his boots.

Complaining about the cold again. "Sorry," I said. "No power, no stove."

I stood and kicked off my story. "The church leaders are planning a coup."

Aaron stared like he didn't believe me.

"I thought you'd be interested," I said.

"How?"

"Popular uprising, I suppose. Can you ask Gray for advice?"

"What's your proof?"

I handed him an envelope with a copied recording of Father Campbell's anti-corruption sermon and Brother Jedediah telling the sheriff to put God's law before man's.

"There's more," I said after summarizing the contents. "Preacher Bill and Brother Jedediah are planning a big rally at the county courthouse." I gave him the details, which I'd learned last night.

He peered inside the envelope, then met my eyes. "I'll look into it."

I stepped closer. "We need Gray's help on this, but I want credit for the arrests with Lewison."

Aaron rolled his eyes. "Yeah, yeah. I don't have a quota to meet, so fine by me."

"And you should know, some of the preachers are organizing a posse to raid Concrete Arms."

His eyes widened. "What?"

"Part of their crusade to cleanse the town."

"How many people? Are they bringing police?"

"Doubt it. And I don't know how many. But you should contact the owner. The churchies might try to burn his buildings down like they burned down that barn. He should hire guards. Like Pinkertons—they'll do it."

"I thought you hated the Pinkertons."

Aaron and his questions. "I do. But it'll give them something to do instead searching for me. And they're more reliable than off-duty cops."

"I've got some guards."

"Well mobilize them, organize all the residents. A lot of people live there. They can throw back some churchies, easy."

* * *

Soon after I returned to American Cleaners and Fixers, Paul entered with a bulging laundry bag. "Your stage supplies have arrived."

Amos followed him in, carrying a heavy-looking wooden box.

"What's in the box?" I asked.

Amos ignored me and went down the hallway toward the back room.

"More supplies," Paul said. "For disrupting the coup celebrations. Let me show you what I got."

Sarah and I followed Paul into June's office. He shut the door and dumped the bag contents onto the mostly-bare wooden desk. Mostly clothes, but also a gray wig and beard, black-framed glasses, and a makeup kit. And a book titled *The Complete Guide to Stage Makeup*.

I put on the wig and glasses. "Will this really fool people?"

Sarah opened the book. "If you're different enough. I thought I'd make you an old man. You'd be way too ugly as a woman."

"That's meant as a compliment, right?"

"Yeah, sure, a compliment." She rolled her eyes and I laughed inside.

She ushered me to one of the cracked leather visitor chairs and rubbed creme on my face.

Paul sat in the swivel chair behind the desk and tapped the desktop with a finger. "Talk around town is Congressman Caldwell initiated a federal investigation into the Sheriff's Office. Maybe New Bethany in general."

That meant Internal Security. No way would someone steal my shot at five names. "I'll write Lewison. Tell him he should be in charge of all New Bethany investigations, since he already has agents here."

"I can see him agreeing, but do you think he has the clout?"

I pushed Sarah's hand away from my face. "Aaron can tell Gray the same thing. And if they send someone else, I'll introduce myself, tell them I work for Agent Lewison, and be their inside man."

Paul nodded, but his eyes shifted away like he was thinking about it.

"Can I finish now?" Sarah asked.

I nodded. "Sorry."

With a thin brush, she drew lines and dabbed spots on my face. She switched to swabs and small sponges, then stared at me and shook her head.

"That bad, huh?" I said.

"Can't always catch a fish on the first cast." She spent another half hour on my face, glued on the gray mustache and beard, and shoved on the wig and glasses. The glasses had non-corrective lenses, like a display model.

She passed me a hand mirror. "What do you think?"

I looked forty years older, if I'd grown a beard like Grandpa and had to wear eyeglasses.

What were the chances I'd be alive forty years from now? What were the chances I'd last forty more days?

* * *

The day of the preachers' rally, Sarah re-applied my makeup, and I trudged over to the county courthouse. The morning was windy, gray, and bitter cold.

The church leaders would be rabid as daytime raccoons. Aaron had told me several carloads of churchies had assembled in the Concrete Arms parking lot, but a combined army of residents and hired Pinkertons chased them off. I wished I'd been there to watch.

The preachers had set up a microphone and amplifier outside the courthouse, like I had last year. They'd drawn a bigger crowd than Rachel. But it still only numbered a couple hundred, hands thrust in jacket pockets, feet tapping and shuffling. Of course, it was the middle of winter, and the violent crackdown at Rachel's rally might have scared people away.

As before, city and county cops stood around the perimeter and eyed the crowd. A grim-faced man in a wool coat took pictures. I recognized him from Rachel's rally. Another man pointed a long-lensed camera from a courthouse window.

I stuck to the fringes and avoided conversation. I spotted Aaron, but he didn't seem to notice me. An old woman in a bright red coat and feathered hat approached me. "Which church do you belong to?"

Was she an informer? I pointed to my throat and whispered, "Strep throat."

Her eyes widened and she backed away. "You should be home in bed."

Preacher Bill was first at the mike. His entourage of Praise the Lord housewives edged closer. I started my tape recorder.

"Friends," the preacher began. "Brothers and sisters in Christ. I apologize for the cold. We were hoping to meet inside the courthouse, but ill-intentioned bureaucrats refused us."

My phone call or the informer route must have worked.

"So we'll have to make this brief." Preacher Bill flung up his arms. "Let us pray for our town and our nation, and let us cast the Devil from our midst."

His entourage shouted a clamor of amens.

He opened a Bible and began reading in melodramatic tones. "Be strong in the Lord and in the strength of his might! Put on the whole armor of God, that you may be able to stand against the schemes of the devil! For we do not wrestle against flesh and blood, but against the rulers, against the authorities…"

Good material for Lewison.

He invoked Luke next. "Behold, I have given you authority to tread on serpents and scorpions, and over all the power of the enemy…"

More useful material.

Father Campbell spoke next, followed by four other pastors. Each led prayers for the salvation of souls and to cast out the devil. "Lord," one said, "even the demons are subject to us in your name!"

If the Insects weren't demons, I didn't know who was.

Brother Jedediah concluded the meeting. By now, half the crowd had capitulated to the frigid wind and hurried to warmer places.

"We need your help," Brother Jedediah proclaimed. "Contact your pastor. Come by the Baptist Association. If you don't know where we are, we're on Milkweed Lane, near the high school."

Next to him, Preacher Bill exclaimed, "We're all in this together! Let us destroy the works of the devil!"

"Now," Brother Jedediah continued, "the Satanic temple on the Smith farm was demolished and set aflame, but there is another. Some of us went to look, but were chased away by hired men with guns. There are more armed men at the Concrete Arms, defending a drug factory that's killing and enslaving people. We've appealed to the authorities, but they've done nothing."

"They're complicit!" Preacher Bill shouted.

"But all of us together," Brother Jedediah said, "can overcome this scourge. Fix this town. Restore Christian values!"

A city sergeant and a sheriff's deputy scribbled in notepads. But the police didn't move to arrest anyone. Probably because the preachers had a lot more clout than Rachel and I. If arrests followed—and I hoped, for Rachel's sake, they would—they'd be less public.

* * *

The following night, I rode with Amos in our stolen black sedan to New Bethany Baptist Church. We wore standard Pinkerton outfits—gray suits and black fedoras.

We parked across the street and waited for Preacher Bill to head home. I wanted to motivate the clergy even more by faking an assassination attempt. I just hoped I didn't hit our target by accident.

"Heard from your girl?" Amos asked me.

"I don't have an address."

"Paul shouldn't have let her leave. I wasn't there and didn't get a say."

I cast the stink eye at him. "Wouldn't matter, he was outvoted four to one."

"I would have said something."

"She won't talk. If she had, we'd have been arrested already."

The lights inside the church went out. My heartbeat quickened. "He's coming."

Amos put his hand on the ignition key but didn't turn it.

I wrapped a Navy-blue bandanna over my face, just below the eyes, and rolled down the passenger window. I gripped my Remington rifle.

The front door of the church opened. Amos started the car but kept it in neutral.

Preacher Bill exited, keys in hand. I rested the rifle barrel on the window frame and pushed the safety off. I pulled the bolt up and back to load a cartridge into the chamber, pushed it back in, held my breath, and aimed.

The preacher spotted the gun aimed at him, heard the bolt move, or both. His eyes widened and he dropped his keys.

I pulled the trigger. Exploding gunpowder rang my ears. Without pausing, I pulled the bolt back. An empty cartridge case flew out and bounced onto the floor. I pushed the bolt back in, aimed, steadied, pulled the trigger again.

Another loud bang.

Neither round hit the preacher. He dashed back inside the church and slammed the door shut.

"Go!" Everyone in town would have heard those gunshots. If the police caught us, we'd be hanged.

Amos pulled away and accelerated down the street. I yanked off my bandanna, tossed the rifle in the back seat, and threw a blanket over it.

"How close did you come?" Amos asked as we sped out of town.

"Close enough to scare the smarmy out of him. He'll praise Jesus for his narrow escape and tell everyone how dangerous this Satanist conspiracy is."

Sirens wailed in the distance, but as we raced away, they faded.

Chapter Thirty-Five

Makeup, gray beard, and glasses on, I shuffled past a bored-looking Pinkerton guard and into the Concrete Arms. I climbed the nine flights of stairs to Aaron's floor, near winded by the time I reached the top. Not a good place for authentic old people.

The dented steel door to the hallway was grimy white like the walls, paint cracked and flaking. But the lock was gleaming new, and the deadbolt set. I knocked, three raps.

No answer.

I pounded the back of my fist against the door, the thumps echoing in the stairwell.

A thirtyish Hispanic-looking man with a thin mustache opened the door. Joel stood past him with a shotgun.

"You've upgraded," I told Joel. At least he wasn't pointing it at me.

The Hispanic-looking man edged aside and Joel stepped a little closer. "Who the hell are you?" he demanded.

"Here to see Aaron." I smelled iodine in the dingy hallway, and a familiar craving crawled forth. I shook it off.

Joel threw his shoulders back. "He's not here."

Where was he? "Give him a message, would you?"

He tensed and raised the shotgun barrel.

Frustration overtopped fear. I was sick of having guns pointed at me. "Relax. Just tell him we need to meet. Tonight, 8 o'clock at the trailer."

He peered at me. "You sound like Ben."

"There's a reason." I pulled off the glasses, mustache, and beard, and stuffed them in a coat pocket, the one without the camera squeeze bulb. "It's me."

He lowered the gun and waved me forward. "Well in that case, come in. You can wait."

I didn't want to hang out at the Smash factory, but it was easier than regrouping for a meeting at the trailer. Joel escorted me to a mildewy apartment with ratty furniture but no occupants.

"Our guest quarters," he said. "More vacancies thanks to the cops."

"What happened?" I didn't know there'd been a police raid.

He exhaled. "Police came the day after we threw the preachers back. City cops, it's their jurisdiction. Aaron paid them off and they left, but they took a few people in for show, ones with old warrants."

"And they haven't been back?"

"Nope." He pointed at a tattered blue sofa that smelled like puke. "Make yourself comfortable. Need Smash?"

I remembered the rush and bliss, then the terrible withdrawals and my need to focus. "No thanks."

"Aaron will be by as soon as he can." Joel and the other man left.

Good job, Jake said.

What?

Staying strong.

I wished I knew if he was really talking to me or if I was crazy like my Aunt Sybil.

Behind all sanity there is madness. But behind all madness there is sanity.

I peeled off my gloves and turned on my tape recorder. Once anyone began talking, the tape would start rolling. I'd copy anything useful later.

After a while, Aaron entered, Joel following with his shotgun. Aaron stared at me as Joel shut the door. "That's Ben," he said, initiating the recording.

"It's me." I removed my hat and wig.

Aaron grinned and nodded. "So it is." He sat next to me on the sofa. Joel stood by the door, trigger finger tapping the shotgun grip.

"Where'd you get the disguise?" Aaron asked.

"Friend who does theater," I lied. "Got me past the Pinkerton downstairs."

"So what brings you here?"

"Can we talk alone?"

Aaron turned to Joel and waved a finger toward the door. Joel frowned and left.

After the door closed, I continued, "It's time to turn people in."

Before the authorities figure out they're being scammed, I didn't add.

Aaron raised an eyebrow. "I've been filing reports. Sidney's coming down to meet with the sheriff."

His handler was coming here? "What?"

"I talked to him on the radio."

"What radio?"

"A techie dropped it off after my last report, and showed me how to use it. Anyway, your congressman is throwing fits about these Satanists, and Sidney was ordered to investigate in person."

"Is Lewison coming too?"

Aaron shrugged. "Not that I know of."

Bad, bad news. "When's your handler coming?"

"Tomorrow afternoon."

Shit! No time to prepare. "What'll he do when he gets here?"

"I told you, investigate the Satanists."

"Yeah, but how?"

He shrugged. "We'll find out when he arrives. Gray's interested in the preachers, too. I admit I embellished a little since they tried to shut me down. And he asked a lot of questions about the Sheriff's Office. I think he wants to take it over."

"What do you mean?" Earlier, Aaron had claimed the Insects wouldn't arrest a sheriff unless he was a foreign spy.

He smiled. "We have incontrovertible evidence of corruption. Sidney can use that as a lever, threaten to press charges, unless the sheriff cooperates on an ongoing basis. Lewison has you and maybe some of your friends. Sidney, on the other hand, has half the Concrete Arms and soon, the whole Sheriff's Office."

Trouble was, some of that evidence was faked, like the document naming Sheriff Johnson as my uncle's insurance beneficiary. As soon as he examined it, my gig was finished. I hadn't thought this through well enough. Hadn't expected agents to come in person so soon.

"Can we call Lewison on the radio? I have to talk to him." I had to control the investigation somehow.

"I only have Gray's frequency and code."

"I'll ask to be transferred to Agent Lewison."

Aaron scratched his forearm, then nodded. "I'll make introductions."

He led me to his apartment a few doors down. He unlocked his bedroom door—it didn't have a lock before—and motioned me inside. Next to the typewriter on his desk and piles of paper and office supplies, sat a shoebox-sized black radio with a confusion of knobs and dials. A phone handset ran to a jack on the lower right. A thick wire ran from the back, up the wall, and disappeared into the ceiling.

Aaron sat at the desk and switched on the radio. "Being so high up, this thing has great range, and there are repeaters in every county—probably at the police stations." He flipped another switch. "I'll put on the speaker so you can hear."

He opened a desk drawer and pulled out a small notebook. Then he turned some dials on the radio and flipped a switch. "Control 17 Foxtrot, this is Kingfisher Eight. Control 17 Foxtrot, this is Kingfisher Eight."

Kingfisher? "Is that Gray you're calling?"

He nodded.

An indicator light turned red. A thin, treble-heavy voice sputtered from the radio speaker. "Clubhaul deify refine nailhead bankroll whisk."

Aaron flipped through the little notebook, which had six columns of words on each page. The even pages were alphabetized, but the odd ones weren't. He put his finger under a row of words and spoke in the microphone. "Clock mascot penman matchbox clapper firewood."

"Go ahead," came the voice from the speaker.

"Trader Five Romeo would like to talk to his controller. Transferring."

Was that my code name? Was that what passed for Lewison's sense of humor? I took Aaron's place in the desk chair.

"Trader Five Romeo," the treble voice said, "can you tell me why you're on this radio and why you want to speak with your controller?"

"I hear you're coming to talk to the sheriff," I said.

"I am making a field visit, yes."

"Is Agent Lewison coming too?"

"Not that I know of."

"I have to speak to him. It's urgent."

There was a pause. "I'll put him on the line. Keep the set on."

Aaron asked me, "Can I get you anything?"

If he meant Smash, I didn't even want it within sight. "Staying clean."

He shrugged.

"I only care about one thing," I said. "Five names."

He sighed. "Never act so desperate." He patted my shoulder. "I feel for you."

Lewison's surly voice radiated from the speaker. "Kingfisher Eight, this is Control Ten November."

They exchanged more strings of nonsense words and Aaron transferred the call to me.

"Trader Five Romeo," Lewison said, "what is it?"

I picked up the phone handset and flipped off the speaker switch. I told Aaron, "I need to speak to him alone."

His eyebrows raised. "Why?"

I scrambled for an answer. "I want to ask about Rachel, and some of it's personal."

"I can't let you use my radio without supervision," he said.

Ugh. I spoke into the handset. "Can we speak privately?"

"Why?" Lewison replied.

Stubborn sons of whores. "Because you're the one I work for. I have information for your ears only."

A long pause, then Lewison said, "Just us on the line. Is Kingfisher Eight there?"

I faced Aaron, who was still standing next to the desk. "My controller would like you to give us some privacy."

"I'll need confirmation from Gray."

I covered the microphone with a palm and told Aaron, "He's off the line. But my controller wants to speak privately and wants you to leave the room."

I prepared myself for a long argument, but Aaron grumbled under his breath, stuffed his code book in a pants pocket, and shuffled out of the room. He wasn't as motivated as me, so I wasn't entirely surprised.

"Kingfisher is giving us privacy," I spoke in the handset as soon as the door closed. "There's a lot happening here. You should be a part of it."

"Be more specific," Lewison said.

"First, how's Rachel doing?"

Even through a tinny speaker, Lewison's voice sounded gruff. "She'll be fine as long as you do your job. You'd better be calling about something more important than that."

I remembered Aaron's words that Lewison was having trouble getting ahead. "Gray's coming down to take over the whole operation. I'll lose my five names and you'll lose Southern Illinois."

"We're all on the same side."

A tight-lipped man, but I tried again. "So you don't care if Gray gets the glory and ends up your boss?"

He didn't snatch the bait—maybe I was too obvious—but his voice became deliberate and staccato. "Have you found the lumber company arsonists?"

"Rumor has it, the company did it themselves for the insurance money." Lying came easy now. Which bothered me. "I'm looking for hard evidence," I added, "but it doesn't surprise me, considering all the other insurance scams we discovered."

We went over my reports and tapes, and I told him what Aaron and I had discovered about corruption in the Sheriff's Office, the cult and its conspiracies, collusion between the Baptist Association and the Empire of Japan, and how the preachers were trying to take control of the city.

"Did Gray pass any of this along?" I asked.

"Some of it," he said in stressed tones.

Meaning Gray hadn't been forthcoming and Lewison could indeed lose his operation. "We need a sit-down, the four of us," I said. "There's too much going on, and we need to sort out who gets to, I mean who does what."

He paused. "Gray shouldn't be going on his own anyway. And I should see the place for myself. Also, it's obvious you need a radio. You shouldn't be using someone else's."

I had him! "Where are we meeting?"

"I don't know yet. Kingfisher Eight knows the meeting place and time. Ask him."

"We should meet separately from him and his controller."

"So you can bite my nose off? I don't think so. Control out." I heard a click and the connection light went off.

Paranoid son of a bastard.

Aaron's typewriter caught my eye. This might be my only chance to use it. The last part of my plan, discrediting the government, could use more evidence.

I fed in a sheet of paper and started typing, trying to imitate Aaron's style from the exercises Paul had kept. All I could remember, really, was that he didn't make mistakes like I did. Not that it mattered; his typewriter had those offset 'd' and 's' keys.

```
List of topics for meeting with Gray:
Need more money. Informants cost $100/week.
Want to buy Concrete Arms and provide free lodging
for my followers.
Need a better forger.
Need more bugs. Use to blackmail everyone important
in town.
```

What else? Maybe I could pin the Pinkerton murders on him. Slimy, but I was coated in slime already.

```
Tell him I don't like working with Pinkertons.
```

Someone knocked on the door. "What are you doing?" Aaron's voice.

"Just a second," I called out. I finished the line.

```
What if they find that detective?
```

I pulled out the sheet, quickly folded it, and stuffed it in my pants pocket.

Aaron opened the door. "Are you done with the radio?"

"Yeah. Thanks, I owe you one. See you tomorrow."

"What were you typing?"

I thought fast. "To-do list from Lewison, so I'd remember. Don't worry, it's vague."

"A pen would have been easier."

I shrugged and played dumb. "We're supposed to use typewriters so that's what I did."

* * *

"I'm meeting two Internal Security officers tomorrow," I told Paul, Sarah, and Amos as they sat talking in the front room of the cleaners' building. My stomach was still knotted at the prospect.

Their eyes widened. Amos snuffed out his cigarette in an aluminum floor stand ashtray.

"My controller and Aaron's," I continued, "are coming down from Decatur."

"Why?" Sarah asked.

"To interview the sheriff and probably everyone else we framed. Our congressman apparently raised a fuss about the outbreak of Satanism."

Amos chuckled. "We sure stirred up a pot of shit!"

Sarah frowned at me. "Do you remember who you framed for what?"

"This is New Bethany," I said. "A land of cliques, gossip, and closed minds. It doesn't matter if the stories are tangled and contradictory. People will grab onto those stories that best fit their view of how the world works. That in itself will deepen the conflict."

She smiled and gave me a look of appreciation.

Paul didn't look so happy. "Certainly there's lots of pointed fingers now. But our conspiracies are built from straw. If these officers are good, they'll kick it all down and find us in the center."

"They're not any smarter than we are," I said, hoping that was true. "We can fool the Insects like we've fooled everyone else. It'll just be a little harder."

Paul crossed his arms. "We've got to clean up anything that points to us."

"What do you mean?"

"For starters, Aaron and Joel have to go."

He was probably right. But murder? And I needed them. "We can use Aaron and Joel. Better that than kill them."

Sarah turned to Paul. "I sure as shit ain't murdering anyone."

Paul ignored her and exchanged glances with Amos.

"And as much as I'd like to," I said, "we can't kill Lewison, or Rachel will never be released."

"What's your plan, then?" Paul asked.

"Convince them I'm right," I said. "I know how they think."

I had to try. I couldn't let the Insects lobotomize Rachel.

Chapter Thirty-Six

The morning of my meeting with Lewison, Gray, and Aaron, I left Micah and Beth's house and hiked through the snowy woods to American Cleaners and Fixers.

Amos opened the back door for me. "Early start?"

"Can't sleep through the revolution."

I greeted the others. The front room stank of burnt, bitter coffee. June bought the cheapest coffee available—heavily cut with chicory and acorn meal—and only she and Amos ever touched it.

June drove off with Sarah and Mary to clean houses, while Paul and Amos answered plumbing and heating calls. I stayed at the office and agonized.

The meeting was at 7 p.m. at the Stay-A-While Motel, Room 9. New Bethany's only hotel, the Stay-A-While abutted the state highway a quarter mile west of the Concrete Arms. It was mostly empty this time of year.

I planned to arrive half an hour early, well before Aaron. If he mentioned Paul, I'd stick with the story that he worked for Internal Security in Chicago. The news had surprised me, I'd claim, but it had been ten years since he left New Bethany.

June, Sarah, and Mary quit at 5:30. They almost never worked double shifts. Sarah hugged me before leaving. "Are you sure you don't want me to stick around?"

"In case something goes wrong, I want you as far away as possible."

"Be careful."

"Of course."

They left in June's car. At 6:15, I put on my coat and checked the camera and tape recorder.

Paul jangled a set of keys. "I'll drive you. It's a little early now, though."

"I'm aiming for 6:30. I need to talk without Aaron around."

"But—"

"And I don't need a ride. It's only half a mile from the cleaners."

He shook his head. "It's not safe for you to walk or take the streetcar. Cops and Pinkertons are everywhere. We'll drop you off near the motel."

That made sense.

Paul had bought another used car, a dented black sedan with fading paint. I took the front passenger seat, which had a crack down the middle. Amos followed, carrying a garment bag, and hopped in the back.

I turned to Amos as Paul started the engine. "Why are you coming?"

"Backup." He peered out the window.

"Is that a gun in your bag?"

"Protection, just in case."

I got out a few minutes later. The single-story Stay-A-While had been built around the same time as the concrete factory, and hadn't been refurbished since. Long, narrow wings of weather-beaten wood formed a horseshoe around a gravel parking lot that glistened with ice. Dirty snow had been plowed into a huge, dark gray pile in the middle, obscuring half the motel.

Except for the numbers on the doors, the rooms looked identical from the outside—aluminum doors, small unwashed windows, and protruding air conditioners. Faint voices sounded from door #9. It sounded like an argument. The curtains were drawn.

I planted my ear to the door, but couldn't make out the words. I looked damn suspicious trying, though. I knocked.

A clean-cut man in his late twenties or early thirties, wearing a dark suit and fedora, opened the door and stepped aside. His face was tense. Agent Lewison stood between the twin beds and the dresser, jacket open, 9 mm automatic in his right hand.

"You're early," Lewison snarled, dark eyes boring into mine.

I paused only briefly before entering. "Surprised I'm not late?"

The room reeked of mildew and cigarettes. The younger Insect shut the door.

Jake and Rachel had spent many a night at the Stay-A-While, especially after he enlisted and could better afford it. It wasn't the luxurious suite I'd imagined.

I offered my hand to the younger man. "You must be Agent Gray."

He smiled and shook my hand. "And you must be Mr. Adamson. Can I take your coat?"

Something a mom would say. Or someone checking for weapons or spy gear. "No thanks."

His smile vanished. "I'm afraid I must insist."

Lewison aimed his pistol at my chest.

I shed my jacket. Gray searched it and shut off the tape recorder. "You were going to record our meeting?"

"It's set to activate automatically. Sorry."

He patted down my back, sides, legs, and ankles. "No weapons," he told Lewison.

"Of course not," I said. Gray missed the folded letter inside my right wool sock, just below the boot collar. It was too thin to make a bulge. I hoped to plant it somewhere if given the chance, although trading five names for Rachel was my main priority.

With his free hand, Lewison pointed at the far bed, a dark-covered queen-size, snug against an off-white wall. "Sit."

The bed creaked and sank when I sat on it. I kept my boots on the floor. I started talking before the Insects could grill me about the tape recorder. "Before I started working for you, I had only the vaguest idea of how corrupt this town is. Everyone knows the sheriff and his deputies take kickbacks. But I had no idea they were in a Satanic cult, or murdered people for insurance money."

Gray stepped closer. "We were asked to look into the Satanist allegations. We'll cast a light on all the nooks and crannies."

Lewison scowled, but slipped his pistol back into its belt holster. "It's the Baptist Association I'm more interested in. Conducting espionage for the Japanese Empire?"

"The churches think they know better than the government," I said.

The Insects stared at me.

"But the bankers and sheriff," I continued, "are breaking laws and should be punished too. Corruption destroyed the Romans." Something I remembered from high school. "Do we want America to suffer the same fate? Or should we make an example? If New Bethany is this corrupt, think about big cities like Chicago and St. Louis. Sweep up here and it sends a signal."

Lewison nodded. "You show promise sometimes."

I had him on the hook. He must know his glorious America was rotting and unstable. "You can't trust local law enforcement to do the right thing. They're only out to pad their wallets."

"We'll see about that."

I caught Gray's eyes, then Lewison's. "Aaron told me you see this as an opportunity to expand your control down here, blackmail the sheriff and his cronies into working for you. If I were you, I'd punish them instead."

Lewison emitted malice from his giant pupils. "You seem to think you're running things."

I waved a hand. "No, I just want to make sure I'm not cast aside. Aaron and I gave you a lot of names and Rachel deserves to be released. She's suffered enough."

Lewison's face relaxed and he sighed. "I'm a man of my word. Five arrests and she goes free." He turned to Gray. "Which means I have to process them."

Gray rolled his eyes. "I've been over this with Kingfisher. I don't care about your numbers game. It's a little premature anyway."

Lewison grunted but the corners of his lips inched up a bit, just for a second.

I'd finally done it. Rachel would be freed. I could almost kiss the Insects' faces, although I'd have to gargle afterward. Jake whooped and hollered inside my head.

Someone knocked on the door. "It's me." Aaron's voice. He was early too.

Gray went to the door and opened it. Lewison stayed by the dresser and pulled out his gun again.

A shotgun went off, the deafening blast echoing off the walls. Gray fell backward against the near bed and collapsed to the floor, blood spurting from his neck.

Aaron stumbled forward into the room, eyes wide with fear. His hands were empty, but Lewison leveled his pistol and shot him in the chest. Aaron's mouth opened and a quick gasp came out.

Behind Aaron, a broad-shouldered man with a black ski mask, holding a shotgun in gloved hands, grunted. The round had gone through Aaron and hit him too.

The masked man pumped his shotgun, ejecting a red case. He fired at Lewison but missed, blowing a hole through the thin wall to the bathroom. Acrid smoke scented the air.

Bleeding from the chest, Aaron tripped over Gray's prone body and sprawled to the floor.

I had no gun on me, no way to defend myself. I ducked into a crouch between the two beds. There wasn't enough space beneath the beds to crawl under. I'd never make it to the bathroom. Maybe I could go for Gray's gun, but it was on the other side of the bed and I'd make an easy target.

I heard the intruder pump his shotgun again. To my left, Lewison fired his pistol again.

The shotgun went off at the same time. Lewison's right arm flew back in a spray of blood, and his gun fell to the carpet with a thump.

"Fuck," the intruder uttered.

I recognized the voice. Amos. I peeked over the bed.

Amos threw a hand against his bleeding chest and staggered out the door.

A taped bundle of thin red tubes flew into the room. Seven sticks of dynamite with a lit fuse. It landed on the near bed in slow motion. A gloved hand—narrower than Amos's—slammed the hotel door shut.

Dripping blood, Lewison stared at the bomb, then faced the door.

That much dynamite, there'd be nothing left of me. But Jake wouldn't panic and neither would I.

I scrambled onto the bed. The fuse threw off sparks and smoke, closer and closer to the blasting cap. I grabbed the bundle of dynamite sticks with my left hand and the fuse with my right. Beneath, the bedspread smoldered.

The fuse burned past my pinky. Searing pain. Detonation seconds away. Heart pounding like a kettle drum, I kept my grip and yanked as hard as I could.

My hands flew apart, burning fuse in one, blasting cap and dynamite in the other.

I tossed the fuse aside, then slid the neutered dynamite underneath the bed in case it was old and unstable.

Outside, tires screeched. Paul's sedan, no doubt. Amos had burst in with the shotgun and Paul must have thrown the dynamite. My right hand screamed in pain where the fuse had burned past. Paul and Amos had tried to kill me.

I glanced to my left. Lewison's arm was a mess and bleeding badly. "Are you alright?"

"Gray," he said, face white and slack.

I ran to Gray, motionless on his back near the door. Half his neck was missing, spurting bright red blood onto the carpet. His eyes stared at the ceiling, pupils dilated. Dead, or seconds away.

Lying face down, blood oozing out a hole in his back, Aaron was unconscious but still breathing. Nothing I could do for him, though. I checked his jacket. No tape recorder.

I yanked the cover off a pillow and rushed over to Lewison, now sitting on the floor against the far bed, holding his tattered arm. I heard distant sirens, getting closer. I rolled up the pillowcase and tied it around his upper arm. As much as I hated him, I couldn't let him die. Not until Rachel was released.

I passed the room phone to Lewison. "Tell the operator to send an ambulance."

While he was on the phone, I returned to Aaron and slipped the incriminating letter in his pants pocket.

The sirens grew loud. I threw my jacket back on and decided on a misdirect.

"Don't let the county cops near you," I told Lewison. "I'm going to find the attackers. I think they're Pinkertons."

I wished they had been. Instead of my comrades.

Burned fingers shaking, I dashed into the bleach-infused bathroom, opened the grimy back window, and vaulted out.

* * *

The phones were probably all tapped, so I trudged through the snow to Micah's house, circling north of town and sticking to woods wherever possible. All my stuff was at their house, and I needed my gun.

The lights were out and the doors locked. Strange, but doctors kept weird hours, and people had been hurt at the Stay-A-While. I picked the back door lock and let myself in.

I loaded my rifle and grabbed an extra box of ammo, a flashlight, and a heavy blanket. My right fingers weren't burned as badly as they felt, but I slathered ointment on the red marks anyway. Then I hiked back through the woods to American Cleaners and Fixers.

The lights were off there too. Amos had installed combination locks on the doors, a type with separate number wheels that I wasn't sure how to crack. The windows were bolted shut.

Paul would appear at some point. I'd been totally unprepared for his betrayal, although I should have expected it. When in doubt, kill—that was his motto. Jake had a moral awakening from killing civilians but Paul just changed sides.

The railroad ran past the back of the building. I nestled in the trees and shrubs on the opposite side, wrapped myself in the blanket, and waited.

Wake up.

I heard tires crunching over snow. Cold tore at my face and hands despite my winter clothes and blanket. A dark sedan pulled into the small parking lot, headlights off.

I wiggled my fingers and toes. They were stiff but still worked. I threw aside the blanket and slipped over the railroad track embankment, as quiet as if I was hunting deer.

Someone got out of the car, a man with a dark face and white fedora. Paul.

There was no cover on this side of the tracks, just shallow snow and cleared asphalt. I circled behind him.

Paul strode to the door, stopped, and looked around. He spotted me. His eyes widened and he reached in his coat pocket.

I pointed my rifle at the center of his chest. "Don't," I said, just loud enough for him to hear. "Put your hands up."

He hesitated, then whipped out his pistol.

I fired.

The shot echoed off the building. Everyone in New Bethany would hear. Paul dropped his gun, then collapsed to the ground.

I ran to him. "Why?"

His arms flopped and he grimaced. "Damn dynamite must be defective."

"I pulled the fuse out."

He blinked, stared, then glanced left and right. "I can't get up. Can't feel my legs. You've got to get me out of here."

"*What?*"

"Police tie me to anything, my family will pay. Keys are in my pocket."

He was right. His family might end up in the camps. And I couldn't have the Insects investigating American Cleaners and Fixers and torturing Sarah. I slung my rifle over my shoulder and picked up his pistol. Finding no other weapons, I dragged him into the passenger seat.

I didn't want to pass the Concrete Arms or the Stay-A-While, where cops might be congregating. Keeping the headlights off, I took the first road north—Lake Drive. I kept one eye on Paul but he didn't move much. I drove past snow-covered fields and skeletal trees.

Lake Drive led to the reservoir. Too bad it was iced over. Beside me, Paul coughed up blood.

"Why'd you try to kill me?" I asked, fingers clenching the steering wheel, eyes straining to keep the sedan on the unlit road and not hit anything.

"Never trusted you after Beth saw that spy gear. I would have killed you then if it weren't for Sarah. And your operation was genius, turning our enemies against each other."

"I'm not done yet. And I never did anything to betray you. You should have trusted me like Sarah and let me finish the plan."

He coughed again. "With those Internal Security investigators here, I had to get rid of everyone who could finger us. I killed Joel. Smash overdose, then dumped the body. And by now, Aaron's dead."

"Micah finished him off at the hospital?"

Paul didn't respond. I spared a glance—he was still alive, eyes blinking, blood dripping from his lips.

"What about Amos?" I asked, returning my eyes to the road.

"Died from his wound." Paul gargled his words. "I was sorry to see it, he was a good man. He's in the trunk. His body can't be found. But the damn ground's frozen. Gonna need acid."

"It's your fault he's dead."

"We all die. At least he took out a fascist enforcer in the process."

I shook my head. "You were a killer for the government and you're still a killer. You quote your hero Biafra and preach cooperation, but your instincts are warped and you murder anyone you can't control. You're no different from the government."

He coughed again, making a wet frothy sound. Probably his lungs were filling with blood. "Revolution's a messy business. Your hands are just as dirty."

I did feel bad about setting up the pastors, but I'd try to get them off, and discredit the government in the process.

"You destroyed our cell," Paul said. "Everything I worked for."

"You did that yourself. Killing that Pinkerton and his lady friend. Disrupting our operation—"

He talked over me. "You and Sarah and your archaic morals. You can't see what needs to be done."

I gripped the wheel tighter. "Without morals we might as well be Insects. Too bad you didn't let Sarah run things. We're not giving up, and we're better off without you."

'We'? Not 'they'? As soon as Rachel was free and the local authorities, businessmen, and churchies at each others' throats, I had planned to return to Talitha. But there was so much more to do, and Sarah would need my help. Could I do both?

I passed the turnoff to the reservoir, searching for an alternate hiding place. Couldn't stay on the roads, police would block them off. Not every day a federal agent was murdered.

"How... long you think I have?" Paul sputtered.

"Couldn't say exactly. You shouldn't have gone for your gun. Or thrown dynamite at me."

"You fucked things up."

Dogmatic to the end. "I could have shot you in the head or heart, killed you right away, but I needed an explanation, why you would do such a thing. And if you want, you have a chance to pray for forgiveness."

Paul wheezed and gurgled. "Prayer... is for the weak. So is forgiveness."

"Anything you want me to tell your parents? Sarah?" His poor mom.

He didn't respond, blood drooling from his lips.

I pulled into a clump of trees and bounced through snow-hooded shrubs until the tires stuck, spinning useless in snow and frozen muck. Choice now—hide the car with branches or set it on fire?

Paul had stopped breathing. His eyes stared into the darkness ahead, unmoving.

I got out and opened the trunk. Amos's blood-soaked body filled half the space. Next to him was a bundle of dynamite.

Option B, then. I found a lighter in Paul's coat pocket. I twisted off his silver ring since it might survive a fire. I unscrewed the gas cap for oxygen, lit the dynamite fuse, and sprinted away as fast as I could.

Behind me, a huge blast sounded. Tree trunks flashed orange, and hot wind almost knocked me over. I looked back. A column of flame billowed into the sky where the car had been.

Chapter Thirty-Seven

I sat at a wooden table in a brightly lit room in the Internal Security Service's Illinois headquarters in Decatur. No chains, at least. State Director Herold Pillett, Lewison's and Gray's boss, sat across from me and opened folders full of papers. He was flanked by two other Insects, younger men who didn't introduce themselves. One scribbled on a note pad and the other just stared at me. Video cameras were mounted on the walls.

This was my last obstacle before freeing Rachel. The last obstacle before seeing Talitha. I'd wean her off Smash, if her doctor hadn't already, and spend the rest of my life in her arms.

"Your name and address for the record?" King Insect began.

"Benjamin Adamson, from New Bethany, Illinois." I gave the farm address—even though the bank had sold our land to a big developer out of Chicago. My toes clenched. Before long, the fields and woods would be gone forever.

"Let's start at the beginning, why you and Rachel Tolson were arrested last year, and how you were recruited."

Lewison had coached me what to say, to make him look good to his superiors. "Rachel and me were traumatized by my brother's death overseas—"

"Your brother's name for the record?"

"Jacob Adamson."

"Proceed."

"We came to question his death," I said, "and organized a public meeting in front of the county courthouse. It was unnecessarily confrontational, and we were brought in for questioning, to see if we were part of an organized anti-government movement."

"And were you?"

"No. We did it entirely on our own. Agent Lewison convinced me we were wrong, that Jake died a hero and we should be proud of him. Which of course we are. I volunteered to help Agent Lewison uncover any actual anti-government activity in New Bethany. My experience is that the city and county police are mostly interested in lining their own pockets and can't be relied on for anything else."

"Can you expand on that?" King Insect said.

"Sure." I told him about the shakedowns, the insurance fraud, and all the other examples I knew of, including how city jail guards tried to rape Rachel.

To his credit, King Insect grimaced. He examined his papers. "You'll be happy to know, all four have been removed from duty."

"They belong in prison," I said, "on the other side of the bars."

"Let's move on to your activities for Special Agent Lewison."

I described, mostly fictitiously, how I talked to people around town and reported my findings. "I followed Aaron's lead for the most part, since he had a lot more experience as a spy."

"Aaron Little?"

"Yes."

"So you knew he was an operative for Special Agent Gray?"

"Yes, he told me."

King Insect frowned. "The police found drug labs that Mr. Little was supposedly in charge of." His cheeks flushed. "Did you know about this?"

"Aaron bragged about how good he was at making and selling Smash. He said Gray knew he was a dealer and not only looked the other way, but provided finances." That wasn't strictly true, but neither man was alive to object.

"And did you participate in this operation?"

"Not at all. All I cared about was finding subversives for Agent Lewison. I heard the local clergy wanted to shut down the drug labs but the cops wouldn't help, and Aaron hired Pinkertons to chase them off."

King Insect asked for details, then said, "You were wanted by Pinkerton detectives, is that true?"

This was the hard part. The key was to play dumb, like I'd done with Lewison. "Yeah, I told Agent Lewison. First Consolidated Bank took our farm and I went to the house to get some of my stuff. The bank sent Pinkertons to find me."

"You admit committing burglary and theft?"

"Not at all. It was my house and my stuff. No one told me I couldn't move it."

"Was there anyone at the house when you went there?"

"Not that I saw." I'd practiced the lie until I believed it myself.

"A Pinkerton employee named Everett Sherman, and his apparent mistress, Veronica Burns, went missing from that house, and evidence of gunplay was uncovered, along with traces of blood."

I went through my prepared story. "I saw the reward flyers, but couldn't believe when I heard it was my family's house they disappeared from. I mentioned it to Aaron, but he said not to worry about it."

King Insect pushed a piece of paper toward me, sealed in a plastic bag. It was the list I wrote on Aaron's typewriter, asking Gray for more money, help with his forging and blackmailing operations, and how he was nervous about working with Pinkertons and hoped they wouldn't find the missing detective.

"The New Bethany police found this note on Mr. Little. They examined his typewriter and confirmed a match."

I peered at the note as if seeing it for the first time. "Sounds like something he might say."

"Why would an experienced operative type a list that could be used against him?"

"Agent Lewison made me memorize everything," I said. "But Aaron was high all the time. He had trouble keeping things straight sometimes." I'd practiced this lie also.

"It's odd. There's no other evidence linking Mr. Little to the Sherman-Burns disappearances. No motive either."

I shrugged. "Maybe this detective was investigating him. Pinkertons aren't afraid to play all sides, from what I've heard."

King Insect drummed fingers against the table. He plucked a sheet of paper from one of his folders and read out the names of the arrestees: Brother Jedediah, his four staff, Preacher Bill, Father Campbell, the Methodist pastor, and four others. "We have your statements to Agent Lewison regarding these people, but I'd like to hear your thoughts myself."

I told him the pastors and their flock put God and Church before the government. And the Dominionists, none of whom were arrested, thought they should run the country and other elements purged.

"What about this devil worshiping ring?" he asked when I finished.

"Doesn't surprise me. Everyone knows how corrupt the Sheriff's Office and bank are. And who's the Lord of Corruption? Satan—at least that's what they taught us in Sunday school."

King Insect examined his notes. "What do you know about Earl Brogan? The manager at First Consolidated Bank?"

I told him Brogan was the sheriff's chief financial backer and they apparently worked together to run the county as their personal fiefdom. "Are you going to press charges?" I asked. "Clean up New Bethany?"

"We're weighing all options."

Which probably meant blackmail, like Gray had planned, instead of prison. I suppressed my disappointment.

"So about these devil worshipers," he continued, "have you personally seen such activity?"

"Not personally, but I don't fly in those flocks."

He flipped through his papers. "Now let's talk about the attack at the Stay-A-While Motel. Tell me everything that happened that day, and who you think the gunmen were."

I told him Agent Gray arranged the meeting, and Lewison decided to come along. I thought we were probably attacked by Pinkertons, but didn't know for sure. I knew Aaron had hired them, but they also worked for the bank. "I bet they double-crossed Aaron, considering how much more the bank could pay."

"Agent Lewison spoke highly of you, said you saved his life."

"We both would have died if that dynamite had gone off."

He nodded. "Why would a banker order the killing of federal agents? It's not very wise."

I'd let him draw his own conclusions, which he'd be more likely to believe than anything I made up. "I don't know. Aaron and Gray must have been onto something. Or maybe the Pinkertons found out Aaron killed their detective, if I read that note right."

"So all you can do is speculate."

I shrugged. "You asked my opinion. Aaron didn't always tell me what he was up to."

King Insect reached his last page of notes. "You were originally asked to investigate a case of arson and the placement of provocative signs. What did you find out about those?"

I told him I'd heard the lumber company fire was an inside job, that they burned it to collect insurance money, like all the other insurance scams in southern Illinois. As for the roadside signs, I never found out. Probably drunk college kids.

King Insect shook my hand at the end. I managed not to recoil.

"Thank you for coming," he said. "We'll be in touch if we need more."

*　*　*

Lewison met me in a courtyard of the sprawling complex. "How did it go?"

"Your boss doesn't blame you for Gray's mistakes."

His face stayed still as a statue. "He shouldn't."

I winced inside. No gratitude. I should have killed him when I had the chance, or at least ruined his career. But Rachel was infinitely more important than revenge.

"In fact," I said, "I wouldn't be surprised if you're promoted."

His lips curled into a fleeting smile. "Why do you think that?"

"Twelve arrests so far, maybe more to follow. And Internal Security has complete control of New Bethany. The State Director seemed pleased." I certainly wasn't pleased about it, but I'd make sure their control was temporary.

He smiled again, and this time it lasted. "Good work, Benjamin. And you handled yourself like a soldier during the attack."

"I assume you're releasing Rachel, as agreed?"

"She's learned her lesson. I signed her release papers, and her psychiatrist agreed she's no longer a threat to society."

"She never was." I regretted my words. This was a bad time to piss him off.

He frowned. "You were both disruptive anti-social elements. The evidence was clear. But sometimes correction works." He called for a guard. "Escort this man to the hospital entrance lobby." He turned back to me. "You can wait for Miss Tolson there."

Sitting in a wooden chair in the undecorated lobby, I watched the minute hands inch along the wall clock. Behind a plastiglass divider, the receptionist and guard ignored me.

The inner door opened. Lewison strode through, carrying a briefcase. He was followed by Rachel, unshackled, a silver-shirted guard behind her.

She was wearing the funeral dress she was arrested in. Spring green eyes, perfect nose and cheeks, cascading black hair—the most beautiful girl in New Bethany. But her eyes blinked like a metronome, like when I visited on Christmas. Something inside her was broken.

Her lips parted when she spotted me. I rushed toward her and she lurched with stiff legs, like she'd forgotten how to flex her knees.

We embraced. She squeezed me tight and sniffled.

"Rachel."

"Deerslayer."

I fought not to cry. "Are you alright?"

"They told me I'm free to leave."

"Yeah. Yeah."

She gazed in my eyes, her blinking under control. "It's finally over—it's hard to believe. Like waking up from the longest, worst nightmare ever. Agent Lewison said I have you to thank."

"Let's get out of here," I said.

In my peripheral vision, Lewison crossed his arms. "This is just the beginning, you know."

Ice squeezed my heart. We stared at him. "What?"

"I envision a lifetime partnership."

The ice pumped through my veins like an injection from the frozen lake of lowest Hell. "We're done." My words were almost certainly futile. "We just want to go home and repair our lives."

Lewison's dark eyes narrowed. "Your skills are needed. And don't forget, I can have you two re-arrested whenever I want."

Rachel looked ready to cry. "You can't."

Cold dizziness gave way to erupting rage. I tried to tame it. "I gave you twelve names, way more than the five you asked for. I helped you at the inquest. And I saved your life."

"And I thank you for it. But it was your life and Rachel's you were saving, too. I agree you've been valuable. But America needs your continued cooperation. Our purpose in life is to serve the State and keep America on course. To fulfill the Will of History. "

I should have known.

"Was that your plan all along?" I said when I could finally speak. "To enslave us the rest of our lives?"

"You shouldn't think of it that way, Benjamin. You're a trained, experienced operative now. Who knows, maybe you have a career at Internal Security ahead of you. A good job with a pension and other benefits."

The government would keep us in bondage forever. Keep everyone in bondage. Until it was overthrown.

"I expect monthly reports," he continued, "to fill me in on any subversive activities or thoughts in your town. And I'll need enough evidence for arrests—at least three a year from each of you." His dark eyes focused on me. "Except during your military service, of course."

Rachel didn't speak, her shoulders deflated, eyes flat. The old Rachel would have argued until the Mississippi went dry.

"We can handle that," I managed. The important thing was to get Rachel out of here. Time would heal her, I hoped.

"Good. Three a year isn't much at all." Lewison opened his briefcase and passed us a small paper bag. "Here's $500, to get you back to New Bethany and set up. I'll open accounts for you at First Consolidated and wire a monthly stipend. It won't be enough to live on by itself, but I'll help you find jobs—places that need eyes and ears. And if you want a career position and comprehensive training, I'll make it happen."

I wondered if Lewison started out that way—a coerced informer who joined his captors. No—he was too dogmatic. He was born for this. Or unlike me, Rachel, and Sarah, Lewison's lifelong indoctrination had settled into the folds of his brain and formed impermeable armor against contrary thoughts. Love of Country, Love of Duty. The Biblical City on the Hill, Triumph of Collective Will. Only the insane could believe otherwise.

Rachel and I left without saying anything else.

At the bus station, I bought Rachel a ticket to New Bethany, with stops in Springfield, St. Louis, and Sparta. The next bus on that route would arrive in half an hour.

She studied her ticket. "Why'd you only buy one? Aren't you coming?"

"I will, but not today. I promised Sarah I'd come back, and I have unfinished business there." I hoped to negate the evidence against the preachers and expose the Insects.

"But it'll just be temporary," I continued. "I can't live in New Bethany any more. No family, no farm." And the Pinkertons were still searching for me despite my misdirects.

She hugged me. "My dad told me what happened to your father. I'm so sorry. It's not fair."

I savored the hug. "Thanks."

"You can stay at our house," she said. "We'll make room."

My heart fluttered, then settled. "I'd love to stay with you. But I thought I'd make Decatur my new home."

She let go. "This place?"

"Yeah. There's this girl, Talitha."

"The girl who came with you on Christmas?"

"Yeah." I missed Talitha, but tears of guilt gathered behind my eyes. No one would ever understand Rachel the way I did, understand what she went through, and now I was abandoning her. "I'll come down whenever I can, though. And we can write and talk on the phone." We'd have to find a safe way to do it.

"What about Agent Lewison's assignments?"

"Don't worry about that. I'll take care of it. Don't mention it to anyone, even your family."

She didn't speak as we trudged to the diagonal parking spot for the bus to New Bethany. We sat on one of the chilly metal benches, the other bench occupied by a bundled-up crone hunched over a Bible.

Rachel slipped her fingers into mine and locked bright eyes with me. "I'll miss you. You're the only person I can relate to now."

"I'll always be there if you need me." If only we could spend our lives together. I loved Talitha, was connected to her, but I felt a different love toward Rachel, a bond beyond anything I could define.

But eventually someone would find those bodies in the reservoir, and there would be a backlash once I publicized the government's schemes in New Bethany. I had work to do up here, too. Rachel would never be free from Lewison's clutches as long as the bastard remained alive.

Don't endanger her, Jake's voice said.

I won't. Are you still with her?

What do you think?

Let her move on when she's ready. You should move on too. I don't need you in my head any more.

No response.

I love you, Jake. Maybe that's an unmanly thing to say, but it's true. I want you to know your death did mean something. Everything we did was because of you, trying to end the wars and brutality. And like you asked, I looked after Rachel and Pop. I'm sorry I failed Pop, but I tried. At least Rachel's out, and I'll make sure she stays safe.

As for the rest, I'm just beginning. I may be starting my own family now, but that's an even stronger reason to fight the Insects and their masters. Ours should be the last generation in chains. I just have to be careful.

And if I fall, before that happens, I'll plant the seeds of revolution in others, like you and Rachel and Paul and Sarah planted them in me. The dictatorship built a seemingly impregnable prison around us. But I'll keep kicking, driving wedges, recruiting, till the walls come down.

No verbal response, but a buzz of release echoed through my head, a lifting of burdens, a quiet embrace. I was on the right track.

And maybe I'll find this Captain Tannin, the intelligence officer who probably had you killed, when he returns to the States. Pay him a visit.

Rachel peered at me. "Are you okay?"

"Yeah." Still holding her hand, I whispered in her ear. "Do you still talk to Jake?"

She nodded and whispered back. "I wouldn't have lasted otherwise."

"You're smart and strong. You don't need him anymore. Let him move on."

"He needs justice."

"We all do. I aim to see it happen."

The old woman on the other bench stared at us. I pulled back. Whispering was suspicious, but I still had a lot more to say.

Rachel might try to contact Paul, not knowing he was dead. Only his cell knew; to everyone else, he'd vanished back to Chicago. There wasn't enough left of him to identify, just scattered bits of bone and teeth, mixed with pieces of Amos. When I told Sarah, she took it hard, cursing both of us, but especially him.

I hugged Rachel and chanced a final whisper. "You'll be watched, so you have to stay away from Sarah and the others. You'll put them in danger."

I ended the hug and squeezed her hands. "Focus on recovery," I said in normal tones.

"I'm in your debt."

"I don't want you in debt. I don't want anyone in anyone's debt. We should all be free."

She kissed me, driving the cold away. Tender at first, our lips squeezed together in solidarity. She pressed against me and I ran fingers through her hair. I disappeared in her scent, into a soul ancient from a lifetime of accumulated knowledge and battered by captivity and suffering. Lost in thoughts about what could have been and what life might be like in a better world.

I waited with Rachel for her bus, holding her hand. The bus arrived on time, like they always did. She boarded and we waved goodbye to each other.

Then I took a local bus to see Talitha.

* * *

The dog didn't bark when I knocked on Talitha's front door. No one answered.

I peeked in the living room window. The drapes were open and a lamp was on inside. I returned to the door and knocked again.

The door creaked open. Talitha, her blonde hair a tangled mess, stared at me with red-rimmed eyes. "You're too late." She started crying. "Where were you when I needed you?"

My heart seized. "I'm sorry it took so long." Four weeks instead of two, but I had worked as fast as I could. "I succeeded, though. Rachel's free. I have more to do, but I'm back and I'm here for good."

I moved forward to hold her but she whipped up her hands and backed away.

"What's wrong?" I asked. "Didn't you get my letters?"

Tears poured down her cheeks. "Some. But I needed you with me. You said we'd be together forever."

My skin froze with fear. "What happened?"

"When I came back to Decatur, and visited my doctor the way your friend Beth said, they put me in rehab. They took Ladonna away." She buried her face in her hands.

I held her as she cried. "They still have her? Who's 'they'? We'll get her back."

She shouted. "We can't! She's dead!"

My blood stopped flowing, the world contracted and darkened to shadow. "What?"

"Her liver failed, they told me, then the rest of her little body. She died all alone, without her mommy." Talitha squirmed out of my grasp and heaved with sobs. "The Smash before I knew I was pregnant... it doomed her... she was doomed before she was even born... I KILLED MY POOR BABY!"

I stood there unable to speak, the plug pulled from the universe. Sour thickness oozed down my throat and curdled in my stomach.

After a while, she choked out more words. "After they stuck me in rehab, they arrested Edna."

"She's in jail? Is that why the dog's gone?"

She fixed me with double barrel shotgun eyes, glimmering wet. "Kaiser starved to death, or maybe it was no water."

Poor dog.

"Edna," she continued, "Edna hung herself. She's dead, my big sister... My sister's dead! She fucking hung herself. You fucking asshole, where were you? WHERE WERE YOU? The withdrawals must have been so awful. I know mine were, it was days and days of torture. But for her, there were no doctors to help and no one to care. She was in such torment, she went and killed herself..."

Talitha dropped to her knees, wailing.

Poor Edna. Poor Ladonna. I couldn't see anything through the tears. I kneeled with her and tried to offer some comfort but she slapped my arms away.

Talitha was gone from me. That part seemed inconsequential. My life of pain was nothing compared to hers, the worst agony possible, worse than the Insects' most evil tortures.

She pressed hands against her face and shook off the worst of her sobbing. She rose, eyes avoiding me. "I have to leave. Get away, as far as I can. As soon as, as soon as I sell the house. I'm not even asking much."

"I... is there anything...?"

"I thought about killing myself like Edna. But I'm gonna change my name, make a new life. Forget this one, like it was just a bad dream."

I started to say I was sorry, as if words could compensate, but she backed into the house and slammed the door. The deadbolt clicked, then the curtains slid shut. On the other side, Talitha screamed and wailed.

Chapter Thirty-Eight

Starting over was Talitha's best course now. I would be a bad reminder.

Once the shock settled into mere horror, I bought a notepad and pen from the grocery store up the street. I returned to Talitha's, sat on the back stoop and scribbled a short letter.

I'm so sorry. I didn't know about Ladonna & Edna. I would have dropped everything and come to help if I'd known.

Would I have? Would it have meant sacrificing Rachel? No, I would have found a way, even if it lengthened Rachel's captivity a few more weeks.

I know what it's like to have your whole universe ripped away. I wish I could go back in time and make things better, for you and everyone else in this fucked-up world.

Ladonna, Edna, Jake, Ma, Abby, Pop... A tear splashed onto the page and smudged the blue ink.

If you ever need anything, put a classified ad in the New Bethany Bugle *and say it's from Sweet T. Stay clean and be kind to yourself.*

B.

P.S. Burn this note after you read it. Always be careful.

I slipped the letter under the front door and trudged to the bus stop.

Having no place else to go—the Tolsons' house would be watched—I moved into Amos's old room at American Cleaners and Fixers. It had no windows and stank of cigarettes, but contained a drop ceiling I could hide above in an emergency.

My first instinct was to drink myself into oblivion. And maybe head to the Concrete Arms for some Smash, assuming Internal Security hadn't purged the place.

But that was the Ben of the past. I was a different person now.

Sitting on my sagging bed, I told Sarah, "I can't fix all the awful things that happened. But maybe I can help stop more people from dying, more people from imprisonment and torture. I'm going to destroy the Insects and the rest of those bastards who make life such a hopeless nightmare."

Smelling like lavender and coconut, Sarah sat on the bed next to me and kissed my cheek. "I'm with you."

"Thanks." She always had been.

"So is June."

The three of us were the last remnants of Paul's cell. Micah and Beth had retired from the revolution business. So had Mary, grieving over her brother's death.

"I'm sorry I was down on Talitha," Sarah continued. "She meant a lot to you and would have been good for you if she weren't an addict."

"I was weak too." Never again.

Sarah bit her lip. "If it had to be between you and Paul, I'm glad it was you."

"Even though he was kin?"

"You're my kin more than anyone." Her molasses eyes shone.

We held each other and I felt strangely safe, like the two of us were fishing together on a warm summer day, at some hidden pond where no one would ever bother us.

We had responsibilities, though. No one could live free and happy as long as the Insects and their masters ran the country. "So what do we do now?" I asked. "Paul said there'd be a big push on Liberation Day. How do we coordinate with the other crews? Where are the drop sites?"

"He told us where two of the drops are, up in Marion County. He taught us one of the code systems too, a word substitution using an old edition of *Leaves of Grass*."

Rachel would love that if she knew.

Sarah led me into the junk-filled back room. She showed me their copy of *Leaves of Grass*, then unscrewed the top of a surplus water heater. "Paul said we'd be part of a nationwide effort, destroying symbols of the oligarchy—as he put it—and mobilizing the public. For New Bethany, we decided to blow up the Lindbergh statue in front of City Hall."

She pulled a black plastic bag out of the drained water heater and passed me one of the flyers inside. "We were going to release these afterward."

```
50 Years Since the Coup. 50 Years of Oppression. 50
years of Poverty. 50 years of Misery. Enough is
Enough! We Demand a Return to Democracy! All Men
and Women are Created Equal! We the People Hereby
Reject the Dictatorship and Throw Off Our Chains!
```

"Sounds promising," I said. "But we don't have to wait until Liberation Day. There's a lot I still need to do, and I want to start now."

* * *

In the shelter of my room at American Cleaners and Fixers, I began the last phase of my plan. I photographed all the documents I had that incriminated the Insects, and wrote how the federal government turned people against each other so they could maintain control. I embellished a little, saying Internal Security was trying to purge the Christian element from the ruling clique, and had built a network of drug addicts.

I made tapes with conversation excerpts, like Joel saying, "Police came the day after we threw the preachers back. City cops, it's their jurisdiction. Aaron paid them off and they left, but they took a few people in for show, ones with old warrants."

I included Aaron describing how his handler wanted to arrest preachers and blackmail the Sheriff's Office. "Gray's interested in the preachers, too. And he asked a lot of questions about the Sheriff's Office. I think he wants to take it over. We have incontrovertible evidence of corruption. Sidney can use that as a lever, threaten to press charges, unless the sheriff cooperates on an ongoing basis. Lewison has you and maybe some of your friends. Sidney, on the other hand, has half the Concrete Arms and soon, the whole Sheriff's Office."

Confirming government support of Smash production, I included Aaron saying, "I'm glad to be here. It's like owning a franchise. And Sidney provided a comfortable allowance."

The Insects would know it was me, but it wouldn't matter. Rachel had been released and only Lewison was keeping her on the line. The Insects didn't seem to share their agents, one of the ways they compartmentalized and competed. And as soon as I took care of Lewison, I'd be long gone, fighting revolution from the hills.

Once I had bundles addressed to every church in town, I sat with Sarah and June in the conference room.

"Can you drop these off before our big attack? You don't have Pinkertons looking for you."

Sarah stared at me. "Big attack?"

"We're still going to blow up the Lindbergh statue?" June asked.

"I've been thinking about it. It's great symbolism. But it would be even better to destroy the one in front of the state capitol building."

"In Springfield?"

"Yeah, a dress rehearsal for Liberation Day. We'll hit at night when no one's around to get hurt, then toss flyers out the windows on our way out of town. What do you think?"

Sarah smiled. "Way more visibility."

"And it might actually be safer," June said. "There's a lot more security in New Bethany than there used to be. An attack in Springfield might catch them off guard."

I nodded. "We'll have to scout it out first."

June unfolded an Illinois road map on the table. It included close-ups of Springfield and other cities on the back—just the major streets, but we could buy a better map once we were there. We brainstormed how to pull off the operation.

"What do we do afterward?" Sarah asked.

"I have to disappear," I said. "The Insects will be searching for me."

Sarah leaned toward me. "You know I can't let you wander around on your own. You might do something dumb."

I gave her the finger and she laughed.

"I'm with you, too," June said.

"The Three Musketeers," I said. "We could hide in the Shawnee Hills or Ozarks, live off the land. Turn more factions against each other and recruit more cell members for the main event in August."

June nodded. "The Ozarks are beautiful, and I know people there."

Sarah grinned. "I've had enough of being a townie."

* * *

I watched Rachel trudge down the trail through the reservoir woods, rubber boots tromping through the melting snow of fading winter. She looked healthy, with alert eyes and smiling ruby lips. I ran to her and we threw arms around each other. She smelled of summer roses.

"How have you been?" I asked. It had been difficult to arrange a rendezvous without someone noticing.

Her soft hair brushed my cheek. "Better. I'm working at the bookstore again."

"I saw you through the window. I saw Will Coulter in the store too."

She drew back enough to share a mutual gaze. "Yeah, the police forced my father to hire him. He doesn't do any work—just watches me and the customers and writes down what people buy."

"That must be good for business."

She half-grinned at the sarcasm. "I'll find a way to get him fired, don't worry." Her smile broadened and she rubbed my jacket sleeves with her mittens. "Guess what—I'm going to U of I in the fall. Finally."

My elation might have exceeded hers. I hugged her tight. "That's wonderful!" She had a future.

"Finally escaping New Bethany." She stepped back and her smile faded. "Lewison will find out. He'll make me inform on everyone on campus."

I gripped her hands. "Don't worry about Lewison. Don't contact him or any other Insects. I told you I'd handle that."

"How?"

"Best that you not know."

We kissed for possibly the last time, a kiss of solidarity and cautious hope.

* * *

I sat in a makeshift chair in the covered bed of the pickup truck. We were parked in front of a shuttered store along the feeder road between the Decatur prison complex and the intercity highway, wheels pointed toward the street. I scanned the approaching cars with binoculars.

Behind me were boxes of dynamite, detonators, and timers, separated until my task here was complete and we headed to the capitol. Wearing a broad hat and sunglasses, June sat in the driver's seat, and Sarah in the passenger seat. My partners. I wished Rachel could be with us too, but her safety was too important, and besides, she was being monitored.

I glanced at my watch. Almost six. Was he working late today? New prisoners to annihilate?

Spring had finally arrived, meaning not only the migration of millions of waterfowl, but that each day was longer. Still, the sun was nearing the horizon, and once it slipped under, it would be too dark and we'd have to abort.

There! Through the binoculars, I spotted Lewison's black sedan approaching. On his way home to Champaign, fifty miles northeast. He drove alone, not high-ranking enough to rate a bodyguard.

I banged on the truck cab window. June started the engine.

I yanked the bed window curtains shut, except for the one facing the cab, then picked up my rifle and loaded a bullet from the magazine. The pickup pulled onto the road and accelerated.

In the cab, Sarah turned around and gave me the okay sign. She hadn't been happy about killing someone but understood it had to be done. As for me, I'd long fantasized about this moment, but all I felt now was dull anger that I'd been forced into it.

I opened the back curtain, then popped the window up. We were moving fast down the left lane of the road. I clicked off the safety.

We passed Lewison's sedan and maneuvered directly in front of him. I held my breath and sighted the rifle between his dark eyes. We were close enough that the slight breeze wouldn't matter.

You should have left us in peace.

Lewison spotted me. His jaw dropped. Too late.

I squeezed the trigger.

###

Dear Reader,

If you enjoyed this book, please consider taking a moment to leave a review at your favorite retailer and/or book review site. It will greatly help other readers discover the book.

Thanks!

T. C. Weber
https://www.tcweber.com/

ABOUT THE AUTHOR

T. C. Weber has pursued writing since childhood, and learned filmmaking and screenwriting in college, along with a little bit of physics. His first published novel was a near-future cyberpunk thriller titled *Sleep State Interrupt* (See Sharp Press). It was a finalist for the 2017 Compton Crook award for best first science fiction, fantasy, or horror novel. The first sequel, *The Wrath of Leviathan*, was published in 2018, and the final book, *Zero-Day Rising*, came out in 2020. He has other books on the way as well. He is a member of Poets & Writers and the Maryland Writers Association, and has run writing workshops and critique groups. By day, Mr. Weber works as an ecologist, and has had a number of scientific papers and book chapters published. He lives in Annapolis, Maryland with his wife Karen. He enjoys traveling and has visited all seven continents.

For book samples, short stories, and more, or to contact the author, visit https://www.tcweber.com/.

Made in the USA
Monee, IL
24 June 2021